BREAKING DANCE

J. BLISS

BOOKS BY J. BLISS

Chance Series Titles by J. Bliss

Not By Chance

Taking Chances

Last Chance

No Chance

Additional Titles

Perfect Imperfect Christmas

Perfect Imperfect Christmas II

No, I Do, In My Future

I Do, In My Future

Breaking Dance

Night and Day: Sr. Rodd

Your Chance: Hunted

Legal Chances

Running Back

J Bliss Books Publishing Company

Atlanta, GA USA

www.jblissbooks.com

ACKNOWLEDGMENTS

I am grateful to the following people for their support:

My heart, my inspiration, my husband, Jerel, thank you for enduring the many changes, supporting my dreams, and helping me remain focused. You help me dream like I have never known an obstacle and I know it is with you by my side each challenge met I will overcome, making life meaningful.

Thank you, Bryan, Cookie, my children, and parents for always believing in me.

Thank you, Lydia Moore and Trescina Bell for being supportive. Thank you for your persistence in asking for clarification, getting annoyed with me about characters going through what I call 'roller coasters.' Every emotion you express about my stories help bring them to life and I am thankful. You have a way with reminding me of my mother's words: *Never Stop Writing*

Thank you Sinsual Bliss Readers it's worth the wait and your support is amazing!

THIS ONE IS DEDICATED TO YOU, QUEEN MOTHER IMANI...FOR I SHALL NEVER QUIT WRITING.

Breaking Dance

By J. Bliss

ROMEL

*R*omel
  The last day of the work week was Thursday for me, three-day weekends are the best. My plans for the evening are comprised of me unwinding from a working man to transitioning to doing whatever I like. My school load has decreased and play time has increased.

I lounge on the couch and my roommate, Drew walks out of the room. I think Drew has dedicated the entire term to seeing how many females he can fuck before graduation. He is out more than me and that's a hell of a lot considering I go out perhaps three times a week as a minimum. No regrets for me, living my life is about experiencing life.

Tap, tap, tap. I glance up at my roommate stretching as he walks across the kitchen. "Are you expecting someone?"

Andrew Rodd is like a second brother. I rarely call him Andrew unless he is not taking me seriously. My biological brother, Rico is seven years my senior; he always calls his ass Andrew. He does it on purpose to fuck with him. He's overseas in the military. I miss him but respect his choice to serve in the military.

Drew's brows rise. "Hell no."

I frown knowing his ass probably told a girl to come by and he forgot. I am not a fan of letting females know where we stay. It's not like he picks ordinary females. Drew's type is the crazy, wild, and never cool chic. This is the second time we've been roommates since college.

Although, growing up with him living around the corner meant most of our days we were together.

Our freshman year our parents made it mandatory we live under the same roof.

By the time our sophomore year rolled around we both had our own spot and kept getting into our own shit.

Drew's ol' man was livid with both of us. We were the typical college students, high off life, finding trouble. It's our senior year, and we have calmed down, mostly. I have the appetite to always live on the edge, but I manage it better than before.

As for Drew and his flings, he thinks nothing of it, our motto is 'it's only for one night.'

Although, he has had women that don't agree to that motto. I guess that got him into older women. Drew claims they are not clingy and don't expect a relationship. It's his life and if that's what he wants I am cool with it. I can't judge him, hell I have my own demons of preference. It's just the crazy aspects of a female I go after the woman portrays in bed. I can be an intense lover so I can't just fuck with anyone.

After, my encounter with one female from Spelman I learned my lesson. Stay away from people that think your lifestyle classifies you as a monster because that's what she wanted everyone to believe. It's not my fault she couldn't handle me; that trick recorded me as if I was out to rape her. It wasn't long lived after she got kicked out of school. Thanks to my hacking skills my mother never saw the light of the scandal. I guess that's my reason for not going out with any female I just fuck up and leave out.

It's only one female I'm interested in pursuing and she is off limits with her 'I want to stay friend's' ass.

The knock sounds off again. Shaking my head, I hope the one at the door is not one trying to renegotiate terms with Drew.

He walks to the door looking suspect. "Who is it?"

I chuckle; it's one of his victims. He cracks the door open. "What's up?"

He doesn't even let the female come in. Wearing nothing but pajama pants, I rest on the couch with my head on the pillow. My ringer goes off, Victoria's face is on my screen and I grab my headset off the table. I should have turned my phone off. She's like eye candy. I shouldn't touch, at least I keep telling myself that, but I am not that convincing. My fingers flex around my cell, seeing her picture on my screen makes the vascularity of my lower arm visible. My veins swell against my skin almost to a point of transparency.

Damn, Victoria is calling. My memory flashes to her big, beautiful brown eyes and long, dark wavy hair; every one of her features drives me crazy.

I answer, "Yeah, what's up?" Not only does her beauty urge my body but her craving to stay fit makes me fight my temptation to fuck her on sight. She's the nineteen-year-old that makes me want to pin her ass to the wall and make her scream sultry shit in my ears until the entire neighborhood knows my name.

I'm sure if I so much as tasted her skin I'd be like Denzel Washington was to his wife in *American Gangster*. She's talking about boxing classes.

"I'm not going today. We go Friday."

I happen to fall upon her defensive training classes and instead of her falling for it she just wants to fucking fight, for real. I turn my head and notice a cougar looking chick at the door glancing at the waterfall mounted on the wall. She stands in place as if Drew told her ass to freeze. He is a trip bringing this 'mom I'd like to fuck' chick in this house. I know she's somebody's mother.

"Rom, I'll be back in two hours." He fists bumps my hand. "Alone."

I tilt my head. "Alone…I gotcha. Hey, bring back some breast milk." Drew bursts out laughing.

He opens the door and the woman steps ahead of Drew as he shuts the entry behind him. He swings the door back. "Fuck you, Rom."

We laugh. I situate the earplugs to my ear.

Victoria is calling my name, though not exactly how I envision. "Yes, I was listening to my roommate. I got off work like an hour ago. Why are you trying to go today?"

She is going out of town. "Oh, so you want me to get up just because."

"Yes, you are my brother." I hang up the phone and it rings instantly.

She makes me explode inside, fighting against me. It's who I am, the contrast between us draws me to her. How can she keep denying how she feels about me? Does she think I make myself available for her to be her damn friend? I release a breath of air.

After the third ring I pick up. "What's up?" She is going on as if the phone lost a signal.

"No, I hung up."

I smirk and it drives her mad. "Why did you hang up?"

"You said I was your brother…if my brother called asking me to come pick him up after I got off work…" My shoulders shrug. "I would have hung up."

She is sulking like a kid acting alarmed going on about me being her Morehouse brother. I shake my head.

Here she goes with more 'I'm her brother shit.' I would be a lot more if she stopped acting like a female version of Drew, dating everyone. "Why can't you go with the guy you were with last week?"

She chuckles telling me she doesn't share time like that with him. I think she resists me mostly because of rumors. If she ever built the courage to ask, she would find out I was not the villain in that situation. That girl had her own motives.

I twist my lips sideways. "So, what about the boy that came to the party with you a week ago?" She acts like she can't recall who I am referring to. "Shit, where is your roommate, Jasmine?" She's probably with her boyfriend.

She snaps, she can't stand for me to say one curse word. It aggravates her so I keep doing it. "Fuck, Victoria. I'll see you in an hour."

She growls enticing my dick and I hang up the phone. Why I keep chasing after her I can't answer myself. You would think a senior of Morehouse would know better but she's the prey I'm after.

I lay back and my phone rings. I answer without looking at the name. "What the fuck?"

I sit up hearing my mother on the other end. Oh shit.

"Yes, ma'am. No, I didn't realize it was you. I thought it was someone playing on my phone." The truth is, I thought it was Victoria being persistent. Over the last year of getting to know her as a freshman she has become comfortable with me.

My mother doesn't sound right.

Her voice worries me. "Ma'Dear, are you all right?"

She is nagging saying she would be fine if I used the manners from the classes me and Drew went to as kids. I hated those etiquette classes.

"Yes, ma'am. I meant nothing by it, Ma'Dear. I'll do better for you, my number one."

She giggles and for a moment it makes me feel okay. "Hey, I should drive down to visit you this weekend. We can hang out and watch a movie." She is begging me not to come. I guess she is hanging out with Mrs. Rodd as usual.

She asks me about Drew. "He's fine, you just missed him, he stepped out." Now she acts like she is worried about me. I should head to Dallas, anyway.

Her voice does not sound right. "Ma'Dear, you know I have been going at this college thing now, for, four years. I am cool. I got accepted in the Master's program." Her voice shrills with excitement, but she rushes me off the phone.

"I will call you later, love you." The call ends and I stare at the phone realizing it's the anniversary of the day that changed our life. Fuck that's what is wrong with her. Looks like I'm making a trip to see her. My fingers glide to pull up Victoria's name and text her.

I'm on my way now, be ready.

She responds.

I'm already ready.

I smirk. Standing on my feet I step to my room to go change into my workout clothes and go release some steam. I hope she's ready because I am not going light on her today.

Victoria

I STRETCH LOOKING in the mirror searching for imperfections, turning to the side. "What imperfections?" I blow myself a kiss. "Yes, she is beautiful!" My brows rise noticing my purple duvet is a hot mess. My pillow shams are screaming 'no ma'am.' I need to work on that, the elaborate headboard is not fitting for an unmade bed, mental note to self.

I do a once over of my body and grab my ass. This came

from my daddy's side, no questions! "No cellulite…I'm keeping it tight."

Smiling at my reflection, I grip my breasts, mother dear was giving. "Yes, everything is nice."

My hand crawls up from behind my head lifting my dark brown hair, mother was most generous. I strike a pose, pursing my lips…"*Gracias, Mami.*" Me thanking my mother as if she is present is a sight to see, I admit.

Enough admiring myself for the moment, I have to finish getting my items packed.

Stepping in my room the portraits of myself, my sister, and both my chicas from childhood smile back at me from the walls; they're accented by illustrations from my lovely chica, Jasmine Chance.

She is the most underrated artist I have ever known. I tell her how wonderful she is, but she's so modest about her gift. Twisting my lips, I remember my earrings are missing and I want to wear them.

"Jasmine!"

Where is this girl? If she is ignoring me one more time for that damn boyfriend of hers. I exit my room storming through the living area. Her door is shut.

Tap tap.

It is quiet, so no one is in there, I push the door open. "Jasmine, are you in here?"

The sound of the water being shut off explains why she didn't answer me. Jasmine pulls the door to the bathroom open. "Victoria." She is standing naked with an alarmed look on her face.

I lower my body on her made bed and toss her the red towel that was blending with her comforter before I sit back. My eyes blink recognizing how picture perfect her room is compared to mine. It looks like it's a showcase for a furniture department store. I adore her images of the lake, you would think she stole

Mother Nature and brought her in her room. Yes, I need to do better in managing my room.

"Girl, don't flatter yourself, I am still strictly dickly."

She bursts out laughing, draping herself as she shuts the bathroom door. "Chica, what do you want sitting on my bed looking like 'I'm out to steal your man?'" She jerks the door forward holding up a finger. "Wait, chica can I say one more thing."

She keeps talking without me granting her. "You over there sitting on my bed looking like ready or not here I come, ass." I smirk this is why I always say encouraging words about myself...she plays too much. I love it, so she is fine.

She shouts and flashes the door again being dramatic. "Come through, Victoria... yes, honey! Okay, I'm done but..." Her fingers spread in the air. "You have no sense of boundaries, woman!"

I laugh; she is a mess, my mess. "Awww, chica, thank you."

She jerks the door open wearing a pair of jeans that are loose and a fitted shirt. "That was not a compliment."

Jasmine searches out her closet as always. You would think she doesn't live here the way she never knows where her own items are.

It's because she spends too much time with her boyfriend. She's my roommate but I have known her since middle school so we are more like family. "I take it as a compliment, perspective is everything. The women in my family would be proud to hear you say I have no boundaries."

She steps out of her closet with her shoes and sits down next to me, smirking. "Victoria the women in your family associate boundaries with sex. I can't visit your house one time without your mother comparing food to some body part." We giggle but she is correct. *Papi* always leaves the kitchen, and that is where we would start our honey pot chats.

By the time I turn sixteen, my Aunt Helen and more of the

women joined our talks, and it became our ritual. "You know I am going home this weekend."

"Tatiana has officially been sixteen for six months." She blinks her eyes sliding her foot in the second shoe. "Let me guess...she will be inducted in the honey pot chats."

I fall back on her bed. "It is tradition! She will finally learn the true meaning of the statement, 'Stay in Touch.' I am so happy too because you did not respond how I hoped when I told you about it."

Jasmine is on her feet standing before her mirror brushing her hair. "Chica, I am just not into vagina meditation sessions, as you call it."

I rise, leaning back on my elbows. "You never have been...I know. I hope that boy knows how to please you because you are the most stubborn student learning how to please your damn self. I bet you are." Hell, if he was sexing her right she wouldn't be able to wear those jeans either...Her ass would certainly spread. I must keep my thoughts to myself and not be disrespectful.

She snaps her head and interrupts me. "My relationship with my grandmother was different. You know this, chica. I was told not to touch myself and my so-called mom... well...no need to explain, the verdict is still out on her claiming such title." I touched a nerve.

She takes in a deep breath. "Your family is different you all talk to one another." I stand behind her as she situates her hair.

"Forgive me, chica, I didn't mean it like that." I embrace her shoulders and kiss her cheek. Her hand touches my hand, assuring me all is well.

"Forgiven, don't worry about it. I have something for you to give your sister in honor of your tradition." I love gifts. Jasmine pulls back the closet door and gets a second pair of pants while grabbing a slender package on the floor. "Open it!" She jerks the tag off and changes into the second pair of pants.

I unlatch it from the top and pull out a sketch of a glorious vagina. "Hello kitty! Yes, honey! Awww, I love this. I want this for me!"

Jasmine turns around I smile. "You look cute, chica; those are sexy on you. Get in front of the mirror! You are giving me life! No wait, it has to be me giving you life!"

She stares at herself and bounces like we are at a club. I jump to my feet and grind as if we are on the stage. "Yes, chica! Yes, own it!"

She stumbles back against the wall laughing at me. "Victoria, you are a hot mess!" She shakes her head and passes me a sketch in a frame. "I am already prepared for you."

I yell loving what is in front of me. "Now I can have a visual with my meditation." I am impressed, her drawing skills are fabulous. "You are the best!"

She blinks several times. "Chica, please don't run off telling people I drew you a picture of a—"

I interrupt, "It's a beautiful honey pot...come on Jasmine. You mean you don't want me to even tell my family you drew this colorful pussy for Tatiana."

Her face frowns as she stares in my eyes. "See how that sounds, Victoria. No, please don't tell people I am drawing kitty cats that purr in the night between your legs."

I twist my nose. "What purr in the night?"

"Victoria, that just sounds like your version of the story." She has a point I would embellish.

I giggle. "This once I will keep my mouth shut. But looking at the details of this clitoris, check out the labia...pure beauty...it confirms you might have been having some 'Stay in Touch' time." I roll my body in excitement. She shuts me off as if I never said one word. Only she is skilled to do this.

"Whatever, did you need me for anything?" She knows damn well she has been observing her private parts more. Why does Jasmine act this way? I thought once we went to college she would open up more and adore everything about her body. She's had it rough, but come on, enjoying yourself intimately is orgasmic, literally.

Jasmine is staring at me waiting. I almost forgot why I came in here. "You have my earrings."

She points to the side of her bed. "They are right there; thank you, sweetie. I forgot about it."

"*No problema*. So you are going on a date for the weekend?"

Her lips twist. "Maybe or a party." Wow, I am happy to hear that. "My boyfriend..." I stop listening once she mentions that jerk. Not that she shouldn't have a boyfriend it's just he is not worthy for such title. She has shut down auditions for another to be the leading role. I guess I should be a better friend and listen, at least she is going to a party, I was just hoping it wouldn't be with his controlling ass. "So are you happy about the party."

She shrugs her shoulders. "I don't know."

"The correct answer would be 'no,' Jasmine. Tell him you are going to Dallas with your chica."

She shakes her head staring in the mirror at her beautiful reflection to make sure she is not forgetting anything. "You need to be with Tati alone, chica, plus I am sure she will find a way for me to go see Franklin."

We burst out laughing like high school chicks. "Franklin came out of your mouth not mine." I flash my eyes. "I know you like caramel in your coffee...so I am certain he wouldn't mind licking it off of you."

"Girl, no. He is a friend...only a friend." Who does Jasmine think she is kidding?

I lower my voice seductively. "A friend that wants to be more than a friend. Funny he always finds you." My eyes narrow down at her. "Snap out of it."

She looks at me all knowingly. "First of all us going to school together doesn't suggest he finds me. Second of all he never really asked me out, he only implied and lastly...I am aware of a guy trying to be more than *your* friend." She moans teasing me and I stand but she pushes me back in place.

I bend over grabbing my stomach laughing and Jasmine keeps going in on me. "Chica, I can tell you like him and if I discern right, he is lurking after you. Chica, you know Romel likes you." I love this girl, but I can't be attracted to a guy with a slight reputation as he has. He's my Morehouse brother although I find it interesting how he became my brother when Jasmine's Morehouse brother is in the same class as us. Romel is a few years older than me.

Bang bang bang.

Great, saved by the prick at the door.

I tease Jasmine. "Franklin finds you even though we are out of high school he always knows when you are in Dallas. Besides, Jasmine, Romel is only my Morehouse brother."

Some girl claims he was rough with her in bed. I struggle to imagine if this is true because it goes against what I know of him.

She turns and exits the room. I follow behind her. "If that's what you want to call it…you can't think when it comes to him."

My mouth drops and I stomp my feet at her audacity. "I know you lying!"

I push my hair back from my eyes and my entire body is moving as if it is speaking another language at her accusation. She is laughing at me as I try to pull her from the behind. Jasmine continues to walk, almost falling in the hall from me jerking her. "No, chica…throw that plan away. You like him." This is how Jasmine thinks, really.

Jasmine stops in her track and looks at me before opening the door. "Why are you running from him? You give all the other guys your time of day…what's wrong with Romel?"

I bat my eyes. "Nothing, he knows too much about me just like Franklin knows too much about you." She smacks her lips. I knew that would divert her thoughts.

The door opens, and she tells dick head she's on her way. She cracks the door before leaving. "Victoria, the same way you want me to live my life and be happy, I want you to be happy. He seems decent unlike the other knuckleheads that run after you. Remember 'staying in touch' doesn't mean shutting down your shop for entry from a guy you like. What's the worst thing could happen…you fall for him?"

I bulge my eyes in disbelief. "I would have to see you fall for one guy. I would pay for that."

My legs lead me to the door urging her to leave and notice Romel's car approaching the parking lot. "Chica, leave…I will be okay."

"I know you will."

She starts twerking. "You got your 'please don't hurt em but you better stare' outfit on. Let me guess…you have an audition in mind but you don't want the role with the guy."

Ugh, I hate she knows me so well. I push her further through the door and she blows me a kiss. "Love you, chica…just be happy. I am okay."

"I want you happy, not okay."

Shutting the door, I run to get my purse and glance in the mirror. "I look cute." My hand reaches for my lipstick and I slide it over my lips. I stand tall. "Great, I am ready to go!"

Romel

MY FOOT TOUCHES down on the brake. I press the removable power button from the dash as the engine from my V8 silences ejecting it from the ignition and I open the car. I step out, situating my sweats, and shut the door. As I walk to the front door, I wave to Victoria's roommate as she leaves with her boyfriend. She is always with him.

I reach my fist to knock on the door.

"Damn." I muffle as Victoria is in front of me looking like she's ready for me to turn her ass into my snack. "Where the fuck are you going dressed like that?" Her legs scream to wrap around me so I can dive up in her guts. More than likely she doesn't have a clue I notice her sexiness.

She blinks her dark brown eyes. "Really, Romel." She turns around locking the door and giving me an eyeful of her ass.

Got damn. "Who wears makeup and dance clothes to fight class?" Is she meeting up with Beyoncé or some shit? I mean she put leggings on but that top looks like she is going to a dance recital choreographed by the Beehive.

She faces me, staring at my body as if I'd steal the breath from her lungs. Her sinful thoughts are loud; she can't resist imaging what I look like naked under my compression shirt. The force of her attention is strong as she contemplates if I'd crush her curvaceous petite body as I do when we workout.

Tell me she does not have on lipstick on her pursed lips. "I do, let's go!"

Most females wear yoga pants and a push-up bra but she has on an outfit. I take training serious.

Uncle Senior had us in fighting classes when we were in middle school with his brother, Uncle Jay. He looks more like Drew's father's twin. We had to promise not to tell Mrs. Rodd and my mom. He called it 'man time.'

Victoria is dressed like she's competing for a *Single Ladies* video and it's a distraction to my eyes. I don't necessarily like to play with my cardio.

I shake my head. "I'm gone make you sweat all that shit off." She frowns with a slight boil of anger rising with her brow. Threatening the likes of what she calls art work on her face is a risk I clearly welcome. She doesn't need that shit, anyway.

My eyes follow her lips as she snaps. "Romel Adcock...stop cursing!" Damn she's beautiful with her sassy ass. I ignore her knowing it will annoy her.

"Only if you go inside and change." She walks ahead of me to my vehicle and I pick up my feet. My arm extends opening the door.

She sits inside. "Victoria, yo ass is fucking around you are not trying to work out."

She giggles. I shut the door walking to the driver's side. Pulling the door ajar I sit and Victoria is texting on her phone.

She turns looking in my direction. "Romel, just because I don't wear sweat pants and a long sleeve shirt as you it doesn't mean I am not serious." I shake my head and the door slams.

"Whatever." My finger presses along the multi-button controls on the steering wheel turning up the music. The backup camera appears on the seven-inch LCD display and I reverse the car.

She rolls her eyes. "Did I upset you?" I can tell she's trying to read my body language.

"I'm straight, I have something on my mind. I'll be better after we leave the gym." I turn the music back up and drive to the gym, avoiding talking.

ROMEL

*R*omel
I pull the handle of the door and she steps ahead. The clerk notices us and tilts his head. I wave two fingers, nodding my head as we pass. I grab two water bottles off the counter and pace to another set entry.

Heads turn as we walk forward and Victoria is giggling, waving at some dude in the spin cycle class that is admiring her. I could destroy him with one blow to the neck, but I digress. My arm reaches to pull the door.

"So is he joining us for warm-up?"

She marches through like she's on the drill team, rolling her eyes. My head jerks back as we stride through the spacious gym floor. A girl from her school, with big hair looks in our direction and she smacks her lips.

"Is she joining us?" Victoria's annoyance is obvious.

My brows rise. "Shit, I don't know, Spelman Sis, go ask her. I don't mind." Victoria knows damn well I'm not interested in this chick that looks like she existed before the Clone Wars. But if it breaks the strange hold, she has over me, I'd accept it.

"Whatever, Romel."

I'm fucking with her, but when she lifts weights, she's gone give a show to the girl side-looking at me. She does it every time someone looks at me. My arms spread as I speak sarcastically. "Hey, I'm not feeling the family love."

She laughs and her smile is contagious. Most people think I am motivational, the truth is I can be very moody. Working out helps me stay disciplined. Victoria sounds chipper. "Okay so what are we doing first?"

"Warm up…you know this. Why ask?" She walks over to get two towels. I head in the opposite direction grabbing two mats and return to our typical spot placing them on the floor. Victoria sits the towel next to the water bottles and stretches. I lower to the mat and she follows suit facing me pushing her toes against mine. We both lower in a push up position.

She peeks her head. "Ten reps is a set, right?" Typically, we do one set and move on. "Not today we are doing three sets."

She pouts. "Romel, it's a warm up."

"I want to make sure you feel the burn." We curl our bodies and push up with a clap syncing our movements. "That's it… motivate me."

She is moaning as if she is not pleased. "You're ridiculous, Romel." Our hands clap. Is this her idea of motivation? Maybe she's flirting?

We finish the first set and I rise and she lies on the mat. "Get up…you called me to come here. Up now!"

She curls her upper body. "Is this better?" She high fives my hand.

We move faster completing the second set. She twists her head as the girl from the school walks by. She increases the speed of her push up and I match each aggressive hand clap. "What's wrong, Victoria? Do you want more company?"

I know I have upset her; she snaps her head and then lays

back. As she rises, she claps my hand and grips my palm. Victoria is getting stronger, her neck pops. "Wheelbarrow."

She stands over me. I stare in her eyes gritting my teeth. "What, are you training me now...or do you think I'm your bitch?"

She stomps her foot. "Come on, Romel. Flip...I am not trying to."

I jump on my toes towering over her. I lower my voice knowing she's doing this power shit because of the female. "Don't think you came here to train me."

All of this would be fine if she'd just admit she wants me. I'd let her dominate me then. She takes in a deep breath. "Romel, will you plank? I get a better work out when I lift your legs."

She's correct. She's weightless. I lower to the floor and flip over. The wall mirror allows me to watch her position. "Victoria, remember, proper form as you elevate and go down."

She grabs my legs. "I know, Romel, you are watching me." She squats holding my legs as I remain in plank position pushing up.

As she completes her set she growls, "It burns."

"Come on, Spelman Sis...you got it."

She glares at her reflection. "Look at me...I love myself." She's definitely in love with herself. Victoria drops my legs. I crawl until I am on my feet.

"You're so selfish."

She walks over to get herself a bottle of water from the other side of the mat. "What?" She acts clueless and I bend over to grab my water bottle.

"It's cool I'll make you pay for your selfish acts. Plank and jump is next." I suppose us to encourage each other instead her ass is admiring her own body. Her eyes bulge.

I bite my lip. "Don't you even think about it, I'll be on the floor."

She hates this, but I enjoy watching her reflection as she jumps up and down. This lets me take advantage of her so-called workout attire.

She needs etiquette classes; I pick up the towel and throw it to her. "Thank you, at least I'll be fit and fabulous." This woman.

I position my elbows on the floor while my feet rest on my tippy toes. "Remember, I'm watching you. You jump over and between my legs." I spread. "Come on, you know this is a good cardio fit." She pouts.

Victoria steps over instead of jumping. I twist my head in her direction. "Stop playing and jump. Come on, you are going for fit and fab remember…jump high. You'll appreciate me when you are out there dancing, let's go!"

"I'm already fabulous."

I shake my head. "Yo ass better jump, Victoria." She stops stepping and jumps between my legs huffing and puffing.

She moans. "This hurts my stomach."

"Great…it's working. Keep building your core. Let's go, baby!" I chuckle and she jumps faster. "I mean Spelman Sis…let's go."

She chuckles and completes a set. "I'm done, Romel." I stand up and pat her midsection. "You're building a strong core…big baby."

I point to the floor she frowns. "You cheated when we were doing push-ups. Make it up." She lowers on the mat and with ease she completes her set without direction. She knows how to do all of this stuff. She has a disturbing expression on her face.

"What is it you want to achieve? Are you doing this to be tone, lean, and look good or be how you already are?"

Victoria has a questioning stance, and she grabs at her hips. "Is something wrong with the way I am?"

I shake my head pointing in front of her. "I'm not the mirror. Check the mirror and answer for yourself."

"Romel, I'm not big or bulky like you, but my ass…"

She knows I will not baby her. She has a daddy for that shit…now if she wants me to be her daddy I'll baby the fuck out of her. I lower my body squatting near her as she is completing her final set thinking of her ass. "Your glutes."

She giggles. "My rear ." She wiggles on the floor laughing at me. "Romel, my glutes and legs are much better thanks to you." I accept the compliment even though she is complimenting herself at the same time.

"Damn, dat ass though…Spelman Sis." She hits at my chest; I chuckle losing my breath.

"I will slap your ass so hard you will cry." And beg me to do it again.

She turns her nose. "No, you won't." She jumps trying to agitate me.

"Victoria, stop playing before you get hurt." She pushes me in the chest and I reflex hitting her. Her eyes grow as if she finds pleasure in me hitting her.

"It might be the other way around if you keep testing me."

She sticks her tongue out. I take in a big gulp of air composing myself. "Focus, Spelman Sis."

Her nostrils flair and I chuckle. She can say whatever she wants I know she wants to be more than my friend. Right now she wants a compliment.

"I've noticed changes in you, Victoria." I tilt my head wiping my hands on my legs. "There's a misconception about lifting weights for a man and woman. Not all men get bulky as you say, nor do all women."

She breathes in and out. I hit her lower thigh. "Come on push…let's go lift."

She pushes up and I nod my head. "I'll be back."

I know this makes her more confident in herself I can see the difference even when she dances she feels stronger and better about her body. I grab two more water bottles and return. She has her hands on top of her head breathing.

I toss her a bottle. "Warm up is over, let's go to the weights." Victoria is staggering at a slow pace behind me. Passing through the gym on my left, my eyes catch sight of the Cardio Theater.

There are a few people using the treadmills staying entertained in their own world with headphones facing the floor to ceiling windows. My head shakes as I spot one guy, it's embarrassing to get killed by a machine. This place is not as busy today.

She looks at me as if she's trying to read me as we approach the free weights. "You are not in a good mood, Romel, you don't want to talk?"

"Nope."

I blink sizing up the tires on the opposite side of the room. I walk in her direction. "What do you want to talk about, Victoria? You said you wanted to come to the gym and we are warming up before we go in the ring."

She is pouting. "I want you to talk, give me instructions."

"You already know how to do this. We have been doing this since last year." She's right, I don't want to talk, I want to relieve my stress. She bats her eyes.

"Romel, I will just go home."

She attempts to walk off and I reach for her wrists. "Calm down. I'm just dealing with something about my mother that's all. I will go see her but I didn't want to talk about it. Let's train."

"If either of us is upset, we will have a bad set. So talk about what is bothering you so we can move forward and fight." She is jumping up and down encouraging my dick to rise. My hand grabs her waist and she stops.

"I don't typically talk to anyone about what I am feeling right now. This was a hard day once, and today is the anniversary of that hard day." I pull my gloves out of my pocket and reach for hers in my second pocket. She will have no excuses about weights.

"Romel, what do you always tell me?"

"I'm training, I say all sorts of sh—"

She interrupts narrowing her eyes, "Say it, Romel Adcock."

My hand rubs my wrist; damn, so she is my weak spot. "Your weakness can be a tool, if manipulated properly." I toss her the gloves and she slides them on. She doesn't know they drilled this into me as I trained as a kid.

"Whatever is bothering you, Romel, take your own advice. Manipulate it to work for you, not against you." I push back my gloves, tucking the leather strap on my wrist. At the moment I am manipulating my craving for dismantling her by staying disciplined and focused on training.

"I'm good, now get over there and lift woman."

She looks. "What are we lifting?"

"The tire…Tire flips…let's see if we can flip the tire. You can try."

Vic squats and grunts squeezing her face. She yells out. "Ugh!"

She pops back up and tries again but it's not happening.

She stands and I high five her. "Good effort.

"I can do this." She nods her head agreeing.

I squat and grip my fingers below the edge of the tire. I pull the tire and she is screaming. "Romel, you are lifting it!" I elevate the tire to my thighs and rest it for a second repositioning my grip. Taking in a deep breath and boost the tire more until I push the tire over.

"Romel how much does that thing weigh?"

"Twelve hundred." I laugh.

Her face is full of astonishment. "Twelve hundred pounds, Romel?"

I chuckle. "Look it up. Come on let's partner flips with the tire."

She stands as if this is a dare she wishes not to comply with. "Come on…Fit and fab, remember. We will flip it and then do box jumps onto the tire."

I gulp and concentrate on the task. "We flip the tire and jump on side of the tire building the jump by each flip until we reach the opposite side of the room." You can discover a lot about a woman when you work out together. Her excitement lets me know anything I do she wants to be a part of it. She complains, but her eyes display excitement and she's for me.

Victoria

SOMETHING TERRIFIED me when I first worked out with him but Romel pushes and motivates me. I don't know if I do the same for him.

The receptionist tells us all the time how we are kicking each other into shape but he might be lying. Romel is a beast with this exercising. I wish he would not cover his damn body with all the clothes. The only flesh I see is between those damn retro leather bracelets he wears. I guess I get to imagine the bare skin.

I am happy he is my Morehouse brother because he's a gentleman even though I see him spotting me, watching my upper body. He doesn't stare at me but his work outs are ripping me.

"This destroys me, Romel."

My saving grace is diverting my sexual tension to exercising. The darkness about him makes me so curious, but based on the whispers I'm not sure if I want to know the truth. Could he hurt a girl like I've been told? I'd rather not risk my friendship, at least with not knowing I can still hold on to seeing his biceps flex through that damn shirt.

He shakes his head. "Nope, this builds you and you're killing it keep going."

No, I am not, I am barely keeping up in my classes lately. Jasmine is out with her boyfriend so much I feel lonely. If I masturbate one more time, I think my body will be set on orgasm mode permanently. Ugh, I am hopeless no matter how many times I try to persuade myself I always end up feeling the same way.

Did they have to put this much space in the room? I mean come on a bench would have easily cut this room in half. He is excited, flipping this tire even though he is demolishing me. "I'm also bleeding right now." We make it to the other side of the room.

Going to the gym with Romel is more like a couple's workout of us being supportive of one another. I guess overall I enjoy his company and feel less lonely in the world.

Romel is super motivating while we flip the tire. He claps my hand. "Good work."

My breathing is growing deeper and Romel gets me another bottle of water. It's like he never makes me wait or has to guess if I need water. He already knows somehow.

"Two-minute rest and we are doing it all over again." He is dangerous in a sexy kind of way. I can't believe he wants us to repeat the tire flip.

"So push it back to the other side of the room?"

He nods his head. "That's it, you can do it. We already did once, let's go!" There goes the zealous incredible hulk. I am happy I am doing this with him. I know it takes him away from working out with his roommate.

"This is so much more fun, Romel, working out together." I bend over. "I think I hurt my knee." My fingers pull my leggings I see a cut. "I knew it. When I came up, I bruised myself. My legs were heavy. Ugh."

I giggle at Romel pushing his hand aside. Mr. Tough Love.

"Walk it off, you're doing good. It will heal…that's a good bruise." I clap my hands against his and he takes our empty bottles, tossing them.

"Breaks over; let's get it."

Ugh, here we go—flip, jump, flip, jump. We make it to the middle of the room. I hold up my hand.

He claps his hands. "Come on, a lot of fight is in you, let's get it!"

With those words I am back on track. We finish the set and I have to catch my breath. Romel is walking behind me. "You good?"

I pace, growling. "I'm good, Romel." My heartbeat slows and I follow him over to the one place I do not want to go. He knows I don't like doing this mess. "Romel, I don't like the weights; it's just us bickering."

He smirks at my comment. "We do resemble Tom and Jerry, but today your ass will lift weights, you called me, so lift."

My shoulders drop. "Romel, if we do this I don't want to fight. You will throw me around and these weights will destroy—"

He doesn't deny it but cuts me off, "You'll thank me later." He strides his chiseled ass across the floor, it's interesting even with him fully clothed he commands the room. I wish he'd let me peek, but we are college siblings; I am really not supposed to stare at him like this. One day I will stop lying to myself.

"Romel, remind me why we are doing this?" A frown grows on his face.

"My achievement at the gym is not the same as yours, this is my lifestyle. I don't come here to work on a body part. I stay ready, so I don't have to get ready."

I twist my head away from him. "Maybe this will be my lifestyle if you stop being so mean." I stick out my tongue.

He shakes his head. "You called me."

I lift my hands in the air. "How could I forget?" He pushes

me in front of the dumbbells. I grab a set. He watches me, as I prefer. I can sense that trifling ass girl from school looking at us. She can hardly be missed. I hard blink, what is Chewbacca from *Star Wars* really saying on top of her head.

If this girl gets any closer, I think I can hear her hair howl.

It's time to cancel! My chest lifts as I take in a deep breath, pleased Romel can't read my thoughts. I know we are not a couple, but she doesn't know that. I hate disrespectful ass bitches.

Romel commands me, "Lift to your chest…don't go higher than your chest, elbows out." His hand glides over my shoulder and he pulls out my elbow. "Torso straight."

I am not concentrating and that bitch sees him touching me. Romel is gritting his teeth. "Return to the start position…Let's get it!"

I follow as he instructs and give the little trick a show; since she wants to watch a workout porn flick I shall oblige. I curl my hands perfect. Romel is an inch away from my back. He whispers in my ear, "Good concentration, are you inspired?"

She is looking at us wondering how we look so freaking hot when working out. Poor thing, she looks like a red bell pepper right before explosion noticing us the moment we step in the gym.

I alternate hand curls. His hand follows down to my knee. "Stand with your legs slightly bent…You do this to offload the weight of the dumbbells onto your legs. Don't overload your spine. Watch…then you do it together." I put the weights to my side and observe him. His body looks like it was made for this. He is so serious. I wonder if he thinks of me like this when we work out.

He is calling my name, "Victoria, keep your back straight."

Romel sets his weights down; I guess he can tell I was off in another world because his hand glides along my back. I let out a heavy moan giving it to the universe staring at the bitch trying to call in all things which do not exist for her.

Her childhood story has to be Pinocchio; she is looking at me like she is wishing upon a star. She looks away…that's right your dreams are not coming true.

He is steady, staying in control while I am having a mind fight with a chick over a dude that is not my man. I need to stop this. I take in a deep breath in and out. "Arms next to your side as you grip the dumbbells. That's it neutral position as your palms face inwards." I position my body away from the female and Romel turns my face. "Look in the mirror. You see your forearm."

My head turns. "Yes! This is destroying me in the inside, Romel. It's ripping my body."

He chuckles. "Nope, your forearm is flexing. You will thank me later. Keep those elbows as still as possible, Victoria, no playing."

My eyes see my reflection. "My arms are hot!"

"Yeah, let's get it! Lower your forearm slow and repeat with the other arm." He is not even paying attention to any other person here. I blink my eyes. Fuck, Romel likes me, but he knows I mess around. Does he? I shake my head.

He is celebrating my stance. "You got it."

"Romel, my biceps are not as big as yours."

He laughs, that was not a joke! One minute I think he likes me the next he acts like my sibling, ugh! He clears the grin from his face and set serious eyes in my direction. "Nope…but they are good, strong, breathe and concentrate…no cheating, Victoria." How does he know I am arching backward?

He snaps, "I will have you on that damn bench if you cheat again."

Am I aroused by that visual, my head twists? "No concentration bells. No, no."

I am trying to finish the last set. He is hyped now. "Life is full of walls, push through that shit. Don't let it stop you...One more set, let's get it." No more sets. I question him.

"Last set?" Please let this be the last set.

He smiles. "Last set, best set...let's get it!"

***

Romel

A SMILE GROWS on my face as Victoria exits the bathroom in her natural state, all the glam is off her face. Finally.

She walks in my direction and I wait on her. "Now you look like you are going to a gym. Your face does at least."

I shake my head. "That outfit is another story." My feet step back away from Victoria and she leaps in my direction.

She slaps my arm. "Shut up, you made me work out like that on purpose."

A mischievous smile grows on my face. I wave at the clerk as we exit the building. "You don't need all that, anyway." She pushes at me and I stop. Victoria sizes me up as her target, focusing on my upper body. Her fist is tightly curled, and she throws her weight toward me holding the heel of her palm toward my neck. I dodge moving out of her reach. "Expected!"

Without delay I push my elbow pitching my body forward into her and Victoria's body swings against the wall. She gulps as her eyes grow big. "Always do the unexpected, no pillow fight dueling. We have gone over this...hurt or be hurt, woman."

I back away and she's whining in a sexy pitch. "Romel, you are bigger than me, you can throw me around." I can, this is true, and I would welcome every bit of throwing her around. Time to switch my thoughts.

"It's not an excuse. Going for the neck is good because I am bigger." I grab her hand trailing it down my neck. "The carotid vein is a bigger target. Stun the attacker; use your elbows and your knees."

"Romel, I will not think of all that punching."

I narrow my eyes. "Victoria, this is not a game." I point to my temple stepping forward. "It's a mind game be strategic, use your body weight, it is your weapon, if another person is coming for you. Pillow fighting will not help." I catch her chin in my hand gently and make her look in to my eyes. "Focus, Victoria."

Her breathing grows heavy. "I'm focused." I pull her in. I keep my eyes steady in her direction. "When someone strikes you, everything is going on around you. Focus, you chose to be successful at your point."

She hits my hands and speaks in an all knowing manner. "I got it, nothing matters, my injuries are irrelevant, use my body weight as a weapon."

I stop walking, she is not being serious. This is why make-up should not be a priority when working out. She stands upright and I am lecturing her as if we are in fight class. "Victoria, the body cannot take the injury, that's why you must be strategic. Our body can handle non-specific trauma. You can get knocked around and your body can take it…it's not an injury." She stands with her hand on her hip.

Shaking my head, I point my finger at her chest. Through clenched teeth, I tell her, "You are the one to deliver the injury; the toll of violence is available to you, so use it. Stop thinking you are not big enough."

She walks to my side and I push the door open. "Thanks, Romel." It's hot as hell walking across the parking lot. I look in her direction.

"No problem, where am I taking you?"

I need space right now. She flashes her eyes. "Wow, I typically cook for you after we work out. You can take me home if it's not too much."

We pass several cars until we are next to my vehicle. "Next

time, you can cook. I need to get to Dallas and see about my mother."

Her face looks concerned. "I hope everything is okay, Romel." I open the car door.

"It works out no matter what." She gets inside and I shut the passenger door.

VICTORIA

I glance into the store fronts briefly as I hurry by. It's impressive how they make the stores at the airport look like those in a shopping mall. It seems a bit pointless though, doesn't it? I wonder how often people buy a fifty-dollar neck pillow they could easily get for fifteen dollars or less. I enjoy shopping, but the prices for these items are ridiculous.

Spotting my gate, I slow my pace as I hear the sounds of excited children and soft music echoes in my ears. An announcement is blasting about my flight. "We will board for flight 232 to Dallas momentarily, please have your boarding passes in hand. We are asking passengers with small children or in need of special assistance to please form a line. Regular boarding will follow."

I giggle as the children spring forward as if Santa himself is boarding the plane. One little girl looks at me and I wave. She has her hand on her hip and speaks. "I'm not supposed to speak to strangers but...girl, your hair is pretty."

I bat my eyes as I cover my mouth and I push my hair back whispering, "Thank you, little princess. You move along, don't talk to any other strangers though." She covers her mouth as her eyes bulge and nods her head. I lean back and watch the family board the plane. I hope this two-hour flight doesn't have me sitting next to a creep, or better yet, bouncy little people. I need a break from kids before I'm back around my little sister when I reach my parent's house.

My eyes close but the attendant is now asking for the remaining passengers and I stand. Soon I will be in Dallas and I am excited to surprise my little minion.

GOING to my sister's school with my family brought back memories I didn't know I forgot. High school was all about me and my chicas, Jasmine and Chantal. I'm looking forward to a little bonding with my sister. Being in college has been a different experience, while I enjoy the freedom, I get homesick. Maybe I thought my sophomore year would bring me fewer days of missing my family. Let's face it, not being able to see my sister Tatiana as frequently as I want has been a pain.

I miss my parents, but I mostly missed talking to *mi hermana*. She can be such a thorn in my side, but no matter what she's my baby sister. I turn my head looking in her direction. She has every right to be proud, her dance group was on point during her school's play. She has the biggest smile on her face.

"Thanks, *hermana,* for coming to my show."

I place my arm around her shoulder pulling her in as we follow behind *mi papi* as he opens the door. "Anything for you."

She has a sarcastic grin on her face. "Yes, but I know you are still spending the weekend with your—" Tati curves her fingers resembling air quotes as we enter the house. "—High school dance team."

I snarl at my sister looking like a cross of our parents and she chuckles.

As I step inside, I take in the scent of my mother's famous

enchiladas. I walk to the coffee themed kitchen noticing the many red utensils she has pulled out. This place has not changed, even my mother's pots and pans match the theme of the kitchen. "Mama, did you make the *rojo* sauce or *verde*?"

I can smell the slivered bell peppers marinating in the sauce. My eyes glance taking in the sight of her go-to dessert, *tres leche* cake. It is so good. The icing is never too sugary, it's perfection.

Looking at her is like seeing my reflection in a mirror. Her hair is tied in a bun as she slides over grabbing items from one counter to the other side wearing her sassy apron. It resembles dancing attire more than cooking wardrobe. Daddy turns on the music which encourages *Mami* to sway her hips. We bounce playfully to the Latin beat, while *Papi* grinds *Mami* from behind. These two make being in love look too easy.

I think she made sure her daughters experienced dance. She used to dance before we came along. She always says your responsibilities change when you have children. I don't know if she tells me that to scare me to not have kids or because she really misses not dancing. Who knows but I want it all, dance, a husband, and children! I stick my finger into the pot of secret sauce to get a little taste. I'm close to replicating the recipe myself.

Her hips bump me away. "*Mija*, get out of my kitchen while I am cooking. Whichever sauce I make, red or green, you will eat." My mother doesn't like anyone disturbing her domain when she is cooking. I promise you if anything is off she blames it on the traffic from people entering her *cocina*.

Tatiana pops up around the corner. "*Mami*, don't you have tortillas for Victoria to make? She misses her days in the kitchen with you."

Learning to make tortillas from scratch as a kid was fun, but I am not interested in cooking. Knowing how to cook is mandatory for the Water's girls. My daddy says my mother's cooking brings life to this house and the way he moans eating her food you would think they were having sex at the table.

She sticks her tongue out, teasing, and my eyes bulge. "No, *Mami,* Tati is playing she is trying to get out of going with me after dinner."

She smiles at Tatiana in love speaking. "Victoria, you came home early to surprise your sister. Surely you are spending time with her."

"Yes, *Mami.*" I narrow my eyes looking at my sister being annoying on purpose. "As long as Tatiana has her items ready to go, she can hang out with me and the girls this weekend."

Tatiana's eyes dance with her rosy cheeks. "Sis, can we stop at the mall first? I want to get something cute if I am hanging out with your dance team from school." My cell phone vibrates, and I pull it out of my back pocket. I swipe the screen seeing a notification from my *chica.*

My father's fingers grip my shoulders. "Baby girl, what have I told you about the phones in the kitchen." Twisting my head in his direction I put the phone away. Disrespecting my six-foot father is not something one does lightly.

"*Papi,* I am not a little girl anymore." A smile grows on his handsome mocha complexion face as he embraces me with a bear hug.

"As long as I am still breathing, you two girls will always be my baby girls...my beautiful baby girls." I shake my head. He has treated us like princesses all our life and our mother is his queen.

"Yes, *Papi,* I know."

He steps forward walking to the living room. "You two girls be sure to help your mother. I don't want my queen overworking." She smiles staring at him as he walks to his recliner. I pull my sister by the hand.

"*Papi,* Tati has girl talk to tell me."

He stands to his feet saying my name assertively, "Victoria."

My mother flashes her hand urging us away. "King, let them be. I want the kitchen to myself." He sits smiling. I think he adores her calling him king. It always gets him to go along with her plans.

———

I'M sure my mother will join us the moment she gets all situated in the kitchen. I will get things set until she enters for our session. I walk in my bedroom placing my assorted purple, white, and black tushie cushies in the center of my room. These comfortable pillows make sitting on the floor enjoyable. My sister walks in like a bouncy kid. I can't believe she is sixteen already. We celebrated her crossing over with the family at her birthday party, but this session is the intimate one my mother takes pride in. Here comes my gorgeous *mami* holding a gift. She unties her apron setting it on my dresser as her eyes watch Tatiana situating herself on the purple cushion.

"Knowing yourself is all about staying in touch."

The doorbell rings, I didn't know we were expecting company. But from the aroma stealing my attention I know who brought *pepian de pollo*. God, they are amazing!

Tati keeps playing with her hair as if her husband-to-be is about to walk in the door. *Pay attention little lady* is what I want to scream. She darts her eyes in my mother's direction. "In touch with whom?"

I stare at Tati with an eagle eye. "Yourself."

A familiar voice hits my ears as I glance to the door and see my favorite aunt. "*Tia* Helen!" She's holding a gift bag and passes it to my sister as she kisses the top of her head.

My mother and her carry on a conversation in their native tongue, speaking as if time is not on their side. Finally, my aunt speaks in English. "Sister, stop it. I am here. You just started, I didn't have any one to close for me today. My son was late. Let's carry on for my niece, *hermana*." My mother gives her a side look.

"Helen you better be happy you are my sister."

"Selena, if it weren't for me you wouldn't know all those special moves with your *papi*."

Focus. We are here for Tatiana. "*Tia*, you are talking about my dad. The image of my *papi* and *mami* is not what I want to imagine."

My mother laughs. "It is love, *hija*!"

My aunt pushes at my mother's leg as she lowers next to her sister. "I think she has someone else she wants to imagine…do share, *patoja*."

I settle my hips as I rest, crossing my legs. Whoever invented these made them a delight of comfort for lounging. The cushion raises my bottom just enough that my legs don't crash into a deep sleep.

My mother places her hand on my knee, continuing where she left off. "Helen, this is not about Victoria. Tati, it's important for you to know the map of your body just as you are clear of the map to get to your home."

Tatiana reaches over grabbing a throw blanket from my bed. She acts as if this is her room the way she is just rearranging things. I shake my head…life with a sister. My sister does not seem too sure of us having this conversation. She reminds me of Jasmine when I attempted to talk to her. Tati takes in deep breath as she clings to the pillow on the floor. "Okay, *Mami*, did you tell Victoria this?"

Aunt Helen interjects, "I told your *mami*, listen."

I nod my head. "Yes, *hermana,* this is our way of learning about us, as women. *Mami* has taught me so much, but I have learned more on my own. It's fun. Don't worry." My mother is shaking her head at how I am responding. I have been waiting for what seems like forever for this moment with my sister. Once my mother opened me up to this bowl of knowledge, it was like entering a paradise. I walk over to my dresser and place the gift Jasmine made for her setting it on the floor in the center of our circle of cushions. My *mami* has her gift in a jewelry box. I know without needing to look that it's a sacred honey pot charm. Tati is at the beginning of the journey of womanhood. Also, a letter from our father is presented to her. I still have the letter *papi* gave me. I imagine this letter was a challenge for him to write. But as a young lady it is a letter I treasure from my father as he celebrates my transition into becoming a woman.

Tatiana reaches for the gift and my mother gives her a stern look. "Tati you will open your gifts later. First, we must speak of your assignment." Her face looks so puzzled.

I whisper in her ear, "This will seem odd first but trust me the more you embrace it the better it will become."

She shakes her head and blurts out, "Do you two think I am clueless about sex?"

I snap, "I would hope not, *hermana*. What we discuss in the honey pot sessions is not to say you know nothing. It is to make sure you understand what is correct. When I was in school, I remember a certain friend of mine thinking she could get pregnant from a kiss."

My mother chuckles and interrupts, "You can get pregnant, but it is not the kiss. A kiss can be orgasmic, Tati, but without penetration from the male, sweetheart, you are not getting pregnant."

Helen interjects, "*Oye...*kiss is how my son was created. Your uncle." She smacks her lips and my mother giggles as she continues. "Oh, my *papi* was so delicate with me when we made your cousin."

Tati's eyes are growing wide. "*Tia porfavor.*" If anyone didn't know better, they would think my Aunt Helen was my mother. We both enjoy this topic. She keeps chatting and it's safe to say with my *tia* here my father will stay out of the room.

Her hands move as she speaks. "Oh, child, I said please on many occasions to your uncle…he is so intense."

I thought my sister would close up, but she surprises me.

Tati shakes her head. "Kids at my school don't talk about a kiss on the mouth, *mami*."

"Really, what type of kiss do they speak of?"

Her eyes roll to the top of her head and she points to her midsection. "Here kissing here." My sister has a look of embarrassment growing on her pretty little face. I know she's a virgin, but it doesn't mean you may not think or say things.

I look at her all knowingly. "Sis, speak, the word will not slap you." Her eyes grow wide and she realizes my mother is in agreement. She shuts her eyes.

"Kids talk about sucking, you know or eating…come on, do you say these words to *Mami, hermana*?"

I nod my head. I speak in a singsong pitch, "Absolutely, my pretty little pussy, my vagina, my honey pot is beautiful and I have no issue saying what it is in front of *Mami*."

My mother chimes in. "Tatiana, why do you have a concern about referring to your body part as what it is? Your vagina, your pussy cat, your precious honey pot? Do you think I don't say this?"

Aunt Helen blurts out, "Aya ya!"

Tati's eyes are so huge they look like they might pop out of her head. "I think I don't imagine you saying the words. People don't talk like this in front of their parents. I mean—"

We laugh and my mother interjects. "Tatiana, you know your father and I conceived you having a night of passionate sex. "

Her face cringes and she muffles her words, "Yes, I know this but do I have to imagine it."

I smirk. "Of course not, sis, you typically imagine who you will one day have sex with, but understand your body. If you don't then how will you know what satisfies you?"

She shrugs her shoulders. "I guess I never considered that."

My mother passes her a letter. "Tatiana, this is from your father. Read it in your own time when you have some privacy. When you are ready to speak to your father about it you can, but know he is supportive of you knowing your body."

"*Mami*, if he is supportive why isn't he here?"

Mami smacks her lips, keeping her composure. "I designate the initiation of these conversations for just my girls. Aunt Helen is here because she is my sister. As Victoria is here as your sister."

She is looking at the letter in a strange way. "So, I have to tell *Papi* 'hey I read your letter and thanks for the vagina advice?'" We laugh.

"Sis, no, I mean…unless you want to say that. The letter helps you not think our father is ashamed of you learning this. It is like a letter of confirmation of what he thinks and or believes so you don't assume."

My mother picks up the conversation. "Tati, sometimes when a woman has sex she can take shame in the bedroom and that shame causes you to not be expressive to the one you love. Sex is a beautiful act, and it is meant to be enjoyed, yet when a person thinks of it in a shameful manner it affects the sexual act." I can tell my sister is trying to digest what we are saying. I pick up my gift and pass it to her.

She holds it. "Sis, it feels like a picture or something?"

I laugh and nod my head. "Don't tell Jasmine, but she made it. She doesn't want me to tell people she created it. Yet, I want you to know because it's for you to know she is supportive. As you get older and learn more about your body, you must select people as a to go-to person to help you learn more. "

"Can I open it?"

I shake my head. "Not now, sis. *Mami,* you have a question right?" My mother repositions and speaks softly.

"Tatiana, I have a statement more than a question. Learning your body helps you understand why you respond a certain way.

When you buy a car you learn the car to know when gas is needed, an oil change, or needs new tires, yes? You learn so much about a car to keep up the maintenance and when that happens the car lasts longer."

"So you are saying when I learn about my body it lasts longer?"

I twist my hair pushing it away from my face and respond. "Well, yes, but you also know what it needs and how to give you what you need."

"So our body needs orgasms and kisses?" She smirks looking like a bashful kid.

I interrupt, "Yes, Tatiana, your body needs this, it's a chemical reaction of feel good that your body needs and craves."

"Tatiana, I am not always going to be around but know I will be here for you. I want you to learn the anatomy of your body. Understand the parts of your vagina and what it is for. Your assignment is to look in the mirror and touch your vagina and know what those parts are. I want you to know this as clear as day, just like when we go to the ice cream shop and you automatically know what ice cream you want."

"I think this is the strangest homework I have ever got, *Mami*. Victoria, did you do this?"

I nod my head. "Yes, I did and understand I am still learning my body. I know when my cycle will return. I understand why I feel drowsy during the menstrual cycle. But I also know if I kiss a guy and sparks don't go off it's because well, he is not the one." My face glows as I speak. "Kissing is the interview."

My aunt makes her moaning noises, and it makes Tati laugh.

She smirks. "Well I talked to Jasmine about this guy you like at school or I forget maybe he likes you. Anyway, do you not like Romel because you kissed him and no sparks followed?"

I narrow my eyes. "I will get Jasmine at another time, but for your information I have not kissed Romel. He is a friend. We're supposed to be discussing you."

My aunt interjects, "So, she wants to imagine Romel."

"Yes, Aunt Helen. Jasmine told me he's tall and big." Aunt Helen is over the top with her facial expressions.

"So, Romel is so strong, Victoria?"

I growl, "This is not about me besides he's a friend!"

My mother's hands go up in the air. "Hey, you three stop it. Tati, I emailed you your assignment and you also have a few links to guide you to complete the assignment. We will discuss more later." Tati peeks in the bag from Aunt Helen and pulls out a night gown. "Thank you, *tia*."

"To remind you how precious you are. Wear it with pride, princess." She smiles and my mother puts the box holding her jewel in her hand. Tatiana opens it. "Thank you, *Mami*, it's just like Victoria's." Her mouth drops. "So, you gave her this...oh when you gave her this it was because she was learning about herself."

I chuckle. "Yes, sis, it is your initiation into the honey pot conversations. Nothing is off limits."

My *mami* pushes my shoulder. "Hey, calm down, *hija*. You are to guide not act like it's a joke."

"*Mami*, I am guiding."

Ugh, she is so serious about this. My mother thinks if we joke too much, we will make Tati uncomfortable about talking about her body or sex. I disagree, if we act relaxed she will be more opt to speak to us. Tatiana looks at both of us as if she is grading our behavior. "*Mami*, I get it and I will look over the information. I am happy we talked about this. It was strange, but I think I will get it." We stand share in a big group hug. I adore this moment. Tatiana releases from the hug and takes up the gift, ripping off the wrapping paper. My mother sees the details. "Awww, *hija*, it is great!"

"*Mami*, it's a vagina, it's so colorful, pretty like." I laugh.

"Sis, you are supposed to think of your body as pretty; love your body and know it's fine to think of your treasure as a priceless jewel." I can tell she has some getting used to but in time she will learn the vagina is a tunnel where life enters and it should be cherished. She shakes her head.

"I'm guess I might hang this in the closet. I don't want *Papi* talking about this right now. But I want to go to the mall, Victoria." My mother walks out of the room and I roll my eyes.

"Don't keep it in the closet forever, sis. Go get ready to go." Hopefully by the time she reads *Papi's* letter she will understand it's okay to hang her picture where she wishes in her room.

VICTORIA

"Tati, why on earth do you have me at this mall?" She is trying on earrings, reminding me of myself with her prissy behavior. "So, *hermana,* do you have a special guy you like?"

I shake my head. "I don't like those, sis. Try on the sparkly ones." I pass her a pair of gold shiny earrings. She holds them up to her ear looking in the mirror. Tatiana twists her lips.

"Sis, you love anything that shines. How is Jasmine?"

I roll my eyes and shrug my shoulders. "You know, chica, she and her boyfriend are so in love. I am not trying to have one boyfriend, sis."

She laughs. "You are so funny. I will be like Jasmine; I want one boyfriend. You and Chantal have too many."

I look in her direction and groan. "I date guys, Tatiana…how am I supposed to find the right guy if I only date one?"

This guy walks by that grabs my attention and I tilt my head. "See, sis, check him out. I wonder if he's a souvenir we can pick up."

Her hand covers her mouth and she giggles. "Victoria, shhh, what if he hears you?"

My eyelashes bat. "Girly, he has on earphones he can't hear us." I spot the cookie store my *papi* loves taking us to get sweets for his sweets. "Tati, let's get cookies."

A cashier comes over to assist my sister. "You go ahead. I will catch up."

I pause noticing this guy in passing is giving my sister the eye. "*Hay una linda triguena.*" My brows rise and I notice her blushing. I am not being overbearing; I think it's cute that a guy thinks she is pretty. What is concerning me is how she overlooks him calling her *triguena*. My parents never liked us to get caught up in the color of our skin and here it is she is welcoming this guy saying this stuff. I roll my eyes. Her in between complexion is gorgeous no matter what. I don't want her giving a guy power to identify her by the color of her skin.

My mother told me when she was a kid her grandmother treated her sister different because she was not *blanquita*.

How do you think it's acceptable to mistreat a person in your own family because of the color of their skin? It's a matter that exists sadly. Puerto Ricans, like African Americans, are an array of colors.

Hell, I see my family as humans, not blended races, just a loving family. However, growing up not looking like most of the in between colored members meant they were taught to dislike those that are *blanco*. If you were *blanco* you were taught to dislike those that are *trinquena*. Not in my household; *Papi* was not letting that happen.

She holds up the earrings glancing in my direction as he walks away. "I'm getting my jewelry."

I walk off. "Okay, I will wait for you. Don't worry I will get your chewy pecan cookies." She smiles as I promise; she makes me giggle looking like a blend of *Mami* and *Papi*. I hand sign I love you and she blushes, painting a heart in the air.

OUR COOKIES IN HAND, I turn around looking for my sister. It was like any other day with her bouncing around wearing her favorite color, the one that *Papi* taught us both to adore.

He always would say 'my princesses' wear purple, the color of royalty. The strange thing is I can't find my sister or the color purple.

She's not a baby anymore, as her sixteen-year-old sassy mouth confirms, but as I look in the crowd my heart is racing and I'd give anything for Tatiana to sass me. I walk further down a dark hall and scratch my head. Where could she be? I pace in the direction of the restroom. Two arms jerk my body, dragging me backwards while two guys dressed in dark clothes walk in my direction, one gags me and I am pulled out the exit. I am kicking my legs, squirming, but no one notices or can hear me scream. A door opens from behind and I am forced on the floor of a car until I pass out silent.

MY EYES BLINK FEELING DISORIENTED. I turn to the left, then right. I moan; my hands attempt to reach my face but I can't release them. "What just happened? Where am I?" My legs jerk pushing at what I think is the side of a door. I must be in a car. It's so dark, I can't see out the window of the vehicle. "Help me!" I try screaming and the car slows. A man's genuinely deep, creepy, dark voice covers the space. He startles me as his eyes keep me trembling in fear and anger. "Shut up!"

I yell, "Where am I?"

"We will kill your sister if you don't shut up. Stop screaming." My body is covered with chills as his evil pitch lowers. It's frightening seeing the person that holds life and death before you.

I can discern the side of his dirty face, it has a scar trailing to his neck. "There's no hope for you no matter how loud you scream." My heartbeat is pounding through my chest and I can't get up to see my surroundings. The car comes to a stop.

Twenty seconds pass and another car stops on asphalt. Thirty seconds pass and the squeaky noise of the opening of the car hits my ears. I don't utter a sound, afraid for my sister's life. Two rough hands grab at my feet, yanking me out of the car. My body is being rushed in a house against my will, everything is moving so swiftly I'm unable to recognize anything around me. I am shaking as the men drag me into a room and throw my limp body in a beat up room. It has a filthy mattress on the floor.

As tears roll out my eyes, two men hold me up, stripping me of my clothes leaving me bare. I stare to the wall beyond the men avoiding looking in their eyes. They jerk my wrist and tie me to a wall with a rope like a dog. There is no doubt my situation has lead me to unthinkable trouble. I will die. I gulp at the thought of not seeing my sister again, disappointing my parents not being able to save her.

Once the men secure me, I turn my head. My eyes come into focus; there's another girl in this filth trap of a room. I cry silently, recognizing it's not my sister. But seeing this girl's young body in the fetal position, rocking back and forth, made me think of my Tati. She wails as if she senses something evil approaching and the door swings open. It's one of the men that grabbed me. He barges in with flared nostrils and punches the young girl in the back of the head.

She sinks backward, and he spreads her legs wide. She screams out a plea. His hands open her legs wider. Her pitch is deafening. Her cries are so loud that hearing anything else is impossible. My stomach tenses. He's raping her in front of me, *dios mio*. The young girl's screams pierce the small room until her yells can no longer be heard. She lays silent, naked. The guy punches her in the face as if he is craving to hear her yell. However, she remains shut off from sound and movement.

My eyes shut as my breathing is out of control and the door

crashes open. Keeping my eyelids shut my ears capture the sweet sound of my sister's voice. My eyelashes flash, aware of the man holding my sister by her hair, dragging her into the room. I growl wanting to rescue her, imagining my parents clueless of what is going on because they think we are away for the weekend. Gritting my teeth to control my outburst I wheeze until Tatiana is in the opposite corner, hostage, out of my reach. Inside I am shredded to pieces.

Hours pass. Several men come in over and over as if they were there for a wine tasting. But the only tasting they are doing includes forcing themselves on the helpless young girl that screams on the floor. I growl, wanting to help her, wanting to stop this from happening and hurt the men that are doing this.

Yet, as my thought grows a man comes in probing me, his hands clutch my chin, forcing me to see his red-rimmed eyes. He has a grotesque stench as spit drools from his slack jaw. He nears me, showcasing the tattoo on his neck and every muscle inside me tenses as his rough fingers skim over my skin. My heart falls right through my ribcage as he grabs my breast. He jabs my arms punching me as if I am a bag meant for beating. I kick, fighting for my life, recalling *hurt or be hurt*. He stumbles back, as the door widens I spot the evil demon claw tattoo on his neck. A man with disfigured face comes in with an identical brand on the flesh of his throat. They get into a confrontation and in seconds I am unleashed from the wall and dragged on the floor. Someone snatches my sister, we yell and they shout at us in unison. "You will learn the ways around here."

My loud pitch is upsetting the customers, they scowl, dragging me in another room.

I can hear the other girl's earsplitting yelps for her life as they take advantage of her. The man tightens the rope on my wrists and backhands my face. "You bitch, shut up." Fire spreads through my body of pure rage. His blistered hand trails across the shape of my breast. "No communication is allowed!"

His gunmetal eyes stare at me. I peer sightlessly in the dark distance, knowing he is nothing but wicked; that mark on his neck doesn't even expose half of the demonic spirits inside him. I lay there until the house grows silent and the light from outside turns dark. My eyes shut and I pretend I am at the mall with my sister. I imagine not going to get cookies alone but instead waiting by her side and eventually I fall asleep.

I JOLT from my sleep hearing my sister moaning from afar. She is scared, calling out for help. The door crashes open. A light from the hallway beams into the room as the man with the scar on his face pours hot water on me. I grit my teeth as my back arches in pain, I want to scream, narrowing my cat eyes. He bends over and slaps my face forcing me to the mattress. "Good, you have learned restraint."

Tears roll from my eyes and he walks out. Soon after he returns with my sister, kicking and screaming. In the light I catch sight of purple marks along her lower body. I hush her. "Shhhh, please, shhh."

She looks out of the corner of her eyes and comes to a silence, somehow knowing they united me with her because I learned to be quiet. The man walks to the door. Her arms, hands, and legs, are trembling in fear. She is moaning in the corner, reaching her fragile fingers toward me.

She whispers with cracked lips, failing the final syllable, "*Herma...na.*"

The man turns and lunges his body toward her. He grabs her by the ankles. My body is rocking and I keep shaking my head. Her eyes meet me and she doesn't utter a sound. He releases Tati and heads for the exit. Taking in a deep breath, I never welcomed darkness as much as I do at this moment. I look to the window, searching for stars. I wonder if God is afraid of the dark. My sister is crying pleading for me. *"Ayuadame"*

I whisper, "Shhh *hermana, estoy aquí para ayudar.* I am here to help...shhh.*"* Although I feel I have failed her, I have to tell her, even if it's a lie. I can hear the other girl from the room wailing. I think she has been crying for over an hour in anguish. Loud voices from several men arguing are echoing outside our room.

My hands cover my ears until a gunshot ricochets across the house. My sister stops crying, the men stop arguing, and I no longer hear the wailing cries from the young girl.

The door swings open. I push up against the wall and jump afraid as my heart pounds as if it's about to explode. The man with the scar on his face grabs my cheek gazing at me with his demonic eyes. His voice is deep and gravelly as he speaks, the veins pop on the atrocious tattoo on his neck. "You're so pretty; we don't want to have to do to you and your sister what we did to the other girl."

I shake my head, gulping at his words. I'm going to die. The man stands there, studying me. His creepy, coarse hands force between my legs and he moans. The surround sound of his night-stalker voice comes at me from every angle. "You behave so you may live." Why won't he kill me already? He releases me and walks out of the room, slamming the door behind him. I know he is doing this to torture me and my sister. Is this one of those walls you have to push through? I want so badly to scream but I choose to live, at least through the night as I stare over my shoulder out the window—scared.

ROMEL

I flinch as my feet touch the cold floor. I go into the stall for my post-workout shower. I reach my hand adjusting the jets as it pours down my face, my thoughts shred and my eyes fill with tears recalling the memory of my father. Not having him here leaves an emptiness in my soul. The steam from the water diffuses the aroma of eucalyptus to my nose. It calms me, fading away the memory and desire to disappear, to not exist.

The second jets flow from behind and the water trickles down my back. I inhale deeply having images flash in my head. My palm pounds the wall and I bend my knees releasing a yell. My voice can be heard across the room. It's safe to say Drew has been alerted. Sitting on the shower bench my palms press against the hard surface and I wail with the force of a person's heart being ripped out, missing his presence.

He can't hear me; I know he's not walking through that door to demand for me to turn the water off. I'd give anything if he would, my mind swirls while the steam builds up in the shower. I hear the door unlatch and the concerned voice of Drew demanding the water to shut off. "Alexa, turn off shower."

The lights from the shower head fade the moment the water stops. A lump forms in my throat as my voice cracks trying to speak. "Alexa, turn on the water."

The stream returns. Drew shouts, "Alexa, turn off the water!"

The voice command feature is something my mother insisted on installing considering past acts of my behavior. I don't utilize it often, somehow chatting with a shower is dim-witted. Silence and hot water running down my skin is the only relationship I want with a shower-head. My breath stutters trying to take in a deep breath.

Drew speaks, "Rom, you alright in there?" The steam is so thick in this bathroom it blocks me from seeing Drew but his demanding voice confirms his presence. I know he is just making sure I'm cool. My heartbeat slows and I relax my breathing.

He repeats his words. "Romel, answer me. Are you alright?"

I clear my throat. "I'm good, bruh. Get out so you don't get intimidated by my fucking glory." I hear him chuckle as his feet turn to exit.

"Glad you think so highly of yourself. My shit does have a lasting impression." I chuckle at his arrogant words and he continues, "My pops sent the falcon to take us to Dallas. Get yo ass out the shower so we can go to Dallas."

As expected, Uncle Senior never forgets this day and I am honored to have him in my life to help me through this pain. It's nice having access to your own plane to leave when you want to and not worry about an airport. "Get out of here, Drew!"

He slams the door and my thoughts are on track, time to go see the family.

ROMEL

"Hey, M'Dear, how are you?"

"I'm fine...I see you listened and stayed at school." I smirk.

"I had to come check on you." She leans into my chest as my arms wrap around her. I had to see her to know she is well. She is looking pass me. "Romel, close the door."

"Drew is behind me he will be in. Is Rico here?" I push the door without shutting it all the way. Her head is nodding as she walks ahead of me going to the kitchen.

"Yes, he is in the game room, probably strategizing a new plan to guard this house."

I laugh at her antics. He is on some special forces since he's gone to the military. "Your father is all in that boy's head. He got upset with one of the security guards Senior had over here and told him to leave."

I frown while she carries on washing her hand before returning to cooking. I notice she has a bowl full of peaches. Next to a ball of dough, it looks like she made pie crust. I take in the flour spread across the island. "Why did he tell them to leave? Did they touch you?"

She has a disbelieving glare looking toward me. "I told you I can handle myself. I don't need you going out there getting in trouble, Romel."

I walk to her side and kiss her cheek. "I am not getting in trouble. Can I help you with anything?" My mother likes no one in her way when she is in her zone cooking. She smacks her lips.

"Romel." She bats her pretty eyes. "You can get the sugar out the pantry and then leave. I will let you know when I finish the peach cobbler. I have something I want you boys...well men...to take over to Janice's."

It's no secret as to why Uncle Senior made sure we lived around the corner. Mrs. Rodd and my mother act like sisters they never had. Anytime, I visit her she has something for me to take to Drew's house. Or I am loading something back to my mother's because Mrs. Rodd got her a gift. I shake my head grabbing the stone countertop in thought of my father.

Drew enters and holds his hands up being extra. "What's up, M'Dear? Did you do all this for me?"

These two love each other. She is grinning. "Drew, don't you touch my peaches." He embraces her as if she is his mother.

"M'Dear, how are you and where is the dude that is supposed to be on post?"

She takes in a deep breath. "You all know I can handle myself. I don't understand why you think I need all this protection." Her eyes get teary and she turns away and pulls open the refrigerator door. I put the sugar on the counter and a loud silence is in the room. She shuts the door holding a stick of butter. "Drew, you and Romel still don't have girls you fancy at that school in Atlanta?"

I step away knowing why she is asking this. She knows if she asks about me having a relationship I will walk away. Drew grabs a few grapes out the fruit bowl popping them in his mouth. "I have females I fancy but not worthy of being in the family. Romel on the other hand..." He grabs the back of my shirt tugging me in reverse as I attempt to inch away. "Rom, tell momma about the girl you like."

"It's nothing." She is adding spices in her bowl of peaches. It smells like cinnamon. My mother reaches for her spoon that Drew is in proximity of and he passes it to her. Her eyes bat.

"Well, Romel, I am waiting."

In a nonchalant manner I respond. "I talk to girls but I am not serious with anyone, Drew is teasing." I can hear footsteps clinking on the stone floor heading in our direction. My eyes survey around the corner spotting the man that resembles my father so closely it is as if he is him reincarnated. He reaches his hand out and we bump fists and join in a hug.

"What's up, bruh? M'Dear, what you gone do with this sexy mother—"

I cut him off. "Watch your mouth, Rico."

He has no sense of boundaries, neither of us do, but I am more tamed around my mother. Drew is laughing as he and Rico are bumping fists and hugging. "What's up, Andrew?"

"Good to see you, bruh...you protecting the house with your special effect muscles?" Drew is concern about his decision to send the guy away. Knowing Shaun he had the guy hide from Rico's sight.

He chuckles. "That man didn't look like he could save a bird. I told Shaun watch who he sends over here." I think no one will look right to him unless they are our ol' man himself.

My mother persists with her question. She pours her peach filling in the glass pan giving me an eagle eye. "Romel, tell Rico who the girl is?"

I fall back a few paces leaning against the counter. "I am not with the girl." Our voices echo loudly in this kitchen.

Drew chimes in, "Her name is Victoria; everyone on campus knows he's after her." My nostrils flare and Rico is officially coming after me.

"Victoria, you say, Drew?"

"Victoria...well why haven't you let us meet her, son?"

I frown. "We are not together Drew is instigating."

I step away from the kitchen and Rico hits me in my back. "I'm investigating M'Dear... I will let you know the details." He walks the opposite direction and motions his hands for me and Drew to follow him. I know what will happen, he will talk to us about life in the military and eventually we will talk about females. He kind of feels like he has to take on my ol' man's role since his death. He's cool but I don't like for him to talk too much because it takes me to a sad place about my pops. Rico looks like him and it's not the best therapy for me either.

We walk down the hall leading to the glass hall off the main house. My mother thought it would be best having a man cave off the house because we can get loud. Drew is walking next to Rico and they are playing tag as if the two are boxing. I can see a security detail in the window's glare; the black Mercedes is a dead giveaway.

My head turns recognizing a bird house in the tree situated the right of the garden. It's beautiful bordering the outskirt of the pond. I remember when we planted that tree for my pops. It was the day I stopped calling Mr. Rodd 'Uncle Senior.' I realized how difficult it was for him to hear us reference him as Senior. Planting that tree was a challenge for us all considering we planted one for the loss of Mr. and Mrs. Rodd's unborn child. It's interesting, we both lost a family member but somehow gained more family with each other.

I step ahead and I see Drew sitting at the table. Rico is shuffling dominos. "Come over here so I can school you in dominoes." My brother is the master of talking trash, it's an art of his. Winning for him is mostly talking trash and less of the skill set. Once he gets in your mind you lose all aspects of staying in the game. I pull out the chair and sit across from him and Drew.

With this game its nothing about brotherhood...it's all about the goal. I started playing this game at a young age. It was a passing of time and a moment to listen to my father give us life lessons. I look at my brother and he is going back and forth with the dominoes. "How long are you washing dishes, bruh? Let's play."

A sly smile grows on his face. "Andrew...I think he might want to talk about Victoria." He tilts his head to Drew. "He might...I know he keeps avoiding the topic as of late."

My brother picks up a domino, here we go. "Every domino is a goal." He pushes all the tiles to the side. His brows rise, and he continues, listening to the sound of his voice. "But as we know the final domino might be the ultimate goal."

Rico's fingers reach for the dominoes joining them together. "But it's no different from the other pieces." This is how his lessons begin, how he sounds like Mr. Rodd and pops all in one is beyond me. I shake my head.

"Can we just play, Rico?"

Drew entertains Rico joining his mind game. "So, bruh, the dominoes are not the problem—"

Rico leans in and continues. "Andrew, these little tiles are not obstacles or even a challenge...they are our goals...small goals." He picks up the domino and flashes it. "You two knuckleheads have to determine the path to reach the goal of trying to stop me —" His voice grows louder resembling Bernie Mac's tone. "— from beating yo ass."

We laugh at his trash-talking self.

He hits at the table. "Now that the PA of the fucking disclaimer has been heard...step aside while I achieve my ultimate goal of winning."

His level of confidence can cut your throat without him even trying. I love this dude. We chuckle and I get up from the table. Drew has a perplexed expression. "What are you doing, Rom?"

Pushing the chair back I rise and pace to the kitchen. "You two want something to drink? I'm sure you'll be sweating once I get in the game."

They chuckle and I reach pulling the refrigerator door open. Any drink you can think of is in here. I grab three beers and return to the table. My arm extends giving the drinks to them. "Thanks."

I tilt my head return to get three more. My brother is at it again. "Thanks, Rom... now that the tea party is over we can move on."

I shake my head sitting in my chair. "Rico, just because you're playing dominoes don't think you hard...it's not that serious."

Drew laughs as he twists the cap off of his drink. "You know this is like boxing to Rico...he is just punching on the table." My brother is a great fighter but he and Drew have an infatuation with guns. I think they memorize them to a science. Their motto is 'bullets are faster than humans.' I'm more hands on. I will use a gun but prefer to strike with my fists up close in vital zones. It's a nice rush.

I open my beer. "Yep, nothing physical all mental, big bruh."

He swigs back his drink. "When I get finish you two will physically feel like I beat you in the ring. Like when Uncle Jay got you in line, Rom'?" He winks his eye as I recall that night.

"That was a wild night... in fact, Uncle Jay was talking all that smack about his nephew coming to get me. He had me so hype in that ring."

Drew is smirking. "My ol' man had no idea we already knew each other from school until we were in the ring boxing." Memories can take you up and down in a moment's time, my head rocks back and forth recalling being nine years old, stubborn as hell. "Uncle Senior walked in the spot with you next to him."

Drew's eyes narrow remembering the day. "I had on a suit and you thought you knew you were about to take me."

A silence grows over me but I push through talking about the turn of events. I can't believe how freely I'm calling him Uncle

Senior. "You changed and came back looking like Satan took over you." Drew laughs.

My brother shuffles the dominos again and looks in my direction. "Uncle Senior was playing with your mind having him show up in that suit."

"Yes, he was...it worked because I was in that gym every weekend." Mr. Rodd was working on all of us with the help of his brother, Uncle Jay. We were all learning to be disciplined, focus our energy and manage it. Considering how he met me in an alley I was completely out of control. Rico stops shuffling and our hands reach in the pile to get our dominoes. Gripping my bones in hand I look for my doubles. I place my pieces face down and grab my double six and slam it in the table's middle. "Straight up...let's go, baby!"

Rico has a cool demeanor, and he is looking at his hand. "It's a strategy to playing dominos. Bruh, your strategy is to get Victoria's pussy just like I am strategizing to take you on this table." I shake my head laughing, but it's true, I have been strategizing over a year now. This will be a long game with him smacking the table and talking mess. You would think he's the UDL champ in here. He slams his domino on the table, yelling out, "Young girl 15."

Drew looks at his hand, then the six three tile and chimes in. "Shit, that's what Romel is messing around with, Young Puerto Rico." My brother is laughing.

"Is that right? Now we are talking." As expected my brother wants me to give him the goods on the girl I like. Victoria's family is Puerto Rican-Colombian on her mother's side. Her grandfather parents immigrated to the United States from Colombia. Her story about how they joined in New York is a classic. I adore that her great grandparents cherish family. She told me how her great grandmother, Alejandra, who is Puerto Rican was friends of the family with her great-grandfather, Victorio, whom she is named after. The fact that her great-grandmother's name is so close to my father's has a certain sentiment. Anyway, their story is like they were a family before getting involved. Yet the moment he was established enough to take care of her he went to her ol' man. It's like they must get the approval of their parents for the union of family. It's honorable. *Dignidad* or as we say dignity, the respect for grandparents, aunts, uncles. It doesn't matter, the way of life for her family reminds me of how we are with each other. Loyalty is to family first it's an attribute she gets without me having to explain to her.

I bite my lip and snarl at Drew. "Hell, you prowling with women bringing breast milk to the house. His ass is the cub to multiple cougars in Atlanta."

We all lean over laughing. Drew speaks up, "No drama, no tricks...they know exactly what they like. Young girls are like an overtime job, you have to put in too much labor and it's still not enough."

Rico looks over and grabs his beer. "Older women take and give pleasure freely...it's a powerful thing. She can teach yo ass how to stay in control." Drew slams the table as if he will break it placing the six two. "Fish and bread keep the po man fed." It's my turn. I have two choices.

I slam down my six five and talk shit. "Break yo back, Rico." He flips his domino up in the air.

"Shit, you still haven't broken Victoria's back but you keep running after my ass." I am laughing at him but staying in the game. He slams a six blank.

Drew moves without waiting. "Next get yo ass up ten, take him to the pen, I knock down Big Ben."

Staring at my hand, I can go either way. "*De cualquier.* Either way, baby!"

They are both laughing at me and I am thinking about being locked up in the care of Victoria. "I'm taking you to the pen all right. Shit, she can handcuff my ass all night."

Rico burst out laughing spitting his beer across the room.

"Shit, she got you speaking Spanish and you ain't even taste her shit? Andrew, what the fuck you letting my brother do in Atlanta?"

Drew puts his hand face down. "You need to talk to him, bruh. He is not trying to mess with any other female since." I give him a side look and he shuts off his words. "You already know, Rico."

My brother is a concern, and I shut my eyes hating that Drew brought up the other female scenario. He pushes the few dominos in his hand and stands. "I'm out." Now we have to listen to his lecture.

My head is shaking. "Rico, you draw from the bone yard." This makes little sense. I flip over his domino. He is lying he could play. Why is Rico concerned like this? I stare across the table. "Drew, what the fuck?" He turns his wrist confirming he meant no harm. That was the shortest game we ever played.

Rico grabs his bottle and tops off his beer. Drew has both his drinks and goes to the chair across from the couch.

Is this an intervention I knew nothing about?

Rico returns with another beer, and picks up the other I already had for him and takes a seat on the couch. I take in a deep breath and sit on the opposite end of the couch from Rico.

He starts a random conversation. "I ran into my boy from school the other day but I didn't see him. Initially, I saw this female, she was walking my way." I think when you go to the Military you automatically become a story teller because he has tales for days.

His eyes bulge as if he can see the chick. "I was like 'baby, shit' and it was like a signal for my dude because he popped around the corner." Drew and I are laughing because Rico has a tendency to air lift a girl from a guy without remorse. He puts his beer on the table next to him and rest his elbows on his knees. "The girl was skinning and grinning and my dude he is cool. I knew it was his girl so I digress and told him." He talks with his hands. "Black, damn yo woman, she looks good." He is motioning his hand recalling the turn of events. "I give a pound and I move around."

I shoot a look at Drew knowing there has to be more to this story. Drew opens his second beer.

"A man knows when he's got something good."

Rico nods his head. "Right, my dude dap me up and we keep moving…but in my mind—" Here goes the rest of the story he doesn't tell his friend. He continues, repositioning on the sofa, "I was thinking, 'shit…I'm giving him a pound but I want to stick that shit.' I am thinking, you know real talk. Can I hit that?" He holds up his finger in the air as he speaks. "Just one time."

Rico's head is shaking his head as if he is imagining her. "I mean the girl was…man, she looks good."

He hits at my knee. "Romel, people want nothing nobody else wants. Mother fuckers compete with me. But I'm like you, coming around here bragging." His fists ball as if he is acting out the scene. "Driving around like you doing something and you haven't even hit that. Get the fuck out of here."

His shoulders shrug. "What am I competing with you? You ain't even fucking her." We laugh taking in his story but I get what he is saying. He says it in a crazy way but I got it. "Rico, I am not thinking she's not pretty enough."

Drew interrupts, "Hell no, Rico, the girl is always meeting up with him to work out. She calls him you know for one-on-one time but he not going at it, at her."

I cringe giving him the evil eye and my brother taps my leg. "Rome,l if she is messing around with another guy—"

Drew interrupts, "Hell no, Rom, sees her with multiple guys."

He frowns. "She's a hoe?"

I stand and knock over my drink. "Fuck no!" They are both motioning for me to sit down. I lean, grabbing my mess and walk to the kitchen. "Every female that messes with multiple dudes are not whores. Drew is a whore?"

We burst out laughing. He chuckles and drinks the rest of his beer. Walking back to the sitting area I take the towel and clean my mess. Rico is laughing, and he clears his throat. "Drew, you are a commanding whore?"

He throws his hand in the air. "You either do what I say or kick rocks. I'm running the show."

"She's the girl I'm not willing to share, so she doesn't have to worry about me interrupting her. She can get that out her system and eventually she will be with me."

He has a filthy expression on his face. "Rom, what are you going to do when a dude with my mentality comes along? She's not coming to you after dealing with me...I'm going for her guts." He grips his fist to his chest and starts grinding then he grabs at himself. "Once I unleash the anaconda and I size you up your ass is mine for the taking."

We all grab our stomachs, laughing at his crazy story. "You don't have an ounce of sense, bruh."

I sit upright composing myself. "I'm good, big bro...I'm confident...she's already mine." Without a doubt I know she is and she will know for herself in due time.

"What's up with you? How long before you have to report in?" My mother is alerting us on the intercom I walk over the wall.

"Yes, M'Dear." She is rambling on and tells us the food will be ready in ten minutes. "We are on our way back." Rico stands and picks up his bottles. Drew passes him the bottles and marches to exit the room. I reach to turn off the light and Rico is coming toward me.

"Romel, you can never tell a dog to stop barking...it's in his nature."

My face hardens in concentration as I flex my chest.

Rico pats my back. "Hey, don't flex too hard and pass out." I chuckle at his remark. "I get it, you are emotionally invested in the girl."

Drew turns back laughing. "Romel is getting hype like he's Kobe in the fourth, sit down, bruh." I rub my palm over my face, reflecting on the conversation and shout at both of them.

"Fuck you, Drew, and fuck you, bruh! I'll let her know." I attempt to trip Drew while he walks ahead, and he jumps from my reach.

"You better tell her, because a dog is always close by."

VICTORIA

I'm exhausted, at this point I think I am going to die.

I don't want to die like an animal; I don't want my sister to see me get shot or watch her get shot.

I don't want to die like this.

Closing my eyes, I remember dancing to a song when I was a kid. I would drive my sister insane and my parents. I'd hum the song, singing under my breath finding peace, the only piece of happiness I had as if I was that young girl dancing. Singing the song over and over in my head imagining me dancing over and over empowers me.

I will not die like this here. My sister will not look at me die and I will not let her die. Pondering our escape, I realize if I get caught they will murder me. But at least I wouldn't die here on this filthy floor as my sister looks at me helplessly. My sister is scared I can hear her whisper, "We will die."

I snap my head up. "No, we will not die." At least if we try, she'll stop looking at me as if I've let her down somehow. At least if we try, we would die trying and fighting. My eyes look up noticing a window; it is boarded up with plywood.

My sister is untied, but she holds her body as if shackles are on her. I whisper for her to hear me, "Tati, I will lift you, but I need you to go as far as you can." She shakes her head and I realize she does not like the plan.

Her voice cuts through the room. "Victoria, we will get caught. I am naked, someone will see me." Her legs are trembling. I move forward and she motions for me to stay.

"Listen, Tatiana we can go when it's dark."

She shakes her head violently, snatching the soul out of my body. I know she's worried, scared, and feels helpless. I feel the same way.

Her eyes grow wide in concern. My bark commands in an aggressive low pitch. "I won't let anyone hurt you. I will insist for them to take me, not you."

Again, she doesn't like the idea and her eyes refuse the notion. I plead, "Sis, you can leave and get away no matter what I will not let them hurt you. You run and don't stop running."

"Victoria, I'm dead if I don't have you." She is shaking all over and I hush her as the morning fades, she cries silently. Tears spill from my sister's eyes onto her bare shoulder. Her lips shiver like a baby as she stares at the ceiling. Static fills my head as the rain seeps inside the bare room. My muscles tense in fear.

A feeling of numbness grows over me. Do I have any more feelings to feel as time is robbing me of my spirit, a deep injury unseen to the eyes? I lean against the wall.

Seeing my sister fall asleep salty tears roll from my eyes to the tip of my lips. Is God afraid of the dark I wonder? I stretch my hand to the walls hoping strength will grow inside...my knees weaken, and I collapse. I have to get out of here. I know I have to still be strong, looking to the window the baby blue sky cascades to lavender. A half smile grows on my face as I think of my father. My legs tremble, pressing against the wall my fingers shake. I lower to the wall crying so silently, holding my chest, I rock back and forth as tears soak through my blinking lashes. I sit in misery, howling inside my core in such raw fashion as my eyes grow heavy into the night. Maybe, that's why God made the stars?

I GULP THE MUGGY AIR, my eyes unable to see beyond the light from the moon. With the passing of hours my senses recognize a permanent stillness is in place. I survey wind and get up grabbing my sister, realizing the house is silent. I lift her.

She is disoriented. "Now…we have to go now."

I practically raise her to the window as if she is a brick I'm stacking on a wall. Her tears fall on my skin. She slams her foot in the window and I push it out. As the realization of her escaping the house grows over her, she becomes alive.

Tatiana's feet are clear from the window and she reaches for me. I shake my head. "Go run please just run." She breaks down. "*Mirar*…look at me. I will get out. I need you to run to the train track." She wails like she is in pain from an open wound and it rips through my muscles. Pressing her forehead against the window I push her. "Please, run." She reaches for me with her trembling fingers and I push her shaking body away.

With a tone of urgency, I encourage her, "Run, Tatiana, or we will not make it." Overcome with emotions she breaks free and her feet kick back through the mud. She makes it across a train track. My heart pounds in relief seeing her as the rain drips over her body.

My ears catch the hint of a noise far off in the building. "Oh, no!"

I can hear the slight sound of the front entrance. My head twist and I see a light come through the hall. My legs jump with so much force.

I must get out of here. I can push through.

I cry as I crawl through the window, naked. The moment the

fresh air hits my face I claw my fingers in the grass, pulling my weight.

A hand grabs my ankle. I'm desperately trying to escape, and his grip never gives up, jerking me back inside. I hear a loud, gruff voice. "You are my bitch!" His accent resembles a foreigner; I didn't notice it at first. My fingers claw at his face as I stumble against the wall. Taking in his sloppy appearance, my eyes stare at the man with the scar on his face.

He stands tall not exactly six feet, but taller than me. His fist hits me on the head making my body twist forward to the wall. Unaware, he knocks me from behind until I am on the floor.

I bring my weight down on the outside of his leg; he is unbalanced as I swing my body weight. Fear boils inside but I'm not letting him win. "Ugh...Not today, bastard!"

My elbow rises, crushing his throat. He buckles at his knees and I ball up my fist, jabbing him in the liver. The man freezes dropping to the floor.

I spit at his face. "Injury is yo bitch." His observant eye watches me, wanting to come after me, but he can do nothing. Realizing he is dazed, his upper body bobs to the right, I am certain there is nothing he can do. I feel as if I am losing consciousness and gulp in the air. The thunder roars, surging a rush of adrenaline inside me.

I jump up to the window, crawling through bare. The fresh air hits my face a second time and I tear my fingers in the grass, pulling my weight until I am no longer in the house. I hear a car door squeak and I lay still, heart pounding in my ear upon the muddy grass. I steal a look, seeing Tatiana's legs from afar. She lowers her body looking for me. My thoughts are racing. Why won't she run to safety?

The rain drops pick up and I lift my head realizing where I am. The wind whistles and screeching noises resonate in my ear as I see a light. "A train is coming."

Becoming more oriented I look around, lying in the grass

bare, cold wind whips across my skin. I am near to Chantal's house; she lives over thirty miles from my house. I pick up my body and run ahead.

A yellow light of hope is growing closer, staring from the rails. My head never turns back my desires and destiny rushes ahead of me as the rain drops on my skin. The sound of the train is closer. I keep running, hearing the rush and rumble of massive metal coming toward me.

Tatiana sees something, and she comes out from hiding. "Hurry. He's coming, sis." She's yelling for me to come. The sound of the long string of metal from the train gains closer and closer. The train block signal descends. I keep my head at the forefront, only looking for my sister. My feet touch the metal bleeding between the concrete. I lower my body under the railway stop signal and tumble, scratching my knees on the gravel. A bell rings in my head as the explosive engines roar steam, whipping the rain and wind around me, as it streaks through the night.

Tatiana's hand is reaching to help me off the ground. I blink as I feel like I'm in the middle of a dream tied to a railroad track. She grabs at me and I know it's not a dream. I rise to my feet. Her voice is shaking. "Victoria, we have to keep running."

My heart is racing, pounding, and I can't believe we made it.

RUNNING as the wind whisks between my legs with the rain pouring over my skin is the most freeing thing at this moment. Looking back is not an option for me or my sister. We have to be four maybe five miles away from the trap house. My sister's pace is slowing. "What's wrong?" Come on we have to move.

"Ugh, I stepped on something." She is pushing me with all the might she has.

"We have to keep going." I see a light coming on in the back of Chantal's house. I point to her home. "Can you make it to the house?" The wind is roaring louder, and the joined thunder adds power to my legs as we run from the hands of the men that promised us death.

"Yes."

I pull her arm around my shoulder and we run.

Our feet hit the alley, I am grateful for the trees towering over us but concerned as the lightning strikes. Looking around the alleyway it's empty, not a person in sight. I imagine most people are not interested in being outside in this weather but for us it's a distraction as we move toward the back yard. I can make out one of Chantal's brothers in a window. How am I going to explain this situation to them? Once they set their eyes on me nothing will stop their rage.

My sister's limp is causing us to move poorly through the dark passage. "We have to go in the house, Tati." She holds at her stomach.

"Can I lay here?"

I shake my head. "Once we get in the house, you can rest. This house, I know where we are."

She is shaking as we hobble inches away from the gate. I eyeball the chain making out the risk of her jumping over the gate. "Please, I can wait, sis."

My head turns back, searching for a sign of someone shadowing us, then my eyes flash to the back door of the house. I know once I jump over this gate the lights are going to hit me and her brothers will not respond nicely. Lifting my sister's body, I position her behind a car sitting on the side of the alleyway. The water seeps through the leaves of the trees overhead, falling on my lips as I speak. "I will get help. You stay here." She is holding her foot and nods her head in agreement.

I take in a jagged breath, imagining the thunder as the fuel that gives me strength as I crawl over the gate. The second my fingers reach the top the lights in the yard's corner flick on. I take in two gulps of air.

Please don't shoot me. Please, just this once, look before acting, I plead as if they can hear my thoughts. Pushing my feet off the metal, I land on the slippery grass and stand still. Another light flashes on. My foot cautiously moves over the soaked land. "Maybe I am undetectable, and they are lost in a movie."

I hope there're no bombs planted out here. I wouldn't be surprised if I get blown away. My foot grazes something hard and I lower my head to the ground. It's the water sprinkler head. My heartbeat is escalating, and I go further trying to reach the door. My head faces the back of the house. "Damn, my moment of being invisible is over."

His eyes glance over my exposed body and I fall to my knees with my hands up. The squeak of the screen sounds and I lift my head noticing Jesse's grip on the gun he holds in my direction. I gulp and plead for his help, "Don't shoot me, please. Help!" Jesse doesn't say a word but his vicious demeanor roars as loud as the thunder with each step he takes.

Omari stomps closer.

"Jesse! Stand down, that's Victoria. Jesse, put the gun down!" I collapse face forward in the mud, in seconds his grip is pulling me off the wet grass. I take in a deep breath and his shouting to Jesse snaps me to reality.

His baritone voice shakes in my ear. "Why are you out here like this?" Omari swings the door further.

I lift my head. "My sister is outside."

Jesse's brutal eyes grow wide. "Chantal?"

I shake my head. "No, Tati."

Omari's body shifts to protection mode, he's Chantal's youngest brother, and he moves forward, passing me. He is the same age as Tatiana, but in his eyes he is a grown man with a huge crush on my baby sister. "Little Ma is outside?" He treads out without me telling him where she is.

Jesse puts me down growling and turns away trying to avoid seeing my naked state. "Let me get you a towel."

"Get my sister!" His eyes connect with my fearful expression and he picks me up by my shoulders until I am back in the kitchen sitting in a chair. "Victoria, Omari is out looking for her."

Jesse walks out of the kitchen and his loud steps thump across the floor. I look over to the living area. Chantal must not be home. Jesse returns to the kitchen with a towel and an over-sized shirt. Standing to my feet I stagger to the sink and turn on the faucet. I hear Jesse opening a compartment. I wipe the mud off my eyes and slide the shirt over my head. Lifting my face, I watch as he secures several guns to his waist.

My neck jerks at the back door as it opens. Omari is speaking frantically, "I don't see her! Victoria, are you sure?" I jump to my feet and rush out the exit. My heart is pounding, and the rain fall is fading as I push the gate open. I go to my right looking to the ground by the vehicle. I left her here, I know I did. "Tatiana?"

I hear a screeching noise but don't see her. Omari steps on the other side of the car. The gate opens from behind, Jesse has something in his hand as he points inside the car. The bass of his voice is so heavy it could scare you into silence or compel you into action. "Open the back door."

Jesse throws a cloth like material to Omari and he pulls open the passenger door. "Little Ma...it's me Omari. Open your eyes."

I rush to the opening of the car and reach for Tatiana, she is backing away on the floor of the car. "Sis, Tatiana, put this over your body come with me inside." Her eyes shine as she takes the shirt in hand.

Backing out to give her space to exit the car, Jesse and Omari share a rage-filled look. "Let's get you two inside; we have business to tend to."

Tatiana clamps her fingers around my wrists as she stands

behind me. "Are we safe here?" I chuckle understanding her timid state.

"We are safe, sis, we are at Chantal's." I don't think she is in her right mind because she still doesn't seem to recognize Omari.

JESSE IS OVERBEARING, not once will he let me explain. He only wants to know where I came from leaving us in this state. "Jesse, let me call Chantal."

Bang! He hits the table. "No."

He throws a pencil and paper on the table and my sister jumps. Omari moves to her side. "Little Ma, you can go take a shower." Jesse's head snaps and his dangerous voice sends chills down my back.

"Fuck no, that's evidence."

I bang the table and he stands I raise my body to his chest. Masking all panic, my voice is stern. "Jesse, calm the fuck down. You are scaring my sister."

His nose flares. "Our sister."

Tears glimmer in his eyes and I realize he is in a state of rage seeing us like this. "I want the person that did this to you both. I am not calming down until I get them all."

Omari holds Tati in his arms and speaks to his brother. "Jesse, look at her, just calm down. Chantal and momma will be here in an hour."

"Where are they? I don't want Chantal seeing us like this, Jesse." I turn looking at Jesse and he sits down pushing the paper across the table.

"We have little time, Victoria. You draw the details. We will take you to the hospital."

Omari stands and holds Tatiana, walking down the hall. Her foot is oozing blood from her injury. He speaks to her in a calm tone. "I will help you with your foot, Little Ma."

Jesse is the most irrational guy I know, he never reasons. I draw him an outline of where we came from before we got to the house. "Jesse, my car is at the mall and my parents have no idea, we have been gone for three days."

His face twists in confusion. "You've been gone for three days and no one went looking for you two?" His calm state is disappearing, and I grab at Jesse's shirt. He jerks his body away pulling out a hand gun from the kitchen drawer.

"Jesse, they thought we were on a trip. It's not what you are thinking." What is he thinking? No one knows, all I know is he has to calm down. Jesse puts the hand gun on the table next to me and I draw out our tracks before we got to the house on the paper.

Omari enters the room without Tatiana. "Victoria, we need to take her to the hospital now. She is not okay. She's in a state of shock."

He looks at Jesse. "Your beast-mode anger is not helping the situation, bruh." I am happy to see he's being rational, but I don't want to go to the hospital they ask too many questions.

"Jesse, I don't—"

Omari cuts me off as if he is my father. How can a sixteen-year-old talk with such aggression. "You two are going to the hospital you can tell them what happened, or you don't have to, but the evidence needs to be accounted for. It deranges Jesse, but your body is evidence." He grabs the hand gun and looks at Jesse. "Where's my friend Mr. Smith?"

Jesse shakes his head. "No, Omari, every time you carry that gun you turn into Black Ops...no!"

He lifts his hand in the air and it's so funny seeing brothers argue over a gun. Typically, brothers argue over shoes or even food, but these two argue over guns. Only Chantal's blood line would be involved in such craziness.

Jesse speaks with a stern voice, "Take the hand gun. Let's get going."

Omari growls and taps on the wall. "You underestimate my skills, bruh."

His brother's eyes grow with concern. "My sis, on the hand, understands me." He is shaking his head. Chantal had that mess installed for him without Jesse knowing. He looks at me. My hands flash in the air.

"I didn't install it, Jesse. Hell, I would have bought him shoes or clothes. Only Chantal buys gifts in the form of auxiliary weapons."

Jesse's eyes narrow in my direction. "I'll deal with Chantal. Omari, you get Tati and meet us in the car out front." Omari is chuckling at his brother and we walk to the garage.

ROMEL

I peek into the kitchen, spotting the granite stone island covered with food. I smile as my mother comes into view; she is beckoning me to work. "Romel, take the place settings and put them on the table. Janice will be here in a moment." I do as she requests. Lifting the faucet handle at the sink in the heart of the room, the water runs over my hands and am eyeballing the peach cobbler.

Considering my mother knows me she politely lifts the dessert from my reach placing it in the oven. "Come on, I didn't touch it."

She smirks, passing me a paper towel. "In your mind that cobbler is good and gone."

I tilt my head, thanking her, and laugh. Rico walks in care-free as my fingers grab enough silverware for six out of the drawer in the island. I look around recalling the last time we all got together for dinner was when we left for college. He pulls open the oven and I chuckle. "Rico, if you don't get away from this cobbler!"

My mother turns him and he is in front of the island.

"M'Dear, I wanted to test it out before the company arrived. I'm sure you will need to know if it tastes good." He acts like he is licking his fingers and steps to the sink. "I can make sure it's perfect for tonight."

She shakes her head. "Get over there with Romel and set the table." Rico grabs the plates off the counter. She never lets us go through her cabinets. My mother knows exactly what she wants on the table and she demands for us to always set it accordingly. He follows in behind me, entering the dining room.

The dramatic oversized chandelier hangs from the tall ceiling making a huge statement as always. I put the settings down one by one on the black, rectangular table. Rico sets the plates on the opposite side in front of the fire place. This room always made me feel as if I am at a five-star restaurant, nothing like our home when I was younger. I don't dislike the dining room, it's just this is the room I imagine my father not spending most of his time. He liked small intimate settings, this area is large.

Rico taps the table. "Go get the glasses and keep your hands out of my peach cobbler." My mother walks through the door and I grab a dish of glazed carrots. Mrs. Rodd enjoys carrots more than anyone I have ever met. I set them closer to the seat she typically sits in.

"Rico, you can grab the glasses!"

My mother returns with wine glasses passing them to Rico and I laugh. He snarls in my direction and I walk in the kitchen grabbing the leg of lamb and steaks dressed with grilled avocados off the counter. My mother likes everything avocado, she watches me as I hold them in the air. "Romel, put those in the center."

I tilt my head being cautious as I stroll in ahead. Rico holds the door open and I hear the doorbell ring.

Drew yells out, "I will get it." Why wasn't he helping set the table? He must be on the phone with some chick. Mr. and Mrs. Rodd's voices echo across the house as they greet my mother.

Drew and Rico rush in with the remaining dishes in hand. Drew sets the Baja chicken and black beans opposite the carrots. Rico has the green beans, potatoes, and a cluster of veggies.

My eyes lift noticing Mr. Rodd, he tilts his head in greeting as he enters with a salad and dinner rolls in hand. I rush back in the kitchen. My nostrils breathe in a chocolate aroma, and I shoot a grin toward Mrs. Rodd and my favorite dish that she is stowing away. "Come on I know you didn't bring those brownies over here for decoration."

My mother laughs and I realize she is covering a pecan pie. Mrs. Rodd grins. "Romel, you will get brownies later."

I turn my head to an unfamiliar face as my mother introduces me. "Romel, this is June, she comes by occasionally." She nods her head.

"Nice to meet you, Romel."

I twist my lips, she must be here to assist with serving and cleaning. My mother finds my eyes and I keep my mouth shut and shake my head. *I don't know her.* My mother smiles and speaks to June as if she and Drew's mother go to a pottery class of some sort together. Mrs. Rose Adcock will not let another woman cook in her kitchen...well Janice is an exception. She enters the dining area with lemonade.

I look at the counter and my mother motions for me to go to the dining area. June is pouring our beverages while Mr. Rodd is opening a bottle of wine. Drew holds the door as the women enter the room. Mr. Rodd sets the wine on the table and pulls out the chair for his wife. Rico pulls the chair out for our mother and we remain on our feet until our mothers have been seated.

Mr. Rodd clears his throat as June has completed filling all the glasses with wine. He stands, holding his glass. "In remembrance of a dear friend, father, and husband, Alexander Adcock."

We all hold our glasses in unison and chant, "We remember you always!" Together we sip from our wine, honoring the memory and time with my father.

Dinners start this way every time we are together, and I cherish it. Rico clears his throat. "M'Dear, everything looks great. I am on a diet so we can skip all this, let June bring out the dessert." She shakes her head and we laugh.

Mrs. Rodd interrupts his banter. "Don't you make me spoon feed you, Rico." He is placing a steak on his plate.

"I am going to eat, Mother Janice." Shrugging his shoulders, he leans in the table. "I just thought I would try, Romel will eat the house if we are not looking."

The sounds of laughter take over the room and love showers throughout the space. I notice everyone has food to their liking on their plates. My mother chimes in, "We have not blessed the food." Her eyes grow wide.

Drew places his fork down and makes a request, "Pops, will you pray? No disrespect, M'Dear Rose, but it will be midnight by the time you finish." Mrs. Rodd turns in Drew's direction giving him a firm look. My mother laughs and addresses my father with a nonchalant, "Senior."

He lifts his eyes. No matter how much time has passed my mother is the only person he cannot stop from calling him Senior. I think it's a memory she shares of stories my dad told her, and Mr. Rodd will only accept her calling him Senior without tearing up. He takes in a deep breath and his wife is smiling at him. Drew is correct, my mom prays as if we are about to float into heaven.

We bow our heads and Mr. Rodd proceeds in prayer, "Heavenly Father, thank you for the cook and bless the food we are about to eat, thank you for this time and memories we are sharing as a family. We appreciate your many blessings…Amen."

Being home eating my mother's cooking is the best. I finish adding more to my plate and Drew speaks out, "I got a call from a Special Agent Charles." I continue eating my food, not wanting to say a word. Mr. Rodd is pissed; he cuts Drew off before he finishes.

"You and Romel will not speak to him, do I make myself clear?" My head shakes I'm sure Drew is not going to take his pops talking to him as if we are still kids. Mr. Rodd is waiting for us to reply. I need them to calm down this is supposed to be a nice dinner. I'm not aware of what happened back in the day, but with someone seeking us out to come work for the government he snaps. Only Uncle Jay his brother can ask us to hack systems to find details. I don't know how Rico got his approval to join the military.

"Uncle Senior, it's cool we will not talk to the guy."

He snaps hearing me call him Uncle Senior. "Ugh, you two don't know everything...you only think you do."

Rico picks up his wine and gives Drew a side look. *Say nothing.*

Mr. Rodd stands throwing his napkin on the table. Drew rises. *Here we go.* "Explain or leave, we are not kids." We hold a silence in the room for ten seconds. I blink my eyes, surely he didn't just say that aloud.

My Rodd's voice resembles something fierce. "If you didn't act so much like a kid, perhaps I could see that."

My mother stands and they sit. "Janice, help me get these men something cool to drink." Mrs. Rodd stands, not responding to them, and she walks with my mother to the kitchen.

Rico wipes his mouth with the napkin and leans in. "You two cool it. No disrespect Mr. Rodd, but for my mother, cool it."

He clears his throat. "Excuse me...I'm straight, Rico."

Drew tilts his head. "My fault Rico and Romel, I'll drop it." My mother returns and I hold the door as she enters.

Rico grabs the pitcher of sweet tea and Drew walks over to his mother to take the dessert she has in her hands. He sets it in the middle of the table on the other side of the veggies "Forgive me, Momma Rose."

"All is forgiven…now let's enjoy this peach cobbler. I didn't make as a decorative centerpiece." Laughter once more fills the room and the balance of love temporarily washes out the secrets Mr. Rodd is keeping from us. It doesn't matter because I want the damn dessert that's still in the kitchen.

ROMEL

$\mathcal{D}$riving directly to work after arriving home from Dallas has got to be the dumbest idea I have made in a while. But I am happy I saw the family. I lean my head over the desk wishing the night would come. I am feeling like I should have called in sick; I don't recall sleeping. Drew turns around and inches his chair behind me. "Check your ten." My eyes raise and a man dressed in a police uniform is walking in my direction. Drew whispers. "Why is his shirt un-tucked?"

Wrinkles form on my forehead and I whisper back, "Drew, where is his gun? What type of officer is he?"

I realize this guy has a mission, as I head to my shit hole of a desk in the room's center surrounded by thirty other desks with people guarding the web from perps. I sit upright and the man leans over my desk. He throws a card on my desk I notice it's embossed with the initials A&R. He walks pass my desk and throws the same card on Drew's desk. We reach for the card and stand. This confirms he knows Mr. Rodd and Uncle Jay. I stride through the rows of desks noticing each person's eyes remain focused on their computer screen. Drew is walking down the opposite aisle giving the impression he is heading to the elevator.

In my view is the guy dressed as a police officer. He pulls open a door to a meeting room and Drew's fingers reach for the door as he follows the man. I pass the door they entered as I cross the second entry the door pulls open and Uncle Jay is in standing against the wooden panel entrance. Stepping inside I see the man in the uniform is next to Drew, entering a side door in the room.

Uncle Jay locks the door behind me and sit next to Drew at the oval table, facing the guy appearing as an officer. An image is being placed in front of us by the unknown man.

"Officially, I am off this case. I need you to use your skills on the dark web to—" He pushes the image closer for me and Drew to see. "—help me find this missing girl."

Uncle Jay interrupts, "Guys, we need you to be discrete." He puts a photo of a girl on the table in the middle of me and Drew. My eyes lift and I look up at Uncle Jay.

"She's dead, Unc?"

Drew pulls the photo of the other image closer. "Isn't she the same girl in this photo?" Why does she have on make-up as if she is a clown? Or a high maintenance doll?

The unidentified officer lowers his voice. "Yes"

He looks devastated, as if something didn't go right. I'm not sure why, but they trust us to help them. What exactly are we supposed to do if she's dead? Uncle Jay puts laptops on the table and he has our attention. "All the information you need is on the computer. We need you to figure out the encrypted code and once you have—"

The officer interrupts and slides his card on the table, "You will contact me to give me the code." They both are on their feet.

I tilt my head and Drew nods. "We will be in touch."

They exit the room and we split, going in opposite directions. I pace until I am at the exit for the staircase. Pushing the door, I step ahead and follow the stairs to the garage and jog with the laptop in hand. Whenever Mr. Rodd or Uncle Jay come by we typically stop what we are doing and head out to work on whatever they ask of us. There is not much of an explanation and I don't mind. I like not knowing more than I need to, but when cases like this rise, it is enough to make myself and Drew draw close to the edge. Seeing dead people and not knowing if we are helping the victim or the assailant can be mind-wrecking.

My feet shuffle, arriving to the garage, and I push the door as I exit the staircase. I see Drew drive off in his Mercedes and I hurry to my vehicle, unlocking the door. I grab my cell from my back pocket and turn on the phone.

I've been working at this location for a year and a half now as a Cyber Security Hacker. One rule states that we cannot have our cell phones on while on the company premises. My phone has notifications sounding off; as I pull open my car door I toss the phone inside and hit the button for the trunk. I walk around to the back of the car and set the laptop inside the trunk of my car and shut it.

Surveying the area, I hear a car approaching. I look up and walk along the side of my car, pulling the driver door. A royal blue car is leaving the premises. I situate myself inside my car and unlock my screen. Victoria still has yet to call me since she went to Dallas. I think that is odd. I see a notification from Drew.

I'm going to our place.

My fingers type a message to his text. *Ten behind.*

I insert the key and drive forward to my apartment.

VICTORIA

J've found that sleeping since escaping from the men that interrupted my life is impossible. Instead, I lay awake listening for the sound of the door unlocking. I lay listening for the voice of the man that stole my weekend of bliss with my sister away from me. I hear the childlike voice of my sister, trembling. "*Hermana.*"

Once the doctors determine Tatiana is unwilling to separate from me, they let us stay in one room, awaiting my parents to pick us up. A police woman attempts to come by to speak but I was not willing to talk to her. Everything inside me wishes I was not at this hospital. Omari is right, our bodies are full of evidence and in order for them to catch the men that did this to us they need the evidence. My sister tugs at the hospital nightgown wrapped around me. "Victoria, what if they come here and find us?" I rub the top of her head and her tears seep through the material onto my chest.

"Don't think like that, sis. We are safe and we are not victims."

My eyes roll to the door as my senses pick up the echo

marching down the hall. The click of the entry resonates in my ear and my body lifts as I hold tight to Tatiana. "*Mami*."

She has a bag in hand with our clothes. Tatiana reaches her arms for our mother and she drops the bag. As my mother's eyes set on her daughters, she gathers us up in a hug. She doesn't question us for now, she just cries in relief that we are alive.

The sound of my father's voice carries from the hall while he demands answers for what has happened to his daughters. My mother notices Tatiana is flinching at the aggression my father is displaying. She hides her face in her hands. "Tati, *Mami* will step out. I want you and your sister to get dressed alright." Silent tears fall from her eyes. My mother reaches for my hand and she pulls me near. Her voice is calm like a river. "Listen, don't you worry about a thing. You hear me, we will get through this together." My arms fall around my mother and sister and we stand crying.

"*Mami*, you go check on *Papi*. Tatiana and I will get dressed."

I RUB my hand across my eyebrow, caressing the stitches, moving my body every bruise can be felt. Shutting my eyes, I hang on to my spirit. A half smile grows as I think about my sister, and I have been stuck together for the past two days. My mother brings in lunch, but it sits on my dresser. We drink the liquids but cannot hold down solids. Jasmine has called my house over ten times and I have not returned her call. My mother told her my cell phone is lost, so instead she calls the house phone.

I wonder if Chantal's brothers have told her about me and Tatiana. I lay in my plush bed holding my sister, she cries out if I leave her side. As I stare at the purple wall feeling less than royal, numbness consumes my body. I stare at my vanity surrounded by pretty jewels.

"Tati, let me comb your hair." She shakes her head.

"I want to lay here."

I pull her chin to face me. "You can return to my bed after I comb your hair; it won't be long." She raises her frail body and I position my hand behind her lower back. My door pushes open; my parents are at the door. Tatiana scoots back. Tears roll down her face.

"It's *Papi,* sis, and *Mami.*" My father stands locked in fear, not wanting to cause more damage. His heavy eyes reveal the pain he has inside not being able to hold us in his arms. He doesn't make a sound. He just stands watching us. *Mami* steps forward and Tatiana moves, it almost as if she's learning to walk when she was a toddler. My mother paces two more steps and reaches her hand, hoping she responds to her.

"Tatiana, it's *Mami.*"

My sister doesn't respond, she walks to my vanity and lowers to the white fluffy pillow until her eyes see her reflection. She points at my reflection. "Victoria."

I nod my head, smiling as a tear falls. I reach for my mother pulling her in view. Tati tilts her head and her fingers slowly rub the outline of her nose down to her cheek bone. She leans looking closer out the three of us. "*Mami.*" My mother rejoices and her arms snake around my sister. Rage lingers within thinking of what those monsters did to my sister, what they did to the girl crying out for her life, and what they did to me. I turn away and my eyes meet my father that stands planted at the door. He doesn't say a word instead he moves his lips. *I'm so sorry.*

My father falls to his knees and my body feels as if it is about to explode. The doorbell rings and I turn to the window noticing the night sky. I speak with urgency. "We have to go now!"

My *papi's* hands are out in front of him. He whispers so softly, "Princess Victoria...you are safe." I look around and I hear the doorbell again, my body jumps. I hear Tati crying and I see my mother holding my sister as my father's tender voice floats in my ear. "Princess Victoria...you are safe." My eyes blink recognizing I am in my room with my family. I rush to my father as he kneels on the floor and he embraces me with his arms.

Life will never be the same for us.

Romel

APART FROM GOING TO CLASS, being locked in my apartment for several days is not helping my mind frame. I don't understand why this task is so difficult. Drew and I never take this long to figure out a code. I'm sitting in front of a computer screen trying to unlock a code. Drew looks up across from me. "Rom, check this out I found a drop box. I don't notice an IP address, but I found more photos."

My computer is still running trying to lock on a code. I stand and circle the table placing myself next to Drew, looking into his screen. I point to the images. "Open that one, Drew." He clicks on the file. What could it hurt if we learn what we are searching for before producing the info over to the officer?

Drew leans closer. "Romel, why do the pictures read as if they are staged? Is this a threat?" His finger glides over. "That photo looks real."

I twist my lips. "It's real, Drew...enlarge that shot."

He increases the size. This is an expression I will never forget for I have carried the memory with me since I was nine years old. "This female has fear and death in her eyes. Whoever this is wants to see their victims at the moment of death." Drew clicks and multiple images emerge. How many people has this person killed? My mind flashes but I keep my head.

"Turn it off, Drew." I lean back to the wall and drop to the carpet. "Turn it off, Drew!"

I push the heel of my palm into my eyes. It's been years since something has triggered me as if it was the night I was in the alley. Drew is in front of me. "Romel, it's okay. We know you were fighting for your—" A buzz from my computer alerts and I snap out of the memory. Drew hits my legs. "On your feet!"

Taking in a deep breath, I rise to join Drew in front of the laptop. There's a chat group of the person trying to meet up with someone to make a purchase. I move the mouse and type, locating more details of our search. "It's a code to a person that bought a photo." Hopefully, this can link the police to the creep killing these girls.

Drew pulls out his cell and calls the officer. "We have it." I don't think I am cut out for the work my ol' man and Mr. Rodd do. Even with him being retired the police still seek him out for help.

———

IT'S BEEN a week and I haven't seen Victoria on campus. Changing into my workout clothes I grab my backpack and throw my gloves inside. I hear Drew in the living room. "Romel, let's go!"

He has been around me more since the night of me flipping out. I am fine. That case was heavy on me. I slide my feet in my shoes and pull the drawstring in my pants. I exit my room grabbing my cell off the dresser. "I'm ready. I am making a stop and will meet you at the gym."

He stands to his feet. "Bruh, you didn't think to tell me. I would not have been out here waiting on you." We bump elbows.

"I just decided, I will see you in fifteen." He is shaking his head pulling the door open.

"I will see you, Rom."

I hustle to my car concern. My phone rings and I pull the phone. It's my mother. "Hi, beautiful."

She is giggling asking me if I say the same thing to Victoria. I unlock the door of my car and toss the bag in the back seat. "No, mother, not as of late." I don't think I have called her beautiful aloud. She is all in my business suggesting I call her beautiful. I twist my lips and enter the car. "I will think about it. How are you?" I look in the mirror and open my glove box reaching for my brush. I start the car and my phone syncs with my conversation with my mother. I place the phone in the cup holder. "Did Rico leave?" She is telling me he is to depart tomorrow. She and Mrs. Rodd are hanging out tonight. Pulling down my visor I brush my hair. I start my car and drive to Victoria's house. "M'Dear, I am on my way to workout I will check on you later." She assures me she will call me back because she has a life and will not be answering my calls. "M'Dear, don't act brand new. I will send Shaun over there if you don't answer my call or I will track you down myself." She is giggling telling me she will beat Shaun if he looks at her wrong. I nod my head and approach a red light. I am certain she will hurt the guy, but beat...hmmm.

My mother is a great fighter and can hold her own. My pops was big on making sure we all knew how to defend ourselves in his absence. I can feel tears coming to the surface as I am pulling up to Victoria's apartments. I wish his absence didn't come so early in my life. "M'Dear, I love you. I will check with you later." She disconnects and I turn the key. Exiting the car, I walk to the door. I spot Jasmine's car. Just as I reach out to knock on the door, it swings open. "Romel!"

Jasmine has a startled expression which I understand, I didn't say I was coming over. "Hey, Jasmine...I was just coming to check on Victoria. I haven't seen her around." She looks worried.

"She hasn't come back from Dallas, Romel. I called her parents' home and they won't tell me anything. I have never known them to be so distance." I rub the top of my head.

"She's okay, Jasmine. I'm sure she will be back soon." My fingers touch my chin. "I'll see you around." Something is going on and I don't like not knowing. Jasmine shuts the door and I walk to my car. I reach for my phone and call Stanley. He answers on the first ring.

"What's up, Stanley?" He is asking me why I am not at the gym to help Drew from getting his ass beat. "I'll be there in a minute. I need you to check something for me." He is laughing telling me how I know how to look into things on my own. "I understand but I have a number for a person, I am concerned about her. I need you to trace her phone. She's in Dallas. Can you find out if she's okay?"

He lets me know he will look into the matter. "Thanks, I will be there in ten." I disconnect the call. I hope she doesn't think I'm intruding but the vibes Jasmine just gave me was like a S.O.S. I could be mistaken but her face was distressed.

Victoria

I'm sitting at the kitchen table when I hear my dad's quiet voice in the hall. He has a smile on his face. "Hi, Princess Victoria." I smile remembering him calling me a princess most of my life. I rise and move to hug him.

"Morning, *Papi*."

"I want you to speak to someone." I step back and lower in the chair.

"I am not keen on talking to the public. "

My mother comes in the kitchen. This discussion is continuing in another direction. My mother lowers her body, hugging me from behind. "Victoria, we need you to communicate with the police."

"No!" I can't talk to the police. What if these people find us or Chantal's brothers? I have yet to even know if they found them.

I stand to leave the room and my father whisks my fingers in his. "Princess, we found your car. The police have your keys and cell phone." I gulp. I hate that they know what happened to us. *Mami* and *papi* are treating us as if we a fragile. I don't like to be looked upon as victim.

"I'm sorry, I didn't mean to get—" He walks closer brushing my hair away from my eyes.

"Princess, this is not your error. We realize you were thought to be out with the dance group."

My mother jumps in cutting him off. "Sweetheart, we expected you two were with the dance group. It wasn't until the officer located your vehicle, we realized you two never made it with the dance group." No, they do not know what happened. Part of me is happy they don't know; the other part of me is concerned because now I know they expect me to tell them.

"I want to go back to school. I have schoolwork to do... get me go back to Atlanta." I can hear another set of footsteps entering the kitchen from the hall. My heart is racing. I snap. "Who did you invite to talk? Where is my sister?" My mother is reaching across the table. "Victoria, please sit down, sweetheart. We only want to help."

My eyes are racing around the room and a police officer enters. She's in a full dark suit holding her badge. Her voice is soft. "Victoria, I'm Lieutenant Nelson from the Special Victims Unit."

I back away. "I am not interested in speaking to anyone."

She nods her head. "I understand not wanting to talk. Your sister told me you saved her life."

Tatiana talked to her. "When did you talk to my sister? Where is she?" I growl and my father's voice finds me.

"Princess Victoria…your sister is fine. If you would sit down, I can go get her for you."

My heart slows as he speaks. "Yes. I want my sister." I run my fingers across the table waiting for Tatiana to enter the room. My mother is moving in the kitchen, grabbing glasses from the cabinet. I glance over at the lady and see her gun holster. "Why did you become a cop?"

She takes two steps closer to the table. "I wanted to help people. What are you studying at school?" She is trying to control the conversation. I narrow my eyes and my sister's face appears in my sight.

"Victoria." My heart races realizing she let my father touch her shoulder.

"Are you okay, Tati?"

She smiles. "Yes, sis, you saved my life. I told *Papi* how you saved my life."

Why did she do that? My eyes grow. "Sis, why…?"

She reaches for my face. "*Hermana*, this is not your fault. Those men took us from the mall. You got us out of that house… you saved us." Her voice resembles a small child.

I peer at the officer. "What do you need to talk for if she's already told you what happened?" My head snaps and I demand speaking to my parents. "*Mami*, I want to go back to school! *Papi*, I have school."

Lieutenant Nelson sits on the opposite end of the table. "I think that is a good idea."

My eyes follow her movement. "Yes, I want to go back."

The officer is surveying my actions. "I have a few questions before you go." She reaches her hand. "Victoria, how did you two get to the hospital?" Tatiana doesn't remember Omari or Jesse bringing us to the hospital.

My sister interrupts. "What hospital is she talking about

Victoria?" She's still in a state of shock, but she remembers being taken from the mall. I scratch my head.

I shrug my shoulders. "We didn't see the people that took us. Don't you have cameras from the mall?" My heart pounds remembering the scar of the man that dragged me in the car, my thoughts flash seeing the man crumple to the floor. I ponder what it would be like to see him sit at my feet in his own blood.

The lady nods her head. "We are going through the footage." Well she doesn't need me.

"I don't know what the men look like."

"Do you remember how many men, Victoria?"

"Over five." She pulls out a notepad and writes notes. What if she already knows and came here to arrest me because maybe I killed the guy and they said I killed the girl?

My eyes shut and she speaks in a flat tone, "Thank you, Victoria. Do you remember the neighborhood?"

"Railroad tracks." That's all I'm telling her.

I stand and my sister runs to my side hugging me. "You're the best *hermana*." I don't feel like the best.

"Thank you, sis." I kiss the top of her head. "I have to get back to school. Help me pack."

Her head lowers. "Will you come back tomorrow?" My insides clench and I stare at my mother. She shakes her head as I realize my sister is not okay.

"I will be in Atlanta okay. I will stay until tomorrow and tonight we can have a slumber party in my room." She squeezes my waist and we walk down the hall until we reach my room.

———

My mother gave me pills to help me sleep but my eyes remain open staring at the ceiling. I sit up against the fluffy headboard and my sister rolls to the side of me. I reach for the water on the nightstand and think of Romel. "Wow."

93

I pull open the drawer of my nightstand and grab my cell phone. It's Saturday again? I have been here for over seven days. I look at the notifications, one hundred are from Jasmine alone. Chantal has left another one hundred text messages. Glancing through it seems her brothers have not told her anything. My eyes shut in relief.

A text comes through from Jasmine. I smirk…my chica.

Chica, I am so sick worried about you. Romel came by looking for you. We miss you. XOXO

I type, responding to her text, *I will be back soon. I love you, chica. XOXO*

She responds instantly, *I love you.*

I put my phone back in the drawer thinking how I will get through this. Romel would tell me this is a wall to push through. Wouldn't he? I am afraid the men will look for us and maybe kill my family. What if I killed that man? They know I saw their faces. I just need to leave, go to school clear my mind, and then I can think better. I hope that's what will help me.

STRETCHING MY ARMS, I flip to my side; a sense of depletion surges through my body as my head turns. The digits on my alarm clock confirm I slept for three hours after three days of no sleep. My hands rock my sister's hips, realizing today we have to part. "Tatiana, it's six o'clock wake up, sis." She twists her body.

"I don't want to get up." I poke under her arms and she rises. A smile grows on her face.

My unfocused eyes stare in her direction. "Get up, you must go to school today."

"Will you come with me?" She is pulling at my arm and I jerk back. She flinches and scoots out of the bed. I scared her.

"Forgive me, sis. I didn't mean to push away."

Tatiana shrugs her shoulders. "It's okay. So I won't see you when I get home from school?" She paces to my door and turns back holding up on the knob. My feet sink to the floor and I pull open the drawer grabbing a shirt.

"No, Tatiana, I will be at my school."

My mother is at the door holding a tray with breakfast. "How are my two princesses?" Tatiana has her head hanging low, and she pushes through, heading to her bedroom.

"I'm not hungry, *Mami*." Why did I jerk away from her? I should not have done that. I stand, looking at my blurred reflection in the mirror. Unable to capture the beauty graced by my parents. My mother's hand touches my shoulder.

"Victoria, I want you to eat before getting on the plane. Your father will go with you." She keeps talking and I go along with the motions unable to hear her words. I walk to my closet, grabbing a pair of jeans I slide my legs inside and realize my mother stepped away. Bending over I grab a pair of sneakers and the sound of my mother's feet entering my room startles me. My eyes lift seeing her standing with a sharp kitchen blade in her hand.

"Forgive me, Victoria. *Mami* didn't mean to alarm you. I was getting a knife to cut your oranges."

She slices the fruit and sets the knife on the tray. "Eat, Victoria, you need the strength." Ugh, her bossing me around is annoying. I reach for the juice and my sister walks pass my room.

"Tatiana?" I gulp the juice and she enters wearing a pair of jeans with a one of my old dance team shirts. My fingers push her curly strands of hair away from her eyes. "Hmmm, you are wearing my clothes?"

She smiles and I lean in to give her a hug. We step toward my door and I set the glass down as we enter the hall. "It looks great on you, sis, you can wear my clothes while I am gone."

Her eyes light up and she runs her hand down the shirt. "I'm taking you with me to school."

My arms wrap around her shoulders. "In spirit, *hermana*. I will be with you always." My father is calling her to let her know *Mami* is waiting on her in the car. She looks at me.

"I love you, *hermana*. Don't forget to call me."

"I love you and you don't forget to call me." She releases me from the hug and walks down the hall. Seeing her disappear down the hall is like the world is ending. An overwhelming voice grows in my head. *You couldn't save her; what type of big sister are you?*

I stomp to my room and slam the door, knocking over the food my mother prepared. Tears fall from my eyes as I bend over to clean my mess.

Tap, tap, tap. "Princess Victoria, is everything okay, sweetheart?" My father asks from the other side of the door.

I respond frantically. "Yes! I just made a mess." I grab my head hoping he doesn't open the door. "I will be ready to leave in a minute."

His voice softly responds, "I am here for you, Princess." His footsteps echo in the hall. Ungrounded with life I plant myself on the floor. My eyes are drawn to the blade on the floor, zoning out, drifting in and out of hope. I stretch my leg and my toes grip the handle of the knife until my fingers have it in hand. I stand to my feet gathering the remaining items from the floor as I toss them on the tray. The knife slips out of my grip slicing a layer of my skin. I flinch as I bite at my palm, stopping the bleeding, able to feel for a moment. I reach for the knife and throw it on the tray and open the door. My father is leaning against the wall.

"I'm here, Princess." I gulp at his stance and he reaches his arms as I pass him the tray. "We can get something else to eat on the way." He looks at my hand as I transfer the food to him. "Victoria, you are bleeding."

My father places the tray on the floor and rushes to my bathroom. I stay and look at the blood seep from the small incision inside my palm to the hardwood floor. My *papi* calls out for me.

"Princess, give me your hand." I do as he requests, and he blots the blood stopping it from flowing. "Keep this pressure with your grip." I nod my head in agreement and he steps by my door grabbing the handle of my luggage as he exits. I clear my throat and step to the hall.

"*Papi*, thank you." My father is grabbing the tray from the floor and he turns, looking over his shoulder in my direction a smile grows on his face. I walk to his side and he kisses the top of my head.

"I love you, Princess."

VICTORIA

*a*fter the plane ride my father made sure I had all my items settled in my apartment safely. He is deeply concerned. I don't think I have ever been so excited to see Jasmine come home. My father would have missed another flight if she didn't walk through the door.

My phone rings. "Yes, *Mami.*" I hope they will not call me every minute of the day. "I am fine. I am resting in my bed and *Papi* got off to the airport safely." She is going on about me having the doors locked. Jasmine is knocking on my door and she pushes her way in without waiting on me. Her body flounces on my bed next to me and she can hear my mother's voice from the phone.

She interjects, "*Hola, Mami!*"

I shake my head trying to distract her from encouraging my mother to stay on the phone. My sister is asking to speak to me. I sit up in the bed and Jasmine is lying next to me she is playing with her hair looking at the ceiling. My sister is so sweet. "*Hola hermana, estoy cansado.*" Me telling Tatiana I am tired does not get her off the phone. She could care less as her mouth is running a marathon telling me how she didn't cry at school. She says some girl liked her shirt, and it made her feel like I was by her side the entire day.

"*Bueno.*" I think it's good for her to be safe. She continues and says my parents want her to go to counseling. My body twists to the side of the bed and my heart is racing. "Why? Did you ask *Mami* and *Papi* to go?" She tells me no, that her counselor at school suggested it because of how sad she was during first period. I see. "Tatiana, be careful what you tell them. I want nothing else to happen." I twist, looking back at Jasmine to understand how much of my conversation is she paying attention to, but she is giggling laying on her stomach texting. "Tati, I have to get rest, the flight made me tired." She sends me her love and tells me to say hi Jasmine.

Looking at Jasmine I put the phone on speaker. "Tatiana, is talking to you." Jasmine perks up twisting her head in my direction.

"I love you, Little Ma!" A silence grows over the phone and I recall Omari. My fingers shut off the speaker mode.

"Tatiana, are you okay?"

She is sniffling but tells me she is okay and will sleep in my room. "That's fine. Love you, sis!" I go to place my phone on the night stand and a notification alerts me. I glance down and see Romel's name, a frown grows on my face and I lay the cell down.

Jasmine jumps up like an energizer bunny. "So, was that Romel?"

I position myself under the covers and speak without emotion. "Yeah, I will talk to him later."

She sits closer and I scoot away. "Victoria, he came over here when you were gone. He is concerned about you. You like him, he likes you."

I shake my head. "Jasmine, I am not interested in Romel. I need to rest." She stands giving me an uneasy look.

"Oh, are we not hanging out with each other? I know you

said you were tired…" Wait she knew what I was saying to Tatiana? Her Spanish is getting better.

"I assumed you were just telling Tati that so we could go out." She likes to go out on Monday to this café where they do spoken word poetry and she draws but I am not feeling up to it. I pull the blanket up.

"You go, Jasmine. I am exhausted and have to get back into the swing of things." She steps back. I can tell I have made her sad. She always looks away when she doesn't want me to know how she feels.

"Well you rest I will see you when I get back." She paces to the door and I sit up.

"I will be asleep, *chica*. I will see you tomorrow."

"Oh…tomorrow." She lets out a deep breath. "*Chica*, whatever is bothering you just know you will get through it." She pulls my door and just before closing it all the way I yell out.

"Jasmine, keep it open!" Her head peeks in my room and rushes to my side putting her arms around my neck.

She whispers in my ear, "Something is bothering you, *chica*."

ROMEL

*S*itting in the class is annoying; I look at the wall clock taking notice of the time. My head turns and I realize Victoria has missed class three times now. I took this damn elective just to see her pretty little ass. The professor is walking in my direction and places our final project before me. Great, we need a partner. I am ready to walk across the stage just so I don't have to do busy work anymore. My phone vibrates and I see a notification about work from Drew.

The professor is wrapping up and I volunteer to partner with Victoria before walking out. Rising to my feet I grab my bag and text him back, *I will be in, I have to make a stop.*

This girl didn't come to class last week, and she's a no show today. I scroll through my log noting that she hasn't responded to my text. What the fuck? I pace across the campus. I spot Jasmine's boy but he has got another chick posted by his car. I chuckle, this motherfucker didn't think to be discrete about his shit. He's foul. My head turns seeing my boy, Chad, hanging out with my frat brothers. This blue-eyed dude is a few years older than me and a strategic fool about who he pursues. He steps to my side and we pound elbows as I situate my cell in my back pocket.

"What's up, Romel?" He looks like he is about to go work out.

"What's up with you, blue eyes? You trying to taste on some chocolate?" He is smirking and walks with me to my car.

"Not at the moment, but I have a few flavors on standby." He rubs his chin. He is concluding his *juris doctorate* at Emory. I don't know how he makes the time to be on this campus as if something is calling him over here. I chuckle as he eyeballs a female and I know exactly what is calling his ass.

"You a cocky motherfucker, Chad. I'm heading to work you going to the gym?"

"I will play ball and then I'll be at the gym later."

My head tilts. "See you around or in court."

He tilts his head and paces the opposite way. "Hell yeah... I'm waiting on my test scores to make my law life official. Everything is coming full circle with my mom hooding me at the ceremony." I'm happy for him. He snaps his wrist as if he is throwing the ball in the air and I stumble as if I caught the ball and make the shot.

"Swoosh....got 'em!"

"I'll see you, Romel."

I TURN THE WHEEL, entering Victoria's apartment complex. This parking lot is full like a party is going on. I circle around and park on the opposite side of the building she stays in. Turning the car off, I open the door to exit the vehicle. I turn back to get the assignment she needs in the passenger seat. I pull the door open and recognize Jasmine heading from around the corner. I step in her direction to go see about Victoria. She looks up at me, surprised. " Hi, Romel!"

I tilt my head and look over my shoulder seeing her boyfriend pulling up in his car. I guess she doesn't know the bastard just left his side chick. Her body movement looks off. I tilt my head and move forward. She alters her direction. "Romel, Victoria is not home right now." I stop walking and twist my lips recalling the last time I saw her she was practically shouting for me to check on Victoria.

"Is that right...so she is still in Dallas?"

She shakes her head. "No, she came back late. Do you need me to tell her something?" What is she, Victoria's receptionist? She doesn't have to play games. I'm good. I hand her the packet.

"Give her this...she needs to find a partner." I guess that explains her not returning my text, she's occupied with another. I rush to my car to get to my job. I don't have time for sophomoric games. Jasmine walks back away from her boyfriend's car. His hoe ass was with a different chick not even an hour ago. Pulling my car door open I enter and start the car.

I text Drew, *I'll be there in ten.*

He responds, *Come to the house. Unc needs us.*

I blast my music, exiting the parking lot and see Victoria getting out of a car. I tilt my head and wait to get a clear visual. Letting my window down I confirm the sights of the guy. "She's with ol' boy from the gym." I have been worried about her ass and he's got her feet facing the sky. Her girl is horrible at covering for her. I engage my car spinning off, making certain I am noticed as I leave the scene.

I PUSH open the door and Drew is in front of the computer screen. Shutting the door, I see pizza on the table and place my items on the couch. He stares at me with a suspicious expression as I walk in the kitchen to wash my hands.

"What's up Drew?"

His eyes don't leave the computer screen, it's like he's watching a video. "You know the IP address with the photos?" He is wiping his head and I grab a slice of pizza sitting across the table from him. He darts in my direction as I eat. "Unc came to the office and told us to look deeper."

"Did you tell him about the pictures we found?" I chew the rest of the pizza and stand to get a drink from the refrigerator. Drew's voice is concerning me.

"Yes, I thought you might want to see this video before sending it to Unc. He says a Lieutenant in Dallas is searching for this young girl but I see…" What is it? I open a soda and guzzle it down. Drew has a serious demeanor, and he is pointing to the laptop. "Romel, come check it out."

I walk around the other side of the table and my eyes burn in a rage. The drink drops from my hand. "Call my mother!" I snatch the laptop. Drew is behind me. "I called her. Shaun is with her and so is my pops."

My heart is racing. How is this possible?

"Drew, tell me what I am looking at on this screen? Who is that? I know that's not who I think it is!" Isn't he dead? I saw him die, didn't I?

Drew is talking and someone is banging on the door. "Calm down, Rom. We are checking into who it is. My ol' man said he is confirming the identity of the man." My hand is shaking and who the fuck is at the door. Drew is not answering the door recognizing my state. In the computer screen my eyes take in a young girl. Recognizing the guy's mark on the film is rattling my thoughts. She appears as if she's overdosed, like she's out of it and several men are raping her. Throwing the computer, I rush to the bathroom and regurgitate the food I just took in. It's all over the bathroom floor. It's as if I am reliving him hurting my mother. I'm unable to hold my body weight and I pound my fist in the wall. Drew is standing outside the bathroom. How can a dead man still be doing the same shit, alive?

"Romel, we will get word. M'Dear is safe." My thoughts flash back to that night to my mother. I reach out shutting my eyes. His dirty face is before me his filthy hands rip my mother's clothes off and my stomach convulses, throwing up a second time in the toilet.

Drew yells for me, standing in what reverted from my insides. "Romel, open your eyes, bruh! You are here with me!" I can hear Stanley's voice as my numb body is being lifted in the shower. Drew keeps calling my name.

"Romel, open your eyes." I hear him command the water on. "Alexa, water on." My body jumps feeling the rush of cold drops revive my senses. My eyelashes flash and Drew shouts. "Alexa, turn water off." He passes me the phone.

"Hello?" I hear my mother's voice and my heart beats again.

VICTORIA

Jasmine and I got into an argument just moments after she tried to get me to pay attention to the car rushing off from the apartment. I guess she thought slapping me would help me snap out. She sounds more as if she is my mother pushing me about my schoolwork. My head rolls back and I look below at the guy attempting to remove the layering of my clothes. He keeps whispering sweet nothings in my ear as if I am in love with him. I can't take this, just fuck me already. I lift my shirt and push him over to his back. I hear the door unlock and I snap.

"LEAVE!" He is looking up at me as I am on top of him. He is trying to rub my arms.

"What's wrong, ba—"

I cut him off, "I'm not into this, just leave." My legs lift and he gathers his shirt from the floor. I hear footsteps barging to my room. The door pushes open.

"Jasmine...what the fuck!"

She snarls at the guy putting on his shirt, "Leave now!"

"I'm going, you two are crazy!" I jump after him and Jasmine is pulling me away from him.

She yells to the guy. "I suggest you leave now!" He picks up his shoes and rushes out of the room. My heavy breathing echoes in the room as Jasmine has me pinned to the bed.

HAVING control over my life seems to be fading day by day. I have been lying in bed, mad at the world, for an hour. I want Jasmine to leave me alone but she is standing in front of my dresser placing more mail on the mess I have yet to open. She throws a flier about a dance competition in my direction. I glance at it and set it aside. She sits in my room as if I am on watch in a mental institute.

Jasmine speaks calmly, "Victoria, you know I love you. You are my *chica* no matter what."

My eyes lift looking at her but my heart is pounding as if I am racing. She stands and walks to the edge of my bed. "Do you want me to call Tatiana for you? Tell me what you need, *chica*, I'll get it." Tears are falling from her eyes.

I drop my head. "Please don't call home, *chica*. I will be okay." She scoots closer to me and lifts my chin.

"I'm sorry for slapping you." I should be the one apologizing to her. Why did I treat her so awful? Jasmine touches my hand and looks at me. "*Chica*, I'll give you some time to tell me what's bothering you. Don't worry about your school work. I will do it for you."

She lifts my head trying to find my eyes. "Victoria, I just want you to get better. I will go make some tea and we can lay here and say nothing." She walks out of my room and I stare out the window seeing the night settle. Standing to my feet I see a tuition payment notice and the assignment Romel gave Jasmine. I know he thinks I am mean for not returning his text messages.

My hand reaches the knob and I push the bathroom door open shutting it behind me. My reflection comes into view seeing my bare skin with nothing but a bra on. Tears fill my eyes. *I'm not a weak little girl crying in this bathroom.*

I touch my face hoping to feel some type of way other than trapped. I want to scream. My eyes lower to the counter and the blades from the scissors come into view. A rush comes over me and I reach for the scissors opening it and I flip my wrist. My eyes inch to my upper arm and I take the blade and strike as I take in a deep breath. The sharp edge breaks the surface of my skin. I exhale, feeling for the first time over a week. Repeating the act once more I feel release from the memories flooding my mind, it's like a high takes over me while my blood oozes.

My mind is in silent in euphoria for five minutes. Hearing Jasmine enter my room, I turn the faucet knob and grab a face towel. I mimic my father, blotting the blood. My eyes set on my mirror image as I acknowledge that I have another *dirty dark* secret, yet this one takes my pain away.

"Jasmine, will you get me a shirt?" I grab the door as it swings open and an artificial smile comes over my face.

"Thanks." I turn, and my back is against the door while I slide my arms through the shirt. I look in the mirror and notice the sleeves don't hide my arm. I grab the towel and pocket it in my elbow as I open the door. Jasmine looks in my direction. She has tea over by my dresser. I walk to my closet and pull out a long sleeved shirt.

She walks in front of the door. "What was wrong with the shirt I gave you?" I shake my head, shifting the shirt over my head. The sensation irritates my skin and I grip my arm.

"Nothing, I'm just colder than I thought. The tea should help."

She looks at me with concern. "Hmm, I guess." Within a matter of minutes, I'm lying to my *chica*...what has my life come to.

Walking out of the closet I step to my dresser and grab my tea. "Thanks, *chica*."

She grins and it's like I am being stabbed for lying to her.

ROMEL

$\mathcal{I}$'ve been going to the gym before work to straighten out my thoughts. It helps me stay centered and the probability of running into Victoria at five in the morning is slim. My head turns as the door unlocks. I smirk taking in the sight of who it is. Drew and Chad walk in from the side door. I tilt my head knowing they only came here to check on me. These two only rise this early for pussy. We bump fists and I eyeball the dick on the opposite side of the room. Drew is twisting his neck. "You come to fight, Rom?"

I tilt my head and motion my hand for him in the room's center. Chad chuckles. "I think he might kill you, Drew, look at his hungry eyes." I am jumping in place ready to go. My fingers push back my gloves. Drew looks into my eyes.

"What you thinking about, Romel? You are in a different mode."

I tilt my head over at ol' boy. "That ugly motherfucker, his sperm is rotten." They turn their heads.

Chad chimes in, "Yeah, that shit is wasted."

We all laugh. Drew has an evil smirk on his face. "He

was with yo girl?" He is intentionally trying to make me respond. I jab at his face and he moves.

"Fuck you, Drew."

Chad punches at my stomach, I swing my hand back, dodging his hit. "What do you want to do?" I plant my feet and look out the window. Drew swings across and I grab his wrist.

"What the fuck is she doing here?" I haven't seen her for the entire week. She hasn't been to class, and she prances her ass in here now.

Chad shakes his head and I step toward the door. He is calling after me. "Romel!" The guy is in the corner hitting at the punching bag and I mean mug him. Drew hits at the back of my knee and I drop.

"What the fuck, Drew?"

He is shaking his head. "No, bruh, you have to calm down." I growl remembering the last time I got out of hand.

Chad pushes me back away from the door. "Reconsider… remember you are a senior. Be smart, Romel." He is testing out giving wisdom, I notice.

I gulp in the dry air and spot her walking out the door with Jasmine. Since when do they come here in the morning? "Let's go to work, Drew."

Chad pushes the door open. "I have class, see you two later." I need to take a shower.

STANLEY HAS BEEN ESCORTING me and Drew around since I flipped out about my mother seeing that video. I am fine knowing she is safe. I just want to know who that man is on the video. Drew has been arguing back and forth with his ol' man. I guess this has a way of making you feel you are a child. Stanley lets the partition down. "Drew, you have an appointment to view the penthouse."

Drew has been looking for a place of his own to break the ties with his ol' man. Stanley passes me a card. "Romel, this is the information you told me to gather."

I tilt my head, looking out the window and see that we are two minutes or fewer from work. I wanted this information when Victoria seemed to give a fuck. "Thank you, Stanley." I place the card in the pocket of my blazer. You would think we own Rivalry Software the way we dress going to this place.

The car pulls up to the office front doors. I push the door open and Stanley gets our attention. "I will be close by, you two."

Drew laughs. "Should we expect anything less?" I exit the car chuckling, knowing he's not the only one watching us. I see an older woman walking by and I step up to open the door for her. I read her name tag. She works here as well. She nods her head. "Thank you kindly, young man."

"You are more than welcome, Ms. Cynthia." She walks through and Drew follows behind me and we walk toward the opposite hall from her.

Drew is tugging his blazer and looks toward me. "One day me and you are walking in the same direction as her, going to the top floor." I smile and he has an all-knowing look in his eyes. "You watch, Romel."

"I believe you, Drew, we will own this place." Continuing straight ahead I pull the door to our exciting room of silence.

No one turns their heads, they stay glued to the computer screens like zombies. My feet arrive to my cubby of a desk and I take out the information Stanley gave me. Sitting in the chair I place the contents on the desk and push the button on the computer screen until it powers up. I'm itching to know what Stanley found out, so I take the envelope and unseal it.

"It's a code." The sound of heels is inching in my direction. Lifting my eyes, I am not enthused be the person coming toward me. What is this, a test of my patience? You go to school day after day to prepare for adulting with mindless people that bicker over the petty shit, take Angie for instance. She looks in my direction as if I gave her an invitation to speak. "Hi, Romel." Her frigid voice makes my skin crawl.

My lips curve in a hospitable manner without alerting her to how I really feel. She's holding a box. Angie has a diaper bag on her shoulder. "So, Dwight, is upset with me." My brows rise and I assume she thinks I am supposed to know who this guy is she is talking about. She keeps talking. "I told him I am perfectly fine with taking care of a baby." Does this chick have a baby at work? Did she not notice there are not any other children running around this office? When will she stop talking? I sit in front of my desk without uttering a sound. I guess this is how Dwight feels at home or wherever he is. She stands in front of me pulling a bottle out of the diaper bag that matches her pin stripped pants. My head tilts and I am pondering where is the baby that is in need of that bottle?

Her hand lowers over to the box and my eyes grow wide seeing her throw a bib over her shoulder from the container. This doesn't look right. I am so confused at the sight before me. Angie dunks her hand once more and pulls out a...no not a baby, but a squirrel. You've got to be shitting me, there is no way this animal is for emotional support. Did I not get the memo that it is officially okay to bring your fucking pet to work? I shake my head and Angie words are like diarrhea of the mouth. "Romel, I want you to meet my baby."

She stuffs the bottle in the rodent's mouth. Drew is passing by and acts as cordial as ever. He speaks professionally in a fading tone. "How swell, Angie, you have a baby—" She cuts him off as she turns around, exposing the fur ball and Drew's face drops.

"Yes, I have a baby squirrel. Isn't he precious?" He nods and paces away as quickly as he came by. My head lowers wondering where in the hell she got clothes for a squirrel...I need fresh air. I can't have spent four years in school for the likes of episodes like this on a daily basis.

VICTORIA

*I*t is unusual seeing his caramel skin glide through the
AU Center after work. I have not been myself lately
and I don't want to get into it with him. I try to minimize
harming myself because I know Jasmine will call my mother if
she finds out about anything. Romel walks toward the table and
looks me in the eyes.

He forgoes greetings. "I'll be straight…I've been watching
you with ol' boy—" he licks his lips as he continues, "—but just
tell me, do I cross your mind?"

Where did this come from?

My eyes bulge and I bite my lips, unable to tame my sinful
thoughts of him. Why is my body responding like this in his
presence? Ugh, I reposition in the chair, wishing I could tell him
what happened because he helped me train. If it weren't for him,
I would not have been able to escape the sickos that tried to turn
me and my sisters into sex slaves. I attempt to play it off and
change the subject…hoping to not sound interested. "I have a
man or two."

"I know you're taken by a few." Damn, he knows there is
somebody else. It's really not somebody… it's more like when I

want to be bothered with someone, I make a call. I blink my eyes and push my hair away from my face.

His eyes size me up and he is looking as if he is about to devour me. "Maybe you have the two because they can't give you what I got." I am not used to him being this way. I guess he is not interested in hearing the 'I am like his sister' line.

I bat my eyes...he looks like he could give me all I want. Wait did I admit that in my thoughts? I take in a jagged breath. "You can come through and we can always play you know." My eyes squint with curiosity as I return to deep thought...I hope he knows I am only playing.

"How do you know what I want? You are my Morehouse brother...let's not play like this." He grabs my hand as I attempt to move and my emotions shift. *Calm down, Victoria, this is Romel he cares about you.* I take in a deep breath and shut my eyes. "I'm not interested in being involved with anyone. What we have now is cool."

Romel stands from the table. "Your loss, I guess." Okay, he had better stop acting. I have too many things going on to think of him as more than what he is. My coming here is a promise I made to Jasmine because I don't want her to worry because she will call my mother.

Jasmine is walking in my direction. I put my head down. She sits in the chair across from me. "*Chica*, what the hell is up with him? So, have you decided for him to be your victim?"

I slide down in my chair. "*Chica*, he has been my Morehouse brother for some time now. But I think he's not interested in just being my friend."

She interrupts, "Victoria, I am feeling like you are not telling me the truth." She blinks. "Why are you wearing long sleeve shirts all the time now?" Does she know?

"Jasmine, I think—"

She cuts me off, "Victoria, I already told you Romel likes you. The strange thing is how you have been acting since you came back from Dallas. Did something happen with your family? Your wardrobe has changed—"

She knows I don't want her to know. "I will be okay I just have practice with dance and it just leaves me drained." This is the only thing I can think of to make her believe I am moving on with life. I guess now I will officially enter the dance contest and tell India and Jade about it. I am the lead dancer considering I have been dancing practically all my life and I'll come up with the choreography. They are part of a dance group I put together. I'm certain they will take part considering money is involved. The truth is Jasmine doesn't want to know what I do to make myself cope every day. I can't tell her...I just can't come to terms with telling anyone what's really going on with me.

She pushes her hand in my direction jerking me. "I can't believe you will keep lying to my face, *chica*. I am not stupid. Something happened when you went to Dallas. Even Romel knows that much and I thought maybe he was being overboard." She gets up huffing and puffing. Romel knows.

"Jasmine, sit down." She lowers her body in front of me. "Something happened, it was not with my family. I ask you to give me a little more time; I am struggling with it."

Her eyes beam at me. "I'm giving you twenty-four hours and I expect some kind of an answer or I am calling Chantal and your parents." My head drops. I know she is concerned, and I love her for caring so much.

"I will tell you. I promise."

ROMEL

take in a deep breath as I roam the campus. I see the security as my feet crosses the street. It feels great out here, under the stars. I've been in Atlanta for four years and only until recently have I started really thinking of my past. I thought that man was dead…I know I was young, but I never forget the sound releasing from the gun. I turn my head as I hear music coming from a nearby building. I follow the sound to see what's going on.

The closer I get I realize the noise is coming from the performing arts studio. I pull the door and it's locked. I reach for the handle in the middle and the door swings open. The hall to the left is dark it smells like dust and sweat so I go to my right and the music grows louder joined with a wailing sound. I look through the window of the brightly lit room and turn away from view. Victoria's in the dance studio. I take in a deep breath and decide to just be her friend and check on her. I lightly push the door open and she doesn't move from her position. Does she think she's invisible? I stride to her knowing she can hear me on this polished, hardwood floor. I think I can see my reflection as I look below.

Victoria is not herself dressing in this edgy attire. Wait, she wears clothes with flair but the long sleeves are unusual for her. Her arms are almost always exposed, showing off the work we put in at the gym. I guess she is trying out something new with that hooded shirt with slashes layered over that black sports bra. That gypsy 'I Dream of Jeanie' pants are nothing like what I am used to seeing her in.

"What are you doing in here at one a.m.?" I walk ahead looking at the mirrored wall. Victoria has her head down, curled into a ball. She looks as though she in a cocoon. She lifts her head her eyes look like she's been crying. Clearing her throat, she speaks in a soft pitch.

"Nothing, I am fine." She is not alright.

I step closer to her speaking in an aggressive tone. "It's too late for you to be here." I can tell she is used to holding her head high and not letting others know what is wrong. My pops didn't like us hiding what is bothering us. He would tell us it causes mental problems and refused to believe expressing your emotions was a weakness. We all knew at our house hiding emotions weakens you. I guess that made him and my mother click.

She smirks and I reach my hand for her. "It's too late for you to be in here, Romel. I have permission to be here. How did you know to come in this room?"

"I've been looking for you." I shrug my shoulders; I guess I got worried. "You've been MIA since returning from Dallas." She takes my hand, standing to her bare feet and prances to the handrail mounted to the wall. This girl walks like she is doing ballet. I chuckle and wonder why she is grabbing her items.

"I was practicing a dance step and lost track of time, Romel. I am fine." She should be aware; I'm not buying her story.

"You love dance huh?"

She steps closer to the mirror, grabbing her shoes. "Yes, I adore it...I guess you can say that." It is obvious she loves dance. Her feet can bend metal the way they point, I bet she gets more excited about getting dance shoes than thinking of her first kiss.

I pull out my phone. Walking away from her I march by the piano slapping my hand down as I take hold of the remote. I link my Bluetooth to the sound system. Speaking as I walk in her direction she listens, "My brother has a way of speaking through playing dominoes. It's a manly conversation. We play, he talks shit." She narrows her eyes, holding her items as if she's ready to leave.

Victoria smacks her lips. "Interesting, Romel."

My hands grip her items and she releases them as I watch her motion with each breath she takes. She is gorgeous beyond words.

Victoria is hiding something, and I am not letting her leave. I step in front of her. "How about you talk shit through dancing? You tell me what's wrong by dancing."

She smirks, batting her pretty eyelashes. "Really, you said it was too late for me to be here." She mumbles as if I can't hear her speaking, "*Hipócrita*"

My head rocks as I find the song that my mother plays throughout the house any time something is bothering her. "It's too late for you to be alone and I'm not a hypocrite." Victoria has an alarmed expression on her face. I speak Spanish perfectly fine, she can't hide. My finger presses play and she grabs the phone from my hand. I have the remote, what she is doing is unnecessary.

"If I am dancing, I have to feel the song."

She puts my phone in my palm and I set it on the piano. I hear Stevie Wonder professing on the song he speaks fluent Spanish. Victoria prances as she paces her feet across the floor, she turns with the rising of her arms twirling to the center of the floor. *Man, she's beautiful.* I kick off my shoes and mimic her movements. She is laughing and I am happy to see her smile.

The beat drops and the look in her eyes shift. She kicks out her foot, drops her leg, twirling her hips. "Oh, I see you're adding ballet and modern dance with a touch of salsa to it."

She laughs surprised I know something about dance. I know more than she thinks but it can be quite a little while longer. I will tell her in good time. Her eyes dart in my direction. "You are interrupting."

My mouth turns down. "Do it again."

Her shoulders drop. "Ugh." I cut her off and pace to the piano walking to get remote. "Don't worry about a thing as Stevie says. I'll start the song over."

Her head leans, and she stretches aligning her body. "What are you doing I have to hear the song, Romel, loud." I ignore her and study the remote to be certain the song plays loud. She has a confused expression.

"Calm down and dance. I put the phone on the piano. I can do everything from the remote."

The room is silent for a moment in seconds the song plays and she repeats the same movement. I follow her body like a magnet it's like she enjoys giving a show, a show I like to see. I stop the song and repeat it. Her foot stomps on the smooth surface. "Romel!" I wonder why she is not dancing with her shoes on.

I jump and rush to her side. I am following her moves and she's in total bliss. I hear Stevie draw out the note and I add stepping back like I'm talking shit.

She folds her stomach over laughing. "You are a mess, Romel. I like it though." She steps behind me putting her hand on my hips. "When you move your center loosen up, think stripper pole."

I laugh and touch her hand biting my lip. Hell, I can do stripper pole. "I got it, you can stay right here to make sure though." She stands to my side and we dance side by side, I follow her lead. Stevie gets to his ripple, stressing his note and I kick on the note, dancing like Michael Jackson in "Thriller".

She laughs so hard and I love it. Stevie's voice is complemented by the brass it's as if he's in a round with the trumpets playing in the song. I step, doing the meringue. She jumps in an open double foot hold, but she pulls me closer, putting her hand on the back of my hip. She starts with her left foot dominating me to follow with my right. "I know how to do this dance, Victoria...my mother and I dance to this song."

She blinks. "You do the meringue with your mother?" She keeps dancing bringing me closer and the temperature of my body is rising even as she is leading. "Romel, you have no problems with forward back step up?"

I take lead starting with the left foot going forward. Then push her hand with my left hand, as we step back her fingers slides over the top of my other hand. I recognize her ability to exchange lead as she becomes confident, I can handle the steps. We pull back in and she smiles. I notice she is turning her body to three o'clock and I follow raising her hand. She's adding her hips in a sensual form. "I see what you are doing, Victoria."

She is taking her time turning trying to make me suffer. I stay connected moving my hips holding her hand as she turns. I keep her fingers within my grasp, and I turn to the right, flirting with her, forcing Victoria's hand to rub against my shoulder. The tempo of the song increases, and she takes my challenge. Victoria turns to her right swaying her hair and my eyes take in her body movement as she motions down. Dancing with her is like being at a club and we are the entertainment. I take in her eyes as she is playing with me. She's flirting purposely. I pull her in, whispering in her ear, "I don't like getting fucked...unless I'm fucking."

Her eyes grow wide and with another turn she looks away trying to not look in my eyes. We chuckle, staying in rhythm as Stevie Wonder sings his heart out. She is completely herself with me, dancing, lost with the time. The music slows and I stroll to the phone to turn it off. My eyes see the time it's almost two in the morning. Victoria calls to me, "Wait"

My head turns. "What's wrong?" She is next to me going through her belongs next to the mirror and she throws me a water bottle. Wow...this is totally not like her. "Thanks." I open the water and drink it realizing she doesn't have one. I pass her the bottle. "Here you can drink the rest."

She smiles and her voice is high like a little girl. "I don't know where your mouth has been."

I push the water bottle in her hand insisting. "You can find out whenever you are ready."

Her eyes follow me up and down. "You thinking about that shit aren't you." Spreading my fingers like a v' over my mouth I stick out my tongue. Victoria's upper body is shaking as she laughs at me.

"You are laughing now...but I know you'll be dreaming about it." She drinks the water, and she shakes her head.

"I don't know what to do with you, Romel."

"I have some ideas, don't worry." She can't say she's not aware I am more than interested than being her friend. She finishes the water putting the bottle in her bag.

"Romel, will you look at something before I leave? It will take only a minute."

I size her up. "Victoria, why are you fighting sleep?"

She shrugs her shoulder and with a low voice she speaks. "I can't sleep."

I know what that's like, something is weighing on her. She's rubbing her eyes. "Just let me show you a dance and then you can go to your apartment."

My eyes flash. "You think I'm leaving you here alone? I know you're fucking lying."

Her eyes roll. "Mouth, Romel" She stomps her foot.

I chuckle. "I will watch you, but I am not leaving you here. I can take you to your place." She takes in a deep breath, pulling back her curly hair and walks to the radio. Damn, I'm sleepy but I can look at her all day and night without complaining about the loss of sleep.

Bending over in front of the mirror I watch her; a song comes on. "Who is this?

"Zedd Marren Morris singing 'The Middle.' I am working on something."

I watch her reflection as she is rocking her body waiting for a certain part. The bridge of the song plays, and she dances like she has a swagger about her movement. Her body flows to every beat of the song. Damn, this girl. A smile grows on my face as she rocks her hips. "Do it again." I know she's hiding something and this entire new look she's flaunting doesn't help. It actually makes it more obvious. Everyone knows she doesn't cover up her arms like there's a blizzard outside; even when it's cold outside she doesn't dress warm.

She does so without a complaint, playing the song from the beginning. I love seeing her dance. We stand silence as she waits for that certain spot. She moves, and the music takes over her body. She is gorgeous, every time I look at her time breaks away from me. I give her the compliment she wants from a friend, knowing if I open anything else her feet will face the sky. "Short, but worth every second. I see you added a jazz feel to it."

Victoria

I BAT MY LASHES. "Romel, thanks for waiting around."

Working on a dance for a contest has helped me occupy my thoughts and fight sleeping. Dancing is how I create art and feel; wow, my thoughts are everywhere.

My expectations of myself are high which helps me remain centered. It's funny how passion can motivate you.

I couldn't stay home any longer, to move forward I had to return to school.

Being at this campus gives me the inspiration I need to push through; my teachers and peers are inspiring.

I slip on my shoes and I grab my bag, putting it on my shoulder. Romel rises reaching for the bag off my shoulder. I never have to ask him to take my items, he just knows. "No problem, you don't have to thank me...so you want to tell me why you are losing your mind?"

He steps in my personal space adjusting his leather wrist bands that he *always* wears and my heartbeat is increasing. "Or is it you just need me in the middle?" My breaths flutter and I push him back, touching the imprint of the word beast on his shirt. His chest bears a resemblance to a body builder. My thoughts keep imagining him as a stripper. Romel doesn't move that far. He looks appetizing in his ash grey, baggy, hip-hop dance slacks. I can see the shape of his ass and I can only wonder if that bulge is slightly hard. I am so grateful he cannot hear what I am thinking, hell I can't believe I am thinking in this manner about him. I flash my eyes trying to focus on my words.

"Romel, what makes you think I am losing my mind or want you in the middle?"

He walks away a few steps, rubbing his hand over the top of his head. "I know you want me in the middle, but that song you picked," he keeps going without taking a breath, "I think you selected to dance off that song for a reason."

He adjusts his leather bands on his wrist as I try to explain. "Something has me feeling like I'm losing my mind but it's not you. I'll work it out."

Romel twists his lips sideways. "So, you use me for company and don't tell me what's bothering you."

He reaches for the door and I step ahead. "I will be okay." I yawn and the clink of the door locking makes me jump. Romel shoots a cautious look my way. "Let me take you to your place. I will give you your space, Victoria, but I know something is not right. You can't hide it from me."

Newsflash, it turns out you and Jasmine both know, I just don't know how to actually say it aloud.

ROMEL

*T*wist the doorknob to my room thinking about typing the code Stanley gave me in the computer to see what he found. I opt not to and I fall on the bed. I hear Drew entering the front door. I can hear the chants from the crew as if they are doing a pledge of some sort. Drew's voice is getting closer to my room and the door swings open.

He drops down on my bed. I jump as several of our frat brothers barge into my room. "What are you guys doing?" They are attempting to lift me and are failing tremendously. Drew shouts, holding me up with the other guys and Chad has a big grin on his face as he shuts the door behind us. "Tonight, we are hanging out with the frat doing wretched shit." I guess Chad is part of the frat now. I shake my head and go with the flow of things.

WE ARE AT A DARK LOCATION. There are no signs, but the parking lot has cars. Stanley is escorting us to our after-midnight charades, and he pulls up to the front. The guys all fall out the car. There is a lady dressed in lingerie opening the door. We all step inside and it's dark. No one says a word. "Where are we?" They all shush me in unison. I do not understand what they are up to, but I think it's some freaky fun. I welcome that at all costs. We stand for ten seconds and a small window opens. I hear a female's voice and she calls out some broken chant. A male's voice follows filling in the words of her chant. The gush of air is felt from our left. We slide to the left and the voice of the woman is in my ear.

"Enjoy yourselves."

Walking forward my thoughts of Victoria are pushed to the side. We walk for what seems like half a mile and they require everyone to drink something from a shot glass before going further. I take the glass and turn it up ready to play.

My head turns as I take in a room filled with whips and chains. Oh shit! Drew hits at my chest as we take in the scene. My eyes view a female dressed in black leather lingerie, tying someone up. A dude enters wearing a thong, he has whips in hand as he walks toward the lady blindfolded and hanging on the wall. I enjoy tying up a woman. We continue walking further in the back and I twist my body to the right making out another room. It looks like you are entering a galaxy with stars every-where, a big bed sits in the center of the room, sitting up high. People are looking out a window on the side.

I walk off from Drew. "I will see what's in here." He tilts his head and a half naked woman is following his steps with satin ribbon tied to around her wrist. "I will see you around."

The room is pitch dark but the floor highlights your path as you walk ahead. "Fuck…the people are watching people fuck." Man this is some untamed shit. I turn and see a man and woman going at it on the other side of the bed. This looks like something Rico would see on his military tours. A woman walks in my direction with a mask on. She rubs down my chest and I politely excuse myself from the room. As I turn, a guy is staring in the mirror jerking off as he watches the others through the window as they go at it. This shit is wild, how the fuck…he is real comfortable with himself beating his dick with all these people in here. This is some uncomfortable shit next to this guy.

I exit the room and walk down the hall recognizing Chad with two nice Georgia peaches hanging around his neck. Shit they are Augusta fine, he loves himself some chocolate. He tilts his head looking like he is eager to spread love to and call out to the wild with a spanking strap in hand. I chuckle when I see their faces, they are twins.

I enter another space with dim lights. It's set up like a loft with people enjoying life on antique furniture. I hear sex sounds all over the place. Seeing couples lose themselves in front of other couples. This man is aroused seeing another person go at it. This shit is seductive. I'm roaming around like I'm wondering what's on the menu in this piece. I'm getting turned on staring at this woman's eyes as she is eating the other female out. Her screams are so loud as she orgasms. I regard this beautiful naked woman with long legs, her eyes are enticing me, filling me out as I walk pass.

This woman greets me, she's informing me that's her hubby. I nod my head noticing he's engaged with two women. My eyes survey the dark, intimate aspect of the room. The lady pushes me against the wall, hypnotizing me in her spell. I am fucking aroused with her going after what she craves. She gives me a towel. "Take it and sit."

I put the towel on the bench, making sure no one is near us. She kisses on my neck, making her way to my chest pushing my shirt up and she grips my dick through my pants. I keep my eyes on her. She must be in her mid-thirties, taking what she wants from me. Her fingers unzip my pants and she feels my erection. I look up noticing another person walking in my direction. Fuck.

She's lowering herself to go down on me. The man draws closer, and it's her husband. My face frowns and he has a chair in hand I am pushing her and she thinks I am playing. My soul is in shock. The man she claims to be her husband sits in the chair and begins to ejaculate. I grab the woman's face. She looks at me. "I have to go to the bathroom. I feel woozy I need to go to the bathroom."

The lady bats her eyes and says to me, "Come right back!"

I stand and hustle out of the room and walk down the hall. I don't mess with married couples. Turning my head, I view the big screens displaying porn and my pace slows as I spot the dance floor of people dancing. The music in the room is so loud. I walk to the bar and lean back noticing a pair of familiar legs wrapping around a pole.

What the fuck is she doing here?

SOMETHING COVERS HER ENTIRE BODY, but I still know her body. I eyeball Drew and he has some cougar with some handcuffs, and he enters a private room. I step to the dance floor and tunnel through the crowd.

The music is fading signaling for people to go off to those they select to fuck. A man grips her wrists, and she pushes him away. He grabs her hips and I stand behind her. The music has completely faded out. My tongue runs under my lower lip. "Certainly, there's no problem."

Drew turns his head and I tilt my head confirming all is well. She looks at Drew. Her hands push the guy away and her shocked eyes find mine. "Romel."

"Victoria, is there an issue?" The club's security stands at the entrance and the man backs away. Something in her eyes is off, it could be the late hour.

"Perhaps, you need a lift home." Her shoulders drop as if she's embarrassed. I have never seen her humiliated. I lift her head. "No worries…I won't tell anyone."

She looks relived but something about her demeanor is off.

"Thanks, Romel, I was just dancing." Victoria can come dance naked with me all night I wouldn't mind.

"You don't owe me an explanation." She walks ahead and I push the door for her to exit. "Victoria, if you don't want to leave you don't have to."

She shakes her head keeping her face from my view. "I'd rather leave." Her feet are moving so fast. I hope she doesn't think I am judging her for being here. Seeing her here is not a deal breaker, maybe she's curious and sees something she wants to explore. I reach for her wrist. She rubs her skin as if it's irritated.

"Hey what's wrong?" She looks off showing her side profile.

"Romel, will you take me home?" Shaking my head, I guess I am taking her home.

"Sure, Victoria, no problem."

VICTORIA

*M*y eyes open to the darkness and silence grows loud in my ears. Twisting my body, the heaviness of my arms descends to the tightening of my back. The reality of the turn of events settle in as my fingers touch the stitches on my face. Empty is the feeling I am feeling. I push myself, rising from my bed as my feet find the floor. I reach for my phone and a light knock echoes in the room. The door pushes in and I flip over, pulling the sheet to my upper body. Jasmine voice is light as she speaks calmly. "Victoria, are we going to the gym?"

I release a sign and yawn. "No, not today."

I finally managed to sleep after dancing at the studio and finding Romel at the one place I thought of as my escape. For once I caught some shut eye without the assistance of sleeping pills. She flicks on the light and I squeeze my eyes shut. "Jasmine, what is it?"

She steps closer the light is still on. I cover my head. Jasmine yanks the sheet off exposing my body. "You are naked!" I tug the covers to my neck, my eyes are failing to adjust to the light. She sits next to me. "I will let you rest considering you stayed out all night. But I expect you to talk today." She passes me my mail.

My eyes take in the financial aid notice. My parents paid up my tuition the first semester and a partial payment for the second term. Even with a scholarship I still have a balance. It is annoying. Ugh, I know I need to make a payment. Jasmine continues talking as if she is my mother. "The next time I will not be so understanding."

I nod my head. She holds her hand on the door. "I will be at the park." My body twists away from her. I muffle my words.

"I will tell you, Jasmine. Just let me rest for now." She lifts from my side and flips the lights off, shutting the door behind her. I grab my phone and note the time, it's five in the morning I need sleep.

ROMEL

I climb the stairs from the thirtieth floor ascending to the roof. My hands and feet feel like I am on my way to a mountaintop. Pushing the door open I step out onto the wood paneling searching for Drew. I turn my head seeing Drew posted along the glass half-wall. He is pulling off his blazer, taking in the air. I step closer and he fists bumps my knuckles as I lower, sitting on the ash grey lounge chair.

"About last night?" I chuckle and shake my head. "You were gone with some lady and I noticed Chad looking like cream between two voluptuous chocolate cookies." Drew laughs and sits on the patio sofa across from me.

"He had a two piece rolling through by his side." He narrows his eyes in my direction. "Who the fuck was climbing down the pole?"

"I didn't make out who it was." I reposition in the seat.

"I know you're fucking lying. You are aware of exactly who was swirling her ass on that pole." He hits at my knee, laughing, and I rub my face trying to stay alert.

"I'm getting too old for you and the crew to be dragging me out, bruh. Victoria is like a splinter in my damn mind." I twist my lips. "I dropped her off at home. So I was like 'how did she get there?'"

His head falls back and his body breaks in a full laugh. "I noticed her instantly, bruh. Victoria's eyes found mine I was like Oh shit!"

I am shaking my head. "The cats out the bag and I was ready to play with her kitty cat." I lean in and release a deep breath. "Tell me why she acted like something embarrassed her." My arms lift in the air and I get passionate in my conversation, speaking with my hands. "I'm like...we grown, whatever you came here to explore I will be more than happy to oblige. But something has been off about her for a minute."

He rubs his chin. "I can't answer that, but I know you are looking into it. I will be happy when you two get it over with and fuck."

My head turns with a gust of the wind. "Yeah, you and me both."

"I peeped you trying to fuck it up with a cougar for a minute. I was passing through and she was pulling you in a room."

I snicker at that memory. "I got the hell out of there. She was gorgeous, seducing me. Her husband came, and I was like what the fuck. She told me to come right back."

I rub the top of my head. "No, I didn't come to play like that with you and your husband. Hell, his ass might see me pull out an orgasm his ass cannot do. Shit, then he'll be ready to fight."

Drew is laughing. "He might not get her off."

I laugh. "I'm not signing up for that playground." I narrow my eyes looking out beyond the sky and switch the conversation. "What's up with the penthouse?"

"I saw one in Atlanta, but the one I like the most is in Buckhead. I want us to invest in these rental properties in North Georgia." He hands over his phone and it shows an image of a cabin on the screen. Drew continues and I scroll through the display. "I saw these when Stanley sent me the properties."

"These are good investments." I tilt my head. "I agree people are always traveling for an escape from day to day routine. Hell you and I can do things with the properties. How many are available?" I have been saving my money for a while since my father passed. The only thing I have been interested in is putting it with something that will work for me while I am sleeping. I give Drew his phone back. He is going through looking for something else.

"I saw a place in Buckhead. It's a home, but considering yo ass eats all the time we should think about partnering up in a restaurant. We have to be silent about that."

I agree. "Your ol' man will not act right about us making several investments at once. I will be a silent partner with the restaurant. I can lead a rental property and as you detach from your pops you can lead on more rental property." Drew agrees by tilting his head. Keeping details from Mr. Rodd is difficult. He hacks shit just like the both of us; knowing his ass he knows we are on a break from work on the roof when we are supposed to be at our desk.

I rub my sleepy eyes; I'm exhausted after staying out so late last night. I clear my throat and ditch out my thoughts. "I'll ask Mrs. Maddox to look into the paperwork to make sure everything is a go."

Chad's mother is an attorney and she will keep our matters out of sight from Mr. Rodd until we complete everything. I think Drew's ol' man keeps close tabs on us because he is just being a father to us both.

I grab my cell from my pocket knowing we are not supposed to have the system on but we are not physically in the building. I disregard the rules for the moment along with Drew. Turning my phone on I disengage the Wi-Fi and pull an image up and show Drew my phone. He looks over the picture.

"What is this? A dance competition?" He shakes his head. "Victoria will be there?"

I shrug my shoulders. "She hasn't mentioned it. I want to go in case she is but that five grand is easy money."

Drew tilts his head. "I'm down for whatever. You tell me what to do. Dancing is your territory, I play around just to mess around with the ladies. Speaking of playing around, spring break is around the corner." Last year we went to Sex Con and more than likely we will go again. Drew passes me my phone. I look at the time and turn off the phone.

"We need to get back downstairs. We will have to think of something epic for spring break, it's our senior year." Standing to my feet my arms stretch to the sky. "Damn I need this day of work to end so I can go to sleep."

Drew is up and walking to get his blazer. "You and me both."

I yawn and push the door open stepping down the stairs to go act like I am working.

VICTORIA

*J*olt awake and see the sunlight streaming through the curtains. My thoughts are flooded by what happened in Dallas. Shutting my eyes, the image of the scar appears and I open my eyelids. I rush to my bathroom and grab the scissors, staring, as a constant wheel of guilt covers me. What type of person am I becoming?

Standing upright, I hear my door swing open, and Jasmine yells at me, "What are you doing in there? This room is dark and you need to talk to me now!"

How did I not hear her come down the hall? I grab a towel and cover my body and turn the knob. "Jasmine, I will be out in a minute."

Her eyes squint and she pushes the door open. She looks around like I have drugs in the bathroom. She reaches for the scissors on the counter and I gulp. Jasmine's face wipes of all emotion.

"Victoria, why are you cutting yourself?" Her eyes gaze at my exposed arm and I cannot lie as she blocks the door.

My words follow a serious tone. "I have been having a hard time, Jasmine." She is not speaking only waiting for me to tell her the truth. "Can I at least put on clothes?" Her head shakes, opposing the suggestion. I sit on the edge of the tub and look at the floor. A thick layer of heat covers the space as I speak. "When I went home someone snatched me and Tatiana when we were at the mall."

She moves in front of the vanity. "Did you think I would judge you for telling me? I mean you know about my past and never judged me." She clears her throat. "Chica, I hate that you were kidnapped, you say snatched, but you were kidnapped." My eyes look in her direction. "You are a hero, sweetheart, you escaped and managed to get your sister out safely." My mouth drops as I know her burden of thinking she never saved her sister. She walks in my direction and leans over to hug me. "I love you, chica, and you having a toxic relationship with a blade is not healthy. You are a great sister, friend, and woman." Tears are falling from her eyes and I don't want her hurt.

"I will stop, Jasmine."

"Promise me when you feel, or don't feel, you will talk to me or dance. Do what makes you feel. Not this. You always tell me you want me to draw because it makes me feel...Living is about feeling. I'd rather look at you and cry seeing you alive than seeing you in a casket." My arms swing around her neck and we cry. She pulls back from me. "Go put on some clothes woman... if someone saw us they would get the wrong impression!" I chuckle.

"Hell no I am strictly dickly!"

"Exactly, get yourself together. India stopped by earlier about the dance competition." Jasmine stands and steps to the door she snaps her head. "Hey, you have to dance right, get up, go practice, get your ass out of this room!"

I follow after her. "I am getting up."

IT's my mother with a voice of concern. "*Si madre, como estas?*" I notice me telling her I am fine, is not calming her down. She's avoiding telling me how she's doing which makes this entire conversation alarming. "*Despacito, mami. Donde esta padre?*" When she is frantic, it's not best to talk to her. I have to ask her to slow down because she is talking so fast but not saying anything. I need her to get my *papi* on the phone. He takes the phone and I can hear uneasiness in his voice, but he is trying to hide it. "*Papi*, I want you to tell me what's going on." I reposition on the couch as a dead silence takes over the room. "I know something is wrong, so just tell me. I can handle it."

I already know about the tuition so I know it must be they don't want to tell me about the money issue. Jasmine walks out the room smelling like peach Bellini. I shake my head and motion for her to keep quiet. She walks past me to the kitchen. My attention returns to my father he is telling me about my sister Tatiana. "*Papi*, I will call her, and I am sure I can get her to talk. I know what she feels like remember I was there." Jasmine walks by with a water bottle she air hugs me and her head rest on her hands as she has them folded in a prayer position. I blow her a kiss knowing she is on her way to bed. My father is going on and on about my sister, but he says something that makes my heart feel as if my heart will fall out.

"*Papi* is she okay? When did this happen?" He tells me she tried to kill herself or at least he thinks she did. She told him she wanted the marks off her wrist from the monsters."*Papi*' I am working on my tuition matter. Focus on Tatiana."

He tells me she's in a rehab center and I grow mad. "Why would you let her go there?" He professes he's concern about her killing herself and he needs her monitored twenty-four seven. He's trying to come up with the money for my tuition as well as her doctor bills. "Papi, don't worry about me only focus on Tatiana *mi' dios* get her out of that place. I know what she feels like she shouldn't be there alone." He tells me how mommy goes there with her throughout the day. Tears roll to my cheek. My heart is aching for my sister. My *papi* tries to comfort me. I tell him I will do everything I can to help and he refuses he only wants me in school so I can finish school. *"Te amor padre."* Saying I love my father typically comforts me, but not this time. I am heartbroken. I have never been in a place like this at least when we were captive, I was with my sister. I have never even shared with Jasmine what happened. I don't want to worry her she has so much on her plate and I just didn't want her to feel sorry for me. She's always been like a little sister, like my Tatiana. She needed me to be her sister not a point of depression. My father attempts to convince me he is working on the matter and I should get rest. I end the call crying myself to my room, I feel like cutting myself, but I promised my chica. I must help my family without harming myself. Maybe I can check out ways online to make money as an option.

I TAP Romel's number on my phone. I am not telling him everything I know I owe him an apology. After this call I am done, I have made enough amends. I hold the phone to my ear. Romel answers it sounds like he is busy. "Hi Romel, am not trying to keep you I just wanted to apologize for how I have been acting lately. I am going through something that's a bit personal." He is asking me about how I got to the club last night. I can't believe he even mentioned it. "I called a cab… it's not against the law." He is funny but I appreciate he is more focused on how I got there instead of why I went. Romel's level of concern for me is intense.

He understands me it seems. "Thank you for not hating me. I will push through it. I have a dance competition I am focusing on right now." He is telling me whenever I decide to tell him what is bothering me he will listen. "It's nothing with you or me. Romel

I had things take place when I went to Dallas and something else just popped up about school. I will be okay." I discern from his voice he knows I am trying to buy time from telling him the truth. He knows me too well. "I will talk to you later." It's one day before this dance competition and I need to focus on that. I end the call and take the rest of the day practicing in my room.

VICTORIA

*T*his club is so lit. Streaming lights are flashing in sync with the pounding music. People are jumping up and down as the DJ keeps the crowd hyped. I scan the room before going out on stage. As I look in the right corner I see my chica is pumped, ready for me to come out. I have put my worries in the back of my mind for a moment. Tonight I am competing in a dance off in hopes to win the five thousand dollars. I have to split it with Jade and India; I am dancing with them, but hey it's better than nothing.

The DJ makes an announcement signaling for my group to come out and I am so nervous. This is nothing like the conservative dancing my parents sent me to school to do but a girl's got to make a living.

I see a female swing across the floor from the ceiling and that is our cue to take our positions. The curtains open and I drop to the floor in the dead center of the group. I need these two girls to stay on point so we can win the fucking competition.

If I can get them to stop focusing on the guys leisurely walking around half naked, I think we could win with ease. For me tonight is all business but I notice a few sexy guys roaming around. Finally, the bass lines of the song drops and the rhythm of the song possess me as I become one with the music. The crowd is screaming so loudly. Jasmine is yelling from the floor, she seems so excited! She is the most supportive when it comes to me, no matter what I do she is always in my corner.

From each step my body parallels the sound of the music, using each step to each hand movement. Dancing is like a natural high for me, my body rolls like an S form. I sway from the floor until I am on my feet. My head drops back with a big reveal of my clothes. I am out of my jacket, swinging it to the floor as I step, placing it between my legs and the judges are most impressed. I smile with confidence glaring at the judge and a grin of appreciation forms on their face.

The crowd is winding down and the moment they think it's over; I drastically vibrate to the floor exposing my back then the shape of my breasts, our bodies flip in unison, exploring the length of the stage, our legs dancing from the tip of our toes. I sexy crawl toward the crowd and I'm back up on my feet perfectly in a beat. We break off and free flow. One girl is popping her booty, moving her body like a snake, while the other is twerking. I turn flirtatiously from the crowd and grab my ass, sexy walking away from the center of the stage. The crowd is hollering; I killed it and I am feeling myself as the curtain closes.

That was so hype. We rush off the stage to see the next competitors. Jasmine is in the crowd and she is hollering, "Chica, you murdered that, you were a savage out there!" I blush and she politely greets the other ladies cheering them on.

I yell amongst the crowd. "We smashed it!" The girls tell me they will get something to drink.

I look over and a group of girls are coming in my direction as if I called them. I can't stand these fake tricks.

I roll my eyes and the DJ announces the next group coming up. One of the girls makes her way over to me, I can't stand her and she talks as if she is welcomed to be heard.

"You know you can make anyone question their sexuality with the way look at the audience."

Her sidekick interrupts, "That shit was so transfixing." She puts her hand on my hair and Jasmine jumps in between both of them. These girls are the worse. My chica yells for the next group and the curtains open while the two girls disappear in the crowd. I know Jasmine reads the silent thank you written across my face; I was about to forfeit my group by getting into a fight with those chicks.

Jasmine's boyfriend walks up from behind her. Ugh, I can't stand him. I paste on a fake smile out of respect for my chica. A male dance group is on the stage. It is so like his ass to get protective because a male group is on the stage. He is so insecure of himself. I mean, what are they going to do, take her away from him because they dance on the stage? Jasmine looks at me with regret in her eyes. "I have to go, chica!"

I nod my head. "I understand. I will see you back at the dorm later, hopefully with good news." Winning is my goal. She embraces me and my eyes notice the guys on the stage.

I yell, "Damn, the stage is in sexiness overload!" Her boyfriend escorts her out and the two girls in my group return.

Damn, I can't tell who the guys are because they have masks on their faces. But that guy with those gripping, caramel arms is someone I would love to dance with. I have a dead lock on his body and his dancing skills are mesmerizing.

The music they selected is hypnotizing. Their body movements move at each beat making you see beats in the song I didn't pay attention to before. I look at the dark chocolate guy and his fucking wing tattoos are summoning me to the stage. I have to admit I am surprised by their selection.

The girls ask me if I know who the guys are. "No, but that caramel guy can slide his ass by me any time he wants." He has mad skills, his moves are so fucking sharp, such a great dancer. They laugh.

India leans in my ear. "Yeah, the caramel and the dark chocolate dude dance like strippers but with a purpose." The choreography is different…it's like they were going for sexy but a deeper meaning. This shit is fire and the girls are screaming as if it's a Magic Mike showcase, well I see a few guys hollering over the dudes on the stage. I laugh but they look delicious.

The song fades and the curtains lower and my eyes survey the announcer. He calls the participants to the stage. We run to the stage and stand on the side. He is holding the results in his hands. The crowd is screaming our names. I overhear people calling out the male frat from Morehouse and I am so pissed. This shit is not fair by any means with the frat involved.

The crowd separates, and the frat begins all their stepping and I am more than pissed now. Everyone is hype and all the happiness evaporates from me. The guys stroll in echoing like they are in the club and huddle in a circle. Even in my annoyed state it's easy to see how crunk they are. They step in unison in a circle and then one guy backwards flips and the guys stand at attention to hear the judges call out the winners. Silence falls in the club and just as I thought the guys with the masks on win. I smile and hug the girls.

Jade embraces me and says in my ear. "Next time, Victoria!" I don't know when next time will be; I needed the money for tuition.

"Thank you, girls."

The crowd is celebrating the victory of the guys. I can't be upset they did a great job.

I walk to the back, away from the noise and gather my items.

WALKING THROUGH THE DOOR. I bump into the two tricks I hate with a passion. One passes me a flier. "Maybe you can make real money using your talents elsewhere."

My eyes fall on the paper. I look at the girls and the door swings open. My Morehouse brother and his frat brothers barge through behind him. "Hey Victoria!"

I shake my head and realize the girls disappeared. My suspicious eyes stare at Romel Adcock.

I smile sideways. "Hi, Romel."

The guy from the group comes out. He is putting on his shirt and has a girl on his side. I notice his tattoos.

He interrupts, "Hey, Rom. I'm on my way out you good?"

He tilts his head and grins. "I'm good, bruh! You go have big fun."

They bump fist in a choreographed hand shake. He looks up at me. "Hey, you are from the girl group!"

I smile realizing he saw my group. "Yeah, what is it to you?"

He bites his lip and shakes his head. "Nothing…shit, we won. But you were good." His eyes size me up and I notice Romel looks tense.

He interjects, "I'll see you at the after party, Drew." His friend walks off with the girl.

Romel looks at me curiously. He's become a close friend although he seems protective. I chuckle. "What was that, Romel? He was with a girl so I don't think he was flirting."

He shakes his head. "I know him better than he knows himself. Trust me, if he wants you that girl would not be able stop him from his advances."

We both laugh. I grab my bag and he offers to take it from my hands. I pass him my bag. We walk along the sidewalk and he looks around. "Victoria, how did you get here?"

"I came with my group, but I'm on my own now. I am just going to walk." He stops walking.

"I'll take you to your spot. It's no problem…unless you have plans with another dude."

Here we go. "You know I think you take being my Morehouse brother a bit too seriously."

He chuckles. "Cool, so I guess you are riding with me."

I sigh. "Romel. I need to walk, I have so much to clear in my mind." He walks as if I said nothing.

"My car is around the corner. It's the black Mercedes." I know which car is his. He loves that damn military looking car, it stays spotless, as if it's in a competition. I used to detest seeing it, but watching it…I don't know I fell for it, that might have more to do with the heated seats. A SUV on the luxury side, but the rugged demeanor…lets just say the car is fitting for Romel. I shake my head.

"You are not taking no, for an answer."

He tilts my chin. "Are you learning your safety is important to me? Whoever the guy is you are trying to clear your mind from will have to be cleared sitting in my vehicle."

He is so off. My worries are far from being about a guy. I have financial issues among others but that's none of his business. We step by his truck and he opens the door. I sit and he asks me a question. "Victoria, what would you have done with the money if you won?"

"I didn't win, so it doesn't matter. I bet your friend will have fun with it though, him and his group." Hell, I need to pay a tuition fee but I am not telling him.

He shuts the door and walks around the driver's side. I attempt to unlock the door. He has to have a remote because the engine sounds off and he sits down. I notice his arms look bigger than usual. Turning his head in my direction something fills his eyes with concern. "What's up with you? I have known you long enough to know when something is bothering you."

I don't enjoy discussing this with him. "I will be all right… sometimes life is just hard. But I will make it through." He takes off from the parking lot, driving like a bat out of hell. I secure my seat belt and look out the window. He turns on the music and we ride down the road until he makes it to my place ten minutes later. He swishes the car in the first parking spot next to Jasmine's car.

Shaking my head. "My life is in danger in the car with yo ass. Get me out of here, you drive like *diablo*."

He bursts out laughing. "I don't drive like a fucking devil."

I unbuckle my seat belt and he grabs my bag. "Do you want to come hang out with us at the party tonight?"

My head falls to the head rest. "I'm not really feeling like it tonight."

He opens the car door. "Oh, I get it. You have an audition to oversee, I'm sure you'll update me about that shit." I notice his tension as he assumes I am hanging out with some dude. I promise you he has been acting more protective lately. My eyes bulge.

"Romel, what is going on with you? I know you and I have this brother and sister friendship but you have been a bit challenging." I reposition in the car and he moves as if he is getting out but I grab his arm. Damn, his arms are so big. I don't think I ever paid attention to his arms.

"I'm good. You have fun on your date. I am sure you will share the details of one of your many fuck ups of a date."

I blink my eyes, okay he is getting too comfortable. "Is this your idea of a brother sister relationship? Do you talk like this to your siblings?"

He looks me in the eyes trying to hold back his emotions. "Victoria, don't worry about it. I'm me today and tomorrow. By the way, you did good up there on the stage tonight." Not good enough. He exits the car not giving me an opportunity to stop him.

The door opens and I stand in his personal space, he steps back. "Thank you for supporting me, Romel. I appreciate it and thanks for bringing me home." He is being so extra.

He tilts his head. "It's no problem. I'll always be supportive or here for you, *soy tu hermano correcto.*"

He bumps my hip his tone sounds more like he's trying to convince himself that he is my brother than agreeing to it. "Yes, you are my brother and I'm your sister."

We walk to the door. "I remember the induction ceremony." He chuckles. "That was wild, Victoria, you brought me a flower and said the flower I gave you was not the right color."

I shake my head. "Yeah, you gave me a yellow carnation."

He stops, stepping after me. "No, you gave me a yellow carnation. I gave you a yellow rose. My flower was meaningful. Your shit meant nothing." I leap over holding my stomach and laugh.

"I didn't know you'd understand the meaning of the flower. I wasn't even thinking of the meaning." We make it to my door, and I pull out my key. I hold my hand out for my bag. "Romel, I wasn't rejecting you. I know that's what the flower means, but I didn't know what to get. My mom always gave my dad flowers. That's what came to my mind. I should have just gotten a keychain." He laughs and passes me my bag.

"Shit, are they working on a divorce." I laugh and Romel pushes my hair away from my face. I stand in silence and Jasmine swings the door open.

"Chica, stop playing at the door. You two scared me. You are either in or out." She shakes her head and turns. "Hi, Romel."

"What's up Jasmine?" She walks off. "I guess we will talk later." He tilts his head and walks off. I step inside and call out to him.

"Romel, what did you think of my dance?"

He grins. "You were good, Victoria; the other girls were unnoticed dancing next to you. Perhaps, you need other people... you know." Wow, that was a nice compliment for me but not the group.

"Like what kind of other people?" He shrugs his shoulders opening the door.

"Someone that will compliment your dancing and that has

more control over their body as you do when you dance. Think about it." He waves his hand saying farewell, and I shut the door. I narrow my eyes.

What does he know about dancing control? He only dances with his mother.

I barge toward Jasmine's room. "Chica...we need to talk!"

ROMEL

I lounge on the couch and two girls walk out of Drew's room half naked. Drew is behind them with his sweat pants on. One girl notices me and squeezes her little ass on the couch so she can sit next to me. "You were on the stage last night with Drew, huh?" I frown and don't move from the couch. Drew and I share a lot but not women. She needs to move.

"Yeah."

She giggles. I look at her then the other female; I chuckle, hell, they are twins. What's up with him and Chad and the double mint twins? Drew snaps his finger, and she pops at his attention. He opens the door and outside they go.

"Alexa turn on the TV." My phone vibrates from the dining table. Drew walks back inside. He is about to say something but I interrupt. "Drew, give me my phone off the table."

He snatches it off the table, talking trash. "Bitch, why are you laying yo buff ass on the couch like you are tired?"

He throws me my phone and I catch it. "Thanks." I tap in my code unlocking the phone and recognize an alert from Victoria. I shake my head. Drew sits across from me on the other couch.

"What's up, bruh? Did you talk to Victoria?" I grit my teeth and shake my head. He throws the pillow at me taking my attention away from the phone.

"Stop playing."

I reposition on the couch and Drew is carrying on. "Fuck you, Rom, your ass is dead watching that girl dance on the stage. You fucking drool over her."

My attention is away from my phone and I burst out laughing. "Shit, I give her my undivided attention and need a fucking condom just watching her. She's a bad girl."

He laughs. "My thoughts exactly, she freakin' killed it."

I sit up on the couch. "She crawled her ass on the floor like she was fucking liquid, bruh. I was ready to make it rain and throw fucking dollar bills off the stage at her ass." I prop my feet on the coffee table "Bruh, Victoria literally had my ass slain, she was rolling her hips like she was fucking Ciara on that damn stage."

"I sense your eyes on her like you are watching porn or some shit." I laugh at Drew and clear my throat.

"Her ass is still talking about me being her fucking Morehouse brother." I frown. "Shit, I got some 'more' dick for yo ass. She needs to stop fucking playing. She has dudes running around here after her ass all fucking day."

"Rom, I told you not to hack the system and force being her Morehouse brother."

I rub my hand down my face. "I'm aware, but man the moment I saw her I couldn't help myself."

"Well we are going to Chicago for Spring break so you will need to get this out of your system."

"I am cool. When are you packing yo shit and moving?"

"Bruh, I told you I would only stay in an apartment for a minute. I have been here for over a year with your ass." I am used to him being here even though I am ready to not have a roommate. We need space.

"Yeah, whatever, did you get the keys to the penthouse yet?"

"I did. Stanley has already planned it out so when we come back from Chicago all my shit will be out of here. And I will see you what...two hours after I move."

I frown, but he is right, I will use his pool. "What, fuck you, Drew."

"I know you can't live without me, Rom. No, but for real, my place is your place; just don't walk in on me fucking." We burst out laughing.

Victoria

I NOTICE an unpleasant stare on Jasmine's face as she is sitting on her bed. "*Chica, que pasa?*" She turns her head, rubbing her eyes then sniffles.

"I think."

She places a picture of her boyfriend on the other side of her. This guy is such a jerk. I wish she would leave him alone already. I narrow my eyes knowing she is in this 'my life is over mood' because of something he did. My life issues consume me and not being there for her isn't right, I need to listen to my chica.

"Jasmine, what did he do?"

She faces me. "I am not sure yet, but I sense he's messing around." Finally, she has figured it out and we can move on from this guy in her life. I want to tell her I overheard a chick talking about him but I can't. Jasmine is stubborn; all she will do is tell him, they will have make-up sex, and I will want to kill his ass. I lean up against her dresser.

"Are you going to tell me why or is this a damn guessing game? He's not your husband you know." She stands and goes around the other side of her bed. I know I touched a nerve. She pulls open the closet.

"I know, chica. I never said he was." She pulls out a change of clothes that look more like she's going to dance class. I know it's the clothes she wears around the house.

Sitting on the bed I pick up the photo and place it on the dresser. "Chica, you can date other people. The last time I checked he didn't put a ring on your finger. If you think he is fucking around, then you go fuck around."

She chuckles. "Chica, I am not into all that, I need a vacation. I have work in the morning so we can strategies how to fuck over my man another day." I laugh and Jasmine carries her items to the bathroom talking as she walks. "Enough about me, I can assume you didn't win but you and your so called Morehouse brother seemed comfortable at the door the other night."

A frown of curiosity grows on my face. "Miss me with that... you are right, we didn't win, which is part of the reason I came in here. But..."

Jasmine returns in my eyesight hanging on the edge of the door with her toothbrush in hand. "But what, chica? I suspect Romel likes you. He is always around telling you how great of a dancer you are." The consistent reminders from her is insane. She leans back away from the door. "Granted your ass is top notch. I saw another dance competition; I will send the information to you."

She gyrates her body mimicking my dance moves. I practice so much around her that I believe she can reenact most of, if not all, of my solos. "Yo ass is a beast out there dancing. The judges know who they want to win because there is no competition. Everybody in the club knows your dancing skills are fierce."

I laugh because she is still mimicking me dancing, dropping to the floor and curling her body up in the position I did once the curtains opens. Hell, maybe she needs to be out there with me, but I know not to ask with her having this stupid boyfriend. He stops her from living; I think that's what I hate more than anything. She's gone through enough and college days are supposed to be fun. We laugh so hard until I catch my breath.

"Thanks, chica…I know it is not just what the judges say, it's the votes from the crowd too. Besides, Romel is just being supportive. That's what brothers do." Why did I say that? Her demeanor changes at once as I mention the word brother. She walks away from my view. I know she is thinking about her brother, he died and she never likes to speak of him but her silence is loud and clear about her missing him. I feel for her not having her brother and not knowing where her sister is. Sometimes she will talk about Mimi when she lets me read the countless letters she has written her. It's like her mother acts as if Jasmine doesn't exist. The entire time we have been in school her mother has not contacted her and her sister never writes back. I guess this is why I am so protective and hate her boyfriend, she has enough people that treat her like shit. She turns on the water and begins brushing her teeth.

I try to change the tempo to get her to continue talking. "Hey, we should go somewhere for spring break, just the girls." She scurries back to the entry way.

"That's a great idea but something tells me wherever we go your Morehouse brother will show up."

I lay back on her bed and toss her pillow up in the air. "Whatever, I need to get money first. You know I have the tuition dilemma, but I will check around for some places to go?" Plus, there's my family issues I have not mentioned to her.

She closes her bathroom door. "Victoria, don't worry about it. I am sure together we will have enough money, hell, I have enough for both of us. So let's plan it!"

I sit up happy to hear her say that; I was definitely thinking about surfing the web about making quick money. My ears fill with the sound of my phone, it's my mommy's ring tone. I better answer it before she freaks out. Standing up I throw Jasmine's pillow back on the bed. "I'll look some stuff up, we can talk tomorrow."

I STROLL over to the couch with my phone in hand. I dial Romel's number. He answers on the third ring. He must be occupied.

"Hey, can you help me with a dance?" He pauses in silence. "Romel, I need the money and need to win. Will you think about it? Meet me at the dance studio?" He chuckles as if I said a joke I'm uncertain if he can pull off what I want. He agrees.

"Thanks, Romel. I need the money for school, Romel, not shopping." His voice alters and I roll my eyes knowing he thought I just wanted money to play with. "I have to contact my girls, if you can get two guys that will be cool." He agrees and I end the call.

ROMEL

I pace across the hardwood floor heading to Victoria wondering why a crowd of people are here. I thought we were just practicing. My eyes memorize the shape of her body as if I was preparing for a test. I clear my ears taking in her words.

"Hey, Romel, we need three guys."

Drew pushes the door in behind me and I notice a crowd standing up against the wall by the handrail. I tilt my head and introduce the two. "Victoria, this is Drew." She nods and her face is so fucking serious.

I shake my head. "It's cool, Victoria, my boy will be here he is on the way. Show us what you and your girls are doing and I will show the crew."

Drew falls back against the wall posted by some females. I see the two girls she dances with walking to the center of the floor. They are dressed in camouflage. Victoria is watching them.

"Romel, this is India and Jade." They are grinning, dressed as if Tina Knowles coordinated their trail blazing army wardrobe. She has on a long-sleeved warm crop-top, I am tired of her hiding her damn skin. She should have no issues about her appearance, if she thinks I don't know something is up she is out of her mind. Although, Victoria's shorts are hypnotizing me. It's as if she is playing peek-a-boo, exposing a few inches of her thighs. I guess I should have told her to dress as if she is going to the gym. I can't see her legs through those damn camo over-the-knee, thigh-high socks. She's killing me with distraction. The earth tone colors are a new look for her and the ladies. Nevertheless, I do like seeing her in those combat boots, she can walk all over me in those. I tilt my head and get out of their way. Victoria still hasn't figured out that I am the dude dancing with the group that beat her ass. I don't know why she is still dancing with these other girls. I told her they don't compliment her. I'm sure we will work it out. I prop my leg against the wall by Drew and the song "Take You Down" by Chris Brown blasts in the room. Drew's eyes find mine, he is chuckling. "We are going to kill her with this song choice."

Victoria

MY EYES FOCUS on the den of iniquity mirror seeing my image. We look cute in our camo but these colors are expressing how blah I feel more than anything. I move to the center of the floor with the ladies and we do a half jump and sway our arms seductively to the side. Romel is watching and the crowd is cheering as we dance but the look Romel is giving me is not right. We prance along like we are strippers and I get lost in the song. As my hands rise to the back of my neck, Romel is walking to me as if I summoned him on the dance floor. I bend and twist my ass. Romel is standing behind me rubbing the top his head. He walks off. He and Drew are caught up in some type of banter, laughing.

I am annoyed. The girls are still dancing. I walk away to grab the remote and start the song over.

I hear Romel yelling out. "Just set it on replay, Victoria." I think I am officially upset with him. Taking in deep breaths I calm myself before returning to the floor. Romel and Drew are up. A frown grows on my face.

"What are you two doing? Romel, you interrupted me and my girls while we were dancing." I'm eyeballing Drew with his ripped jeans. He moves his upper body like he's doing jumping jacks with his chest muscles then takes his shirt off displaying his tattoo of wings. My eyebrows rise as I turn away.

He chuckles. "Victoria, whatever is on in your mind is interfering with your dance. I have seen you dance and at this moment you are pissed. Let Drew dance and you fall back. Don't worry he will follow what you have already choreographed…for now."

"What?" He grabs my wrist, escorting me away from the center of the room. I am not happy, but I call on India to dance with his friend. I know she has a crush on his sexy, chocolate ass.

Pushing my hair back I attempt to ignore the unwelcome stares from those in our presence. The sound of the audience fades as the music drops at last, Drew and his partner tap their feet in sync with the beat of the song and half jump in the air. Drew changes the move and slow grinds. He flicks his wrist as if a whip is in hand and drops to the floor. I interrupt their dance and stomp over to the sound system to turn the song off. Both he and Romel are laughing like this is a game.

Romel follows after me along with the eyes of the others. He whispers but I am sure someone is reading his lips. Damn, why are his lips so sexy? "Victoria, just let him finish the song." I restart the song and he reprograms it to auto replay. I should have done that but I am frustrated.

"You said he was going to do what I said, Romel." His hand is rubbing on his chest trying to distract me.

"Victoria, calm down. I'm the leader of this pack."

This cocky asshole. My eyes watch him as his shirt releases from his skin. I think I am suffocating as I eyeball the muscular definition of his physique. Oh my God! How did I not know his ass was the dancer on the stage? I blink in his direction. The females are howling as if he is presenting his strength before them, flexing his ripped, vascular look. Breathing is officially a discomfort as tension is building in my shoulders and heat rushes between my legs. He speaks to me and I can't seem to focus on the air escaping in and out of my lungs.

His words float in my ear. "We practice to win, so trust me, whatever money you are trying to win, you'll have it." I roll my eyes and walk off. Romel grabs my wrist, he should not touch me. *Don't give in, Victoria*, my head snaps. But why is my mouth growing a light smile as my mind assesses the silliness of my behavior. Naturally the semi-autonomous process happens as the contact of his skin merges with me, as if I am at the very end of being out of breath. It's as if my body's surface has come alive as he is mere inches from me, radiating energy. It has a different feel to it, as if I ran out of something and now I'm empty, at his beck and call. His velvety voice is alluring to me.

"With me, you'll win, trust me. The step needs to sell sex, not your dance lessons." The dominance, confidence, and sexiness of Romel's vocal cords gives me chills. What is happening to me?

I chuckle at his explanation, maybe he has a point, but I am not giving in that fast. At least I am not trying to and failure seems to resemble the same at this moment. He never mentioned he was on the damn stage with Drew. My voice lowers in a sugary pitch. "I have been dancing all my life, Romel."

He steps ahead talking as he walks away from, me rolling his body like...my lips part. Romel's hips roll...work! He's hot as fuck! God almighty...please stop that camel roll. He's so fine. I love the way his body moves. *CONTROL, VICTORIA!* His full lips are moving, speaking to me.

"This is street dancing...not your class." I stomp away, hating that he is correct. Why is my body responding to him this way? I should throw in the towel, self-help is not working today.

He continues speaking in a nonchalant manner. "You will be officially pregnant after watching this dance." I might be pregnant now...I need my water to break looking at all his glory. He winks motioning for his friend to carry on. "Go ahead, Drew."

I guess I will watch him. I am afraid I want to do more than watch him. He is coaching India on the moves and touching her hips. I shake my head...assholes. Romel counts them off and everyone is watching.

The song replays and their dance moves repeat . Drew slow grinds India. My brow rises seeing him slide, following India's ass nice across the surface. Their gaze remains locked and the crowd's response of the hyperventilating chicks is alarming. It's like they are having a screaming contest. Her hips slow grind, his hands are on her hips. I shake my head watching Romel jump up and down behind them as the pair dances. He is so hype, yelling, "Boy, if you don't stop!" He looks cute, excited about them dancing.

The beat of the music changes to Silk "Freak Me Baby" and the two drop to the floor as Drew's hands slam to his mid-section his legs spread apart. He looks like a fucking stripper ready for me to throw some dollar bills at his ass. The way India is looking at him it's like she's in a daze. Turning my head, I see how excited everyone is, maybe my negative energy is spilling over as I dance. Oh my God! I'm looking at this man on the floor as his pelvis is rising in the air. Romel walks to my side and whispers in my ear. "Don't look so sexually frustrated."

Asshole. He hops his hype self-back on the opposite side of his little sexy friend. I eyeball Drew as he flips over, grinding the floor. I take in a deep breath. Damn. Drew is eyeballing her, seducing the freak out of her ass while they dance. Hell, if she's a virgin she's lost all aspects of it. This one female keeps screaming. I think we might have to mop the floor, their damn ovaries are going crazy.

Romel stops Drew for some reason. He is walking his sexy ass in my direction. I look off. He stands in my personal space.

"You got it?" I shrug my shoulders. "We will add yours with what me and my fellas will do. It complements the song." Asking him to partner with me is not about him being in control I admit to myself. I am on the edge of losing myself watching Drew's ass dance with India. "I guess, Romel...as long as my girls don't oppose."

They chime in like little high school chicks. "No...we don't mind." I hear the door unlock and all heads turn. I pull my hair back and in sixty seconds it's returned to a bun. *Calm down, Victoria, everything is alright.* I narrow my eyes, focusing on his highlights.

"Who is blue eyes?" His slim swag pants fit him perfectly as he treads through the crowd. Is Romel's crew the ultimate ladies men, just flirty shades of sexy?

ROMEL

I reach my hands through the sleeves of my shirt until it is back in place. I chuckle, loving her doubt. I point to the other female. "He will dance with the other girl." She looks at me.

"Jade...you want her to dance with him?" I tilt my head and Chad hustles to us over the crowd talking.

"Chad, this is Victoria." He reaches his hand and her fingers follow his.

"Hey, beautiful." I give him and evil eye, his hands release hers. "Romel, catch me up, my fault." I tilt my head and walk it off.

"Blue-eyed motherfucker." Chad is laughing and Victoria walks away. The song is on instant replay, so I brief him on the steps and he nods his head. "Remember the after party..."

He nods his head. "Yeah, I remember the steps...you and Drew, man." My eyes grow and I laugh. "Shhh, that's our business." Victoria settles the crowd. She will flip out when she sees him dance.

Chad enters the center of the floor, bouncing, and I step to his side. He tilts his eyes assuring me he has the dance. The song drops at Chris Brown singing and we both whip our wrist in sequence. I step back and Chad is following my lead and we break dance. I step back. His movements are in tune with the slow music. Chad falls to the floor on one knee as if he is pulling to the other side of the room. He shifts his gears, letting the crowd know he should not be underestimated. My eyes set on Victoria ogling him with the surrounding girls. I chuckle as Chad gives them their little sex fantasy while he licks his lips and the ladies are screaming. He grinds the floor like he's a stripper. He wins the crowd overall

I am yelling, "Hey, hey, hey!" Hyping him more and more. Chad breaks off doing his own thing, the audience screams as he rolls his body with his tongue flicking out his mouth. The wild-eyed faces of the crowd are lost in screams.

Me and Drew jump on his shoulders, pointing to him. The room is on fire!

Drew slaps my hand, hyped, and I yell out, "Shit, we getting people pregnant up in here." We all burst out in a full body laugh.

The song is looping again. I stare at Victoria and she looks as if she has calmed her nerves. Walking to her side I reach my hand and she gives me a suspicious expression. "Come on, girl... I won't bite." Unless she wants me too, the heat between us is growing by each second, along with my heartbeat.

"I know the dance, Romel."

My lips turn down and I whisper in her ear. "I don't like being fucked, unless I'm fucking. So grace me, dance with me." She walks to the center of the room, releasing her long, curly hair from the bun. Damn, she's so gorgeous. My eyes are hunting her body movements.

As the music drops I circle Victoria like she's my victim until I am at her side, our gaze remains locked. The audience applauds as we tap our feet with the beat of the song and half jump in the air slow grinding to the audio. Everyone is screaming. She looks as if she's coming for me. Shit she can discipline my ass all night and day. We dance in perfect sync to my heart. I drop to the floor, relaxed, sliding on one knee following her ass, nice and slow. A smile forms on my lips.

The song progresses, as she collapses on her palms, leisurely grinding her hips. The yells are as surreal as the beat of the music changes to Silk "Freak Me Baby." We drop to the floor as my hands slam to my mid-section. I see Victoria from my side view mimicking me. She splits to the floor, legs spread apart, as I sink to the floor we lift our hips in the air, flipping over, humping the floor.

The beat is pumping; I can hear Drew yelling. "Hey, hey, hey, hey." I rise as she is grinding the floor. My hands motion as if I am sprinkling something at her contracting ass from side to side. It's as if my hand movement possess her body at my demand. Victoria is on all fours pushing against the floor. Shit, she has my thoughts caught up in the rapture of taking her on this floor. She smacks her ass and rises from the floor with her feet part. Damn, that pose in those heels I slide between her legs, pointing, saluting in her direction from the floor and she grabs her midsection, smiling. Her eyes are inviting me to heaven. We jump back to our feet and the chorus runs again. Everything we did was perfect, in sync as one. I am falling deeper for her but when will she know. If all was taken away from me at this moment, I would understand why.

Victoria

I MIGHT BE LOSING my mind dancing with Romel. Something about his eye contact makes me burn inside. It's like we are seductively break dancing. My whole body and soul is communicating at once, connecting a feeling with music and this man inspires me. Hearing the audience is giving me the most incredible sensation as if dancing with him is perfect. Romel does his classic backward, talking shit move. I follow him and throw my legs like I'm on the drill team.

Fuck! He lifts my ass, rocking it. Everyone is cheering as if they are waiting for their best friend to finally get their crush on. Romel points, smiling, and I slide my hands to the wet juices he's demanding to flow between my legs while I lower my body. I rock my hips and this boy keeps flirting with me. I love every bit. This is a straight turn on, he's rough and I like it! To say he appears to be a beast in the sheets might not do him justice.

Romel's hand trails down the center of my stomach and we are back at seductively break dancing. I catch him off guard and flip my legs over planting myself on my palms. He smiles as if he can smell my juices spilling over. Romel runs his fingers spreading my legs and I wrap my legs around his waist. I'm tossing my head, throwing my hair, and he is slapping my back, pulling his hand to my ass.

I hear one distinct scream from the right corner. She might be pregnant or dislocated three vertebrae simply watching. He pulls back, releasing my legs to the floor. DAAAYYYUUUMMM!!

I flip over, motioning my finger for him to come here. He moves as smoothly as water flows, and he is so sexy. He should drop the pants. The song is dying out and Romel points at me in appreciation. He steps like he is pledging, while raising his shirt and watching me as I crawl back on the floor. I smile as he reaches his hand, lifting me from the floor and speaks in my ear. "We might have made everyone thirsty." I push at his chest and he laughs. My heart is pounding as my eyes are sizing his wildebeest ass.

I take in a deep breath. "Hell, I'm thirsty."

His two friends walk to his side and my brow raises. I am silently praying to the dance gods for forgiveness. The entire act resembles us going at it on the floor, but I loved every bit! Damn blue eyes and that tongue releasing from his mouth gave me life. I notice Jade's eyes are watching the tall, vanilla man. India and Jade stride out to my side, clenching my wrists, jumping up and down in pure excitement.

ROMEL

$\mathcal{I}$ push the door open. Chad and Drew follow behind me loud about the class. I step in the kitchen, grabbing bottles of water feeling more like I just left the gym. Chad sits in a chair and I throw him some water. Drew walks to his room and opens his hand catching the bottle. "Thanks, I will be back. I need to change."

I sit at the table facing the couch looking over at Chad. "So what you thinking, Chad. Will your schedule permit time for this?"

He nods his head. "Hell yeah, I'll make the time." He is stomping his foot on the floor. "That was everything, Romel."

I tilt my water over while agreeing. "Man, Victoria is a work of art; she did that release split, falling on her hand."

Chad repositions in his chair frowning. "How did she flip into a split, bruh. I'm aware she's your girl but her ass had my fucking attention."

My body leans over in the chair as I laugh at Chad.

Following with a hand salute, I shout out, "I'm ready to report to duty, you hear me, bruh!"

He is looking confused. "I figured you were about to take her all the way down, when you did the freestyle." Drew enters the room with a change of clothes on. He was sweating like a beast when we were dancing. His mouth is open with a surprise expression on his face as he walks toward me.

"Rom, yo girl a rookie but you were bringing some shit out of her dancing. I could tell you were testing the waters to see her response."

I laugh while clapping his hand. "India had your ass..." I twist my lips knowing he was messing with the girl. "*Woo*, I saw you looking at her like don't touch your booty."

Drew walks to the other side of the room and sits across from Chad as he interrupts smirking through his words. "Drew, you rubbed your damn fingers across that girl's clit." Drew leans in laughing slapping Chad's hand.

"Hell yeah! Shut all responsibilities off, it's going down." Drew was looking at India and crushing it. He is shaking his head in a hard motion. Chad and I are laughing at him. "India jumped on my body sliding down...I was like I got a pole for your ass to slide down." He jumps to his feet imitating her acts. He is still turned up. "She put her ass on my dick grinding, like, take this shit."

Placing my bottle on the table I keep laughing.

He looks across to Chad frowning. "Blue eyes walks in the place like a pro. Everyone was screaming at you sliding on the floor."

I hit the table recalling his dancing. "Chad, you had the tongue work going for the ladies like...I'm getting pussy from somebody after this dance. You wild, bruh!" We were all crunk, sweating and dancing. Chad speaks through his laughter.

"Romel, that song had us all going crazy, the remix was fire. Once you heard the word baby something freaky just took over everybody. I had to lick my tongue to let them know I'm not playing."

Chad narrows his face. "The girl I danced with had a fat

ass...so I was like..." He rubs his hands and continues his statement, "It's going down. Romel, I see why you over there thinking you need a dancer in your life."

Drew sits up and turns in my direction from the couch. "Did you tell Victoria to throw her legs on your waist, bruh?"

I shake my head. "No, but I was like that position will get you pregnant." I stand imitating as if she wraps her legs around me. "I was looking at her like she is ready for my anaconda with her fit ass."

Tilting my head my mouth drops staring at Chad with his eyes glossing in surprise. "I need it in my life! Her legs were up in the air and you snatched her."

Drew interrupts him, speaking slapping his chest. "You damn near went at it."

He hits his chest again trying to compose his laughter. "No, no, I was like class is over in this piece. She was ready for that shit, bruh."

Drew lies back, speaking in a curious pitch. "That beat dropped. How did she cartwheel into a split?" He jumps on the couch yelling. He rocks and I am laughing at him recall the turn of events. "I was like hey, hey, hey...you two were fucking shit up."

Drew pauses reflecting on his words. "I am looking at you with her." He jerks his body and asks of Chad, "Didn't it look like he was sniffing her ass? She was seducing him out there, Chad." He is stomping his foot laughing, looking in my direction and Drew continues. "I knew you were into it, Romel, Victoria did the slow twerk and you were like...let me look at you twerking on this floor." I can't stop laughing.

My eyes grow as my mouth drops, holding a surprise expression and I chime in, "I was looking at her like, can we do an instant replay of that shit?" I was definitely living the dream, grinding her ass.

Chad stands to his feet. "Romel, you been working her ass

out in the gym, bruh. She is the grind queen up in this piece, for real." He is not lying, her hip rotation was on point, having me salivate with her arch of the back. Damn, she's sexy.

Chad walks down the hall to the bathroom, laughing. My thoughts are recalling Victoria saying she needs money. I grab my computer and do something I know I shouldn't do but I need to know why this girl needs money. Drew is walking in the kitchen talking on his phone to some female about his plans after the dance off tomorrow. I hack into the school system and pull up her financial statement.

"Oh, damn!" Drew is walking behind me and stares at the screen. I push him off. "Talk on the phone, bruh."

He laughs and ends his call. "How in the hell are you pushing me away when you are hacking into shit? Whose account is that?" I chuckle at me hiding hacking from him. I move over and he looks again. "Romel, stop hacking into Victoria's shit and tell her you like her already." I enlarge the screen.

"I'm concerned asshole."

"Damn, this could explain her stress. She needs six thousand dollars..." He lies on the couch. "Tell my mother...but don't tell M'Dear." Then he sits back up wait. "She will know if you tell mother."

I nod my head. "Yep, I have to figure out how to disguise it. I know if I asked the cause is worthy but because we are trying to not let them know about the investments." I stand to my feet.

"I will tell Chad." He lays back down. "Chad can handle it!"

I stand in front of the couch. "She needs six thousand dollars; I'm not asking him for six. All of us can give two thousand and we will avoid our parents noticing."

"What the fuck, Rom? How are you just going to spend my money on someone you are not fucking?" I hit him in the back of his head and he laughs. "I'm good, you bully. I will give you the money and you can do as you please. I don't want you coming back saying I gave your girl shit? Just get the money out of my account." He grabs his phone. "Tell Victoria to send me India's number I'm fucking her ass. If I am spending money, I am getting her ass." I burst out laughing and he gets up to walk to his room. "Not really she's too young for me." He is crazy.

"Thanks, Drew—"

He interrupts, he hates if I thank him for anything. "*Mi casa es su casa*...if I have it you have it, right." This is how we live our life. It works. I hear him speaking on the phone and he shuts his door behind him.

VICTORIA

I have slept most of the day. My body is tense. I take in a deep breath and reach for my cell. Chantal called, chica left a message and she's at work. I slide down and open the message from Romel. Something about seeing his name on the display is comforting. I read his message.

Hit me up when you get a sec.

I press the screen to type a message but my text is interrupted by Chantal. My other sister from another mother, after graduating from high school she was the one not interested in leaving Dallas. She enrolled in college and enjoys her life working as a project manager locally. When she is not off being wined and dined by some guy she allows the privilege, as she says, to have her time.

I answer the call.

"Hey, chica! What's up, sis?" She is popping off at the mouth, fussing at me for not returning a call or a text message of hers. I was concerned I wouldn't know what to say. It's not like her brothers told me anything. Wait, is Jesse or Omari are okay?

"Awww, sis, I was busy and wait, wait…I have to tell you something."

Taking lead of the conversation will help avoid having her ask me anything about coming to Texas. "So you know I have mentioned Romel. Well, chica has mentioned him to you more than me." She recalls and rushes for me to get to the point.

"Okay so we danced the other night...it was more like rehearsal. We will be in a competition. His ass can dance, you hear me. I am not talking about electric slide dance. No gurrrrl-ll." She is giggling as I illustrate my story. "Sis, his body moves like...take me now! I am serious. We were grinding. Chica was out with her dude so she can't attest. But I promise you my head was in thought of if he moves like this he might fuck me into a coma." She is hollering, telling me to stop lying. Chantal cannot believe I am thinking about having sex with him. I typically tell her how he is my brother. "I am for real! On everything holy, I knew he would carry my ass to the hospital from the dance floor."

She clears her throat and is asking me questions about Romel having a brother. "Girl his brother is much older and lives in Dallas, so that might work. Anyway, his two other friends were dancing with us." She cuts me off demanding to know who is the 'us' I'm referencing. "India and Jade were dancing with his friends. They were sexy too." She is not at all interested in hearing about them dancing with the other girls. I can hear her mother yelling her name. "Tell Momma Ann I said hello and yes, I am behaving in school...just don't give her details about how I am behaving, woman." We laugh and Omari's voice comes in. He speaks and I am rushing off the phone. "Tell Omari I said hi. I love you, sis we will talk later." She tells me to hug Jasmine and from the sound of her voice she knows nothing about what happened when I was in Dallas. I end the call.

I flip my screen and start typing a reply to Romel. I don't want to sound desperate.

Okay, I will. I am packing to go on a trip at the moment. Thanks for helping with the dance. I will hit you up later.

I press send.

MY HANDS RUB the top of my arms as the chill rushes through the attire I opted to wear for the evening. We are back at the club and there are so many people here trying to win. Some are here for the love of watching. It is fun, I admit. I hope Romel is not upset because I didn't call him back. I didn't know what to say to him honestly. I can't stop thinking of how he danced with me, maybe that's what he wants to talk about.

I notice India and Jade walking in my direction. This is the first time we don't look like we're members of an all girls' group. Instead, we are wearing whatever made us feel like we would have fun. Jade is stepping high in her red pumps matching the red bra that is peeking out through her unbuttoned baseball jersey, she's paired it with low-cut booty shorts and fishnet stockings. India is definitely dressed to demand attention in her all black, leaving no room for imagination.

Those thigh-high boots are gorgeous. She throws her arms around my neck. I whisper in her ear. "I love your no rules shirt." It hits just below like a halter top. She turns as her fingers touch on the laces that tie at the hips of her mini skirt. I smile knowing she is definitely showing her ass off tonight...Literally. I guess these guys bring out their wild side. Jade joins us in a hug.

"Where are the guys?"

I shrug my shoulders. "I'm not sure. They will be here."

India screams at my appearance as we thought in harmony with the thigh-high boots. Although I have the white version and mine have laces up the front.

"You look cute and covered."

My head lowers. Come on, my outfit is see-through. I smile. "Thank you, slut."

She giggles I know she is not used to the change of clothes I am wearing. We still all look cute and ready for pictures. I pull out my phone and we capture the moment.

My eyes survey the room and I don't see chica. I text her the photo and notify her that we are going backstage.

She replies, *I am in the parking lot, sexy ma.*

I grin and turn, bumping into Romel's delicious chest. I gulp at his appearance. Something about him in these jeans make me want to rip them off. His bare chest is something I am growing to enjoy.

He whispers in my ear. "I see you don't have time to talk but you make sure I spot yo ass bedazzled in this body suit." He takes my fingers and lifts my hand in the air turning me.

I see his eyes grow wide. Maybe I am peeking below at his bulge. His arms are massive and sexy. Drew shouts out of nowhere, "Fuck, your ass is naked!"

My nostrils flare. I am not naked; I have on a bra and g-string under this. Romel chuckles looking back at Drew and Chad, he bites his bottom lip and walks behind me. His stance looks like he is ready to fight Thanos if he entered the room. Is he guarding me? Why do I feel so awkward around him while he walks relaxed?

I AM SO NERVOUS. Romel squeezes my hand. "We will win, don't worry." We walk ahead entering the stage as the crowd silences the familiar notes of the Chris Brown song plays. The guys invite us all in position. It is so exciting dancing on this stage with Romel. We demand the yelps from the crowd with ease. I think he knew before me he compliments my dancing all along.

We finished our set, but the DJ plays our song again. I turn my head noticing how alert Romel is scanning the floor ahead of him. He jerks me about on the stage and the others have cleared the way.

Something else is happening to this man in front of me, as my heart pounds.

The average person looking might think he is focusing on his desires, forgetting the considerations of me.

His eyes resemble something fierce. I don't think we can do this exactly on the dance floor. I read the guidelines.

What is he going to do is the question?

"Romel." I whisper, "You know all eyes are on us."

Something tells me these three have done something like this before. The crowd yells and Romel is staring at me like no one else is in this room.

It's scary, but such a turn on. I doubt dancing for a competition is anywhere in his thoughts but I think the crowd will not stop us. He responds, "Really?" He squeezes my hand slightly and a smile forms across his face as he twirls me. His words float in my ear, "I have noticed no one but you."

He knows exactly what he is doing, as he advances every move is as if planned yet not forced because my body is on the edge at his command. Chad places a chair in front of me.

I gulp. What have I unleashed in him wearing this outfit? Allowing him to lead, I feel exactly where he is and what he is doing. I adapt to his direction as he demands to control and I trust him.

Romel's hand tilts me like I am a tea pot and I bend over touching the back of the chair with my palms. His tongue lavishes the back of my spine and I shiver.

Fuck, I knew he would send me to the emergency room. I can't believe he put his tongue on me, all my senses are off balance. Romel is behind me with his erection pressing against my ass. I don't turn my head; I let him do as he pleases in front of all these people. I am so turned on. Is he lifting his leg? I feel him resting on my back. The crowd's screams are downright filthy.

Romel is grinding me, my heart is racing; I can feel him on

my pussy. He grabs me by the back of my neck and I am so lost with the freedom I am giving this man over me.

Wait, is this part of the damn act? I am about to unravel on this dance floor. I am standing upright and Romel screams to the crowd.

"You like that shit!" The crowd yells but somehow I feel like he is talking directly to me. *Yes,* I do like that and this moment confirms he will fuck me into a coma. What happens next assures all thoughts are thrown out the door.

He whispers in my ear, "Be still trust me."

I let go live at the moment, as he takes me where he pleases. Romel's hand are sliding between my legs, he clutches his fingers, and lifts me with his strong massive hand. Assaulting between my legs, oh my God, he flips me over. I am facing the floor on all fours, my heart is pounding and he is acting out thrusting behind me matching the rhythm of the song.

Oh my, why have I been forsaken? I am letting him do anything he wants to me on this dance floor. The song plays out and we become one. He balances me upright and I turn, facing the audience with screeching applause filling our ears. I turn facing him smiling, wondering why I didn't see before.

He leans over and his fingers crawl on my flesh as heat radiates from my skin. Taking small breaths, he tilts my head forward. Romel's warm lips graze over my mouth, free from guilt with a boost of desire, and his tongue devours me with deep sweeping strokes, my eyes roll to the back of my head. I can feel every emotion run through my whole body with pleasure. My thoughts flood questioning is he the one?

I grab his hand, scared that this is probably part of the act. But it seems so real. His hand runs through my hair, keeping our faces still, we stand quiet in a room full of people as if we are alone for a moment, noses touching.

In seconds, Drew and Chad are jumping on the stage. I turn

hearing the announcer shout, *"The prize of sixty-five hundred dollars goes to the final contestants!"*

Wow, I think he just congratulated us as winners of the competition.

My eyes bulge, we won!

I grab at my chest and Romel stands there, calm as a river. My girls are at my side, lifting my shoulders and chanting. We won!

ROMEL

y head is hanging back as my eyes look straight to the sky. I'm enjoying the breathtaking views. I hear the door open and I lift my shoulders, sitting upright. Drew is walking in my direction with a grin on his face.

He has a chipper voice. "What's up Rom?" I stretch my arms. "I'm good; what's up with you?"

He sits across from me continuing in conversation. "You know what I want to know."

He is not accepting silence.

"Did you two link up or what? Don't say you didn't know if Victoria was feeling you because everybody at the club knew her ass was yours for the taking. Plus, I didn't come to the house I had some other things on the menu."

Hell, I saw him and Chad leaving with those females. I chuckle recalling last night. My fingers rub the top of my head. I knew I wanted her, but she still was not acting as if she was aware. "Nope, nothing happened. I think she thought I was doing all that for the competition."

He hits at my leg and a frown grows on his face. "No, Romel, I saw that girl, you damn near opened her up on the stage. She kissed you back, I saw her breathing out of control like you to were out in the wild." He tilts his head. "Just to be clear I wasn't watching you I was watching her nice apple bottom ass. Shit it was all out to see."

Victoria dressed like she wanted to be my sex slave but she wasn't acting right and I am not forcing any female no matter how into them I am.

"Fuck you, Drew." He needs to stop playing so much. He chuckles.

"You really think she thought you did all that to win? I mean we won before you damn near stood up in her pussy." I fall over laughing holding my stomach as he keeps running off at the mouth. "Come on all you two were doing was showing your fantasies to one another, publically."

I nod, Victoria had other topics on her mind so I dropped her off to her spot.

"She was thankful and all about us helping her win but something else is bothering her, Drew. She still isn't acting like herself."

He stands on his feet. "It's quitting time around here and we are flying out to Chi Town. Did you bring your luggage?"

"Yep, Stanley is going with us isn't he?"

He steps ahead and opens the door. "You know he is. Pops is over the top right now. I don't know why, but hey, we will get on the falcon, fly to Chicago and hopefully you will find someone to fuck while we are there." I laugh but I need to put Victoria to rest this time. Sex Con is just the place to do that, I just hope I don't run into her.

STANDING in an elevator with a casual suit on seems unusual as I twist my head and notice that the crowd heading in the same direction is practically naked. I remember coming here last year and we dressed nothing like this when we were working. Drew is set on getting a device to add to his collection of toys from a vendor before the night gets too late. He looks in my direction.

"We can go to the hotel to change our clothes after I pick up this item." I am fine with the detour. I tilt my head.

"That's cool with me." The doors open and we take in the view in front of us; there's a woman hanging from large rings. I shake my head knowing we will not leave after he picks up his stuff. "Drew, check out that girl."

He tilts his head. "Damn, something wrap her ass in bandages." A group of plus size women walk through in lingerie followed a crew of buff men with jeans and no shirts. I wave and one lady bites at me. Drew tugs at my shoulder. "You know she'll eat you alive."

I rub my hand over my chest. "Shit, she would definitely try to take my ass out."

Walking in this dark area I see the women are naked with body paint over them or lingerie with their ass cheeks hanging out. I twist my head as we continue walking, seeing a guy being interviewed. One lady has on a black corset and pants. The lady on the opposite side of him is wearing a white fitted shirt with ripped, pink boy shorts over her net stockings. They are asking him about his penis to body ratio. He yells out, "It's good." The women laugh.

We keep moving ahead and my eyes take notice of a woman in a purple sequin jacket, black top hat, black stockings, and boots. She twists her body and her bare breasts flash. She looks like she's part of the entertainment.

There's so much going on in this place; there's everything from porn stars, strippers, tattoo stations…it's like one massive night club with every sex desire you might have. I see the bar to my left. "Drew, I'm going to get something to drink."

He tilts his head as I make out the person he's come here to meet. Rashad tilts his chin and I speak, nodding my head. He's a frat brother from Colorado. We met him last year when his company was demonstrating some furniture that I later added to my private space. "I'll be over afterwards."

The live band is crushing it. I pace through the men dancing with women in lingerie until I am at the bar. A waitress wearing a fitted, white t-shirt and black boy shorts speaks, "I'll be with you in a moment." She walks away holding a tray of shot glasses.

This guy comes by and passes me a flier. He is telling me about a contest for best bikini body and ass shaker. My eyes spot this sexy chick licking her lips. She is sitting getting her body painted completely gold next to some woman pole dancing. Drew better get back before I leave the bar to go shake her ass. I turn around as the waiter returns. I shout out, "Do you have Canadian Whiskey?" She tilts her head confirming. "Let me get a snake bite, straight up." She nods and begins to making my drink.

I look across the way recognizing Jasmine. I didn't expect to see her here. Victoria mentioned they were coming but somehow I didn't actually expect to see her here. She's always with her boyfriend. I know Victoria is not far behind her with Jasmine being near. The waitress sets my drink down and I pull out my wallet. She turns, grabbing me a napkin, and I pass her a twenty-dollar bill. I snap the shot back and Drew is heading in my direction. Standing to my feet I turn to leave and this lady is grabbing me to come dance with her. I knew this would happen.

"I'm on my way out to change. We will be back."

She looks at Drew smiling. "Come on, you two." She rubs both of our chests, holding on to my neck tie requesting us to join her. "Come over to the stage and play with us."

Drew shrugs his shoulder. "I will meet you over there, let me get someone to hold this for me." I tilt my head and follow the young lady to the stage.

THE MUSIC IS LOUD. There is a screen displaying the acts of everything going on the stage. I chuckle at the female responding to Drew. He is basically fucking a random chick on the stage as he dances. The crowd is so pumped. This female is walking in my direction, signaling for me to come to the stage. She speaks in my ear, "You go up in one minute. We will select a random female." I tilt my head. The crowd is high-pitched as Drew exits the stage. I walk and the DJ switches the song to "Wet the Bed" by Chris Brown.

As I step closer, I can see a female in the bed in the center of the stage rocking her head. I hip roll in front of her and the crowd is screaming. A smile grows on my face and I circle her like she's my prey. I can't help it, something about Chicago makes me free. I fall to the floor on one knee and lower my body, grinding the floor, crawling to her feet. The chorus sounds off and I stand, releasing my jacket from my arms. Throwing it the floor, I circle around her as I remove my tie and pull at my shirt.

The crowd screams as I slow grind my hips, teasing her. I circle around until I am at her side and I lean into her face. As she reaches for my chin, the crowd is blaring as I center upon her breast breathing on her neck. I lower my body, gliding down her center backing away, and the announcer yells out to the crowd.

Everything is so pumped up. The pack of people is yelling, and I look in the audience as they are pointing for me to turn around. This place is always wild. My head turns, and I take in the sight of Victoria sexy walking in my direction. She is unleashing the intensity of deep desire as she moves in closer. My eyes follow her legs striding in my direction. I admire her black lace bra, gripping her breasts, coming for me to feast on. The high-waist black garter wrapped around her middle is screaming for me to detach it from her skin. She steps to my side in black heels. Saying she's fucking with my mind is an understatement.

I smile as I reach my hand out for her.

Victoria's fingers fall upon mine and she joins the stage act. My eyes blink as I notice Victoria reaches her hand for the young lady and they switch positions. My eyes grow at the view of her ass is exposed from the thong with a heart cutout design. I chuckle recognizing she's not into sharing me even if she's entertaining.

The DJ switches to another Chris Brown song and my ears hear "Take You Down." My fingers cup my chin and I shake my head seeing Drew in the corner next to the DJ. The biggest grin grows on my face. What kind of shit is he up to? His ass is always up to something. I look on the screen and note Victoria displayed front and center for the crowd to view on the bed. The song is so loud and the audience is applauding me on to take her. Red lights blaze to our sides as if there is fire in the air.

I size her up for twenty seconds and unbutton my shirt. The audience is yelling. I hear Drew from the microphone. "Claim her ass!"

She is lying, twitching her body as if not one person is around. I nod my head and my adrenaline is building; she keeps her eyes on me, studying the motion of my body. I lean over watching her closely. My lips are at her ear she grabs my head twisting my face to hear her words. "Are you going to break my cervix?" I'd crush her fucking body on this stage if she'd let me. I take her hand, pinning it above her head. I reposition my head at her ear whispering, "Your ovaries would explode."

She gulps at my words and I chuckle. I slide to her other ear. "I don't enjoy being fucked unless I'm fucking." She takes in the air and I continue breathing on her neck and her head falls back. The crowd keeps screaming. As I lower down her center, I look at her squirming in front of a crowd of people. My head circles around the layering of her clothes before her pussy. I trail my hands down her thighs slowly, noticing her legs shaking she kicks them out.

I back away looking at her like she's a fucking dessert, lowering my pants, and the lights black out. A light center on us and Victoria's eyes are flashing unholy thoughts at me. I grin and the chorus repeats. My hands reach for her ankles and I yank her. She jerks her legs in the air and I watch her grab her head. My lips possess her mouth and I suck her bottom lip. I tease her lips with the graze of my tongue. She's losing it before everyone. Her legs fall, she lifts her upper body coming after me dismissing we are in a room full of people and I snake my hands around her ass. My hips are wrapped with her legs. I pull back, standing to my feet with her in my arms. Her chest is convulsing. The crowd is screaming and we exit the stage.

Victoria

AFTER MIND FUCKING and dancing on the stage with Romel, my mind is scattered. My hand grabs at the hissy fit throbbing below as I stand inches away from my room. My legs weaken and I lean into the entry it's as if I am having voltages of energy ignite the folds of my lower lips. Fuck! Typically, I welcome the sensations growing within but I think my lady below is actually pouting. Why am I having an orgasm walking down the hall, standing in front of this door?

Taking in a deep breath my lower muscles relax. Saying I am sexually frustrated is an understatement, my body is longing after Romel. I wonder if his delight curves or maybe it's straight. My thoughts need to curve from his pleasures. I grab the key card out of my pocket, flashing it across the keypad. I push the door open and these big hands lift me from the floor pushing me inside the room. My heart is racing unaware of who is behind me dragging me to the bed. I descend on the mattress and see Romel in front of me.

"What are you doing?" I think my lower lips got a different message because it's dripping at his strength.

I feel disoriented by the attraction I have toward his sculptured body as my eyes follow the veins in his arms, etched and bold. His chest is bouncing up and down from breathing so hard. Is he okay? How could I be asking myself if he's okay, and he damned near attacked me? Didn't he push me from behind and barge in my room?

My body drifts over and a surge pulsates below. I flinch, resisting grabbing at my throbbing clit. I rub my legs together as if I am in a tight spot and need to relieve myself.

I stand to my feet and move closer to him. Mingling our bodies together was not a good idea, considering my reaction. Perhaps he is drunk. I need to escort him to his room between my attacking orgasms.

I grab at my head recalling we were a bit heated on the stage dancing. He is gradually building up every sense in my body. Teasing my body…and now my body is naturally chasing the orgasm, craving this man.

He stares at me with dark eyes; in seconds his palms cup my face as he assaults my mouth. I taste his warm lips and I think briefly that I should stop him. Romel's arms embrace me like I have never been hugged before. All my blood is rushing to his touch like a magnet as his fingers lowers below my waist. My heat is naturally rising at his demand.

He dances his tongue with mine while his delicate hands wrap around me. For a moment it's as if Romel realizes his actions and he sinks his lips, possessing me. As his fingers touch against my pants he pulls at the material preventing him access I respond to him instantly.

I shatter inside, spiraling out an orgasm over his fingertips that have yet to feel my lower skin. Sexual energy continues to build between us. It has been going on for too long, who am I kidding. I can't remember the last time I had sex, certainly not since working out with him; I have not had a craving for the guys I date. The countless night of tension orgasm is overbearing, I must satisfy myself. I will go with it, connect with my body just this once. Fuck the guilt in the atmosphere that wants to hold me back from taking this man and letting him have me.

His strong, masculine arms pull me closer, eliminating all space between us. Again, I completely lose my willpower at Romel; I no longer can speak to him as my Morehouse brother. I push and he pulls.

"Romel...just."

He pushes my leggings, lowering enough for him to have contact. "You want me... you're purring, drenching wet after me." *Of course I am, you are turning me on... I think. Why is he turning me on?*

Romel's finger pushes my panties to the side, and he circles my clit. *Why does this feel so good coming from Romel?*

He bites at my neck. "Say you like it." No I am not giving him such power. I hope I don't...I am always in control.

I push away trying to tell myself this is wrong but my body gravitates to the pleasure he offers before me. With all my strength I push, feeling his barrel chest that hides between the layers of material from his shirt.

Romel's fingers clamp my wrists. "The more you pull away...." He twists harder as his words spill over me like a chocolate mocha, "the tighter my grip gets."

Without penetration this man has me shaking into another orgasm, spilling over his fingers once more, valuing the pleasure he gives. I go against my fight, against my guilt, and sink into his spell.

My vulva is in for taking a beating that only he can offer me. I will not stop him. "I want you inside me."

Physically, Romel attacks me, throwing my body onto the bed, followed by a gentle kiss. "Victoria…I have to warn you."

He peels my leggings down until they are on the floor. He is so massive it's scary and exciting at the same time.

"Do so…" I am panting. His fingers slide my panties off my hips and he throws them over his back.

"Damn, you are beautiful."

He pulls his arms out of his unbuttoned shirt and I tighten my muscles, reaching my hands out to touch him. "Romel, you look delicious."

He grabs my hands. Tell me he is not stopping me. I growl. "What is it?" He removes my shirt and I can tell what he has to say it's serious. Why are his pants still on? Part of me wants him to talk about it later but I sense it's the rumors. He backs off the bed, kneeling to the floor.

"I can be rough in bed." Pain doesn't scare me from his touch. I roll over inching closer to his face.

"Brutally rough or savagely pleasurable?" He smirks with a surprise expression in his eyes with my response. "If you are worried about rumors…you don't have to be. You can tell me your side of the story if it makes you feel better."

He takes my hand. "I'm not concerned as much about the rumors…that can wait. Unless you don't want it to."

I want nothing else to stop us from what he has for me under those pants. "I only need to know one thing for now." My tongue swirls the inside of my mouth. "How rough?"

He gently kisses the center of my face. The caress of his lips sends a shivering sensation over my body. Nothing about him seems like what others have said. His lips reach my mouth and he climbs on the bed. I roll over, expecting his next touch. His hands lift at my shoulders making certain I am attentive.

"Savagely pleasurable."

I gulp at his words. "All the time?" His breathing increases and he trails his finger down my arm. "Not necessarily." He runs his finger across my lower lips. "Is this your most sensitive spot?"

My, he's good...I love that he's asking. "One of them."

He smiles. I grab his hand pushing his fingers deeper and the sensation is driving me wild. My hips lift. "Deeper...Romel, is another sensitive spot." He bites his bottom lip as if he is pleased to hear my response.

He grinds further. "You have a deep sensitive spot? Hmmm you are aware of yourself." Yes, I am hope it doesn't scare him off. I shake my head.

He stands and I spot his bulge. My eyes flash. I gulp, oh my damn. I inch back watching him remove his pants. How big is he? He might have to break barriers to get all the way inside of me.

A sly grin grows on his face. "Don't worry...I'll be pleasurable and a savage at your request." I'm far from being worried about him pleasing me...more concerned about him ripping my insides. Somehow, I am still craving him, did I drink something? My little cat keeps leaking.

"Romel...I'm not a 'do me' kind of chick." He crawls over me and my heart is racing as I touch his arms coming for me. "I don't just lay here and you fuck me." Romel's eyes flicker past me.

He grips my breast. "Really...?"

With a fixed expression Romel's mouth goes after my nipples as his hands incline to my wrist pinning me down. Our eyes lock in a shared understanding. "Tonight you will."

I yield at his request even as my lips tell him it's as if he has taken over my body. He pulls back the latex to cover his length and my eyes dance with excitement.

He's nothing like the other guys that easily let me have my way. I don't know what's so different with him, or maybe it's me that's changed since...I erase the thought. I need him to take me, reclaiming my body so the negative thoughts of being touched vanish.

Romel's greedy hand goes after me, bending my hips further in the bed. He parts my knees and my legs fall.

I moan and he smiles. "You want me to control you...own you for the night."

My body swaying as if music is guiding my hips, he has a power over me. "Yes, Romel."

A relentless charge grows over my body as his eyes watch me. I moan, guiding my hand down my center as my fingertips crawl to my waist. His huge hand unapologetically bats my touch away, my eyes grow. His eyes are far from being gentle or sweet.

"Say it."

My body squirms wishing he would just take me. "Control me...I want you to control me." The motion of my body stops, realizing the power I am exchanging to him. What am I becoming with Romel?

His ruthless eyes beam into mine. "I will tell you when to touch."

"Romel, now I need—" He cut my words grabbing the water bottle from the ice bucket on the nightstand and pours it all over me. My body balks at the cold sensation.

"Romel!"

"Two people can't lead," he snarls in my direction.

Why did he do that? I wipe the water from my center, glaring at him in annoyance.

"We shouldn't...Romel."

His hand returns, grabbing an ice cube.

"Shhh," Romel whispers, trailing the ice in hand along my lower hips and I forget my thoughts, I let go, my nerves perk embracing the sensation to override me once more.

"I can help you prolong your itch between your legs."

He places an ice cube on his tongue and inserts my fingers in his mouth.

I let out a moan, contracting as he toggles the ice linking my fingers. "Ahhh...Rom." The ice melts and he lowers his tongue, gliding it between my inner thighs. My hands press the top of his head. "Romel."

He keeps building and releasing my tension with his mere touch. My eyes roll to the back of my head. I squirm and he holds my wrists tightly, pressing them to the bed.

"Who is in control, Victoria?" My entire body feels like it's on fire.

I utter my words. "You are."

He goes for another piece of ice, guiding it along my navel up the center of my stomach. Romel eyeballs the honey left from my tea on the night stand. I move my hand and he shakes his head. "No, Victoria...put your hands in place."

I grin as he opens the top, turning over the container. The warmth drizzles on my stomach and his mouth goes after every drop. I grab his head and he presses my wrists above my head.

He clenches his teeth. "Hands stay in place."

Romel repeats his trick with the ice, rubbing it over my nipples; my ass sinks into the bed. My reaction puts a sinister smile on his face. He places the ice in his mouth. Romel is keeping all my regions alert at his command and calm from heat.

I am hot and bothered by his teasing, my moans resonate in his ears and he peeks in my eyes. "Good you kept your hands in place."

I breathe ready to release. "You can touch my head...but no orgasm."

Is he insane? He lowers his body between my thighs, spreading my legs like the wing of a butterfly. His cold tongue circles the top of my clit. I bolt, whimpering his name as the shocking sensation of cold sends shivers down my spine.

"Ahhh...Romel."

My lips are so sensitive. His finger inches at my sensitive spot and I yell between moans. This is the most intensifying pleasure.

Victoria

MY EYES ROLL to the top of my head but not because of Romel.

Bang bang

I hear an abrupt noise from the hall. I shake my head blinking my eyes. "Stop!" I jump and push back. Romel's head turns and I know he hears the yell from the hall. "Get off, you bastard!" That's strange, it sounds like my chica.

I push out of the bed, grabbing clothes as I go. Romel reaches for his pants and I am barging out the door. "Jasmine!" She has her fingers gouging in the guy's eyes and his head is leaning away from her.

I rush to her side and punch the guy forcing himself on her in the head. He stumbles back. She pulls at his ear and I yank his opposite earlobe with a ripping force. His eyes bulge. I jab him in the knee with a kick and he swings, punching me in the shoulder as he buckles to the floor. Jasmine is stomping him in the groin. My fingers clench my aching shoulder. My head twists as I see Romel charge through to the guy. Oh shit, his eyes are beaming with fire. I jump and grab Jasmine away from the guy. Romel takes his brutal finger and yanks it in the man's mouth as if he's caught a fish, dragging him to the side of the wall.

It looks like his skin is elastic, drawing away from his teeth. Romel darts back at me. "I told you to go for the throat." The guy jabs a right hook and my eyes grow.

"Watch out!" Romel's hand blocks his fist. His palm hits the guy in the forehead exposing his neck and Romel follows through with a throat punch. I think he shook the guy's brain.

Jasmine is yelling as if she's having flashbacks.

I hurdle her in the room and notice Drew rushing to Romel. Damn, he stumbles back. I think something cracked. The guy swings a second hook and Romel lowers his stance taking both of his fists in the guy's ribs.

I turn seeing Romel go after him like a mad man. I am at a loss thinking he will kill him. Drew pushes me back in the room. He is yelling, "Get inside, call the front desk." Something tells me he is concerned his friend will kill this guy.

ROMEL

*M*y feet are stomping the ribs of this guy like I am trying to break a skate board. I can hear Drew screaming. "Romel...Rom!" He pulls me back and notice Stanley giving me a look as if he is tired. Victoria is back in her room.

I am panting and the guy speaks in a drunken tone. "Security is here for you now!" I step in his direction and Drew pulls me as my spit flies in the guy's direction.

"Bitch, security is here to protect you from me."

Drew's hand is tapping at my chest. "Look at me, Rom! Checkmate. He's down Rom...let's go!" Drew's trying to make sure I don't go overboard. Stanley is at the end of the hall looking like a stuntman for Men in Black. It's best for me to leave.

AFTER HOW THINGS unfolded I grab my phone to contact Victoria. Her phone rings and she doesn't answer.

Damn, I guess I scared her. Drew walks in and sits across

from me. "Rom, you know this will cause a red flag with my pops. What the hell happened?"

Drew is right, but he appears if he is interrogating me. We are trying to make financial investments and Stanley will tell him the shit we got into. I got into, I should say. I stand to me feet talking with my hands, eyeballing him. "I was going at it with Victoria and we heard someone screaming in the hall. Victoria flipped out of the bed and rushed to the hall." My head tilts as I rub my hair and turn my head to the city lights of Chicago. Was that not her roommate? What triggered her to jump away from me like she did? "Drew, something else is up."

He stands, pacing the room. He crosses his arms, giving me concerned eyes. "Yeah, yo ass is beating random—"

I interrupt. "Drew…you don't understand. We were in the midst of sex. How the fuck do you snap out of a heated moment?" Drew has a suspicious look on his face.

"Don't think I won't contact your counselor, Rom? Your safety is always my fucking concern." He is interrogating me. His hands move at his side and he stands in one place. "Is this necessary? I know you like Victoria, but I am not—"

I interrupt him again. My voice elevates. "If it wasn't neces-sary, I would not have done it. Let's stop this, Drew!"

He sits back on the bed, speaking in a concerned manner, "Any emotional or trauma can, no…will, make you trigger. Good or bad."

I hit at the wall. "I know my triggers." I hit at my chest and Drew stands to his feet and I look in his eyes. "You think I am a child…where's the faith in me, bruh?"

"You're my fucking brother, Rom…your triggers are my trig-gers. I want you safe." I know I am like the only brother he has, outside of me and Rico he's an only child. I lower in the chair, taking in a deep breath and Drew sits on the bed. He switches the direction of the conversation.

"Do you think Victoria was faking?" My fingers rub my chin and I calm my nerves. I think the yell triggered Victoria.

"No, fuck no. She wanted my ass. Hell, you saw her on the stage." He laughs, and that comforts me considering how serious we were a few seconds ago. No matter how much we argue he is always my brother. According to my mother and his father, it was my ol' man's wishes we'd operate as family. I am talking with my hands. "She was all over the place. You know how I snap." It was on her face. "I saw it in her eyes, Drew. Something else happened to her."

Drew interrupts, "Wait, Romel, don't get out of hand about this. Did you find out anything about when she went to Dallas?" My head is shaking, and the phone sounds off. It's Victoria. I reach for my cell and take the call. Drew walks away giving me my privacy.

"Hey, how are you and your girl."

She assures me she is fine and Jasmine reported the guy to the police. "I am happy to hear you two are okay." She is asking about me and moans. "I am fine. Are you hurt?" She is going on about the guy being hurt. "I don't give two fucks about him. I asked about you." She smirks, I know she is not answering me. "I'm coming to your room." She insists for me not to come. I scared her. She tells me Jasmine is having a hard time, and she doesn't want company. "I see." I can hear another female in the background.

Victoria asks to meet me in fifteen minutes. "Where? In my room?" I can get Drew out in two minutes. She is asking me to go to the front of her hotel. I interrupt her, this is bullshit. "In the lobby? If you have a problem with me say it." Her tone sounds uncertain, and she is promising me she doesn't have a problem. "I will see you." I disconnect the call. I stand to my feet and go take a shower.

I AM SITTING in the lobby and two officers are walking in my direction. I take in a deep breath, crossing my leg. The officer walks to my personal space and I notice Victoria has changed. Damn, those jeans are calling me. The police woman clears her throat. "Excuse me, I'm with Chicago PD are you…?" My eyes lift and she has a notepad in her hand that she is checking. "Romel Adcock?"

Damn, she knows my legal name as if someone told her. Victoria's sexy ass walks in between the officers and I stand. She is reaching her arms embracing me. "Officer, he saved me and my best friend from that jerk." Her tone is not convincing me. The officer is waiting for my answer. The male officer questions me while Victoria is hugging me as if they are about to put cuffs on my wrist. "Sir, are you Romel Adcock?"

"I am, is there a problem?"

"Yes, we were called in because of complaints. We have talked to the young ladies, and we wanted to hear the account of the story from you." I grab Victoria's grip that continues to grow on my waist. "I walked out after things were started. The prick… I witnessed him attacking the young ladies." Didn't I, or were they beating him because of what he did? The female officer is writing as I speak. I continue telling the story as I remember. "I reacted and went to remove him from the two and then the guy swung at me. From that point I was defending myself from him."

The male officer asks another question. "Sir, how did you know the young ladies were being attacked if you didn't see it from the beginning?" I look him in the eyes knowing I heard Jasmine in need of help. "I heard her tell the guy to stop. He wouldn't, I could hear him pushing her from the hall. He was attacking her. I know because her voice was in distress. She needed urgent help."

The officer reaches to shake my hand and passes his business card. The female police officer speaks, holding her card out to me as well. "If you can think of anything else, let us know. I need your contact so I can get in touch with you in case anything else develops." I reach for my wallet and pull out my business card.

"I don't live around here. I came here for an event and will leave in a few days, but you can reach me by phone."

The officers tilt their hats. "Thank you." They both march away.

I pull Victoria's hand and have her sit as I squat to looking her in her eyes. "Are you sure you are okay?"

"I'm fine… I didn't tell you thank you." I tilt her chin staring in her eyes.

"You never have to." Her demeanor is odd. "Tell me what is bothering you. If it was because I went after the guy. I was only protecting you and Jasmine from the guy." She is shaking her head as if she is trying to make sense. She grips her arm where she was hit. "Let me get you some ice. Sit here."

I rise and she stands. "No, Romel. I will be okay." She is bothered. "Let's go get the ice together." I touch her shoulder and she flinches.

"Babe…I mean Victoria. Forgive me. Victoria, did he hit your shoulder?"

She rolls her eyes. "It hurts."

I motion for her to walk with me. I need to take a picture and send it to the officers. Her feet are pacing behind me but she's reluctant. I turn the corner and turn the knob of the restroom. As I pull her inside the door locks. Victoria is looking around as if she is trying to confirm her surroundings. She's frantic. Her eyes are doing what they did earlier. She did this when we left the dance studio that night the moment the door locks.

I pull out my camera pulling her shirt over from her shoulder. "No, Romel, what are you doing?" I just touched her, there is no way she should think I will hurt her.

"Lift your shirt so I can get an image." I soften my voice and look in her eyes. "Jasmine needs the photo of your arm for the cops. Remember the man that attacked her." She nods her head. I can tell she is not alert of the here and now. I gulp and a tear falls from my eye. I wish she would talk to me. She is standing almost in shock, part of me wants to open the door to let the lock resound again in her ear. Victoria's body is trembling, she reaches her hand out, but it's as if the rest of her body is paralyzed. I lift her shirt and I hold my phone to snap the photo fast and get it over with. I know this is painful for her, but something tells me she is detached.

Without focusing on details I snap two images and put my cell away. My head tilts as I take notice of her upper arm. She is motionless. I speak to her in a calm tone.

"Victoria, tell me what you feel." Tears fall from her eyes. Fuck, I knew something was wrong with her. It might not be a good idea to speak at the moment knowing she's not clear in her mind. I slide her shirt back over her head. The moment her body is covered her eye twitches. I take her fingers tapping them against mine. I ask her once more. "Victoria, tell me what you feel?"

Her voice squeaks, "I'm sad."

Tears fall to her cheek. I take in a deep slow breath. "Why are you sad, Victoria?" I rub her palm with my fingers while looking in her dilated eyes.

"I didn't stop him…I couldn't." Her voice shakes. "I'm sorry I didn't protect you." Protect me?

My hand rubs the top of her fingers. I speak full of concern.

"What are you afraid of, Victoria?"

Her words are slow and her face twist. "You…your voice." My voice scares her. She keeps speaking, "That tattoo." She points up and then takes her hand grabbing between her legs. I realize she's not talking about me she's remembering. "Don't touch me. Please no," She wails and my insides are boiling over. I compose myself.

I speak with her in a gentle tone, "Victoria, look at me. You are in Chicago… Do you know where you are?"

Someone is pulling at the door unable to get in. She. "What are we doing in here?"

Fuck, fuck… What happened to her? I hold back my tears. "Do you know where you are?" Her eyes survey the room.

"We are in a restroom… Why did you bring me in here?"

I fall to my knees. She pushes my shoulder. "Romel, do you think I brought you in here to—"

I interrupt her. "No, I don't, Victoria."

She steps in front of me. "You are my brother."

This is not the place to be talking about this. "Why don't we go get something to eat?" We can sort this out later; I have to see what Stanley found because she's not okay.

"Romel, can we eat in your room? I don't want to go out." My eyes widen and I twist the knob, unlocking the bathroom door. I think we should go out but I will have to control myself. Pulling the door open, she steps ahead of me. I speak as she passes.

"Sure, we can order room service."

VICTORIA

R omel swipes the key card on the wall and he pushes the door as I follow behind him. His hand is feeling on the wall. I stand for a few seconds until the light comes on and I twist my head surveying the room. I head by the walk-in closet next to the restroom. He slides the door and the double beds are to the right. Romel steps back offering for me to go before him. He's a gentleman by nature. I step and my body twists as I sit on the bed near the window. This room reminds me of a European, United Kingdom vibe.

"Romel, where is Drew?"

He looks up to the ceiling. "In his room why?" I know I heard him for a moment on the phone. He grabs the remote off the wall and falls back on the opposite bed. The screen turns on. I lean over to my side watching him.

"I thought he was in your room." He pulls up a screen displaying a menu.

"He was, then he left. What do you want to eat? I selected what I want." I lift my upper body eyeballing the screen. As I view the cart, I notice what he ordered.

"Romel, who are the nachos for?"

"Me." Okay it looks like he ordered for two people.

"Who is the burger for?"

"Me." I shake my head this man and his eating habits. "I want nachos and add chicken please." He takes control of the remote typing in my order. I recognize he adds cranberry juice without me asking.

Romel looks in my direction. "No black beans, right?" Why didn't he just order for me since he knows I dislike beans?

"Correct, but you know that." His lips turn down and he adds my request and submits the order. He loves technology. He lowers his head and says nothing. "What are you thinking about?"

He rises from the bed. Romel speaks as the weight of his large muscles sink in the floor as he is placing the remote in the wall pocket. "Nothing worth talking about." I stand from the bed as the scent from the air freshener hits my nose like I'm walking in a garden of honeysuckles. My room doesn't smell this damn good.

"Romel, I don't like when you act like this. I mean you are like a bro—" He cuts me off and head toward the bathroom. It's like he is avoiding being near me. His words snap at me.

"Don't call me your brother."

My movement places me in front of his broad muscles. "I don't want our friendship to be wrecked, Romel."

Romel grabs my face, his breathing increases and I gulp trying to measure what he will do next. He speaks in a control manner. "All you do is call and tell me what you want. When the moment comes for us to get involved you pull this brother sister card. Victoria, I need you to stop this." He is accurate, when I call him he is always there.

I grow a counterfeit nonchalant expression hoping he doesn't know. Romel knows so much about me. He is the friend that makes me smile and laugh when my world is breaking apart. My voice is sympathetic.

"I care about you, Romel—" He cuts me off, realizing. He knows I understand his statement. I step away giving him space. Romel reaches for my wrist boldly speaking.

"What fear are you running from? Shit, I'm facing mine." My friendship with him is important, destroying it by entering in a relationship risks me having him as a friend. What if we argue too much? What if he didn't like something about me? Wait, being with him in a relationship what would that actually mean. I've never seen him with a girl. I only heard the rumor about the girl that said he hurt her sexually. Although, it seems false; if he sexually assaulted her then why did she go to jail and not him? Maybe that is what he is afraid of telling me what really happened.

I touch the cup of his chin. "What fear?" He is afraid of something although he looked fearless attacking that guy. Damn, he is an honorable art of manliness. A knock is heard from the door and I release his face.

"Room service."

I step to the table and Romel heads to the door. My eyes set on the window looking across the buildings of downtown Chicago. Being able to see the fifth tallest skyscraper in the world up close and personal is cool. There are so many high-rise buildings here. The beauty of this city is amazing. My hand trails the soft velvet curtain. The ostentatiousness of wealthy people strolling through downtown, riding around in their Rolls Royce and Benz cars...even this hotel is more upscale than the one Jasmine and I are in. We are not in a shabby place, it's just Drew and Romel are not in a hundred dollar a night hotel. His hotel is off of Lake Michigan and I can't help but wonder how can he afford this room? What exactly does Romel's and Drew's job consist of?

I note Romel did not let the server enter the room. I hear the water running from the faucet. I think he is washing his hands. I rise to my feet and as he pushes the cart closer to the table, I go wash my hands. My eyes set on my reflection in the mirror as the water touches my skin. I'm a mess. Pushing my hair away from my eyes I turn my head, looking at the cart and then him as he lowers in the seat across from me. He has placed everything on the table. The moment I smile he reaches below the cart and gives me a single two tone rose. I blink and give attention to his beautiful smile.

"My fear is falling for you…but I think that's too late. I think if I fell from the observation deck of the one hundred and third floor, it still wouldn't equate to how hard I fell for you." My eyes follow as his fingers point to the building.

His words are causing me to erode inside as I take in his charming expressions. I take the single rose, noticing its distinct colors. He doesn't want to be only my friend. The yellow rose with a red tip shows his desires. A smile tweaks at the corners of my lips.

As I watch, Romel go after a nacho from his plate, my brows rises noting his tongue trailing up the back of the chip as the first emergence of ecstasy simmers below my waist. Is it me or does him eating a chip make my lower lips tingle? The color of his never failing skin is clear, striking eyes, full line from his lips. OMG! I shake my head and take in a deep breath. He's just eating a nacho. He takes a second nacho and again that damn tongue is gliding along the backside of the chip, licking the cheese off the back. He makes this sloppy suction sound and instantly my memory is reminded of him between my legs. I am still holding my one nacho and this boy devoured his second one. He winks in my direction licking the cheese from the corner of his mouth. His voice is calm.

"I want to be here for you just not as your brother." I clear my throat and finally place the chip in my mouth with my eyes set on my plate. I am feeling some kind of way I haven't registered just yet. It's only a nacho.

My head lifts and I decide I will not be turned on by him

eating a chip. He is licking his top lip as if he is savoring every taste of cheese. "Has it been a while since you...had nachos?"

He looks at me as if his thoughts are somewhere else and says, "It's been a long time." My head falls back. Okay, he is playing. I take my chip and remove the chicken. I dip it in the cheese sauce and open my mouth as the cheese drips from the chip to my tongue. Holding the chip in the air I dab the chip in an up and down motion, moaning.

Closing my mouth, I crunch. "I guess it has been a while." I look over at his plate of half eaten food. He ate too fast. Romel grabs his napkin and wipes his mouth. He sucks his bottom lip and my stomach is tense as if he is touching me. His voice is low and I pay attention to his words. "I see my acts have you thinking of me. Yet, you might want to draw your hand strokes longer."

He winks as his lips turn up in laughter. "My shit is bigger than that." SEXY ASSHOLE!

I take in a jagged breath, blinking. "Really, Romel?" He picks up his drink glossing his eyes in my direction.

"I'll be happy to let you clarify if you should need confirmation."

I reposition in the chair and he sips from the glass. He even looks appetizing drinking. I need to finish eating my nachos. I take my fork and peck at my chicken. He looks across the table at me. "Tell me why you fight how you feel for me? Don't tell me you are not attracted to me."

I chew my food and look to the floor.

One side of my mouth rises higher than the other exposing my dimples, I am flattered, trying to control myself. I am extremely attracted to him.

He continues. "I know you are, Victoria. You interrupted me on the stage with another female. I practically had your feet facing the sky."

A high pitched sound emerges from me while my body rocks

in a laugh. Romel sits upright with a grin, chewing the juicy double meat burger he ordered. Flashing my eyes, I am trying to take hold of my thoughts while my taste buds have me viewing him as the juicy, hot, one hundred percent beef I want in my mouth. Touching my pounding chest, I take in a slow breath. I reach for my juice. *Please stop thinking this way about the golden man across the table from you.*

My eyes grow wide; did he only take like two bites and it's almost gone? I blurt out,"Why do you eat so much food?"

He laughs as if it's not a problem. "You had no complaints of me eating an hour or so ago."

My entire body is fluttering as I sip from my glass. My hand taps the table like I am a referee in boxing. "Stop it!"

"You might have thought that earlier but..." His tongue is sliding between his fingers and he licks the juice from the burger off. "Your body didn't." My eyes roll to the top of my head, recalling the lapping of his tongue between my legs. Stopping my thoughts, I control myself and point my finger in his direction.

"You had an advantage." A heavenly one at that or was it wicked. "You seduced me."

He frowns. "I know you fuckin lying!" I laugh, I don't think he will stop cursing. It's in his nature. I continue eating my nachos. Romel and I haven't gone out on a date. My eyes travel to the ceiling. Our friendship has been casual, yet prior to me going to Dallas for this last trip we only hung out about once a week. But that was boxing classes...fighting classes. Hmmm. Me cooking for him after we worked out... We always ended up alone the moment Jasmine stepped out the apartment, and the plates went on the table. As I think about it, she always left us alone to eat. My place was a hub for friends but wait a minute. How long has he had feelings for me? I look in his direction.

"Victoria I have something to tell you."

I reposition in the chair and nod my head. "I'm listening."

His elbows are touching the table and his full lips twist. He takes in a deep breath. "When we were at your hotel, I asked you if you wanted me to tell you something and you had your way of responding."

His hands are moving with his words and I rest back in the chair. "A few years ago, a young lady at your school made a report about me." I know, most of the ladies on the campus know. I nod my head. "I'm aware of that."

He continues, "Why did you not ask me about it?"

I shrug my shoulders. "It wasn't my place to ask you about your past."

His head tilts. "Are you saying because you never imagined us as more than friends—"

I interrupt his words. "Romel, I believe if you want to tell me something you will tell me. Why should I force you to tell me anything?"

"The young lady recorded me without my permission. I wasn't aware of her actions. We agreed to have sex and... This is awkward." He pauses contemplating his words.

I give him a serious stare. "If you are uncomfortable, then don't tell me."

He reaches his hand across the table touching my skin and I get chills. What is going on with my reaction?

"Victoria, I didn't...let's just say we never made it to inter-course. She and I were not compatible." He nods his head as if his remarks clears the entire matter.

"So she went to jail because you were not a good mate for one another?" I cross my arms and his head pushes back.

"You know she went to jail?"

"Yes, Romel."

He is using his hands again as he speaks. "Her body would not open for you know..." He looks down in his lap.

My eyes narrow. "Say it..."

"She claimed I raped her and tried to get me to pay her

money. I went to the police and filed a complaint after that but she had already reported before I got there. I was arrested and held for a brief time. Once the video was discovered by the police, they saw she and I never had sex."

"You couldn't? Wow...was she upset you didn't have sex?"

He smirks. "No, me not having sex with her was based on her body not giving to my size." I gulp at his words and listen to him further. Is he telling me her vagina would not let him enter? My eyes blink and he continues, "She tried it with another guy. It's just the cops concluded she was out to make money by scheming guys." He leans in his chair as if he is relieved from the weight he was carrying around. I can see how that could have caused a mix up...but why am I thinking of his size.

"Romel, I would not be your friend if I thought you really hurt a female."

I pick up my drink and finish. I am full and not interested in eating all the nachos. He wipes his mouth and stands, stretching his arms. Interesting, he can spend endless hours with me and not get tired.

"Do you want me to take you back to your hotel or call you a cab?" I thought he didn't mind spending time with me. I yawn.

"Excuse me." He chuckles grabbing his items and clearing the table. "I guess."

He puts the plates on the tray and sets it outside his door. I guess he knows room service will pick it up. It seems like he is used to this. I stand and walk to his personal space as he is shutting the door. He looks down in my eyes. "What, girl..." His arms push me back at the shoulders. I flinch. "Vic...toria. Forgive me."

"I have pain medicine, if you want it?" He turns going after the medicine. Has he always been nurturing toward me? Have I always blocked it out? He reaches for a bag at the top of the closet and I step aside. Romel pulls out pain medicine. His movement is so swift you would think I am bleeding. He grabs a tumbler from the wall shelf and opens the mini fridge. He picks up a water bottle and pours it in the glass. "Here, this should help."

"Tha—"

He cuts me off. "You don't have to thank me." He walks over to the bed and falls on his stomach and I take the medicine. I place the glass on the table and walk until I am facing behind him. He seems tired.

"Romel, can I ask you a question?"

"I will get up, Victoria, don't worry. I am not letting you catch a cab."

"Romel, it's not about a cab." He flips over.

"Ask." I sit on the side of the bed across from him.

Did you feel... How did you feel after fighting that guy?" He looks at me, puzzled, and sits up finding my eyes. His hand reaches my hand.

"I feel fine, but did I scare you?" I look to the floor and he sits on my side leveling my eyes with his. "Going after the guy was a natural reflex for me." He pushes my hair from my eyes and I take his hand.

"You really didn't scare me."

He chuckles. "How did you feel about me going after the guy?" *Safe.*

"I didn't have a problem with it. It's what you have been training me to do."

"You know you protected Jasmine like she was your sister." A tear rolls from my eyes when he says sister. I shake my head.

"No you are giving me too much credit, Romel." He wipes my tears and I relax. His voice is so calm.

"Why would you cry the moment I say protect?" He is most attentive. I sit back and he scoots closer. My eyes wander.

"Romel it is nothing."

"When you fight someone that is hurting someone you are not at fault." I scoot over giving us space. He moves near me ignoring my silent request for distance between us. "When you fight for someone you deeply care about your hits land more passionately." He has his hand balled in a fist, looking at me with great concern. "At that moment your fist is carrying the love you have for the other. You are protecting…that's all. Forgive me, but I do care for you more than you know… that's my fault you don't know." His words melt between every cell in my body and I jump, pushing him back. My hands possess his face as my tongue dives between his warm, soft lips. He lifts me and our breaths are compounding as the energy rises between us.

"Victoria, don't fuck with me like this."

He pushes me on the other side of him and sits on the opposite bed. I stand before him and he gulps at my touch across his face.

"I'm not fucking with you." He looks hesitant.

His voice snaps, "Why are you not being honest with me? I have been honest with you about how I feel about you, as well as the female." He stands and moves to the bed opposite of me. "Victoria, I already know how I feel about you." He tilts his head. He is stopping me from having sex with him because he wants me to tell him the truth. What in the world? Most guys couldn't care less about what I think. The muscles in my face relax as I realize. He *loves* me…he doesn't just care about me.

I sit across from him. "If I tell you, will you not be upset?"

He takes in a deep breath. "I will not be upset if you tell me. But I am not going to lie and say I will not be upset by what you reveal. I have no way of predicting that."

"How long have you liked me?"

He doesn't hesitate in answering the question. "Since the first time I set eyes on you… Now tell me the truth, not this kindergarten shit." I don't think he likes beating around the bush. I place my hand on his knee, he pushes it away. Is he serious? He doesn't even want me to touch him?

He growls. "Tell me now."

I clear my throat. "I like you Romel."

He shakes his head. "The truth... will start with something light. Can you see yourself with one guy?"

Romel

SHE LOOKS uncertain as if the thought of being exclusive is a life decision. "This is all new and so far it sucks...Romel." I laugh at her expression.

"I can teach a thing a two about that?"

She arches her back, rolling her neck until her head slants. "Oh, really?"

I bulge my eyes, that wasn't supposed to come out like that. "Wait, that's not what I mean." I smirk. "I mean...you can determine compatibility with just knowing the dessert a person likes."

"It's okay, Romel. Something tells me you think I'm a hoe." She stands. I place my fingers on her wrists.

"Victoria, listen...you seem to be playing around because perhaps you want to find the right guy that's compatible to you."

She stands straight giving me all her attention. "What makes you say that, Romel?"

The look on her face displays she is curious of my words.

"It's not about you finding the guy...it's more about him finding you." Her brows rise. A smile of confidence grows across my face. "So dessert preference..."

"What will you know about my—"

I interrupt. "Apple pie?

Her face has a confused expression. "Nope!"

"Lemon Meringue," She tilts her head to the side looking out the corner of her eyes.

"Cheese Cake?"

Her lips pucker. "Not as much."

"Chocolate Cake?" Now she's staring at me like she is recalling her last orgasm.

"Mmmm."

"Tembleque?" Her eyes bulge with suspense and terror and she nods her head...

"You have written your own death sentence."

"Perfect." I grin.

She interrupts. "I don't mean to be cruel, Romel."

"So don't."

"Romel...you already said you don't enjoy sharing. I am involved—"

"Fuck them. I don't trust them...and neither do you." I know she dates guys but something tells me she's not having sex with all these guys. If she was, her ability to resist me would not be so high.

She flashes her eyes and smacks her sexy tongue. "What are you talking about, Romel?" I eagle eye her and she is twitching in the chair. I bite my bottom lip realizing she is controlling herself with me. I speak in an aggressive tone.

"Victoria, quit bringing them up. Am I supposed to give a fuck about them? Is that why you bring them up?"

Her face displays a strong dislike, but her body is flinching. She likes aggressiveness and she cannot hide it. She repositions and holds her stare in my direction. "Do you always curse like this, Romel?"

My brows raise, she has heard my mouth say words like this why is it an issue now. "Typically. Why is it a problem? I'm just saying why should I give a fuck about them?"

She takes in a deep breath. "Your mouth, Romel!"

I rub my hand down my face. "What?"

Victoria

HE LICKS HIS LIPS. "We can skip all this and you can get an exclusive interview to see for yourself?" A cocky grin grows upon my face.

"Your mouth is filthy...you curse every other word. My daddy said..." His face frowns but I continue talking, "A person that curses all the time is displaying a sign of their ignorance, a lack of vocabulary."

"I see." Romel stands. "I guess it's your loss."

My face twists at my word. "Romel, what the hell did you mean by that?" Now I'm cursing, ugh. I walk off and he grabs my wrist.

"No, no, that was the easy part. I know how you feel about me without you telling me." He winks his eyes and somehow, I know he detects of my true feelings.

Romel

I RUB her arm where I spotted the marks. "Tell me the truth." I shut my eyes, and she sits down with her back facing me.

"It was an altercation and I—"

I interrupt her and pull my bands off. "Victoria...is it that hard for you to tell me the truth?"

Her eyes measure me as she suppresses her cry. She's not saying a word just standing there.

I speak to Victoria in a calm voice. "One day I couldn't feel... I had too much on my plate. Look at my arm, Victoria."

She looks at my wrist. Victoria's eyes grow teary. My arms

extend embracing her. I know how she feels, but I don't want her to think she is alone.

"Victoria, Drew caught me in the act of me cutting my wrist." She is shaking her head as if she doesn't want to know. Her reaction is alarming, and she's on the verge of tears. It's only one scar. I know the feeling it releases is like exercising or eating chocolate. "Victoria…I am not ashamed of what I did and neither should you be. My pops died when I when I was young. I cut my vein causing my arm to be semi-paralyzed." I bled so much. I knew death was approaching, and I'd be with my father. Funny because today it's the reason I use it the most when I hit, because it goes numb." Uncertainty is on her face while her eyes resist releasing tears.

"Read my inscription." I place one of my leather bands in her hand and she looks, reading.

"Freedom? It reads freedom on the wrist cuffs." Her first tear breaks free, rolling to her cheek. A thunderstorm brews from her as she convulses in tears. Victoria's sobs cause me to ache inside, seeing the redness of her face confirms she's not able to keep control. I wipe her puffy eyes and tears of sorrow continue to flow as her open mouth gasps for air. She takes her fingers wiping the tears from her nose and sniffles. The room is still with only the sounds of her tears hitting the blanket. I lift her head seeing her bloodshot eyes that continue to stream tears like fountains. Her cheeks speak her truth of the pain she's been holding inside. I wish I could do more to help her but all I can do is hold her.

I lean back on the bed with her in my arms. She sighs in relief as if that is the first time she's actually cried. I speak and notice her heart beat is slowing. She takes in a deep breath. I speak to her with a sincere voice, "My scar has healed. Cuts are open and they need to heal. I only did it once…let's just say Drew can be convincing." I chuckle and her breaths are gentle. I have to ask her a question she might not want to answer but I am asking, anyway.

"Are you still cutting yourself?" She remains at a standstill in my arms.

"No, I want to sometimes but I am not anymore."

"Did it start when we...you came back from Dallas?" Tears release on instant.

"Yes, Romel." I wipe her tears and kiss her face. She smiles and hugs me tightly.

"Scars are proof you defeated the hard times. Even in death my father teaches me. I've earned my stripes; my bruises are good bruises. Reminding me I am good. You are good." I kiss the top of her head and continue as she listens. "All bruises are not bad bruises. Some remind you that you're healing or you already healed from some shit. "

She has an agitated breath as she repositions on my chest. I am trying to get her to talk, to just say what she needs to release. It doesn't seem to be working.

"You don't want to talk about it, do you?" She shakes her head and I take in a deep breath. My fingers trail through her soft hair. "Am I taking you to your room?" She shakes her head. Her voice sounds like a sweet innocent child.

"I want to stay with you, Romel." I shut my eyes while holding her, wishing our conversation unfolded another way. I know how I feel about her. I don't want her doubting anything we do because something tells me I will not give her up.

VICTORIA

I jolt from my sleep and look around. Romel caresses my wrist and I tingle. He calms me. My hands touch at Romel's mountain of a chest. He blinks. "Hey beautiful…" I look under the sheets and my eyes grow wide. Okay, it looks like we did nothing. I turn and my spine arches at the touch of… I pull the sheets above my head and slide my hand. Romel flexes his body. "Woman, don't play with me. What are you checking to see if it's real?" No, but I am looking and wondering if he can smell me lusting after him. I should go take a bath.

He laughs and turns his body over. "Romel, why did you stop me?"

"I didn't…I stopped myself." He sits on the side of the bed. I sit up against the headboard. He is thinking about it. I can't stop thinking about it, not just it, but him inside of me.

"Why?" He gets up walking to the bathroom.

Romel blurts out, "So you want to have sex, Victoria?" Okay, this confirms he knows I am thinking about it. Damn, his fucking erection through those jeans is enormous.

"Oh, wow, you put it out there?" I want to have sex with him now and I don't want him to stop me. He looks over his shoulder, walking toward the bathroom.

He speaks as if he doesn't care. "We can have meaningless sex." He shuts the slide door and shouts, "Are you sure that's what you want?"

"Yes!" Wait, is he inviting me in the bathroom and I am still fully dressed? I jump to my feet and take my clothes off and pace. My head lifts and the door slides open. Oh my, am I sure about this? He steps toward me with nothing on but briefs.

"You don't want me to stop myself even though you are not honest with me?" I shake my head in multiple directions uncertain of which is the correct answer as I watch him with a close eye. He is so tall, so big everywhere. He reaches his hand and his fingers touch my hips.

"Damn, you're beautiful."

He thinks I am beautiful. He really likes me. I like him… okay, I like him more than just like.

"Can I just have you as my delight first?" Romel chuckles and I step on his feet. He lifts me and my legs wrap around his waist. He embraces me as he stands in front of the bed.

"So…after we have sex we will just be friends?"

I nod my head. "Yes."

"Is this your typical routine, woman? I'm not opposed to it… I just wonder what makes you think you would want to be my friend after we have sex?"

I have done it before…why would he be any different. "I can handle it…no strings attached."

He lowers his eyes. "I will agree to your terms but tell me what happened, to cause you to cut your arms."

"Afterwards!"

Romel

. . .

VICTORIA'S VOICE LOWERS. "I want to live in the moment with just you." I know this girl will not feel the same way. She already is in too deep, but hey she can figure that out for herself.

"Fine with me." I move to lay on the bed and she stands back, towering over me. This is different.

"You lay on that bed." My eyes blink. Is she ordering me? Perhaps she thinks if she is directing me she can control her emotions. I step back and open the drawer and grab a condom. Sitting back, I place it on the side of me for her to decide just how far she wants to go.

Victoria

MY BLOOD IS RUSHING to my lower area as I have longed after him entering me so much that my little kitty is angry, on the verge of breaking out. He slides his hand up my arm and my muscles contract. He looks in my eyes.

"You think I don't know how to please you, Victoria?"

My lip twists. "Maybe you do, maybe you don't. I am just making sure I am pleased either way." My expression is calm and he speaks in a low pitch. "You are not aware."

He reaches his hand below and his finger touches my clit. "I am not one you have had to teach how to please you." He swirls his finger then grips my clit with two fingers. "I know your senses extend deep in your walls."

His full hand cups my wetness. "Your lips are swollen because you are stimulated but holding the orgasm I call upon your body. You haven't had sex in a while?" My body is weakening as his voice is hypnotizing me.

"No, I haven't…I have wanted no one the way I want you."
My juices are spilling over his fingers and he takes his finger and
licks them one by one.

He speaks slowly. "I can unlock your deepest pleasures."
Vibrations flow up and down my spine. I think he has released
everything already.

I open as Romel touches me. "This has only one job." I take
in a deep breath and love the sensations he is causing to grow
over my body as he teases my clit. He continues speaking, "Pleasure." He is pleasing the fuck out of me and I moan.

I jump on top of him looking him in the eyes. Romel has this
sexy laugh as he speaks. "So you mean business." Placing my
hand on his strong chest I extend my hand and he grabs the
condom. I smile and he opens it. I inch away and he sits me next
to him, removing his underwear. I gulp, he is huge. Romel lies
on his back. I crawl on top of him as he is sucking his teeth. I
think he is not used to a girl taking the lead. He yanks my hand.
My heart rate increases as he brings my ear to his lips and whispers, "Are you going to take all day looking at me?" He looks
beautiful.

"No."

"Are you nervous?"

I lean over and kiss his chest in between my words. I whisper, "No…I'm not nervous." *Maybe I am a little.*

He takes in a deep breath and his head lowers back in the
bed. My hands contact his firm body as my lips bite after his
nipples. He doesn't stop, assuring me to continue. I am so
engulfed with his skin merging with me. I sit up and his eyes are
surveying my body.

He grins. "You are so gorgeous."

He takes the latex and I move, watching him cover every
inch. He grabs my chin and I lower to his face. "Kiss me." I lift
and he charges, pushing me while he takes both my breast in
hand and licks between the center, rubbing my breast against his

face. I twist my body, panting as he touches me. I lay on my back and his warm lips slurp my bottom lip. "Victoria, are you sure you—" I interrupt him and push his shoulder and he surrenders, lying on his back. My hand touches his chest, as I suck his lips tingles rush down my back. I look in his eyes.

"Are you comfortable?" He nods his head and rests back. My hands trail after his legs and he breathes in. "I want you to tell me where you want your big cock." He grins, surprised by my verbiage. I slap his face and I feel his dick jump. Hmmm. He moans. I speak to him a calm tone.

"You like when I hit you?"

He smiles, answering me while biting his lips. "Yes."

"Tell me where you want your big dick." He takes in a deep breath, controlling himself from coming after me taking charge. His words whisper with a sigh, "In your dripping pussy."

Damn, his words grow sensations between my legs, watching his fully erect glory has me in awe. He lifts me, inching me to his face. "Romel...I."

He interrupts me with a chocolate tone. "You can have your way after I prepare you." My insides feel as if they are on fire from our heated energy. I lean to whisper in his ear.

"I'm ready for you...I've been longing for you to be inside me." His hands slip inside my thighs as his fingers fall to the back of my hips, tingles run through my body.

"I'm baptizing your pussy so don't stop me." His words rip through my soul as if air is being knocked out of my lungs.

My legs spread and I straddle his face. He hits my leg, licking his tongue between my inner thigh. My head falls back as my clit is throbbing. "Closer." I yearn as the adrenaline builds through my pores. I scoot nearer, for he's so convincing. Romel's hands rub my lower butt and he pushes me closer to his face, alleviating all space from his full lips to my lower folds. He rests his hands on my thighs as I inch closer to his lips. Romel is far from being intimidated and I am far from his magical touch.

Time slows as his licks possess my lips. My hand grips the top of his head. I am panting in between my words. "Romel...this... feels so good."

His skilled tongue demands my juices, as I contract his fingers grip my thighs. I have never felt this way in my life. I stay in one place, hovering over his face, twerking, and like an animal he rotates his head, making slurping sounds. The noise grows louder and my back arcs as his lips pull my clit, rushing a sensation of ecstasy over my body. My sultry moans bounce off the wall while I fuck his face. I continue to whine after his touch. "Oh, Ro...mel."

He boosts me higher, bouncing me up and down on his tongue. My body has never been thrown around so. His tongue pattern speeds as he laps between my lips. I place my hand on the head board. Romel is a beast lapping my juices, his finger slides across my clit, then he thrusts his fingers deep inside. I brace the wall, balancing. I scream his name so loud. He stops and I look below. "Louder, baby!"

I scream louder. He repeats his acts I'm sure the entire floor knows exactly what we are doing. He holds me, speaking between my legs. "You are so beautiful from this view." I am drenched with cum, it's dripping on his face and he loves every drop. Falling back on the bed, I pull his face and his tongue dives deeper within. My heart beat slows while he holds my hips slowly, I grind his gorgeous face between my wetness. My fingers rub the waves from his hair before I claw in his head. He moans, "Ahhh"

He caresses me with his glorious tongue in delicate circles. My thighs are on each side of Romel's face as I straddle him, giving him a pussy facial. He continues to relieve me of the deep scratch inside, unbeknown to me. Wrapping my legs around his neck, I speak in a low tone, "Don't stop, Romel."

My body moves in sync with the movement of his tongue, gyrating against his face. I hit at the wall. My hand hits the wall again and I'm losing my breath as I convulse. He lifts me, but my legs fall, lifeless.

Romel

THE CLOSER SHE gets to her climax the more her sweetness gushes on my awaiting tongue. Tasting Victoria drives me wild. I bite my lip, speaking with a modulated tone. "Did you enjoy your orgasms?" She is shivering, moaning in pleasure, and I rub below her swollen lips.

Victoria grabs my wrist. Her voice is breathy but sugary, "Romel." She shakes her head. I lick her mouth; she moans at the passing of her fluids from my mouth. My hand lowers and I ease three fingers inside. Her back arches and Victoria is excited, coming after me. Her palms hold my chin while her tongue licks my face clean, tasting her juices. Damn, she's sexy. I stare in her eyes with the resonance of my words are unhurried and low.

"You're dripping wet." I thrust inside her deeper and she moans. Her pussy contracts, expanding to my touch.

"Victoria, let me—" She shakes her head unwilling to surrender. I don't want to hurt her.

Her hand touches my chest and I place her finger in my mouth. She looks in my eyes as she leans forward rocking back. Her other hand touches my dick and I grip her fingers. "Slow, Victoria."

Victoria

. . .

ROMEL IS SPREADING my legs and his touch feels hypnotizing. His hand caresses my breast while rubbing every inch of his length between my aching lips. I want him so badly. Fire seems to rush through my cells.

Everything about his touch energizes me, his tenderness melts inside. My voice softens and I smile. "You go slow for now."

I love his gentleness. He inches inside and I curve my body. He kisses my stomach. "Relax, sweetheart... I'll never hurt you."

I grab his head smiling. "Unless I want you to." He bites his bottom lip looking in my eyes.

"Of course."

My muscles relax at his soft touch. Something about his voice gets me every time. He really knows how to turn me on. He inches further and I moan in slight discomfort. He pauses. I claw at his shoulder.

"Don't stop, Romel.'" *Please go deeper.*

"You want me—" *More than you can imagine.*

"So bad I want you inside of me...please don't stop." He obliges my request, inside a burning sensation starts and his lip passionately kisses me. My legs fall to the bed and he pushes further inside. I whimper, "Oh my." He's so big.

His fingers push my hair back. I love when he touches my hair. His eyes are full of lust, but also concern. "Do you want me to stop?"

My heart will not stop pounding and I shake my head. "No"

He slowly thrusts further inside, and I bite my lip, moaning. He seems to be hesitant because of my response. I grip his ass and push him deeply inside. My voice shrills in ecstasy, "Romel!"

He pulls back. "Breathe, Victoria." Damn, I gulp, taking slow breaths in and out. My walls are completely full, and I don't want to stop. He rotates his sexy abs and I lose control of his muscles as he strokes in and out. My insides expand to his length and I am lost.

"You're so beautiful, Victoria." His mellow brown complexion merges with me like a bath cleaning my stress away. How is it that his touch elevates my mood, building me stronger, is a gift he only possesses? Romel lifts me and I turn over, he slides his hand to my lower back. I drop my face in the pillow and his strong hand grips my butt up in the air while my legs slide between of his. Romel caresses along my back, down my hips and I shiver.

He slides inside and my body surrenders to this man. Romel's strokes grow deeper. I meet him as he thrusts. His fingers grip my hair pulling me back and I pounce harder. His force is so deep, he has me lifted slightly off the bed and his length expands, deep-rooted within my walls. What this man is doing no other has dared to do. My head is tossing in the pillow in a manic expression. He calls for me, "Oh, Vic…"

I am trying to leverage myself on my arms. I can hear him demanding me. "Throw yo ass back." My damn, this beast of a man is pleasing every cell in my body. I push forward and he inches away, we meet in the middle and all you can hear is the sounds of our body.

Clap, clap, clap, our bodies smack over and over. It's like we are dancing in the bed and it is an x-rated, blissful sensation. My motions are as if I'm riding him while I am on my knees, I stay in one place, twerking, building my rhythm. Romel moans.

"Fuck, Vic!"

We are breathing so loud. He pulls out and throws me over on my back. He spreads my legs and looks as if his eyes are taking a picture.

He lowers his body. "Your pussy is so good…had to look at you." Fuck…his words are fucking my head. His hand spreads me as his face grazes my lips and my body caves at the rotation of his hips. His breath covers my skin and I pull his head to my lower lips. He attacks my outer folds and my hands release his head. He inches away and my fingers claw at his head, holding him in position and I yell, "DON'T STOP!"

He increases the tempo, adding pressure to his marvelous tongue and my body relaxes. Romel lifts his head. I don't want him to ever stop. I am whining for his touch and he takes his cock and slams deep inside me. "Oh, damn."

He pushes away and falls to my lower lips, his mouth tastes all the juices he's demanded from my body. Again, he lifts and pounds his glorious dick between my wetness. He's incredible. I have never met another like him. It's like he is escorting me to the moon, launching rockets from my core. Romel's thrust build deeper inside of me and I convulse in a full body orgasm. He does not stop pouncing inside me, my eyes lower and he speaks in a low pitch. "Look at me."

My eyes notice his dick gliding in and out of me, hitting the right spot. He pulls me to his midsection. His voice is so masculine. "Victoria…look at me." I gulp and find his eyes full of sex.

"Yes, Romel"

"After this we are only friends." Oh yeah, I said that…right. I nod my head. Wait am I agreeing to be his friend or something else? He strokes over and over, rotating his abs. His body is beautiful. "You can't come back to me." What *come* is he talking about? I have lost count how many times he has made me cum.

"Okay, Romel, I can—" He thrust me harder cutting off my words. I think he is teaching me a lesson. The deeper he goes the more I spill over his dick. He strokes faster and faster, harder and harder. My legs kick out as my body shakes in spasms and I scream, "ROMEL!"

A sexy grin forms on his face and he releases my body.

Romel

. . .

Victoria is no longer fighting me and her yells rush inside me... I know she is mine. My hand trails from the touch of her skin as I step back, watching her. Turning my head, I pace toward the bathroom and chuckle as I notice she is trying to catch her breath as she sits upright on the side of the bed.

I look over my shoulder, Victoria is attempting to stand to her feet, she stumbles. I rush, lifting her. I find her eyes as I pull her to the bed and lie her on her back.

I smirk. "Are you okay?" She flashes her eyes.

I stand and step to get her water from the mini fridge. Twisting the cap, she attempts to lift her body. I am shaking my head and I sit next to her and hold her head up. She opens her mouth and I pour the water in her mouth.

She moans and whimpers her words. "I'm fine, Romel."

Yes, she is absolutely mine. I lower my voice, "I see you." Soon she will see me as well...but I will play with her for the moment. She can't hide her feelings for me now. I know it.

ROMEL

$\mathcal{I}$ pull the door to the gym back and spot Drew on the treadmill. He is shaking his head listening to his music. Drew removes the headphones and I step to the treadmill next to him. It's nice having the space to ourselves for the moment.

"What's up, Rom? You walk in here innocent." He adjusts his pace so he can speak without breathing hard. "You know Rico is concerned you are fucking garbage cans to get off."

I chuckle at his remark and he continues, "But you know damn well I heard you going at it with Victoria. So, what's up?"

I laugh aware that he and the other people on the floor could hear her screaming. "It was animalistic. I had her ass as if I was the mountain lion out to get the sheep plotting a terrorist attack." He is laughing and I situate the dials on the screen and pick up my pace jogging on the treadmill beside him. "Drew, I had Victoria past the point of no return. She said she wanted a one-night stand and we can be friends."

He laughs out loud and pushes the button on the screen. "Wait, Rom. So, you gave her a go even knowing she doesn't want more than sex?" I twist my lips sideways.

"Trust me she is not going to ever look at me like a brother in her life. My scent is all over her. She will crab walk around for days trying to figure out what is going on."

"Rom, tell me you did not—" I cut him off before he finishes his statement. My eyes look downward and I twist my lips.

"Trust me, if she thinks I am fucking with someone she's beating the door down." I chuckle and spread my legs to gain my balance from falling over. "I got something for her when we return to Atlanta. She better wear those boots when she's knocking on my door." I shake inside just imaging her in those combat heels. Damn. I continue jogging as I set my eyes on the person entering the gym.

"Where is she now?"

"In the room, paralyzed, she is asleep."

He laughs. "Well you better get your stuff together you know we have a flight leaving soon."

I nod my head. "I know is Stanley still here?"

"Yes. He said the police officer contacted him. They called me yesterday as well but I think they have what they need from us."

"Drew, something else is going on with Victoria. She is hiding personal things she shouldn't."

He shakes his head and speaks in a concerned tone. "I get that but I need you to stay focused. Everyone is not as open as you are. I know that's your way and I respect it. But everyone else is not conditioned to speak up about how they feel." He increases his pace and I nod, understanding his statement.

"Drew, she cut herself. I saw it on her arm...there's something deeper going on with her." My eyes are looking ahead seeing his face transform as he hears my words.

He speaks in between breaths. "Did you look at the file Stanley sent you?"

Damn, I still haven't looked at it. "No, I haven't. I will as soon as I get a minute." Drew sets his headphones in his ear and

I set the timer for an hour. My speed increases and I am lost in my workout.

Victoria

MY ARM REACHES over finding a plush pillow instead of the back of Romel's head. I lift my head and survey the room. I call out for him, "Romel!" He doesn't answer. Where is he? I scoot over and my lower body aches as my eyes grow wide. I reach my hand below feeling a pool of liquid. I need help, I am leaking while in pain. I moan in thought of Romel. Mmmm. Somehow the pain reconnects me, turning me on. What has this man done?

I pull my body up, sitting upright against the headboard of the bed and view the dragon fruit energy drink, cranberry juice, and a banana. Turning my lips, my eyes tighten at his actions. How cute he wants to help me restore my energy. I laugh reaching for the notepad by the phone and read it.

I know you fuckin lyin thinking you can just move about. I will be back. I went to the gym. Have a drink or two, relax, and I will take you to your hotel room.

Setting the paper in place, I shut my eyes, grabbing my stomach laughing. Who takes the time to write a letter like this? Where does he get the stamina to go to the gym after what we did? I push my 'I just got sexed down' hair in a bun. I look too crazy to sit in here. I reach for the cranberry juice and open the bottle. This is my favorite drink of all times. I gulp until it is no more. I put it on the nightstand and I think of Romel.

Why is he on my mind? I have to maintain our friendship even though I'm throbbing between my legs. Where is my phone? My eyes locate the special cell I need to call Jasmine; the phone is situated on the small table in the room. I cannot believe

I am looking at the table as if it is six miles away. I will try this again because I was a failure while Romel got a standing ovation for delivering me an unforgettable night of pleasure; mind blowing. *Stop thinking about him!*

I swing my legs to the side of the bed and push myself up on my feet. My body bends, am I cramping up? I slide my legs across the floor, being mindful not to bend my knees. My palms are flat as I walk toward my hands on my toes. If Jasmine walks in here, she will think I am either auditioning to be an inch worm or I was assaulted. I repeat my movement until I make it to the table.

Tap tap. Fucking bite me. Who is at the door?

"*Room service.*" I ordered nothing. "*Mr. Adcock, your order.*"

Great, he ordered something. I take in a deep breath and try to straighten my upper body. The knob twists. I speak quickly. "Hold on, please!" I reach for the robe hanging on the wall. I step to the table on my tippy toes and I can feel every muscle straining in my legs. I don't think I can handle this aftereffect. I clear my throat. "Enter." The door pushes open and I sit in the chair.

Wow, my eyes grow wide at the dozens of beautiful roses. They are duplicates of the single stemmed rose he gave me last night. The guy has on all white as he pushes the cart across the floor. He tilts his head. "Good afternoon." I take the flowers and put them on the table.

I smile, greeting him. He lifts the lid over the plate. It is the healthiest meal I have ever set eyes on. The grilled veggies are so pretty they look fake, there is also a spinach salad and blackened chicken. How generous of him. The gentleman bows and speaks cordially, "Is there anything else I can get for you?" I shake my head.

"No thank you, this is perfect." He pulls a card out and sets it next to the glass of cranberry juice. The guy exits the room and I go for the envelop opening it.

Did you try to get out of bed? Stop being stubborn, relax, and eat. I will be there soon.

I chuckle, admiring how sweet he is. I have not known this side of Romel, I like it. I touch my phone and dial Jasmine's number. She answers on the first ring.

"Hey, chica!" She answers and I push a button and put it on speaker phone. I can hear her as if she is in the room. I pick up my fork, taking a bite of the veggies. Oh, that is delicious. Jasmine has a chipper pitch. "Victoria, what exactly did you do to Romel to have him ordering me room service?"

My eyes widen and I gulp. "He did what?" Her high tone vibrates in the room.

"Yes, I have a note card and it says hoping you are well. Enjoy your meal, signed Romel, Victoria's friend."

What game is he playing? She continues, "Chica, when I opened the door for room service a security guard was at the freaking door. Did he send someone to guard me because you were with him last night?" I finish chewing my vegetables. Romel was concerned about Jasmine and he never mentioned it to me.

"I'm not sure. I didn't know he ordered you food, Jasmine." She is laughing.

"Victoria, I am not upset about him sending room service. I just wanted you to know. You two had sex didn't you?"

I gulp, smiling in the phone, as if she can see me. "Yes, we did. Jasmine, it was a freaking non-stop cumfest. Everything was earth shattering...I think he was trying to break my stomach cavity because I told him I wanted it to be a one-night thing." My eyes lift eyeballing the entry.

"I'm looking at the door right now as if the entry way has turned into the hallway from movie *The Shining*. He is a monster, Jasmine. I saw him walk out the bathroom naked and I

was like where in the hell did his Air Force dick come from?"
She is laughing so loud in between her words.

"You said you like to be completely full. Don't be like that
with Romel." She gasps for air amused with my statement. "I
know you like him. If you didn't, you would not have spent the
night. Hmmm, let me count how many times you spent the night
with a guy…wait I don't have to. NEVER!"

Jasmine has a point; I have not given time to a guy before.
She continues, "I reminded you the night of the competition
when you claimed he was just acting. You can't tell me you saw
his horse dick and thought he will hurt me now. For all I know
his cock grew hard from you teasing him for over a year and a
half. I told you he likes you."

I interrupt, "Chica, no, there is no way you can grow the
titanic out of your pants because you are anxious to have a
female." Her laugh echoes in the room, if Romel is standing
outside he would think she is in here with me. She clears her
throat.

"Well, I saw you on the stage with him at the Sex Con…you
should not have interrupted him with that female. You and I
know why you did it. You heard that song, saw that female on
the stage and was like 'Oh hell no.'"

She might have a slight truth in that version of the story.

"Whatever, chica, I would have gone all the way with Romel
at our hotel had that guy not attacked you."

Her voice is calm. "That guy was a jerk. I was hanging out
with his friend and he followed me. His friend was so sexy and
chocolate…just like I like them." Reaching for the knife, I can
overhear her drinking, she sighs and continues her story while
I eat.

"I was only coming to the room to change and tell you I
would be with his friend."

Did she say what I think she said? "Jasmine, you would
cheat—"

She interrupts me. "I was not cheating. Well, I didn't get the opportunity to, hell. I am sick of hearing rumors or thinking I am being faithful to someone that doesn't appreciate me. So yes, I was ready for the chocolate bar guy, but his aggressive friend interrupted the entire evening."

My voice clears and I speak to her seriously. "Are you feeling okay?"

"Victoria, I am fine. Do you need me to come rescue your paralyzed ass?" She is laughing so hard and I can't with her. She continues, "I know you like Romel...heal from your dick adventure and I am sure you will adjust to him. He must have done something right to get you to open at his command."

She is enjoying teasing me too much. "His foreplay made up for his grand entrance. I think I was a virgin prior to him. Jasmine, I need you to come get me now!"

She is laughing like I said a joke. I hear the door pushing forward and I see Romel standing in the entrance, all sweaty from working out. Damn...he looks sexy as hell. I think I might need to visit with workout Romel.

I take the phone off of speaker. "Jasmine, let me call you back."

Romel

PUSHING the door behind me my feet step further in the room. "I see you made it to the table to eat." I chuckle and Victoria throws a napkin. I think she wants my attention. I will ignore her. I turn back to the bathroom and I hear her standing. I grab a towel and she calls for me in a sugary tone.

"Romel." I can't resist her voice. I turn and look at her but keep my distance.

"What's up?"

She blinks. "Why are you acting different?" My head tilts knowing I am aware of her conditions of us remaining friends. I clear my throat.

"I am respecting your terms, not acting different. Did you enjoy your lunch?" She steps and holds the wall. Fuck, I hurt her. I step closer to her.

"Babe." Her expression on her face is puzzled. I should not have called her that. "Victoria, I was too rough. Why didn't you stop me?" Lifting her I place her back in the chair and she takes in a deep breath of air.

"You smell like sweat!"

I laugh. "I was exercising, I should smell…that's why I was going to the shower." She sits back and touches my face. Damn she is not supposed to do that. I grab her hand. "Don't, Victoria." In order for this to work, she can't touch me.

Her eyes bat. "Romel, I like my flowers." I turn and my eyes grow wide, but I think she is only playing with me.

"Vic, don't play with me."

She interrupts, "Why do you call me Vic?" I chuckle standing over her. I motion to step away and she pulls my shorts. I grab the waist.

"Hey, don't Vic…toria. Let me go so I can clean up." I push her hand to the side and she reaches with her other hand. She is laughing.

"Why do you call me Vic, Romel?"

"Why did you call me Rom?" Her eyes bulge. I'm aware she called me Rom when she had an orgasm. She gulps and her fist hits the table

"I asked you first."

I blink my eyes. "If I am not mistaken, you have yet to answer my question. You got your one-night stand."

She bursts out laughing and I lower my body. My eyes meet her eyes and my demeanor changes. "I heard you tell Jasmine to come get you, Victoria. I can only assume you are trying your hardest to not tell me why you have those marks on your arms. Don't fucking play with me."

"Why are you being so serious? We were just playing, Romel." She releases my shorts. I take the towel around my neck and wipe my face. She is playing games.

"I don't have an issue answering your questions, but you demand me to answer your questions. Let me clear your conscious. I call you Vic because last night you turned into a vixen. Fighting me and it turned me on." I stand as she twists in the chair. "While I am at it...I will answer the questions you will eventually ask me. I sent lunch for Jasmine and a security guard is there just as one was outside the door when I left this room."

She stands and I walk ahead to go take a shower. She yells my name as if I can't hear her in her normal pitch. "Romel, why did you do that?"

I shrug my shoulders. "I'm a friend that cares about your safety. Plus, I knew you were worried about Jasmine; I wanted to make sure no one bothered her. Don't worry, neither you nor Jasmine owes me anything." I slide the door and she forces her way to push the door open. I look down in her direction.

"I didn't tell you...you hurt me because..." She pauses as if she's embarrassed.

"What, Victoria...I'm your friend, remember? say it."

Her face grows red at me referring to myself as her friend. I should laugh in her face, but I won't. She lowers her head and looks away speaking. "I like the pain." I twist her head to look in my eyes. Her voice is shaking. What's wrong with her? "The soreness lets me feel for a while, but it turns me on. I guess it's weird." I lean in doing what I know I shouldn't do and kiss her lips. She clings on to my body. "Rom."

I release her lips. "Now...you are."

She interrupts me. "Yes, Rom, now." Damn, I reach my fingers below, sliding them between her robe knowing I should not be doing this. It totally goes against me respecting being her friend.

"You are wet...for me." She nods her head and her eyes look confused as if she doesn't understand her attraction toward me. I move my hand and shut her robe. "We are friends... I don't want to disrespect your wishes. You asked Jasmine to come get you."

She grips my waist. "Romel." We are planted in silence and she is breathing heavily. Is she having an orgasm? I remove her hand and push her robe open. My body lowers as I slide my hand between her thighs, feeling liquid spill over her skin. I smile. She still has no clue she's mine. She pulls my chin until my eyes are staring in her direction. "Disrespect me...I want you to."

I step back; if this was another woman I would move forward without a doubt.

She takes my hand setting my fingers below her juices. "Romel, I want you. I am not interested in—"

I cut her off, "Being my friend... I know you only want N.S.A. Vic." Her eyes roll to the top of her head.

"Why are you bugging about the friend matter?" She releases my hand. I shake my head unwilling to be her friend with no strings attached. I turn and slide the door to the bathroom shut. She stomps her foot like a toddler.

I say between the door, "I'm respecting your wishes." She never answered my question, even with me asking. I have to pack my things and get back to Atlanta, she can decide what she wants later but for now...I'm not fucking her...I think. The restraint is killing me.

VICTORIA

I am sitting in a cab with Romel and he has his luggage situated between us as we travel back to my hotel. He is serious about a one-night stand. I am frustrated. His flight leaves before my flight with Jasmine. I guess I will see him in Atlanta and we will return to the way we were. The driver pulls the car to the curb of the hotel. Romel exits the car and walks around to open my door. He reaches for my hand and for a moment we appear like a couple. He leans over, pecking me on the cheek. "Call me when you get to Atlanta."

I look up and the massive buildings are in my sights, but he has won my attention. "Romel, you will get in Atlanta before me…why don't you text me."

He stoops over talking to the driver. "Give me a minute."

"I have to go to work when I get back and I don't have access to my phone." His arms embrace me and I wish he was coming to snuggle with me. "I'll text you when I land, friend."

I exhale a jagged breath, my eyes narrow as he releases his grip. He works so much you would think he had a wife and kids. It's a good attribute but… Why am I concerned about his schedule? "I'll talk to you later in Atlanta."

Romel tilts his head. "I see you." My eyes roam to the sky and I wonder why does he say he sees me now? He enters the car and I watch him ride off, heading to the airport. Vacation time is ending for me and Jasmine; we have to get back to school.

ROMEL

I'm happy to be back in Atlanta. I have things to handle so I can move on to Georgia Tech and complete my Master's. I guess part of me doesn't feel much like I am graduating considering I am continuing on through the summer. My big day is when I get my Master's degree. My head twists and Drew comes in my side view as I tighten my tie in front of the mirror.

"You ready, Rom?"

My thoughts are with Victoria as I hear him say Rom. I forgot to text her, it's too late now, I'm in the building. I tilt my head. We came directly to work from the airport. I am not crazy about getting dressed in a public restroom. Drew is brushing his hair.

"I'm ready, grab my stuff, Drew." He passes me my bag on the other side of him.

"I can take it to the locker, Romel."

"Cool thanks." I look over my appearance confirming I look worthy of being at this job even though I feel like crashing in a deep sleep for two days. I push the door open and stride to my desk. Angie comes from around the corner and her hair is flaming orange. My eyes bulge. "Hi, Angie." I wave being polite.

She has such a *Brady Bunch* chipper tone. "Hi, Romel." She is touching her hair waiting for me to say something. I nod my head.

"Your hair—"

Drew walks around the corner and blurts out with no regard. "Damn!" He covers his mouth with his hand. Angie is reading our response opposite from what they truly mean but who cares. She keeps running her fingers through her hair.

"Yeah, I dyed it myself yesterday."

Trust me, we can tell you did it yourself, I think.

She keeps running her mouth and Drew gets by, heading to the lockers. "I was like why not; I should just go for it?" *No the hell you should not have gone for it.* Why do women do this to themselves? She is standing in front of me believing she looks great when in reality her head looks like a flaming hot chip.

I interrupt her. "Well, I am happy you like it. I have to get work done. I will see you around." *As if I can miss you now.* I can see her coming in the dark with that hair. She gives me a wave, grinning from ear to ear. My feet pace and I take notice of Drew sitting at his desk. I shake my head and hold up my fingers displaying six. He turns and sees Uncle Jay and I divert my walking, wondering what is going on now.

VICTORIA

*L*ooking out the window I see the clouds below us. The sight of the ground disappears from Chicago O'Hare airport. Seeing the clouds remind me of Romel's big arms wrapped around me, keeping me secure. Lying in the bed next to him was heavenly. A smile paints upon my face as I imagine his embrace. A sharp jolt from the plane interrupts my thoughts. I turn seeing Jasmine resting with her eyes shut. I nudge her and she groans, assuring me she wants to sleep. I giggle and lie back, his scent is still on me and images of him in my mind will not escape. I need to talk to him. Shutting my eyes, my thoughts sink deeper into all things Romel as we ascend in the air.

ROMEL

e are sitting at the oval table and Stanley enters the room with Uncle Jay behind him. Drew speaks freely. "What's up?" Uncle Jay pushes a flash drive across the table.

"I need you to handle something again. The information you gave me has hit closer to home."

I frown. "Dallas home?"

Stanley shakes his head. "Atlanta home... Did you look at the information you asked me to look in?"

I shake my head. "No, I pushed it aside."

Uncle Jay is persistent about the matter. "Drew, I want you both to look at this together."

I hold my hands in the air. "The information about the female I asked Stanley to look at or the stuff on the flash drive?" He leans over, looking identical to Uncle Senior giving me serious eyes.

"Romel, after what happened in Chicago. I need you to focus. Drew will be with you when you both look into both matters. You will understand once you see the file. I'm trying to trace the IP addresses of the buyers so I can get that information to the officers involved." I shrug my shoulders at Stanley. I hate when these guys act like we are kids and will not understand what we are looking at. I rise and Stanley is mean mugging me. "Stay focused, Romel. We have to let the authorities handle the matter."

Drew pushes his way between the two of us. "We will be focused. Let us go do our job."

Uncle Jay is holding the door open and Stanley walks ahead. We turn around to exit the opposite door Uncle Jay speaks from across the room. "After lunch you two call it a day here. I need the info before the closing of the day." We nod our heads and disperse.

I HEAD over to grab my lunch from the campus. I park near Clark University and spot Chad. I promise you, if you didn't know better you would think he attends school on one of the campuses. He is walking in my direction. "What's up, Romel? How was Chicago?" We dap and I keep moving forward to get me some tacos. I pull out my phone from my pocket, remembering I have not turned it on. A smile grows on my face and I laugh. "It was on and poppin."

Chad passes me his phone. I stop walking and look at an image. "Who is this?"

"I don't know I was hoping you would tell me, Romel." I give him his cell and text Victoria. She hasn't called, she must still be in Chicago. We pass through the buildings and the AU Center is straight ahead.

"Chad, I don't know that beefy motherfucker. He was asking for Victoria. Security escorted him off campus." I snatch his phone and look at the photo once more. "I have never seen her with this guy." I send the image to my phone.

Chad snatches his cell from my grip after I press send. "Don't snatch my shit."

I shake my head. "I overheard the younger guy call out for him, but I couldn't make out the name. He left quickly as if something was urgent." I dial Vic's number and it rolls over to voicemail. She must be on the plane. "Call me when you get this message."

I pull open the door and walk inside seeing a group of females watching me and Chad like hawks. Chad spots the girl he was dancing with. "I'll be back." I chuckle, yeah right. I step up to the counter and I notice it's the female from my class. She and Victoria are in a few classes together. She speaks fast.

"Hi how can I help you?"

"Let me get four tacos."

"Your usual." Wrinkles grow on my face as I nod. She must have been working here for a minute and I never noticed her. "I'll bring it to you if you want to take a seat."

"I will wait."

I am remaining for her to give me the total. Another female in the opposite line barges over and gives her a twenty. I hope she doesn't think I am impressed, it's only four tacos. "Hey, I'm interested and you are?"

I tilt my head. Damn, she's forward. I don't think I have seen this female before. I hold up a twenty and hand it to her. "I'm Romel, you can keep your money. My lady doesn't buy me food. I'm good." She makes some moaning gesture, and the clerk is looking confused and gives the girl her change. I don't have time to play I need to get my food and go to the house. The girl behind the counter passes me my bag and I turn, spotting Drew barge in holding a laptop. I walk to the corner and he paces in the same direction. What is wrong with him?

My phone rings it Victoria. "Hey, what's up?" She is telling me she just finished unpacking. "Cool I am getting tacos at the AU center but I have work to do afterwards." She is whining. I shake my head and Drew is motioning for me to get off the phone. Victoria can hear the crowd in the background. "Hey, I need to see what's up with Drew." She is asking for my help, this damn girl and all her help requests. "What is it, Victoria?" A female hears me say Victoria, and she has yet to take her eyes off me. "I have work…can't you take it to the computer—" Victoria over talks me and wants me to fix her computer. She claims it has a virus.

I bet it has a freaking virus all right. "I'll be here for a minute and then I am going to my spot." She insists on meeting me. "I will wait around for you but I have work to do, Victoria." I disconnect the call and a female near the group by Chad walks in our direction. Drew has that leave me the fuck alone look on his face. The female gets the message and walks away.

"What's up, Drew?"

He insists on me sitting. I lower in the chair and his computer is uploading. I pull out a taco while his computer gets together.

"I got the code from Stanley. We can look at the other matter later. This is urgent, Rom." I am crunching my taco and I move to the other seat so no one can see the screen. My eyes view the screen.

"Where is this, Drew?"

"Dallas, at the mall…keep watching." I see a young girl getting snatched but I can't see her face. Someone is kidnapping her. I pause seeing the neck of a male with a demonic claw tattoo. My eyebrows pull down together as my nostrils flare. Drew's lips don't move but I hear his words muffle. "Keep watching, Romel."

I've lost my appetite. Pushing my food aside, I keep my head buried in the screen and my heart drops. My finger replays to confirm the visual I saw on the video. Shit…she kept this from me. I know it's her. I can make out her body from anywhere, even on this grainy security footage. I shut the laptop and Drew swipes it from the table, placing it in his computer bag. My head lifts and I spot Victoria entering.

I step forward. "I'll meet you at the house, Drew." He tilts his head. Chad looks in my direction and walks over. The females are following him like a magnet. I head to Victoria and a girl grabs me from behind.

Chad speaks up. "Hey, fall back." She seems hard of hearing. I shake my head and move her hand off my back. She approaches us and asks about the dance competition. I don't have time for this. She smacks off at the mouth, "Is there a problem?"

I look out of the corner of my eye and see Victoria coming closer. Chad stands on my side and Drew is near Victoria. I tilt my head. I will stop coming here for tacos. It upset this random woman that I am not paying her attention, blah, blah, blah.

She grabs my arm. My eyes narrow in her direction and I speak to her slowly. "You touching me is a problem." She releases me seeing Victoria march toward me after handing her laptop to Drew. Her demeanor is concerning me as she barges through the crowd. Drew grabs her, but Victoria presses forward. Chad's head turns recognizing the legs coming through. Victoria is watching the female like she is here hunting. I am shaking my head; tell me she is not paying attention to this female.

I think she knows Victoria because she looks her up and down. She speaks to her aggressively, "You are aggravating me. I'm sure you have somewhere to be."

Victoria slides her arms around my waist and I step but am tugged by the sudden stop of Victoria as she overhears the female talking. "I wanted to know his name, what's it to you."

Vic's face is red. Why did the girl say anything? This has to be the most sophomoric situation, but it's a turn on. Victoria's Spanish accent heightens as she speaks in English. "Bitch, his name is 'spoken for'…fall the fuck back." I place my hands on Victoria's shoulder and realize this girl heard me talking to her over the phone. Chad is now trying to get the girl to move away.

This is high school mess, but Victoria is causing my nature to rise the way she barged through the crowd after my ass.

I speak over the girl, attempting to address Victoria. "Hey, she told you my name." I yank Victoria away from the girl and claim her lips, watching the girl do as instructed. She falls back. This is so childish, but I think Vic figured out she doesn't want to be just friends.

VICTORIA

*R*omel is silent as we walk across the campus to his vehicle. I have a feeling something is bothering him, but it's not how I interacted with the female. We cross the street and I spot his car. A truck pulls out and his hand reaches for me, pulling me in. His senses are naturally set in protection mode. Walking along the path I stop and call his name.

"Why won't you say anything?"

I've known Romel for over a year and a half and being silent is not a good sign. He's thinking, processing something. Being in Chicago has changed us. I knew having sex with him would be dangerous. Having him in my life is more important than sex. The fact I am even thinking this is a change scares me. I don't want to be like Jasmine and be in love with a guy that toys her around.

Romel twists his head and steps in front of me. The energy he pulls next to me makes me feel I'm no longer numb. He breathes down my neck as his fingers lift my chin. "We can talk in the car, Victoria."

His lips softly graze my mouth and I am so wet. This frightens me. He makes me lose the one thing I always control in

BREAKING DANCE

my life. With all that has happened recently, sex didn't seem to be a threat, but with Romel sex is earth shattering and it makes me question love. He turns to walk forward. This feeling is scaring me. I reach for his wrist. "Romel, you are scaring me, I mean this feeling is scaring me."

His hand covers my fingers, and he smiles. "Don't be...I'm taking you home." Why would he take me home? I needed to talk to him. We step in together until we are before his car. Romel pulls the door open and I lower myself inside. Maybe I was overboard but I haven't stopped thinking about him since we left Chicago. The more we are apart, the stronger my thoughts for him grow. The more I breathe, the stronger my breath aches for his scent. I can't even drink water without thinking of him, walking and not being able to walk makes me think of him. God, what has this man done to me? Romel enters the car and shuts the door. His body twists while his eyes are set on me.

"Do you have something to tell me?"

Yes, but I didn't want to say it now; I am still processing what I should say. I look out the window and Romel pulls my arm. "You don't get to act shy now, Victoria. Nothing about you is shy."

I take in a deep breath, knowing he expects me to talk, not about what just happened but to talk about the marks. Speaking of the marks is painful because it reminds me of why I did it in the first place. I am not like him. I have not healed...I know I have not healed. My fingers grab at my arm as I gulp and ask him to clarify. "Are you talking about my response to the female?"

He shakes his head and touches my fingers gripping my arm. "You tell me, Victoria... I'm not withholding anything from you." Funny, his touch speaks a language I know, but I don't want to respond. I need more time.

"Are you going to drive?" He doesn't speak, instead he rests his head back and shuts his eyes. I deserve that. Repositioning

251

my body, I face him. "Romel, I can't stop thinking about you and I saw the girl...Well, I didn't want her near you." His eyes slightly open but he doesn't face me. I continue, "I saw her touch you."

I didn't want her next to him and her skin touching his drove me mad. I might need anger management. I know my mother would not be pleased with my behavior.

Is he going to move? Romel is just sitting? I guess after all he has shared with me, I should be willing to at least try to tell him. I don't want to be like we were in Chicago when I was crying like a baby. I sigh and continue, "I've been stressed."

His head turns, and he looks at me. My heart is pounding, and I twist my fingers as I hold my hands in my lap. Romel grabs my hand. "My tuition concern has been bothering me. I went to Dallas and the eye of the storm opened, swallowing me and my baby sister. I wasn't strong enough to save her." Tears fall to my cheek and he takes his strong hand wiping my tears away. He turns the key and the car starts. "Romel, I wasn't finished talking to you."

His eyes look at the time. Did I upset him? I was telling him part of the issue. He doesn't look at me but speaks. "I have to get home and I can tell you are not ready to tell me."

He looks in the display, reversing the car from park. I feel awkward and I don't know why. We make it out of the parking lot and as Romel approaches the stop sign, he reaches for my hand. "Everything is okay. I'll fix your computer and send you a text when I am done, friend."

An evil smile paints on his face. Ugh, my foot stomps the floor. "Romel."

He turns the music on and the song fills my ear. I give him an evil stare and he laughs. I shake my head hearing the hook of the song "Just a Friend" by Biz Markie. *Asshole.*

ROMEL

I walk in and Drew has a board on the wall as if we are police officers. He is serious. "What did you find out?"

He is typing, eyes set on the screen. "I am still trying to track the buyers." His serious demeanor is concerning me as he opens my laptop. Drew is like a machine that can tap into my thoughts, without me asking he knew I would be focused and only want to get answers. It's a unique bond I don't even share with Rico; I guess this links us as brothers. He has his Uncle Senior methodical look concentrating on the monitor to find the IP address as he talks.

"I need you to do your search, Rom. Are you able to center after what you saw?" Since I have been a youngster my family always questions me if I am on edge. I understand why, I don't like it. He can't possibly be talking about Victoria and the high school crap. My voice is muffled as I lower in the chair in front of my computer.

"Victoria and that girl, or the video?" He gives me a 'don't fuck with me' look. I know he overlooked it.

"Bruh, her coming in there is fickle. Did she tell you? Did you ask her about the video?"

"I tried to get her to be direct, but she wasn't ready. She gave you her computer." I knew she wasn't ready to open up to me. My single-mindedness of this matter has alarmed me with the need to see more, to find out if I could handle it. I guess I got concerned about losing it in front of her. Drew steps by the couch and grabs the bag, pulling out her purple laptop. She loves this color. He passes me the computer and walks to the tackboard. He is like a drill sergeant. I turn on Victoria's PC and look at Drew.

"This is what I printed from what I saw." He is pinning up images of multiple young girls.

"Drew, that's an entire group of females." They all have a similar look. Her computer has pop-up ads flashing everywhere. I shake my head and go to the settings. She was downloading crap. I stand and look closer at an image on the bulletin surface.

"Drew, is this female from the video?" He is looking at his screen and tilts his head in my direction. "The one you just saw. I am not sure; I can pull it back up." She favors Victoria slightly. I pace to my room to get the disk for the virus protector. "Rom!" I grab the disk out of my top drawer and stride to the living area.

"What's up?" He is frozen. Damn, should I ask him anything? I take the disk out and insert it in Victoria's central processing unit.

My feet step to the side of Drew and we are both looking at the computer screen.

"They made a video of killing the young girl we saw, but I hear a distinct voice."

Moving Drew my fingers adjust the volume and I fade out the sounds of the gun shot. I press play. Drew is looking in my direction. "What is it, Rom?"

My ear is drawn to a sound.

"I can hear something. I might be wrong..." I stop speaking

and listen. My mouth drops. Drew takes control of the keyboard and fades the background noise focusing only on the screeching shouts. I know he can hear her. The entire floor in Chicago can attest to her screams. He presses play and syncs the volume with the sound bar. I can hear a person wailing, in tears, it's heart-wrenching, echoing in the apartment. A door is heard. I make out someone is crying, pleading *'ayuadame.'* Drew opens his mouth to speak and I hold my hand up. A soft voice travels in the room's space. 'Shhh *hermana, estoy aquí para ayudar.* I am here to help…shhh.' The person whispering, must be her sister.

Drew's veins are growing in his neck and he looks at me. My ears hear a large caliber gunshot ricochet. "That's a nine millimeter."

I nod, assuring him we hear the same. His head tilts as shock grows over his face he speaks hesitantly. "It's her isn't it, Rom?" The audio is still playing and the crying stops and some men arguing fades.

"Yes, Drew, that's her…I know it's her." The visual is picking up a signal clearing up. I spot a dark room but a light is hitting the screen, it's like a flash or something is in their camera. I can see a young girl, she's naked, with fear in her eyes, laying on a floor that looks more like a slab of concrete. The girl is being snatched by a man in all black. Drew stops the video.

"Why did you stop?"

He shakes his head, and he points to the screen. I look close and my chest is pounding, and it feels like my heart jumps in my throat. I wipe my head, feeling more like I'm sweating bullets. I continue surveying the display, bending over. My hands wrap around the screen and Drew places his hand on my shoulder. "Romel…"

He gives me a look reminding me to stay calm. Nothing can change what has happened, but I wish I could. My rasping resembles someone going at my throat with a cheese grater. I muffle my words, fighting for more oxygen.

"I'm focused."

Continuing to view what is a blur of a man standing over a female on the opposite side of the room, I can tell she's kicking the guy and he stumbles over her. The door widens, another man enters, shouting. He seems to give the orders. The guy leans over her, I can't see her. Is she unconscious?

"What happened, Drew?" The screen is in slow motion.

I know I will not like what I see no matter what. His voice is relaxed, in a controlled temper. "Keep looking...Romel, just stay calm okay." With uneven breaths I nod and keep my eyes straight, my body feels like it's burning on the inside. The guy has turned and I can see a scar on his face. Looking below he is dragging someone. I'm praying so desperately that what I'm seeing isn't real, I feel I might explode.

"No, Drew...no."

I shake my head and release the screen. My hands grab the top of my head as I walk away shouting pleading.

"Drew, tell me this is not real!"

Devastation grows as I shake my head in denial; a gut-wrenching yell tears from my throat. My eyes shut as I fight the anger of tears spilling over. I know it's her, but I don't want it to be her.

Drew is pacing a few feet behind me. "Rom, sit down! We don't know enough." My eyes blaze, staring at Drew and I am shredding on the inside. I hit my chest. Sputtering, my voice sounds huskier as if I am exhausted.

"Drew, is it the same man? These people hurt my mother and..."

My legs feel like they will give. Drew is directing me. "Sit down, Rom, you are shaking, sit down now!"

I wipe my face and go to the couch. I know why Uncle Jay told me to watch this with Drew. He knows who these bastards are. If he knows then Uncle Senior knows, as does Stanley. My eyes drift to my trembling hands and Drew is sitting across from me in the chair. He has the laptop. I question him in broken speech, stammering my words.

"Did you...see...t-the entire clip?"

He is scratching his head; his eyes are glossy as if he is holding back tears. The harsh rush of his breath confirms this is agonizing for him to see me like this.

"Most of it." Drew rubs his face taking in a breath. "I can finish...you don't have to look at it, Rom."

"Was she...?" My head is pounding at the thought of someone violating her. I am trying to hold on to focus. Drew's eyes are filled with concern as they dart in my direction.

"Not from what I saw."

I pull up, recognizing my knees are shaking. I rest back and count to ten, inhaling and exhaling slowly. I can hear Drew walking to the kitchen.

Drew paces until he is at my side. He opens a bottle. "Drink this now, Rom before you overheat yourself." Sucking in a deep breath of air, I hold it one last time for ten seconds...and with a slow release, I exhale while my vision is clear. *You can handle this Romel.* I take the water nodding at Drew. "I am good; we can watch the rest." I guzzle the water and Drew grabs the laptop out of the chair. His presence next to me reminds me of being a kid, or maybe I feel like a child, safe, not immature. Opening the screen, I top off the water and a light flashes as the video resumes.

Victoria is yelling in unison with the other person in the room. I hear his dark voice telling her she'll learn their way. I rub my chin and speak in a muffled tone.

"He's trying to scare her, Drew. Look at the other girl...who is she?" Drew interrupts he points to the screen.

"Look how she responds to Victoria when he drags her out the room. She's falling apart." Hell, I am falling apart. Victoria stayed away from me until her body healed from all the marks on her arms. She covered her arms for more than cuts, she has been masking her body...everything. Shutting my eyes, I am certain of the girl on the photo. She is black and blue with bruises. I growl, frustrated. The visual blacks out. Who records shit like this and puts it on the dark web?

"Drew, that's who we heard crying out for help...her sister."

I press the next clip. Instantly, I hear Vic. She's startled, I can tell by her barely audible cry. Screaming, demanding for someone to stop. This view has more light. "She's in a room with windows." I point at the top of the screen. "You can see in this room it's daylight, it's a different day." How long was she there? Drew looks closer and the sound of the man's voice is heavy from the surround sound. My eyes spot the neck tattoo of the guy. He is tightening a rope and slaps her, calling her a bitch. She's trying to control her cries. Rage spreads through my body like a forest fire, Drew stops the video. I snap. "No let it play. I will be pissed. She won't tell me, Drew."

He eyeballs me with serious eyes. Drew is breathing with his nostrils flared. Shit, I overlooked him getting annoyed by watching this. I get up, placing the computer on the table and go get him a bottle of water. Drew has been by my side since I was a kid, watching me spiral out, not wanting to fight to live, until I finally decided to fight to live. He's seen me empty, hoping to die to be with my father. A tear falls to my chin as I reach to open the pantry door and grab several bottles. Maybe we should rest from the video clips, it has us uncomfortable. Walking back to the couch, I notice Victoria's PC is still processing, cleaning the virus. Drew's head is hanging back on the couch. I pass him the water and he opens the top.

"We can stop watching, Drew."

He shakes his head, drinking the water. His strangled voice is not entertaining such a notion. "No, we will finish together." I sit, welcoming the challenge to complete this task and press play, watching the screen from the table. My lip is twitching, viewing the kidnapper's hand trail her skin. Drew leans in but my arm extends, blocking him. How I am building the courage to face this is beyond me. I am not interested in running. She's a person I can't see myself giving up on. I really want Victoria in my life. Facing this truth now is better than turning my cheek. It's difficult, but it's worse to regret not facing it.

"Let it play." The fear of what could happen will not lead to nothing happening. I am focusing.

She keeps yelling in terror and he fondles her. I am fighting closing my eyes as he violates her, touching every inch of her body as she is pleading for him to stop. My heart rate is on fire and Drew stands in a hurry, walking to the kitchen. I can hear a retching sound. He's hurling in the sink.

I walk in as he is sliding against the lower cabinets to the floor, shaking his head. His voice is low. "I'm sorry, Romel." My hand reaches for a towel off the counter and I pass it to him. Drew sits for five seconds and I reach to pull him from the floor. He embraces me.

"Are you okay, Rom?"

I hit his back, and he chuckles. "I still have a pulse. Go clean your dirty mouth, bruh." I walk to the living area. We both know what happened. I am confused. Why would she not tell me? I stand from the table and see Drew in the hall.

"I need to get air."

"I'm going with you, Rom." I shake my head. Drew walks toward me.

"I'm just going to run, Drew." He looks me in the eyes and grabs my fist.

"We will run together, go change." I don't argue with him, my head is a mess. I hear the phone ring and Drew answers. He's talking to Stanley.

VICTORIA

I am laying on the couch and Jasmine enters from the hall. She has a grin on her face. Why is she so chipper? Her voice has a high pitch. "Hi, chica! So I got a video I want you to check out." She sits on the arm of the couch and I look in the screen of her phone. My eyes bulge at the image.

"Where did you get this picture?" She is laughing.

"Girl, I saw him when I dropped you off at the financial aid office. He was lurking around until I told her you were fine."

I take in the phone screen, currently displaying an image of Jesse. I hope he hasn't mentioned what he saw the night I showed up at his house with my sister after we made our escape. What does Jasmine mean he is lurking around? "What did Jesse say?" She shrugs her shoulder.

"He's not the big news. According to several females you were spotted at the AU Center acting like a lioness protecting her property." That is extreme. I was not acting like an animal and he is not my property.

"Whatever, chica. What did Jesse want? I gave him your number and told you are fine. He seems concerned, and he demanded for me not to call Chantal." She falls on top of me like a big kid. "What's up with you and Romel, chica?"

I roll my eyes and tingle inside thinking about him. "Nothing…he wants me to tell him about my marks on my arm." Her back rises as if she was caught in a lie… I chuckle. Jasmine is eagle eying me wondering about my reaction.

"Well…"

"I have to tell him." She is darting her eyes waiting for me to complete my thoughts. "I…" Jasmine slaps my leg. I snicker knowing she wants me to tell her about me acting out with the girl. "Romel is more interested in what happened."

"Chica he cares about you and I know you care about him. Everyone at the AU Center knows because I got several messages about it from Jade." My eyes blink wondering why is she in my personal business.

"What was she saying, chica?"

"She said you and ol' boy from the dance group are doing more than dancing. It's nothing, Victoria." I reposition on the couch. I don't want her saying Romel's name.

"I know she likes him."

She has a matter of fact glare staring at me. "Girl, most of the females on this campus finds him attractive. Don't act brand new."

She's right, I already figured that. "Well, he's mine, she can't have him." Jasmine is laughing.

"He's your what brother…or friend?" I grab the pillow and swing it at her head. She pushes the pillow pinning me down. I am laughing and I hear the phone ring. We stop at once. She grabs the cell off the table.

"Who is it?"

She passes it. "It's your friend." I growl at her and she snaps.

"Lioness!" I answer the call laughing and out of breath.

"Hello." Romel sounds odd. He is telling me my computer is finished. "Okay, thank you." He cuts me off, he doesn't like me telling him thank you. It makes no sense. "I will come over to get it." He has an uncertain tone. I have never been to his apartment. Is he concerned about me knowing where he lives? Jasmine is making noise. She motions her lips as if Romel is kissing me. I roll my eyes. "Stop being petty!" Romel thinks I am talking to him. "I am talking to my chica. I will see you soon, text the address." He agrees for me to come over. I end the call.

"Chica, take me to Romel's house."

She stands with her hand on her hip as if she is my mother. "Wait, did you take care of the money issue? Did they give you an extension?"

I shake my head. "No, the strangest thing happened, I asked them to check twice."

I pull out the statement from my back pocket. She is looking at the paper. "Perhaps, they made a mistake."

"Girl, maybe my pops paid it and didn't tell me. I need to call home to check on my sister, anyway."

I step from the couch and Jasmine pushes me down. She looks down, persisting to get more information. "Now, this Jesse thing, did you do something with Jesse in Dallas?"

I frown. "No way, he is our brother, girl. He is just being protective." Her eyes survey me. I am not sure if she believes me.

"I will stay away from telling sis his ass is here, but if Chantal shows up in Atlanta...You already know."

"Chica, I know the rules...we are family. I wouldn't let him...but Omari. Sis better get her brother from chasing after my Tatiana. She's off limits." Jasmine is laughing and I stand on my feet. She paces towards her room. Then turns her head slightly.

"So are you two a couple?"

"Yes and no..." I smirk and her body leans against the wall in the hall.

"Explain, chica."

"Jasmine, I will tell him I will not date other guys because I can't stop thinking about his 'horse and carriage.'" Her eyes flash and I am laughing. "No seriously, Jasmine, I feel different with him. It's like we have already been together and I'm falling for him."

Her eyes are glowing. "Love, chica…you love the guy, just be careful."

She walks off and I yell, "Careful of what, chica?"

She is shouting, "His dick has you doing things… Be careful lioness!"

My head falls back. "I'm taking a bath, then we can leave."

She hurdles down the hall. "His ass has you preparing to make certain you are fresh upon entering his door."

"Shut up, Jasmine!" So what if she's right; she didn't have to say it!

I step toward my room and my phone vibrates. Swiping the screen, I see a notification.

Are you good, Lil' Ma?

I type back, *Yes.*

Another notification comes through from Jesse. *How many?*

My lips twists…he is talking in a pattern. *I spot three… how many?*

Oh, he wants to know how many was it there.

One injured, right? He texts so fast for a guy. I read his reply. *Two is ghost, one is wishing. How many?*

I take in a deep breath. I can't think of this right now. I need him to know I am fine. *I'm good.*

He responds…*I'm watching… be good Lil' Ma.*

Great, now his crazy ass will see Romel. I hope Romel doesn't see Jesse. Shit just got real. I will go make something sweet for Romel first then I will go take a bath.

ROMEL

$\mathcal{I}$ pull out a box from the top of my closet and pace my feet across the cold floor.

As I stand before the bed I push the king-size pillows to the side and prop my back against the black leather headboard frame. I haven't had a reason to go through these memories, or maybe it was just me not wanting to reminisce.

My hand grazes the top of the box, engraved with my father's name.

My mother placed it in a metal box before I left home. She wanted to make sure not even a fire could break through the memories we shared.

For a moment, I'm numb, my thoughts recall Victoria saying she wanted to feel. I know what it's like to be stunned, walking in a world that revolves yet you stand still in one place. I press in the code and it unlocks. A suctioning feeling caves in at my chest deep inside. I grab my face, holding my eyes as tears run to my neck. Calling out to him...yet I know he will not return with his voice. "I miss you, Pops."

I pull out a photo of us; seeing him smile comforts me but stings at the same time. He's holding me on a bike, lecturing me.

I wanted to go out with Rico and he would not let me go until I mastered riding that damn bike. I take in a deep breath reflecting on his words. He would tell me *don't look back, Romel...that's the past. It's only a lesson to get you to this instant.* I remember his messages as if he is speaking at this present moment. He'd tell me *today is your gift.* I can picture him pointing ahead. I shut my eyes imagining him, imagining his voice. *The future is your motivation son... you are my motivation.* Bike lessons were never just about learning to ride a bike.

This was the day I learned to ride without training wheels. I remember him yelling, *push through, Romel.* My tear falls to the image and I chuckle, that was a fun memory. "I'm pushing through, Pops...missing you but pushing."

Tap, tap, tap

I look up and see Drew at my door. "What's up?"

He tilts his head. "I'm going out to set up things at my new place. Do you want to roll out with me?"

I shake my head. "I'm good, Vic is coming over."

"Awww, shit...you letting her come to the spot. You calling her Vic." I am chuckling, looking away. He steps in the room and elbows my shoulder.

"Does she know she's getting baptized in this piece?"

I am shaking my head at his over dramatic self. "She'll know."

"Call me if you change your mind. I sent the info to Stanley. He says it's another code he wants us to locate because the people are linked to the video and audio we have."

I shake my head. "I got you. I will let you know if I want to leave out. I doubt it."

We bump fists and he exists my room.

VICTORIA

y fist reaches to knock but Romel opens the door and a sly grin forms on his face. He reaches to free my hands from the container. "I see you are showing skin, friend." I roll my eyes knowing my attire looks nothing like I want him to call me his friend. I step forward smelling the fresh scent of honeysuckle and my heels sound off on the hardwood floor. His room in Chicago smelled like this, Romel likes this scent. My ears catch the sound of the water from the three panel wall fountain. Wow, this room reminds me of being outside in a rainforest.

There are several palm-like plants placed strategically, centering the energy of the room. Romel paces to the dining table, reaching for my laptop. He places the item I brought on the table without asking about it. Is he trying to get rid of me? I cross my arms raising my brow.

"Romel, are you sending me home?" I want to see the rest of this place. It is large, especially for a few college kids. I know they work, but hey they are in college. What do these guys do at their place of employment? He'd better not be doing anything illegal. I don't think so, but I know whatever he's doing someone else is helping with this space financially.

My eyes spot three glass ball vases with ivy spilling over the sides. I wonder if they are artificial. "Romel, are those real?"

He motions for me to move forward. "See for yourself. What did you bring with you?" Finally, he asks.

I walk ahead, there are several doors going down this hall. It is like a maze. My hand touches the green leaf. I twist my head as his fingers are trying to pry open the container. I huff and his impatient self, but I am enjoying the view of strong hands, he is sexy beyond words.

"It's dessert, Romel." His lips form a grin and the container unlatches.

I peek closer. Aww, fish are inside, a garden aquarium. "Who decorated this place? It looks nothing like the typical bachelor pad." Kind of but not really. He chuckles and I watch his finger sliding on the side of the cake I made. He speaks and I want him to stop messing up the desert.

"We did, but my mother and Drew's both like decorating. They had an influence on some things. It is like an extension of what we have back home." Wow, they went all out; these guys are spoiled.

His lips part and Romel takes his finger, sliding the icing between his lips, he moans. "Damn, where did you get this from? Red velvet, right?" His eyes roll to the top of his head confirming he is enjoying it. This is his favorite cake. I saw him buy it several times at the school and he gets pissed because it doesn't taste like his mother's cake. I'm certain mine doesn't either.

I smile. "My kitchen, I made it. I thought we could eat it together." He closes the container, looking at me suspiciously.

Romel has my PC in hand. "Where is Jasmine? She's not waiting on you...friend?" I take in a breath of air and grab my computer, setting it by my purse. He looks at me, surveying my appearance. "Have a seat, or stand whichever you prefer." Really? Nothing about my cake? I step away to relax on his massive black sectional sofa, it complements him. I am thinking the guys definitely picked this out.

"Why does this look like a futuristic star ship of some sort?" It's nothing you would see in a store. I guess they need generous seating considering they are tall guys. Placing my purse on the coffee table, I plop down and fall back. This is the most comfortable couch.

"It was designed for me and Drew."

I rise. "Do you two have sex parties on this thing? I don't want to lie on old dried up cum." He smacks his lips.

"You look like you are dressed for a sex party with that shredded, sleeveless dress on. I guess wearing red is a popular choice for you today." He sits down adjusting the headrest, making a growling noise. He seems agitated.

"Do you want me to leave?"

"No Vic...toria, you're in my spot. I'm not used to sitting here. It's not a big—" My movement cuts him off as I lower my body on his legs.

"I can move... it's not a problem."

"Victoria, I don't enjoy being teased." He lifts me, sitting me on the side of him and lifts a compartment grabbing a remote. I can't believe he is acting this way.

"Romel...where is the restroom?" He points to the hall. I have to go but I will wait for a moment.

He shakes his head and presses buttons until I hear that damn song coming from the sound bar hanging below the thinnest TV I have ever seen. The screen is large, but the remarkable thinness of the floating television has the guys' names written all over it. If Biz Markie sings that friend song one more time!

My heel stomps on the grass-like rug, not making much of a sound and I am pulling my dress from my thigh.

Romel teases, "How adorable." He is biting his lip, looking

away toward the TV. He's trying to ignore me but it's not going well.

I snap my head. "Romel, turn that off!"

He looks out the side of his eye. "Victoria...What are you doing coming to my house dressed like that?"

"I dressed for the environment."

"What environment? We are not going out, I ordered in." I stand in front of him practically naked. His eyes are piercing through the slits on my dress, revealing my black bra and boy shorts underneath. I look at his leg and he turns to his side. I smile and speak to him in a sugary tone.

"You are the environment I dressed for."

I get closer to his personal space and he doesn't budge. He speaks as if he wants me to stop. "Go to the restroom woman." His eyes are on the sixty plus inches on the wall but there is no volume. I jump on him and he tussles with me. I need to get up.

"I'll be back." He shakes his head.

"I'll be here I might eat my food without you." He is always eating.

ROMEL

*D*amn, Victoria is in my spot showing out, with my favorite cake. That damn icing made me want to lick it off her ass. She is playing with my head. Her sheer beauty is magical and I adore that she's not covering her marks. She rushed from the bathroom as if I would vanish. Her eyes are sparkling as she is laying on me demanding my attention. I chuckle. "You can't have me. The one-night stand is over."

Her voice is tempting. "Baby…" The nature of the room is relaxing her more than I expected. I blink my eyes I guess I will give her my attention and eat dinner later.

"Yes, Vic."

Her hands reach for my face and she goes after my lips. I clutch her hands.

"I know you fuckin lyin." I stand and she rolls over.

"Romel!"

"Don't fuck with me, Victoria Waters!" I turn the song off. I told her the terms and if she thinks that damn sexy piece of material will make me forget, she doesn't know me well. She is on her feet, looking up, reaching for my hands. She speaks candidly.

"I cut myself because…well it used to be because I was

270

worried about my tuition, but that's not an issue anymore, some-how." My lip twitches and I push away, trying to not reveal my knowledge of her finances. She continues and I sit as she stands in front of me.

She's so gorgeous. I already know what happened, more than I should know. Her feet slide out of her heels and she finishes her statement. She has a slight grin forming on her face as if the feel of the carpet is tickling the soles of her feet. She lets out a slight breath continuing, "Compounded with the financial aid..." Her head twists and I reach for her hand, she steps closer and I wonder if she can hear my heart pounding. She gulps clearing her voice. "I was attacked, kidnapped and held for several days with my sister, and went into shell shock. I couldn't defend myself. I wanted to..."

A tear drops and I pull her. "It's okay, Victoria. You are here alive." I push her hair away from her eyes and I lower myself until I am seated. I don't know if I want her to utter the words.

"Romel, what does it mean to date you?" She switches topics with ease. Wow, this is interesting. I entertain the question.

"What we make it. Why? Do you think you want to have a relationship with me?" She shrugs her shoulders as if she's reverting in a childlike form.

"Yes...I don't know, maybe you complete me."

A frown grows on my forehead. "Victoria, I'm not looking to complete you, only accept you completely the way you are. I would only ask the same in return. You came in the world complete, if not I would have come in with you." She smiles sitting in my lap.

"How do you know you want to be with me, Romel?" I can answer this in my sleep, my lip turns down. I run my fingers through her soft hair. I want to take her but I need to answer her questions.

Looking in her eyes, I respond, "On my ugliest days you are the beauty that lifts my heartbeat." The expression she gives me is as if I stole her breath. Okay, I might not stop myself from the erection growing. She is repositioning herself and plants her legs on both sides of me. Damn, she knows what she's doing.

She whispers in my ear, gripping my head. "Even knowing the crazy stuff about me, you don't dislike me, Romel?" I can smell her wetness; her fumes are flipping my insides.

I shake my head. Speaking in a low pitch I answer her ,"In the darkest sky, one can see the brightest star. Your dark clouds only make you shine brighter."

"I don't want to be your friend...not only your friend." She rises from my chest looking in my eyes. Aww shit, her warm sugary lips infuse my mouth. My body is heating by her touch.

My voice is low. "I'm not the sharing type."

Victoria is batting her eyes, flirting with me. All the blood from my head is redirecting everything to my dick.

Her lips part as her words escape. "I'm not sharing you either,"

Rising from the couch, I lift her in my arms and she steps backwards until her skin meets the wall, inches away from the mounted waterfall. The sound of the water streaming in my ear, standing against my Victoria, is imposing an adrenaline like no other. Cascading over her, I forget all the problems of yesterday and today while losing myself in her beauty. Standing next to her causes a lively feeling to drive me, my hand gently touches her face as my eyes soak in her natural beauty.

She looks in my eyes, panting. Her voice is honeyed, "Take off your clothes, Romel." I chuckle she wants control. My eyes follow her body as she squirms before me.

I remove my shirt and demand of her, "Take off your dress."

She lifts her clothes over her head. Damn, I'm lucky. Victoria is mesmerizing, addictive to say the least. If I pass away now... I'd have no regrets. I remove my pants and her pupils dilate as she catalogues my appearance. I have her undivided attention.

Victoria knows what's going to happen, as sex lingers in her eyes. I will change her expectations. My fingers clamp around her waist, pressing her further to the wall as I tower in front of her, her breasts are motioning up and down from her intense breaths. "I love how your body feels against me." She releases her breath and my skin craves her more.

Her heart is pounding. I run my fingers up her back, grabbing her hair with one hand, while pushing her back as if we are dancing, she doesn't resist. She's got that look in her eyes as if she's ready to go with me wherever I go. I want to taste her, but teasing her seems like a nice treat for now.

I press her against the wall as my body fuses with her. Licking my lips, breathing heavy, centimeters from her face, Victoria's lips part.

She thinks I'm going in for a kiss at the last minute my head slides just below her neck, my fingers brush her lustrous hair to the side.

She moans, "Romel."

Heavy heaving confirms she expects me to kiss her neck, but I take in her scent as she feels the warmth of my breath. "The smell of you drives me fucking crazy." I think she knows how I respond to honeysuckle. Her intoxicating scent is transporting me under her spell... Fuck. She smells like sweet honey waiting for me to devour her juices.

Taking both her hands, I pin them to the wall, taking in her aroma from her neck for mere seconds. "Have you been preparing for me?"

She gulps as my lips sweep, kissing her from her shoulder... with slow soft caresses from my lips. I taste her skin, millimeter by millimeter with each kiss. Her legs weaken as the painful slow motion of my kisses torture her, building her anxiety of having me. I reach her neck and breathe until the heat from my mouth reaches her ears. She takes in a deep breath expecting my wet lips on her skin.

"Yes...I have," she whispers.

I pull away my mouth, brushing past her face, moving my lips as if I will kiss her. She takes in a jagged breath. Repeating the same acts, my lips trail against her other shoulder, Victoria's nails inch the skin of my arms. My eyes roll to the back of my head as pain arouses me.

She moans, "Romel."

Victoria swallows the air while my lips brush her skin, kissing her from her shoulder...with slow soft caresses. I taste her skin, millimeter by millimeter, with each kiss fucking with her mind.

Her legs tremble. "*Senorita*, is this painful for you?"

She slows her breath. "Ahhh, *papi*— agonizing."

Each twirl of my tongue across her skin is torturous, she wants so bad to control.

I look in her eyes. "I will fuck you like no man has before." I have both her hands, hemming them with one hand to the wall. "You'll thank me...tell me I'm the best you've ever had." A sexy smile forms on her face while I smell her neck. It's as if she's dying a slow death of ecstasy in my arms.

Victoria squirms, pushing her shorts below to the floor. She whimpers and my tongue craves her taste, I lower my body, smelling her until I am face to face with her pretty little pussy. Victoria inches her leg to the side, I grab it, kissing her inner thigh as she trembles with pleasure and I slide my finger between her dripping folds. My mouth slurps her juices while my hands go round her hips, rubbing her down.

"Ahh...Romel." After tonight everything will change, but she's what I want, what I need...what I have to have.

VICTORIA

$\mathcal{B}$eing held to a wall with my leg draped over Romel is not what I planned. We were only supposed to talk; I think that's what I told chica…but then I saw him. He is so skilled at making me cum over and over, it's like he's the god that came to crown my kitty cat. How am I supposed to resist this guy? I tried so hard. My eyes roll to the back of my head and his tongue washes my juices away. I whimper, "Romel."

His strong tongue pushes up and forward pulling, his face to forward he is reconstructing my insides as I unravel before him. Romel is anchoring his entire tongue, licking to the tip of my clit. I scream with pleasure a heat grows in my lower stomach, the sensation is so strong. "What are you doing to me, Romel?"

He pulls away from my aching lips. "I want to make you feel savagely pleasurable." Yes, please do, *papi*. I think I will explode, Romel inserts two fingers, locating my spot, beckoning me. He knows exactly what to do…I let out a breath. All of me. "You do, *papi,* my, my, you so do."

His eyes are heavy looking at me as the palm of his hand pushes at my stomach holding me in place.

Romel's fingers push and pull in a sinister motion, a strong sensation keeps building, my body is unstitching every nerve. His voice is so low as he questions me. "Victoria, you will feel you will pee." I clench my stomach and my eyes grow wide. I already feel that way.

"Don't worry, you already went…just let go." He is smiling, and I am confused. How can he make me feel this urgency between my legs? "Relax, baby, you can just let go. Trust me it will be amazing."

He lifts me from the wall and takes me to the couch. My stomach clenches and it's as if I'm convulsing "What if Drew walks in here?"

He is so aggressive, but it turns everything inside of me on. I'm propped over a pillow, my hand reaches to move it and he moves my hand, keeping the pillow below my ass.

Romel takes all of his length and flicks it with so much pressure over and over across my clit. I scream, "ROMEL!"

This man is not a man, he's a fucking savage. His hand pushes my lower stomach down. He takes the tip of his shaft encircling the entrance of my wetness. Where in heaven and hell has this man come from? He's demanding something from me that is unknown and he's taking whatever he's come to get. He's teasing and I'm squirming, breathing heavily.

Romel is beating my g-spot, his fingers return, tapping my inside with pressure. My ears take in the slippery sounds coming from below as he keeps demanding me to get wetter and wetter and he teases me harder and harder. I echo sounds I never knew I could make. He looks at me with such intensity. "You're so sexy."

I squelch sponge-like sounds, my body twitches, and he presses my lower stomach, making certain I don't escape his grip. My nerves shut off and on as he constantly stimulates me… I've never been this excited during sex in my life. He is saturating me with a full body orgasm. "Romel you're the best!"

I am so exhausted it's been close to an hour he's been teasing me.

His massive hand should be tired, but his touch is amazing, attacking my lower lips like a beast. Romel moves over, cupping the palm of his hand on my clit while stroking my g-spot with his two marvelous fingers. He snaps, "The best what? Say it."

He hasn't even fucked me and he's the best. I'm losing control with the urgency to pee, my eyes grow wide and his eyes fill with nothing but bliss, claiming power over the orgasm running up my spine. "I'm cumming!"

Romel

"Let go and I'll give you what you crave for deep, deep, inside, Victoria."

She is shaking her head. "I need to go…"

I grin and keep going, while speaking to her in a calm tone. "You need to let go…"

I cut her off, knowing that's what I am waiting on. She's on the edge, she can't stop herself if she wants to. I tease her wet pussy with the pressure of my dick. She yells like a siren.

"You don't have on a condom!" She'll be fine, I'm only teasing her.

Ten seconds pass and I drive her further, tittering to the edge, and she is shaking in convulsions.

"Just relax… I want to see you let go…you're so beautiful." Twenty seconds pass.

"Romel, I'm cuming."

I thrust my dick harder and harder up her g-spot and snatch it out.

Fifty seconds pass and she screams as if she's being assaulted with pleasure as she soaks the couch. Her pussy is squirting like a busted fire hydrant and I am more than turned on seeing her deep orgasm falling like a waterfall.

Her ass belongs to me and me alone.

I lift her from the couch. She speaks, muffled with slight embarrassment. "Sorry about the mess on the couch. I've never done that." I smile carrying her to what she perceives as my bedroom. Her eyes survey in wonder.

I know the darkness of the hall is questionable especially with the red lights hitting the wall. "It was a complete turn on." I kick open the door to my room. "I'll buy a new couch...no worries." She shakes her head.

I can hear her breathing as we stand in complete darkness. "Thank you..." She gets closer and I wonder what she is thinking. "You're the best I've ever had."

Like a ticking time bomb her words drive me wild and I force her back to the corner bench. Her heart is beating so fast. I lift her arms against the padded wall.

"Do I scare you?"

Part of me is asking her this because I know what happened to her. I will stop if I make her think of that day. She might think another way after she sees what is hidden in the darkness. I reach above her head pressing a button and the dim light hits various areas, limiting a big reveal of the area.

"Romel, what is this room?"

She stands pushing away from my chest and I tilt my head noticing Victoria's eyelashes as they bat. I don't think she's thinking of the guys that kidnapped her. I hope she's not.

"My pleasure sanctuary."

She smirks, watching me step back. Interesting, she's more curious than she was when I saw her sliding down the pole at the club. Her eyes never leave me as I grab a condom from my drawer.

"I only want to make you feel good...if I scare you..." She stands on the bench and reaches for the chains.

"Does this link to the bands on your wrist?" She's not scared at all.

I pace to her as Victoria seizes my face with her soft fingers and her warm lips possess my mouth. I take hold of her and she wraps her legs around me. "Nothing about you scares me, Romel." She's amazing.

Victoria

I SLIDE from Romel's arms, planting my feet on the floor. He's next to me making my temperature rise. Something tells me his mother had nothing to do with the design of this room. My fingers push across the fabric of the bench, trying to distract my thoughts. But this is not helpful. There's no doubt this was made for sexual pleasure, but I think below the cushioned seat of the bench is storage. Maybe more toys. This room has me feeling some type of way and I adore it. Something tells me the experience we have tonight will scratch an itch leaving me dominating the situation.

I'm loving the dramatic edge the wall adds to the room. My curiosity makes me wonder, why does it feel like it was made with me in mind.

I am almost certain having a purple accented wall is not his preference is it. Hmmm, maybe he's like Prince regarding the color. I know this room is made for having fun! I wonder what Romel might think if I make a request of him. "Romel, do the chains connect to your bands?"

My head turns sliding across the panels on the wall. I think he installed these to make the room less noisy. The padding feels insulated, but he made sure it was soft to touch. I wonder what's in the other corner. Blinking my eyes, I look at Romel, he'd better answer me.

"They can."

His eyes sparkle with curiosity of my actions. I stand, walking around, wearing nothing but a bra and his eyes follow every move I make.

Being bare around him is so freeing. Perhaps this space has something to do with it.

"Are you into pain?"

He shrugs his shoulders and his chocolate voice makes me tingle. "It's not so much of a pain as it is sensation…intense sensation. Pain can turn you off, but I trust…from the look in your eyes, I trust you are focusing on intensifying a sensation."

He is reading me well as I pace in front of him. "Why do you enjoy being in control, Romel?"

He tugs in a jagged breath. Romel strokes my hand and I feel like my skin is melting in his touch. "Using power can provide pleasure for the willing vessel."

"Would you be my willing vessel?"

His eyes grow as he blinks his eyelashes. His eyes are dreamy. "You want control…over me?" He is contemplating this idea longer than I thought. Ten seconds pass and he repositions watching me.

"You know you want change…you'll still be…" I lower my hand gripping his dick and he smiles. "…a man."

He rubs his face, pondering. "So, Victoria, I trust fundamentally overpowering me is not your goal. I'll receive as you give?" I affirm with a head shake.

"Yes…do you trust me?" I need him to agree, want him to let me have my way.

His muscles relax and he has the most serious demeanor. "Yes…I see you."

Ugh. "What does that mean, Romel?"

He smirks. "You'll know when it's right for you to know. Just know I see you." I shrug my shoulders and carry on.

"Let's negotiate…" I start. He is laughing as if I said a joke.

"Okay if I say the safe word, you pick our first date; if you don't make me say it…I pick the first date."

This is great, I will make him scream the safe word. Hmmm. I speak in a hurried tone. "The safe word can be *red*!" He nods agreeing. Why does this feel like a game? He licks his bottom lip. The chains above him looks enticing, my eyes slant, noting something it looks like pockets. I'm not sure, there are three sets below. I am thinking it's for your feet, but why is there only one lonely pocket up top.

"Can I tie you up?" I lean over to lick his lips as I plead. He wiggles and I smirk at his reaction.

"Yes, you can tie me up." I kiss him, speaking in a low sweet voice.

"Can I blindfold you?"

"Yes, Vic."

I am so excited. He said yes! Now we have established what I can do, I dive my tongue between his lips sensually with aggression and a warm feeling rushes through my body. His touch relaxes me; slowing my heart beat, I notice his hand grip the bench. He is controlling himself. Leisurely, I carry on savoring the moment. My speech is unhurried.

"Remember, safe word… is *RED*."

Romel

SHE IS EXCITED, rubbing her fingers along the chain. "Have you done this before?" Her eyes grow.

"No, but I'm anxious to with you. I've seen it at the club." I knew it. She's a curious little woman. I bite my lip as she takes hold of my wrist. This woman has to slow down. I adore the excitement, yet I am not in a rush. I reach for the remote on the wall. I can tell she is wondering why am I interrupting her. I chuckle and set the sound system. Placing the hand controller back in place my personal remix is heard in the room.

She looks in my eyes speaking suggestively. "I will tie you up now."

"I'm looking forward to it." Agreeing to this is something I'd never do with any other. Yet, with Victoria I think it will help me know how far I can go with her. After what she's experienced, I need to know my boundaries. I also know how revolutionary this can be for not only her body, but mind…if she wields her powers she can heal.

"Put your hands together." Her voice and the beat of this song is hypnotizing.

I follow her wishes as she has me cornered on the bench raising my hands above my head. "I want you to tell me if it's uncomfortable."

I nod my head. "Are you sure you've never done this?"

She caresses my abs as if I am sculpture she formed with her bare hands. I watch her and she stops. "What?"

I don't want her to stop. She stands and walks and realizes the lights come on as she steps across the floor, she twists her body. "Romel, this room is fabulous."

I laugh not knowing she would say that. I had her in mind as I installed my many toys. I have dreamt about her being here for far too long. Knowing she is excited about it is exhilarating. She steps over, finding what she's in search of. As she is pacing toward me my heart rate is increasing. She stands between my legs.

"Romel, you are so sexy."

I bite my lip wanting her to do something anything besides look at me. I don't know if I will be able to take this for long.

She trails her fingers over my chest and she watches the reflex of my dick and she smiles. Damn. Victoria reaches hooking the blindfold to the bondage chains above my head and accidently finds something in the pocket overhead.

I chuckle. "What is this, Romel?"

My eyes roll to the top of my head. I hope she doesn't think I am...well, I don't know, I hope she doesn't freak out. She grabs the device, looking at it as if it is foreign. I have pictured it attached to her as it records her sex sounds. She lowers, rubbing her wet pussy over my dick. Oh shit. "What is this, Romel?" I'm panting as she grinds, teasing me.

"It's a clip-on microphone. You can attach it to your bra or leave it up there."

She blinks her eyes. "Why do you have this?"

"You like music loud and I like..." My eyes survey her slow grinding. She knows her winding her body is doing something. She stomps her foot.

"Well...finish, Romel."

My voice lowers. "To hear you in my ear loud, it excites me. You can hear your voice." Her head tilts as the slow intro of another song seems to grab her attention.

She fidgets until her finger presses a button. Victoria speaks in a whisper, "This turns you on?" She's fucking with me too much. "Turn it off."

She stands. "Wait, Vic, if you get the mic, I want something."

"What?" Her hand glides over the leather upholstery. I think it's safe to say she likes the feel. I know she likes the color, it's her favorite.

"Push that button." She leans above my head and presses until the lights beam. Her eyes lift as her mouth drops seeing the deep purple velvet curtain unveil the wall.

"No fucking way!"

She sees her reflection, and she walks closer to the wall mirror. I know how much she enjoys looking at herself.

She is standing before me, caressing her hourglass figure reflection. She speaks softly. "This really turns you on doesn't it?"

She does not understand how much she's turning me on.

Victoria walks as I keep my eyes set on her. "I will keep the mic, you and I will both enjoy the mirror."

Her voice can make me do anything right now. I gulp, desperate for her to touch me. I went overboard installing this shit. I only thought about driving her wild, not me. She lowers her body and finally she's contacted my skin.

She kisses around my neck with her soft lips making certain that her wet juices drip upon my skin.

My breath is increasing, and she spreads her fingers like a fan, gripping my chest. Her tongue circles until she bites my skin, I moan, "Victoria."

She inches down, her touch gripping me, pressing into my skin. Until she grips my balls and my stomach caves at her touch, I don't know if this is a good idea but it feels so good.

She flicks her precious tongue out. Oh my fucking god. She lifts my testicles and my eyes roll to the top of my head. She's motioning for my legs to spread and she's clawing my inner thighs.

"Stop teasing me!" I jerk the chain mounted to the wall panel. Taking in a deep breath, why did I agree to giving her this much power over me?

She giggles, shaking her head going against my request. I keep breathing so hard and she is doing something…something I didn't expect. She wants me in her mouth, I see it in her eyes. She is teasing me with her tongue around my shaft. I told her not to tease me. She sucks my tip and I hear her fucking slurping sounds and I will not be able to control myself long.

Her honey voice rings in my ear, "Romel, you are growing."

I am moaning, trying to think about something else. She wraps her hand along my dick. *No, Victoria, don't…I am shat-*

tering inside. The more she licks the longer I grow, and it turns her squirming ass on, she's grinding my leg. Sweeping her tongue, stroking her hand up and down… I jerk my hand realizing she's trying to make me break. I shout her name, "Victoria!"

Fuck no, why did I put Chris Brown on this playlist? Not now. "Take You Down" echoes and she's in her own world, ignoring me while gaining power from controlling me and pleasing me. She's beautiful.

Victoria moans, her voice is embedded in my head. My toes curl as she caresses my balls like she owns my shit. She stops and I am panting to catch my breath. She's not finished. "Victoria…what are you doing?"

She reaches above my head for the blindfold. Seeing her against the purple tufted wall panels arouses me. Wait, I thought she forgot about that item. I am shaking my head. "Babe, no, don't."

"Safe word?"

I muffle between my teeth. "No safe word." She lifts my head. She's driving me insane, but I love it. As she eliminates my ability to see I know she is more than comfortable with me. I know her actions will be a constant erotic surprise as I am unaware if she will give me pain or pleasure. Damn, she's amazing.

Victoria

I FEEL like a porn star in Romel's 'pleasure sanctuary,' as he calls it. I don't know how long he's had this room, but every detail displays my likes. Covering his eyes is the best thing for me at the moment. Dominating him is doing something to me internally. My anxiety is eradicating and his willingness to yield to me makes me adore him more. From what I have seen of this man, being in control is his domain, but he freely agreed to me. Choosing where I want my body to go, uncertainty enters my thoughts...not about my body, but about whether I can take his entire length in my mouth. Lowering between his legs, he is pulling the chain and I whisper. "Do I scare you, Romel?"

I'm calling the shots now, mister.

I grin while slurping his skin. His breathing intensifies. "No, baby, not at all." This microphone picks up his sultry sounds, adding to the intense sensation growing inside of me. I cup my hand like a tube against my lips, wrapping my mouth around his glorious shaft and I can see every vein build. Damn, his dick looks like art work. My mouth joins my hand and slides up and down.

Up and down.

I spit on his dick and he growls, "Victoria!"

I think he loves my lips sucking his skin.

I am making him lose it. Watching him crumble over me pleasing him is empowering. I release my hand, rubbing his million-dollar spot, feeling the ridges as I continue to suck him. I hear him moan, "Your mouth is mesmerizing, Vic."

I release my lips and whisper slowly, "Don't you cum, Romel." He jerks the chains on his wrists. I never knew he had so much constraint. This kind of massive pleasure is priceless.

I am taking his cock for a ride, sliding through my mouth, and he loves it. As I pay close attention to his sensitive head, he reels as my checks suck in. The suction sound echoes and he calls my name, "Victoria!"

My heart rate increases and I race after his cock with each lapping stroke. "Damn, Vic!"

Romel

VICTORIA IS SLOBBERING over my dick, dripping spit out of her mouth. Her motions are so intense.

Her moans amplify the space as if I am in the ultimate sex chamber. I am flinching my leg as she sucks . Hearing her sloppy noises as she pops the head of my dick in and out her mouth is explosive. I can't hold my orgasm anymore. "Vic…" I growl gripping my fist.

She releases me and I am so thankful as I tailspin, spilling over before her. She has me posted up convulsing and I promise you I feel like asking this damn girl to marry me. "Fuck, Vic."

She rises, hungrily taking my mouth. Shit, letting her take control might need to happen on a regular basis. She just ripped my heart out and I am rising for the next occasion. "I need to feel you, Victoria."

A smile forms on her face. She notices the condom and pulls it out of the package placing it properly over my skin. She stands over my head and unlocks the chains, she's got her pussy in my face. I lose it.

VICTORIA

 y heart is racing, unleashing this man seems dangerous. He lifts me, carrying me to another corner and the lights follow him with each step he takes. These lights are extreme, highlighting this lovely chaise, it's tufted resembling the wall, but it's white. Interesting color choice.

He lowers my body, commanding me, "Turn over." I do as he says, desiring him without hesitating.

The mirrors in this room have me feeling myself. I lay on my stomach my skin brushes against the soft velvet chair. Romel lifts my ass in the air, dominating me with a deep thrust. I scream forgetting I have on a microphone, "ROMEL!"

I don't think him hearing me yell was a good idea, he is in full animal mode. He positions me. I turn my head seeing our reflection, we look beautiful. Romel, is a beast, losing it, but I love it. His abs are gorgeous, rotating. He pounds. I feel like I have to pee again. Oh, no not now. "Romel!"

He rushes inside so deep. "Let go, Vic!"

My body is on fire, shaking. He pounces over and over. He will not stop and I have no control. My body is contracting. I am squirming with great force and his strong hands grip me with no escape. How he makes my head spin in manic spells is beyond me. A sinful howl escapes my mouth, "Rom!"

Nothing I can say will stop this man. I'm screaming violent yells of passion.

A force is spilling over as if juice releases from me. I've made another soaking wet mess, passing over into another realm of existence. I feel like I have been spun around in complete bliss. Pleasure knows no limit in this space that only Romel escorts me to. This man is a savage I can't get enough of him.

ROMEL

I think it's safe to say Victoria's baptismal experience by hers truly has her looking like she's on her way to the ICU. My foot kicks open the door. Victoria's head is twisting as if she is going through an exhibit watching her surroundings. I place her on my bed and kiss her lips. Her hand touches my face.

"Don't do that." My ability to resist her is weakening the more I taste her and feel inside her warm juices. I shake off and step away, grabbing my dick. She is laughing.

"Romel?"

"Yes?" I pace to the closet and she's sitting as if she is feeling awkward.

"Why are we in this room?" My eyes widen. What? She thinks I would take her to Drew's room? I pull down a t-shirt and pajama pants for myself.

"This I my space, woman." She looks at the ceiling and spreads her hands back, laying on the bed. Finally, she looks comfortable. She smacks her lips. Victoria rises. Oh shit, I walk further in the closet turning the sound bar off.

"Romel!"

I shake my head. "It's nothing, babe, the microphone is

synced to the Bluetooth on my sound bar." Her fingers unlatch the clip and she removes her black bra. I take in a deep breath, controlling my thoughts away from her full breasts. My fingers reach for the microphone, placing it on my dresser as I digress.

Wrinkles form on her head and she falls back on my bed. I walk ahead pulling open the bathroom door. I like how relaxed she is around me. Setting the items on the counter, I prepare a bath for her. I hope I haven't ripped her insides. I need to talk to her to make sure I am not hurting her. She's yelling my name, "Romel"

I peek from the door. "What's up?"

Her eyes are blinking, and she points to my wall. "Is this wall insulated?" I chuckle, she's thinking about the wall panels in my other room.

"It serves that purpose. I don't need it. You can scream as loud as you want. Drew will not be here."

She shrugs her shoulder. "Black is your favorite color, huh?" It reminds me of my pops more than anything.

"Yes…it is, and purple is yours." I turn the water off and stride to my room lifting her from my bed. "I can walk, Romel."

I shake my head; we are not making this a discussion. "I can carry you…is there an issue?" She shakes her head in a bashful manner. I like holding her in my arms, plus after Chicago I will make sure she's straight after sex.

I lower her in the tub and she sighs as the water touches her skin. "Why do you do all this for me, Romel?"

"I want to…do you dislike it?" She shakes her head and shuts her eyes, lying back.

"Not at all."

I pace to the cabinet and grab a towel before passing her a washcloth. Lowering to my knees, she lifts bubbles are surrounding her and her skin is slightly revealed before her breast. Damn, her beauty is mesmerizing. "Vic…toria."

She snickers and then sighs, leaning back. "Rom."

I put my hand in the water and splash it. "Hey, stop it, woman!" She wipes her face, chuckling.

"You started...I know what Vic means." She narrows her eyes. "What is it Romel?" She lowers her head in the water and flashes up, with water dripping everywhere. This is so fucking sexy. Her hair is a curly, wet mess.

"Babe, after sex with me are you...do I hurt you?" She is lavishing her skin and the fresh tropical aroma fills my nostrils. She has a serious display.

"Afterwards, before, during...it can hurt but you don't give me the impression you are trying to hurt me. I can handle it. I can handle you, Romel. I love how you feel inside me."

She is washing her neck and I have a fucking hard on. She has no idea...I don't think. She keeps talking. "You don't rush inside of me...is that why you..." She is twirling her finger pointing at my mouth. "...make sure your marvel of a tongue demands my juices."

I blink, chuckling. "I only want to provide you pleasure, sweetheart, not hurt." I reach over, turning off the jets that she doesn't necessarily need. The water flow will increase at the floor of the tub and I know she will love me for it.

Her eyes bulge. "What did you do?"

I smirk. "Cut off the jets that aren't needed. Who taught you how to talk so damn erotic?" She is moaning and I think I might envy that water. My tongue runs across my lower lip. Her hand is gliding over her neck and she releases a sigh.

"Don't think crazy, mister..." I'm thinking alright, but not what she thinks. I stand and from the look on her face she's aware of my erection. I put my hand up motioning her to hold on. I walk out to the living area and pick up her purse and grab a chair from the kitchen table.

As I enter my room, I throw her purse on the bed and a book slides out. I look at the author, Brenda Jackson. I keep it in hand as I step to the bathroom.

I plant the chair and face her while she continues to bathe herself. I hold up the book.

"Is this how you know?"

She shakes her head. "Why did you go in my purse?" My shoulders lift.

"I didn't; it fell out when I tossed your purse on my bed. So, you enjoy reading from Ms. Brenda Jackson... Let's see what type of story this is." I read the back and my brows narrow. "The female in this book is named Victoria, and she falls for a dude name Drake."

She is shaking her head, snickering. "I love Brenda Jackson's books, they are my fave. It's a romance, but she's not this little weak female. I like that the couple...well both of them are tough." I can tell she has affection for reading, she carries her kindle like it's her second purse. I wonder how many books she reads. She inches down, sinking further in the tub and releases a deep breath. She makes time stand still as I study her face. Her eyes roam to the ceiling as if she contemplates her next words as her lips purse. "But I learned to talk erotic from my mother and aunts. I mean the books are stimulating, but my introduction to sex came from my mother, not a book, Romel."

I lean over. "Your mother?" I can't help myself, I have to see her reaction. My hand dives in the water and my fingers rotate the jet. Her eyes grow wide and she pulls her knees up moaning. Her eyelashes flash, confirming how much she adores that tickling between her lower lips. Victoria's voice is something I can listen to all night. Her eyes focus on me as she speaks.

"Yes, my mother and aunts." She clears her throat and completes her statement, "They are open minded, some might call it. It's our tradition in our family."

My look has to be drawing her to continue talking because I am curious as fuck. "What do you mean tradition?"

"My *papi*—"

I cut her off. "You call your father *papi*? Vic, you can't call me *papi*. First you were looking at me like I was your brother, then you had the friend lens. I don't want you thinking of me as your father."

She is laughing, relaxing as the jets rush against her body. "Romel, all the women in my family call the guy they love or their hubby *papi.*" I reposition, hearing her words. "It's like you calling me baby or sweetheart. Trust me, the only thing about you that makes me think of about my father is your complexion…well, and your height. Wait, also your demanding side." Her eyes have an 'Oh fuck look.' Please don't tell me I look like her ol' man.

She relaxes her face. "It's cool, Romel…you two have similarities but I don't think of you as my father." I think we should switch the topic.

"Well, I guess it's cool you have a bond with your mother to talk about sex. Does this mean you would talk to her about what we do? Shit, if your ol' man knew what I did—"

Victoria interrupts me and throws water on me. "No, you dick! We ask questions so we are confident about our sexuality." She stands from the tub and I pass her the towel. She continues and I can tell whatever they talk about helps her not have any shame walking around me. "My mother didn't want me to learn from another person. Of course, she doesn't teach me everything but my family has a unique tradition. All the females learn to please themselves; we are to understand our body parts and a man's body part."

"What about the guys?" She shrugs her shoulder drying off her body once more and wraps the towel around her hair. I help her exit and I am sorry my dick is not going down. She looks at me as if I am asking her to take me. She speaks with a sweet pitch. "I don't have a brother and my male cousins don't talk as much about sex, they are more protective."

I kiss her lips. I need a cold shower. "Victoria, I will take a bath…no a shower. I'll be out and we can eat." *Food,* shit. I keep looking at her like I am about to devour her ass. Damn. I reach to get her the t-shirt from the counter. She smiles and steps away.

"Okay, Romel…I'll wait in your room." This will be a long night.

VICTORIA

$\mathcal{W}$alking in his room feels like another side of him I don't know. It's such a distinguished room. The plush bed is simple with a silver platinum comforter. He doesn't have too many pillows, but the subtle, black wall panel spices up the room. It's bold but sophisticated…it's Romel. I wonder if his mother suggested this sleek look. I grab my purse and fumble around until I find my bra and panty set. Jasmine was kind and smart for suggesting I bring a second pair. She knows me well. Sliding into my lace panties my mind wanders. Where are my other panties and the dress I was wearing earlier? I snake my arms through the t-shirt Romel gave me, feeling relief. This shirt is so soft. I can hear the water blasting from the faucet in the bathroom. I walk out to the living area spotting my panties and dress spread across the floor. I would hate for Drew to walk in seeing my items dispersed on the floor. I lean over, picking up my items and set to return to Romel's room. This apartment is so tidy.

I pass by the kitchen, noticing grey panel cabinets and stainless-steel appliances. It's defiantly a kitchen for a guy. I step inside and pull open the refrigerator door. He has food for us. We need to stop having sex so we can eat. I hear Romel's feet stepping from the bathroom. Shutting the door, I pace to the room, my eyes focus on his beautiful catalogue of abs that are just screaming for me to touch them. I take in a deep breath appreciating that he put pants on. "You look comfortable." He smirks and walks toward me.

"You're rather comfy yourself, *senorita.*" He sounds adorable speaking Spanish. I think he wants to eat in the living area. I turn and walk out the room, he's pacing behind me. Someone is knocking at his door. I flash my eyes and turn my head. "Are you expecting someone?" Someone is saying something, but I have no clue.

"Yes, go answer the door." I am a guest, why is he asking me to answer the door and I have on a freaking t-shirt without my bra. He nudges me. "Go, I will warm up the food and set the table."

I roll my eyes and step to the entry. Extending my arm, I pull the door open. A female is standing hold a vase with a beautiful floral arrangement. "Hi, are you Victoria?"

Smiling, the lady passes me the lilies. I think she knows I am the person she's seeking. My eyes are captured by the deep pink petals and lush green leaves. This elegant bouquet was well thought of by Romel. I turn seeing him set the table. "Romel, these are beautiful." The purple petals next to the dark purple calla lilies have so much elegance and mystery at the same time.

He pulls the chair for me and grabs the vase, centering them on the bar. They stand out, perfectly surrounded by the grey. He sits across from me and I stare in his dreamy eyes. Romel is perfect in a rough around the edges kind of way. Where did all this food come from? I only saw a salad in the fridge. He has steak, grilled chicken, and smoked wings. I shift my eyes noticing corn on the cob, wait is someone else coming over here. I shake my head and reach for my glass of water.

"Romel, do you drink?"

"Yes." I have never seen him drinking.

"When?"

He chuckles. "Typically when I am around others that drink."
I know this guy is hungry, but he is not getting anything until I
have my plate prepared.

"Did you take etiquette classes as a child? I am not being
funny..." He clears his throat turning his head away laughing.

"Pardon me...Yes, I did. Am I making you uncomfortable?"

"No, it's not that. You do things I am familiar with."

Etiquette is required if one wants to be a dancer, so I grew
up with it. "I have always noticed your charming ways." My
shoulders shrug "I just never mentioned how you...well you
know. You're a sweetheart, a gentleman." He looks across the
table listening to my words. It's hard looking at him without
thinking of feeling his body against me, inside me, rushing my
senses like heat flashes. "Do you want anything else?"

I shake my head. "No, I'm not eating all this food." I can't
eat all this.

"BABE, I know that I just wanted it to be enough. I eat a lot
but..." His lips display the biggest grin.

"Yes, you do!" But I am not complaining. He smacks his
lips and reaches for wings and a steak. He stands, grabbing a
salad from the bar. "What's different from my salad and
yours?"

He shrugs his shoulders. "Not that much, mine has a variety
of greens and different vegetables that keep me up on my
vegetable intake." He lowers flexing his arms, I can't tell if it's
naturally or because he is trying to make a statement. I think he
needs to put on a damn shirt. I am trying to eat and his body is a
distraction.

"You don't eat dressing on your salad?"

He is laughing. "No, sweetheart, you have never noticed

that?" I feel awful, I have known him over a year, and I did not pay attention. My eyes bulge.

"No!"

"You really looked at me like a friend...damn you had a wall up. Don't look at Romel." He turns around lifting from his chair reaching for the dessert plates. "I can't forget the main dish of the evening...besides you of course." I grin, watching him place the slices of the cake I made before us. Romel takes the fork, and he inserts a mouthful between his full lips.

"Damn, babe, this cake is so moist... oh its good."

I grin. "Romel, dessert is after dinner, not prior." He swallows his serving.

"Royalty eats dessert before, princess." I chuckle, and he leans the fork to me. My lips part and as my eyes shut, heat radiates inside of me. I don't think I can eat red velvet cake the same. Man, he's perfect.

He picks up his wing, pulling it in the opposite direction. He is twisting as if he is deboning the meat. "You like spicy food?"

He licks his lips. "I like flavor, taste." He places the meet in his mouth and sucks his finger. My head falls back as he is wiping his mouth with the napkin laughing. "I know it's not proper Vic...toria, but it's me."

I laugh shaking my head. "No, it's not that. Watching you eat reminds me of other things, that's all."

His head drops and he steps away from the table giving me a side look. "Come on, Victoria...I'm not trying to make you."

He sits in the chair. "Stop looking with that look in your eye...you're gonna get something between those thighs. Behave, woman!" I moan and my fingers wrap around my neck and I am twisting in the chair.

"Should I eat at another time, Vic... shit if I hear you say 'Rom' I am excusing myself from the table. Yo ass is wild." I am laughing trying to eat my food.

"No Ro...mel. I am fine." Placing my hand on the table I plead. "Don't leave."

I bat my eyes and change the topic. "I take it you have studied the Victorian language of flowers."

He nods. "Yes, I have." This man eats like he is making love to every piece of meat he slides in his mouth. I need on blinders.

"Romel, a woman can get pregnant watching you eat." He has his glass in hand, trying not to spill the drink, and bursts out laughing.

"Babe, come on...it's the same way watching yo ass dance." What? "Shit, you have people redirecting their fucking life trying to make way for you." Is this how he feels?

"Romel, what do you mean?" He is chewing his food, so I wait for him to reply.

Clearing his mouth, he looks in my eyes. "You look beautiful, that's all; it's not an insult."

I complete eating my salad, collecting my thoughts. Has he been waiting on me this entire time? My phone rings and I excuse myself from the table. Romel keeps eating and I walk to the room grabbing my purse. I reach for my cell.

"Hello?" It's my sister. She sounds so sweet. I have been wrapped up on focusing on me, I forgot to call. She is running her mouth, talking about counseling. I walk to the window and pull the curtains away to reveal the city below; magic! It looks so pretty. "I'm happy for you."

She keeps talking more and more. I think counseling is helping her because she sounds happy. "Did you win?" Oh my gosh, she won first place. "Where is *Papi* or *Mami*?" My mother is by her waiting to speak. "Congrats. I love you and I am so proud of you!" I blow her a kiss and my mother gets on the phone. Her voice sounds so concerning. *"Hola madre, como estas?"* My mother is very serious... Did I do something? I gulp and she tells me they will not have the money in time for my tuition. This is strange, I thought P*api* paid it. "No problem, *Mami*. I talked to the financial aid officer and I have a statement saying my payment is paid. I thought you all paid it." I was trying to pay it with the money I won from the competition.

This is weird. I don't know what to say, but I know I am not getting rid of the receipt. I will have to ask India to look into it. She works in that office maybe she can sneak and find out. *"Mami,* I am on a date."

She sounds alarmed. "No, you do not know him. I have mentioned him before. His name is Romel."

"Romel Adcock, *Mami* let me get off the phone, I am being rude." She is blowing me a kiss and telling me to be safe. Oh my, I think I am worrying her. *"Mami* send *Papi* my love. I will call you tomorrow." I end the call and walk back to the dining table. Romel is no longer sitting. I hope he isn't upset. I look up, hearing the door knob unlock from the room. I need to stay the hell away from that room. Romel is looking in my eyes with concern.

"Hey, are you okay?" Why is he asking me, if I am okay? I am fine. He walks to the table clearing his plate. "I was putting the microphone away. I came in the room and grabbed it."

I help him pick up items from the table. I feel like I am going through something I don't understand. He puts the glass down. "Babe, I can handle this. Go relax, I'll be in the room." He is most understanding; I don't think he enjoys seeing me stressed.

ROMEL

$\mathcal{I}$ walk in the room holding my cell, speaking to my mother. "I am with Victoria now. Let me call you tomorrow. Love you, beautiful." Victoria snuggles under the covers reading a book. It must be a good story. She has her eyes glued to the words of the novel. Pulling the cover back, I lower my body. Damn wait where is the t-shirt?

"Vic, where is the shirt, I gave you?"

She points to the dresser without talking. I shake my head and put my hand in the middle of the pages. Her eyes look like fire is about to come out. "Excuse me, *senorita*."

I bat my eyelids and she chuckles.

"*Papi* what is it?" She is not in this bed whining, topless.

I tilt my head and motion my hand. "I suggest you go retrieve the shirt I gave you. I just got finish cleaning the couch from the mess we made and in the sanctuary." I shake my head and she is amused snickering. "Put that damn shirt on. I need boundaries. You sleeping in the bed is already fucking my head. Plus, my date with you is at five in the morning."

Her face is still. "What? No, Romel, I am not going on a five o'clock in the morning date. You need to let me rest, mister."

I chuckle. "Okay, I will change the time, but it's still in the morning. I have to go to work, babe. I need you to put on the shirt and we can talk, put the book away." She flips over like a happy little school girl. I watch her walk to get the shirt and she is slipping it over her body, teasing me. I narrow my eyes. "Okay, your actions will cause me to break this damn bed with yo ass. Stop playing." She laughs and crawls in the bed snuggling next to me.

Victoria

ROMEL'S BED IS COMFORTABLE, it's like I am at a hotel. What the hell does he do to afford this stuff? His fingers lace between mine. "Does your mother know me?"

He smiles nodding his head. "Something like that…she knows of you." Interesting, he told his mom about me, I assume he was speaking to her while I was reading. My brows rise pondering what has he told her.

"What does she know?" I told my mother his full name tonight when she called.

"She knows how I feel about you." He talks to his mother about his feelings? I have never met a guy that talks to his mom. I guess that explains why he speaks to her candidly.

"You are close to your mother?" He looks in my eyes giving me all his attention.

"My brother and I both are…and Drew." His hand rests on the back of his head. I think he is trying to relax. How is it he can sleep topless, but I have to have on a shirt? I lift the blanket. Oh, he has on those pants…I guess.

"Romel, Drew is your brother?

"Mostly… not biologically, but he's family. His family and my family are one."

I think it's strange I have known him for so long, but he doesn't know much about my family. Besides about my great-grandparents, Tatiana knows about him more than my parents. My father is extremely protective. He thinks me not having my car on campus will somehow stop me from seeing guys. Maybe that's why I don't talk to Romel much about him. Chica and Chantal know my family, we are practically all family. I guess that's what he means about his relationship with Drew. Hell, this is the first time I have even come to his place, but he has been at my apartment several times. Romel is staring at me. I push his shoulder he grins, and he interviews me.

"Do you have siblings?"

"Yes, I only have a sister. My baby *hermana* is sixteen and you've met Jasmine. Back home, I have another, her name is Chantal." I giggle saying her name. Chantal and I debate often, not as much since we have graduated from high school. She loves being in control. But I love her. "Jasmine and Chantal are my sisters from another mother. We met in middle school." My fingers cross and I tingle as Romel's touch is felt on my skin. He kisses the top of my head.

"So, your parents have two children."

"Yes, we are our father's princesses." His chest is moving as he laughs.

"What's so funny?"

"You're a daddy's girl."

I turn over facing him and he pushes my hair back. "I am not."

Am I a daddy's girl? I know Tatiana is. "Does he call you princess?"

I roll over and fold my arms. He faces me sideways and runs his fingers through my hair. His touch is perfect. I roll my eyes. "Why does it matter if he calls me princess?"

He has a sly look in his eyes, it's attractive. I lean in to kiss his soft lips and his hands trail to my hips. He mumbles between our mouth. "Would he be opposed to Princess Victoria being with a guy like me?" My heartbeat jumps, at the question. My eyes roam the ceiling.

"I...don't know. He's never met a guy I like. My dad is over-board protective."

He hasn't been himself since I was kidnapped. I hear it in his voice, he is disappointed with himself. How was he supposed to do anything he wasn't even there?

"My entire family is protective, I can relate. Your ol' man just loves you, princess." Ugh, he is teasing me.

"Is your father—" Oh shit, I forgot. Why did I ask him about his dad? I typically just listen to him if he brings him up. He never talks about him long but enough for me to know he's no longer alive. "Forgive me, Romel."

"It's cool." He takes my hand and places it over his barrel chest. "My father is inside me...he always is because he lives and breathes inside me through my blood. You can ask me about my father. Don't apologize." I grin and realize he is such a generous guy. How could anyone not love this monument of a man?

"I love your perspective of life. How you find beauty in ugly, stars in dark skies? I think it's perfect." He smiles in a humble manner, awaiting my question, I believe. "Was your father protective?"

He laughs. It's like he is recalling a memory. "My father is still protective... When we were kids, Rico and I, my father made sure our home was small. I mean it wasn't tiny like a shack or anything, it was enough space. He wanted to always know we were close by and he wanted us to learn to live with each other. He said, he didn't want us living in a house not knowing who our family members are. I don't know, Rico said he didn't talk much about his family besides Uncle...I mean Drew's pop."

"Well, why do you and Drew have such a large apartment at least two more people can live here?" My eyes glance over recalling the site of a second hanging TV in the corner near the indoor waterfall wall fixture. It's so serene in there; if they didn't have two flat screens, I'd imagine it as a meditation room. The bottom line is this apartment is big.

He chuckles. "We want it for personal reasons." Does Drew have a play room or something? I am not asking him that, but it is not stopping me from thinking it.

"It's nice you are close to your father." A tear rolls from his eye and he is not ashamed. "I still think you are a momma's boy."

He laughs and speaks in a cheery tone, "I am concerned about my mother. I love her; she's the only mother I have. Her name is Roselyn. You remind me of her, especially when we fight." Oh, now I definitely have the wrong impression about his mother.

"You fight your mother, Romel?" I am not waiting for an answer; my head takes a double look away from him.

"Victoria, what is wrong what did I say?"

I am breathing heavy; I can't look at him right now. Why would he fight his mother? My head is spinning thinking of what Jasmine has gone through with her step-dad. What I went through, my sister went through, I will not submit to a dysfunctional relationship.

"I am leaving, Romel."

Did I hear him correctly?

"What did I say, baby? Tell me?" He is wiping the tears from my eyes and he lifts my chin.

"Romel, I will not be in a relationship with someone that physically abuses women."

He lets out a quiet chuckle, looking confused. "What?" Realization hits him and Romel takes in a deep breath. "I can let you talk to my mother to confirm this, if you want, but I'd never abuse a woman. My mother and I would train. You know, defensive training fight, just like what you and I do, Victoria."

"Romel, *perdóname*. Forgive me for accusing you of such an awful act." How stupid of me to think he fought his mother. I am on edge.

"Baby, why didn't you just ask before assuming I meant I physically fight my mother?

"Romel, I misunderstood your words." I take in a deep breath. He wraps his arms around me I think I could live in this one spot.

"Babe, you have to ask me things... I want you to trust me."

He's been nothing but forthcoming with me about everything. "Romel, I will." He leans over kissing the top of my head. I guess we should get some sleep, I have an early date with him. If he will still have me.

VICTORIA

I can hear Romel in my ear but I am ignoring him. "Wake up."

I twist, pulling the cover over my head, sinking into the comfort of the king-size bed. Feeling like I am lying on clouds does not encourage me to want to leave. "Not now, Romel." His arm is creeping across my hip and my fingers grab his wrist pushing it off the blanket separating him from touching my skin. "Don't, Romel, I don't want to wake up, for real." He pulls me near his chest. The touch of his skin is electrifying. I smile as he leans over, licking my stomach. I push his head back and as I turn, he rises with a pillow in hand, hitting me in the head. My hair flares and I turn grabbing my pillow.

"No, you didn't." I slam the pillow across his shoulder and he laughs. I jump on top of him and his fingers slide from my thighs to my breasts. I grab his face and his morning breath doesn't scare me away. I am craving him. His fingers slide through my hair and he flings me over kissing under my neck, down to my waist. I clench my stomach muscles. "No fucking."

He grips my ass, pulling my panties. "Why are you naked?"

"I have on underwear."

His chest is moving as he comes after me. "No, I told you to keep on the shirt." Romel lifts, pushing my panties down and he takes my legs in the air, spreading them out like a fan. He looks at me with his bedroom eyes. "That shy girl shit needs to stop."

He keeps moving my legs contemplating on how he wants to take me and it's driving me wild. He falls between my legs, reaching for my arms and I wrap them around him. He walks in the bathroom carrying me, planting my cheeks on the counter. He pulls out a toothbrush in the middle drawer and I'm laughing. His voice is playful. "I told you to get up. I guess this is how I'm waking you up."

He opens the container pulling out the item. I snatch it out of his hand and he moves to the second sink brushing his teeth. I watch him, staring at his reflection in the mirror. My clit is throbbing after this man. I moan while I am brushing my teeth. As he finishes cleaning his mouth, I spit, turning on the water as I rinse my mouth. I watch him walk to the wall, pressing the digital in wall receiver. Music from his sex playlist echoes through the room. It's safe to say Romel can read my eyes.

He stands behind me, placing his hands on my hips while his lips chase down my neck to my shoulder. I am panting, moaning. He knows I am aching for him inside of me. "Rom."

"I asked you to wear my shirt. You took it off on purpose."

I'm squirming in front of him as his hard erection grows, looking at the reflection of us in the mirror is more than turning me on. His hand is lowering, gripping as I am dripping between my legs. I'm addicted to this man and I can't keep my fingers off of him. Romel leans me back on his chest as his hand creeps to my neck he whispers in my ear, "I'm eating this for breakfast."

He certainly knows how to get my heartrate up; every morning will start this way with this man. He slaps my hip, motioning for me to turn around. I surrender to his gesture as he lifts me in the air, sliding my clit across his tongue. "Lawdy, lawwwwwd." This savage is so nasty… but so good.

My body lowers and I'm hanging from him with my head facing the mirror seeing our bodies grinding. His voice is hypnotizing me deeper in his spell. "Damn, you're beautiful, Victoria."

I love this; he lifts me again to his champion tongue. He has so much strength, holding me in the air French kissing my lower lips.

He never leaves me, placing me on the counter he falls to his knees. He is touching all over me and I don't want him to stop. I'm losing everything with him.

"Your walls...remember me,"

I want him inside me so bad, I need him now. He reaches for a condom in the middle drawer. He takes the latex and I whimper. I'm throbbing, pulsating as I merely look at his length. He widens my legs. "Open for me."

His voice is like a damn remote, controlling what he desires. He slides inside so deep. I can feel this man so deep in my chest and I growl. "Ugh, Rom...Romel!" I clench, gripping him within my walls.

Romel moans and sets his eyes on me. He whispers, "Ahhh, Vic, I see you."

I clench again and he smiles, growling louder, my nails dig in his skin and he grips my ass. He is thunder clapping me over and over, it's so sexy.

Romel moans louder. "Again, Vic...squeeze it again." He takes my legs as if he's shifting gears and he rotates his hips. I'm shivering, his sweat is dripping on my skin and I roll my eyes to the top of my head. This is beautiful hearing Romel's wicked moan elevating in my ear. "Squeeze my dick again, Vic." I grant his wish and he thrusts deep, deep inside. Our bodies smack echoing, this feels so good. The noise he creates as he penetrates me is so surreal. I squeeze my wall and he thrusts deeper. I'm at my peak, gasping for air, spilling over his dick. I moan, squeezing my pussy. "Rom."

His rhythm is vigorously growing, our moaning and groaning

increases. Romel fills me so deep our sounds resemble a whoopee cushion as he slaps, slaps until my muscles relax in his arms. I'm spinning in a drunk spell and he grins.

"Rom, you are so good."

He grips my hips and kisses me, taking my breath away. I turn seeing my hair is drenched like a washrag. How did this shit happen?

ROMEL

I open the car door and Victoria's face is glowing. "You bought me a gift!" I shake my head. This girl loves gifts; it is her love language. I have seen her freak out when Jasmine gives her the smallest item. I lean over and pass her the box. She takes the top off, grabbing the items inside. She pulls out her attire. "Aww, Romel, you bought me an outfit for our date!"

She rubs my chest and stands on her tippy toes. I lower my chin to kiss her. She teases my bottom lip and I grip her shoulders. "Hey, no teasing me, woman."

She shakes her head. "You are so sweet I love this outfit."

She lowers her body and twists, putting the box in the back seat. I hear her yelling. I assume she found the shoes. I shut the door and walk to the driver's side. She has her foot in the shoe acting as if it's Christmas. "Babe, it's just gym clothes. I can't concentrate with the tiny outfits you put on."

She snaps her head. "There is nothing wrong with how I dress. It keeps your attention."

I start the car. "Vic, you look great all the time, babe. You have no problem with getting my attention."

I grab her fingers, kissing her hand. "I am making a request...help me concentrate and don't wear this dress you have on to the gym today. Considering what took place with you wearing this." I shake my head and bite her lip. She moans.

"Okay, Romel... I appreciate the outfit and I love these shoes; they match perfect." This girl is like a kid with gifts.

———

MY FIST SWINGS at the punching bag and I lift my eyes seeing Victoria. She looks so chipper in her white rose camo leggings. I am laughing at her touching her breast walking in my direction. She cannot help herself; she speaks in a singsong pitch. "So do you like my sports bra? It matches my pants."

"It's cool...I notice you didn't wear the shirt."

I bought her a top that resembles the dress she wore to my house. She flicks her tongue out teasing. "I looked at all the rips in the shirt and thought it might break your concentration." Her tongue is breaking my concentration. She adjusts her gloves and keeps running her little sexy mouth. "I like the shirt." She winks her eyes and waves me a kiss. "I'll wear it another day."

I post in the middle of the room; come on, Vic, you were hitting me in the bed...let's see if you can talk shit now. She is pacing around me. "Romel, you are bigger than me." I grab my dick...she grins.

"You didn't have a problem with that before. Come on, girl." I shake my head. "I told you not to think like that, babe. Be confident like you were in that damn mirror." I rotate my stomach as if I am drilling inside her guts. She laughs. I keep jumping in place. Jabbing, her reflexes are great. Come on, one two swing. She repeats my act, throwing her right fist followed by her left. Her foot work looks nice. I am salivating after her, I need to hit her. I swing jabbing her in the stomach and she lowers. She looks at me like she might want to fuck me up for hitting her. I punch her once more and she blocks me. I grin but nothing on her face is smiling. Good, she's getting focused. We are both bouncing, dancing around swinging and dodging.

"You know you can burn over four hundred calories boxing."

She nods. "Yes, I know but you won't because I am kicking your ass!"

She is buffing her fist. "Warm up, face off...come on, Romel!" Victoria gets closer to my face and I have to move fast.

"Hey, you almost hit me, woman!" I plant my feet and pick her up throwing her on the mat. She jumps up growling, where did all her energy come from? She's like a firecracker. She kicks me in the knee, and I bend. Victoria punches me on my side and right hooks me in the jaw. I frown...okay she is playing with her right hand. She throws her hook and I jab her in the stomach. She lowers and grabs my dick.

I put my hands in the air. "Hey, hey...no punching low unless you blowing low!"

She chuckles and teases, rolling her neck. "All is fair in love and war."

I lower my chin. "You are going to be trying to kiss it out, if you hurt my fucking dick." She walks up to me as if I am a baby. I push her in the head. "Stop that shit."

She stomps her foot. "Romel."

"What, woman?"

She walks off. "Your mouth!" I run, lifting her from behind, holding her in the air.

"What...what about my fucking champion mouth?" She is balancing herself in my grip, laughing. I plant her on the floor, and she jabs me in the jaw. I burst out laughing. "Losing to you is so precious." She jumps up and her fist is fucking fierce coming at my face.

I stumble back, damn she is turning me on. "Babe, how did you jump that high?" Victoria has the biggest grin displaying on her face. I grab my nose. She looks at me with a mischievous stare.

"Are you okay, Rom?"

I tilt my head. "Yes, babe, you look great out there!"

She smirks and her eyes are dancing. "Yes, I do, don't I." I smack my lips, she's feeling herself. Her sweaty body comes closer to mine and I can't help myself, I've been daydreaming about her pussy. Shit. I lower, pecking her salty lips. "Okay, go take a shower so we can go on our date."

She snaps. "Romel, I am not taking a shower here. I prefer to go to my place." She is so picky about this, I am not arguing. She claims the late-night crew does not clean the locker room like the morning crew. I shake my head not having the same issue. I think it has more to do with the fact that the girl that works here has a crush on half the men that workout at the gym. She just takes it out on the females. I take a deep breath. "I have to take a shower here, babe."

She nods her head. "I understand your little girlfriend more than likely cleaned your locker room." Her hands rise in the air and I am laughing at her being dramatic. "You are going to work. I will wait for you on the treadmill. We can go out for lunch." I watch her sexy walk, pushing the door she turns facing me. "I'll wear something revealing." I bite my bottom lip. Revealing... I go to the locker room daydreaming about my Vic.

VICTORIA

$\mathcal{W}$alking outside the air is stale; it's still dark and I am ready to go back to sleep. Romel drives off and I lower my eyes to my iPod, leaning against the building. I hear the engine of his Mercedes, seeing Romel drive to the curb he lets the window down. His truck matches his sexy self. "Victoria, I think you should consider waiting inside. It's still dark out and I'd feel better if you went inside." I shake my head. I spot a message from Jasmine and reply.

I'm on my way home, don't get out the bed. XOXO

I press send as my head lifts, seeing a cab. "I am fine. You taught me well. The cab is behind you, anyway." He winks blowing me a kiss. "We will meet later, *papi.*"

Romel puts the car in park, trying to get out to assist me. "I will get the door for you."

I cut him off. "Romel, it doesn't help me to treat me like a victim. I am safe. You go to work; I will see you later." He looks at me with concern but agrees.

I will be fine. I just need him to know it. He exits the parking lot. My sneakers hit the gravel as I open the car door. Someone rips my bag off my shoulder, tossing it to the ground. With a jerk, someone squeezes my wrist behind my back as a hand is pressed over my mouth with a rag, gagging me. I am screaming but my muffled yells are not heard. My body feels heavy being forced away from the cab. What the hell is happening?

The weight in my legs is eliminating my will to walk. The sound of a loud door unlocks behind me and my body is forced on the floor of a van.

"Please," I mutter, "Stop. Let me go."

My words slur. Pushed forward, someone releases my hand. My mouth has a dry bitter taste.

I'm pounding against the steel floor; peeking through, I look around and I can't see, everything is dark. I feel the van speeding and my body moves with the force of the car turning. My eyes are not able to maintain being open, I feel like I am slipping away. I cry out for help... no one is coming. No one can hear me crying in my mind. I imagine, I am getting up reaching for the back door. My body is not moving; my eyes shut as the sunlight hits through the top window... nothing about the sunrise seems right. Where am I?

ROMEL

*V*ictoria being in the lead is not ideal. It's not the way a man of my nature has been taught, but exchanging power with her gave me life. It was as if she provided me the keys to what I'd been waiting on…the access to love her. She had me peering through her fucking window wishing after her, craving her. Drew might not get it, maybe one day he will. I take a drink from my water bottle as I move forward. Walking ahead I spot Drew and he motions to meet me on the rooftop. I think I need a second bottle of water, so I pace to the lounge before heading up and I catch sight of Uncle Jay.

I tilt my head and disregard the water and take the elevator. What is it now? As I step forward, I notice Angie with her head down. Her hair reminds me of a mop, but she looks sad. She speaks to me in a low pitch. "Hi, Romel."

I tilt my head and she is her usual self-talking as if I want to know her life story. "My baby died." My eyes grow wide; is she talking about Dwight? Her voice is breaking, and I am wondering if I should take her to H.R. She needs a counselor. The silence of the room becomes overpowered by her crying.

"My baby died in my…" She has her hand out, cupping her fingers and I pat her shoulder for comfort.

"My deepest condolences, I didn't know Dwight, Angie—"

She snaps and her eyes look at me with rage. "Dwight! Fuck him, he doesn't care about me mourning." I step back in the corner unaware of what is going on with her. She sobs and I just listen before I exit the elevator.

"My baby died in my hands last night. I fed him every day and laid him to rest in my back yard."

My eyes flick to the side, tell me she is not talking about that damn rodent. She continues, "Dwight was so upset with me. It's no secret he poisoned my baby and I will kill him." The elevator reaches my destination. She lifts her eyes and blurts out her words. "I was supposed to be going downstairs. I forgot to push the button. Thanks for listening anyway, Romel." I shrug my shoulders, yeah right. The door opens. Angie clears her throat. "I am having a ceremony in memory of squirrel, I will get you an invitation. Thanks."

I think I side with Dwight on this one, it was a fucking squirrel. I give her a fraction of a smile, unaware of how to respond about a creature that is supposed to be free, not caged like her personal pet. My feet move without hesitation, I don't think I have ever been that thankful to exit the elevator in my life.

FACING the doors that are shutting in front of me I recall Uncle Jay never comes here this early in the morning. I yawn and the step ahead as the gust of air hits my face. I open the door and turn, seeing Drew posted. My eyes look at the blue sky noticing the clouds. I've always enjoyed this view. I pace closer to Drew and we bump fists. He has a grin on face. "Shit call nine, one, one Drew!"

He leans over, laughing and sits across from me. "You and Victoria had a good time?"

I am smiling, feeling real good about life especially after escaping Angie's horror rodent tale. "Drew, Victoria had me walking around like shit." I straighten my shoulders prowling like a man of honor.

Drew interrupts, "Let me call the policeman. Did she rip yo shit off?" My eyes grow and

I laugh through my words. "Bruh, she had my ass tied up."

A frown forms on his forehead. "Wait, you let her tie you up?" He is in denial laughing. "No, you didn't."

I am nodding like a kid in the ice cream store asking for seconds. "Drew, if you would have walked in you would have seen me posted." Last night was everything with my girl.

I lift my arms in the air demonstrating and Drew falls over laughing. "I was tied, chained, blindfolded..." Drew is laughing hysterically. I continue speaking, "and you would have been on the cell making a report." My hand motions on the side of my ear as I pretend to be on the phone. "Shit the assailant is five foot seven. Come get her."

Drew hits at my knee laughing. "She ripped yo shit...I'm happy for you, Rom. She's a bad girl. I'm calling Rico to let him know."

I shake my head knowing he and Rico will have a blast talking about me. "Everything she did was top ten, bruh. She saw the mirror and found herself." We are laughing and our heads turns as we hear a noise. Drew switches his demeanor. We consider we might not be alone up here. I ask him a question.

"What was up with Stanley? I had him arranging things because we went to the gym this morning. He picked up some items for me."

He shakes his head. "Nothing, it's cool. I considered you would make it in. Stanley had me on the damn phone looking for shit with the codes late last night. He said you were with a lady and didn't want to disturb you."

I hear the door shut and turn my head seeing Stanley pace in our direction. I suspected Uncle Jay was coming up here. Stanley sits with the serious stare. "What's up? I noticed Uncle Jay."

His voice sounds like a marine dictating orders. Something is not right because he is controlling his voice. "Your uncle went to tend to something that is pressing."

Drew questions Stanley. "Are you going to tell us what's up or not? You all treat us like we are kids."

He leans over and we get closer. "We have some information, but I need you two to get me something." I can't take seeing another video.

I shake my head. "Stanley, I understand why you all are asking us I get that but after the last video. I can't... I want do it."

I know my triggers, if I see someone touch this girl, somebody is going to die. Stanley is demanding our help and Drew is going with what I say in support. He speaks low to Stanley. "What happened to the information we already gave the police? Why can't they make an arrest?" Drew's nostrils flare and I am aware he is getting agitated thinking about his father denying him from talking to the Charles guy. "We don't work for the police. My pops...wait you already know that Stanley."

I take in a deep breath. "We are men so let's not get childish; Drew has a good point. Why are we still searching for codes?"

He stands and paces around as if he is having a hard time thinking of what to say. This is unusual for him. I don't like it. Stanley sits and tugs his tie. "The men are here in Atlanta."

My face drops. "Why have the police not gotten them, Stanley? If you know they are here, it would seem like the safest thing to do is snatch them before something else happens." Drew grabs my knee knowing damn well I am not making a light threat.

Drew interrupts, "You can't tell us why you are asking for us to get this code, but you need us Stanley." He shakes his head. Nothing about this situation feels right.

"I'll agree this last time if Drew agrees. You are doing your job trying to keep us safe."

Drew interrupts and looks close to Stanley. "I know you are trying to protect more than our eyes can see. Something else is wrong...I can sense it."

Drew stands and the vibes he gives off confirms he is upset. He wants to work as a special agent, he's never uttered the words but it's what I understand he wants. Since my pop's death the idea of working with Charles will not be entertained.

It seems unfair to be a man yet be challenged about the path you desire to walk as a man. It doesn't seem fair, but I have to side with Uncle Senior besides my pops is not here and I know what that feels like.

I speak up in our moment of silence. "We will help."

Stanley tilts his head. "Go to the blue meeting room on the thirtieth floor. I have a group and the computers are set up."

He knew we would help that's why he had the group on standby. "How are we supposed to contact you?" Drew looks at me in a peculiar manner and he calls out to Stanley as he walks to the elevator. "We don't have access to our phones here?"

"I will be close by in the building. I will get you another phone that connects to me." He pulls open the door. We step to exit the roof top. Taking in a deep breath I am feeling exhausted from a conversation. Damn, I guess I won't see Victoria until after work.

ROMEL

$\mathcal{M}$y focus is on a team of men as I walk into the room. They all appear to be special skilled killers, the way they survey Drew and I as we move into the area is alarming. Their eye movement reminds me of my dad walking in a room. I chuckle, I bet they met my father. Something tells me this is bigger than Drew and I are being led to believe. The question is why are we being kept from the truth. Drew leans in my ear. "The masks on these men are thick, bruh." He senses the same thing. A female walks forward, she looks like Drew's type. I twist around she's the only female in here. When you are in this environment, all greetings are tossed to the side. We have work to do.

"Gentlemen we have an area for you here." She passes us separate phones as she gestures to our seats. "Dial one and you will be connected to Stanley. Any questions?" We shake our heads *no*. I step ahead and lower myself in front of a screen. This is high tech shit. The screens are split with four displays of nothing but codes running through.

A dude dressed in a dark suit passes us files. "You will need this." I tilt my head and open it, seeing a variety of codes and links. Drew whispers in my ear, "Rom, all of these link to the information we already provided."

"I know…what could we possibly be looking for now?" It's not like they tell us. We are just supposed to figure it out when we find something out of the norm and notify Stanley once we locate our findings.

I type in the code and one screen is a personal bulletin board display. An image of the first girl we saw when we entered this case pops up with several folders. I look over at the file and type in the next code, a video formulates in another file.

Here is the code that got us the purchaser information. None of this is new information. I sit back and fold my arms staring at the screen. Drew looks at my screen, it's identical to his.

"Do you see something?" I shake my head it's a repeated code the only thing that is different is the guy we gave the encrypted code to. "Of course, we don't know how that information helped them." I keep looking for codes. I type in a search on the dark web, maybe I will draw out another code. Drew is doing an extensive search.

"What are you looking for, Drew?" He shrugs his shoulder.

"I am searching locals. If they have come from here somebody has to be buying from here." I nod my head that's a good point.

"I'm looking for new codes on the dark web maybe a new video." He grabs my hand.

"Rom, I don't think you should."

"Drew, I already saw what they did to her. I will not flip out. I am looking to see if it's posted; if it is perhaps there's a buyer, if there is a buyer there is the seller."

Stanley did not say he wanted the seller, but if I cross him I'm taking his ass. I will just hand deliver him to Stanley.

VICTORIA

I'm trapped in a room that feels like it is spinning. My head falls in my palms and I blink my eyes, recognizing I am surrounded by other females. I think someone drugged me or something. The door unlocks and the women shriek, running to the other side of the room. I stay planted, leaning against the wall. I look up and shiver at the sight of the tattoo. He leans over, looking at me with a sinister glare. "Get up!"

I scream, raising hell I kick as he barges closer.

I shout, "Fire!" I'm just hoping someone hears me so they can alert the authorities. I don't want days to go by like the last time. I have to get away from these creeps. I kick and slap the guy. This is the bastard that had me in Dallas. He's pissed, holding an axe as he comes for me. A girl tries to help me and she risks her life, pulling at me. He swings. SPLATTT!

Blood sprays across the wall, the other ladies move further in the room's corner.

Two men come to take the dead woman away as red spills, trailing across the floor.

His hand comes for me, feeling on my body.

I shut my eyes. "You bitch! You had my men killed!" He yells as if he is heartbroken shouting like a mad man. "My family!"

Remorse is far from my thoughts with him...I wish him death.

"What is he talking about?" I shut my eyes, trying to shut him out from my thoughts and I remember. Shit, Jesse...well he didn't kill you. Lucky is what you are. He pulls my face close and I punch at his stomach, I claw my fingers at his tattoo and gouge at his eyes. He punches me, knocking me to the floor and the ladies scatter, making certain they stay out of his way. He is using me to torture them. The asshole places me in a chair and I snap. I'm not fucking scared of this bastard. If he's in mourning, he will take his time with me.

"What do you want from me?"

He laughs his voice is brutal. "Whatever I fucking want I will take from you." He calls out for one of his men. On demand a man dressed in black steps in; he looks so young. He smells like alcohol. "Take this one away and don't touch her. I want her for myself." I spit at him and he drags me out like a rag doll.

ROMEL

I am looking at my computer screen, it's well past six and I have not eaten since lunch. I figured I'd hold out for dinner with Victoria. My hand reflexes open as Drew tosses me a snack. If he throws me one more granola bar I will turn into one. Leaning back in my chair, I stretch. My monitor is making a noise and I can over hear a few people making a crowd. The glass wall does not hide their voices so I sit tight and eat this so called diversion from dinner.

It's the code and it looks like it links to the person who bought from the other seller. I point to my screen and Drew is pointing to his screen. We both found something. "Drew, what did you locate?" Our heads lift noticing a female's handbag on the screen. Why does that look like Victoria's bag? My screen is signaling me to look. I catch sight of an IP address I think this might be what I am looking for. I return my focus. "All right Drew, I have something."

I click and find a file. He is uploading a file. "Rom, did you notice how silent the room got?" I nod my head. I open a file seeing a transaction being made. The lady walks in and speaks to the group. She posts a note on the bulletin board and holds a remote in her hand.

"Gentlemen, based on our time stamp this is the guy we are looking for." I am looking at the screen. Drew speaks up, "I have four profiles; it matches the person based on the location of the time stamp."

She interrupts him. "Excuse me, how do you know these people you have profiles on" I interrupt her and stand, demanding the attention of the group. "Miss, their location matches based on what you provided. You can clearly see. The cell phone towers confirm they were all close enough to the location according to your time stamp."

I tilt my head and peek over at Drew. The time stamp is today.

Drew leans in my ear speaking low. "Rom, isn't that the gym?"

I narrow my eyes and turn, looking at the bag I witnessed seconds ago on the screen. *It's here?* This bitch is playing. I get up from the desk and walk in the room Drew, is watching me. I step closer to the table and pick up the bag. My hands pull out a purple laptop. I turn and my eyes meet Drew's. I walk out of the room and slowly step by Drew. The lady is updating the team and Drew speaks.

"So, what now?"

A gentleman looks up, speaking, "It's eight o'clock, no one is working on the detail we have gathered, if we call the cops..."

Stanley enters, he has a serious look. "We still don't have, proof calling the police will not be of use at this point." He has a stress ball in his hand. "Nice work, crew, at least we have narrowed down a few possible assailants. We will resume tomorrow."

I move away without speaking and my insides are on fire. I turn back and blurt, looking at Stanley in the eyes. Drew sees me and stays planted. "Stanley, you used me like a fucking puppet." Disrespected doesn't begin to describe how I feel.

Drew is walking closer, merging Stanley in between us; a few of the people are surrounding us in a circle. I step closer and my voice rockets. "Vic could be one of the girls being sold in those pictures. You have been distracting me all this time. How in the hell did you get her bag?" He can stand there and lie but I know it's her damn bag. "All this time you had us searching for shit. You made a decision to not alert me that you found Victoria's belongings outside the gym?" Stanley is silent staring, unapologetic.

The officer that brought this case to our attention speaks up, "We are uncertain about details. With her being close to you we didn't want to—"

I cut him off. "You keep this shit...from me!" I hit the wall in anger. Drew has an uncertain expression.

"Rom, what is it? Tell me, Stan, you did not keep this, not this information."

I storm off not knowing who to trust at this point. I must get out of here and Angie can help me get a clear phone line. Drew is yelling and asking Stanley to tell him something. I swing the door open and turn back exclaiming to clarify matters, "I'm done."

Walking out a few men are standing in my view; if they think they are stopping me they can try. A man stands in front of me he stretches his hand to greet me. "I know you don't know who I am."

He passes me a card. "Place this number in your cell. I'm a former CIA spy, requesting permission to tag along."

Drew steps out, and he is behind me breathing heavy in anger. I keep my eyes on the man.

"I'm Elliot and I know your father; it would be my pleasure to assist you unofficially."

I tilt my head "Give your info to Drew." I move forward and push the door heading for to the stairs to the roof.

Victoria

IT'S NOW night and I've been left lying next to a man that hopes to take me back to the house; I've been separated from the other ladies. I think spiting in his face might have triggered him in some manner. He said my behavior is not his way. My fingers continue to claw at the rope clenching my wrist together as I lay eyeballing the cell phone inches away from me. My mind ponders escaping staring at the dingy, crumbling walls in this room that echoes with pain. How many young girls lay here ripped of their bright smiles that once shone like the sun? What causes a person to be so evil that they start thinking of people as property?

Lifting my eyes to the sections of the ceilings that hang low I whisper a prayer.

Dios mio dios ayudame. My God, help me get out of this rope. Wriggling my body, I keep rotating my wrist, tears flow to the side of my face and my level of discomfort continues. My breathing is growing hysterical as I take in the claw under the man's neck. *Calm down, Victoria, push through.* How many are like him?

I keep rotating my wrist back and forth, loosening the rope. Bending one arm upwards stretching the bonds my wrists gives and gives and I have a lot of slack now. I can't stop, I must get away. My thumb is pulling between one strand and I am working it back and forth, back and forth, it's peeling it away from my skin. Friction is building and the sting from my sweat burns me on contact. I pause and I am breathing as calm as possible facing the low life that is seconds away from taking my existence. The rope still feels tight so I maneuver my thumb, my skin is perspiring and it's slipping as I try to grip the strand. *You can do this, Victoria, push through.* Finally, I pull, bending my arm upward further and I breathe as my heart pounds in my ear, my wrist is free from bondage. I want to run but something is telling me, not yet. I peek around noticing the trap he has created. There's a rope trailing from the night stand filled with empty beer cans and a syringe by a valve with foil wrapped around it. Shit, if I run to the bathroom the bells will sound off. I have to make a tactical exit. I lie still with my eyes shut, I'm just barely peeking through my eyelashes, trembling. *Be still, Victoria.*

He flips over and his back is toward my face, releasing the fumes of alcohol. He smells gross. I lie waiting for the best moment as sweat drips from my forehead. I wait praying this man keeps his back turned. I look at him, paying attention to his skinned head. They must be some gang; he has a small claw in the lower center of his head. It's like the man's in Dallas only his was on his neck.

In my head, I count to sixty on repeat, keeping time as I restrain the fear from seeping within. My thought to yell and kick this sorry excuse of a man in front of me is pressing. I want to scream and ask God why. Is this what forsakenness feels like? Why is this happening to me? My muscles tense as I pant, counting my last round in my head. He's been still for over ten minutes. *Stay ready, Victoria, push through.*

I have to escape but my limitations are high with the bell trap concoction. I gulp, taking in the sweaty stale air, I reach for the phone and place myself back in position. *Please don't wake up. Please, Victoria, don't freak out. Push through.* How am I supposed to call for help? What if this phone does not work? What piece of shit leaves a phone out? The shit next to me sleeping without a care in the world, high off of whatever he's been smoking. *Fuck it, I'm calling for help.* I press the screen and a light beams into the darkened room. *Fuck, fuck, please don't wake up.* I shut my eyelids, thankful the phone works. My heart is racing in fear, my trembling fingers press nine one one, a dispatcher answers.

"Nine one one, what is the address to your emergency?" I burst in silent tears. "I don't know," I mumble. I hope she can hear me. *Keep calm, Victoria. My throat is closing, it's as if the oxygen is being cut off while my heart pounds. A choked cry creeps through the face of my death.*

"Right across the street from a dollar store near Evans Mill." I don't know where I am I remember seeing Panola and felt the exit was not too far away. I saw a sign, it was a café, I think so. The dispatcher has a calm voice it helps me focus.

"What's the problem?" Everything! I'm next to my captor and if you don't get here I will die.

My voice is cracking through my short breaths. "I've been abducted."

"Are you at the dollar store?" No I am near the store. Oh please tell me she can trace my location. I whisper.

"No, I'm in a room with him. It's a bedroom."

"Do you know the color of the house?" I know it's dark outside. I don't know the color on my own hair at this moment. I just need help.

"No. Please hurry."

"Does he have a weapon?" His fist, his entire body is a weapon, just get here. I look around remembering he shocked me but I don't see a weapon out.

"I don't know, he used a taser on me."

Speaking out in a hushed voice I insist, "Please hurry."

The fear in my voice is plausible as I plea for her assistance. She is trying to keep me on the line asking me questions. I am trying to stay calm. The length of one standard size pillow separates us and she wants to stay on the fucking phone. I take in a deep breath listening to her questions.

"Can you get out of the building?" My fear is boiling into anger, she will not find me, tears are flooding from my eyes. She can't lock in on my whereabouts. Trying to make logic out of her questions. I stutter in fear...this will be my last conversation.

"I don't know...I will wake him, I'm scared." I profess my fear.

She rushes her questions. "Is there a bathroom in the house?" My head lightly twists in a breathy pitch I respond.

"The room is shut, it's like a trap. He will hear me move." There are bells that will alert him of my movement if my feet inches to the bathroom I am dead.

"He will do something to you if you go to the bathroom?"

He and his friends kidnapped me, what type of bullshit question is this. I need help now, my legs are shaking and I shut my eyes.

I'm going to die.

I release a slow breath and it's as if I'm slipping away. "He had me tied up."

Her voice reminds me of Tatiana and it warms my heart. "Are you tied up now?" I'm not sure she can hear my low voice. I speak broken through the phone.

"I freed myself." I lay in a puddle of my tears. She is trying to keep me calm. I need to get out of this place.

"Stay on the line until the police arrive to the house." Does she even know where I am? He moves his legs.

"Oh shit, I woke him up." I inch the phone behind me and his head lifts. I can hear a woman screaming and crying in the background, someone is beating her. I wonder if the dispatcher can hear her. Her shouts turn into grunts, you can't ignore the sounds escaping from her. She silences and the bastard looks me over and returns to his slumber. Will the unknown lady be the last person I talk to? Will this be the final moments of my life, terrified? I am not moving.

ROMEL

rew and I get out to thank Angie for getting her cell at the front desk. I'm not too sad about the rodent but I will send her something for her help. With everything in my being I am trying to get to Victoria. We are sitting at Chad's place trying to narrow down the last link to get the female that dropped off the bag. Drew is in front of the computer typing like a madman.

"Why is it taking so long?" Everything comes back full circle so we have to find her. I am looking in the camera and a tear falls from my eye. It's like picking at a scab waiting to release the information. I growl.

"They distorted the video."

"If you all find out—" I interrupt Chad.

"We will find out."

His hands are in the air. "I am just saying at least try to get the woman to tell you something before going in the house."

I give him a side look. "Say something like what, Chad? 'Hey is your old man a rapist?'"

He shrugs his shoulders. "You will need defending if this

doesn't go right. I am just saying at least have it where it looks like you tried to ask if she needed help. Just be safe."

Chad is looking over my shoulder he points. "Go slow, there is a reflection in the mirror."

Drew yells, "I got it!"

I take in a deep breath. "Slow on the image, bring it in." My eyes grow wide and I am in shock. It's the guy with that fucking tattoo. He's got an axe in his hand scaring the ladies as they run across the room. This place looks more like an operating room. He swings the axe and blood spurts on the wall.

Chad blurts out, "Jesus fucking Christ." He is storming off.

"Drew, get Elliot on the phone!"

Victoria...my Vic is there. I study his hand movement as he pushes her in a chair. She has pissed him off. He gets closer, and she kicks him. She spits on his face and the screen goes dark. I pull the door open, heading outside, screaming and kicking at the bushes. I grab my keys out of my back pocket. Rushing to my car I take in a deep breath, situate the car, and take off to the address we located hoping I find someone.

ROMEL

*J*approach the porch of the house slowly and can see a woman just on the other side of the screen door replacing a lightbulb in the overhead lamp.

"Who are you?"

"You don't know me…I might know you. You have a guy in your life. He worries you; maybe you found something that caused you to face a fear you have. A fear you know about him, it caused you to deliver the item you found hoping someone would hear what you were really saying." This house looks like it belongs to a loving family, but the shutters reveal more to the story. There is no family here.

Her voice is shaky. "I don't know what you are talking about. You should leave my property…before I call the police." I look around seeing the dead grass and bare trees. This house is a trap house of some sort.

Come on, lady, show me some sign, I know it's you. I saw you on the video. I shake my head and step slowly. "If you were going to call the police you would have already, but you are not. You know someone will die because of what this guy is doing." I take another step and she remains where she is, giving me her attention. "You can turn him in. If you think what you have done is enough you are mistaken." She fidgets her hands, not moving her legs. I see in her eyes how frightened she is. "You know this friend I am speaking of and I only want to ask you to turn him in. I have people that will take care of your safety. He will never hurt you again." Chad's way is not working.

My foot touches the step. Wondering if Drew or Chad hears me as I approach, I adjust the earpiece. "Turn him in so he won't hurt anyone else again."

She opens the screen separating herself from me. "Get off my property."

I pull a card from my back pocket and lower it to the first step. "When you change your mind, call me."

I shake my head. She is scared so I walk off.

Drew, is yelling in my ear. "Romel, I know you are angry. Rom, we will send a crew." In my head I agree, I should wait for Drew but the screams of panic are growing louder. It's coming from that house. I hear Drew but my heart is telling me to go back to that house.

"I'm not perfect, Drew."

I turn my feet around remembering what I saw on the video. Hoping God remembers what I saw on the video. Hoping God remembers what I do on this day is to help those women. My body moves with a force that won't consider stopping until I get the monster.

I speak updating Drew. "I'm going back Drew." His voice is frantic. "Rom, please I'm on my way don't do this. I'm on my way. Wait. I'm asking you to spare your life, the moment you walk in there you could be dead."

"I'm at the front door Drew."

"I will not talk anymore… it's cool I see you bruh. You know that but I can't turn on these people. I see you bruh. I hear the despair in their screaming they need help." The yells increase.

Drew is shouting in my ear. "You need help Romel. I'm coming bruh, I see you."

I disconnect and focus going ahead.

ROMEL

$\mathcal{I}$ barge in the front door of the house and at least five women go running out. The lady from the front porch is guiding me to a basement door. She is shaking her head and her lips are trembling. I knew she needed help. She hugs me and whispers in my ear, "Thank you." I can hear Elliot in my ear but I have my microphone off.

"Romel, the authorities are close by."

I pat her on the back. "Does he have weapons?" She nods and I motion for her to leave.

My feet step below and I listen for a sound. It is dark but a light shines on one side of the space. As I plant my foot on the floor, I see a room that looks out of place, it looks almost medical in nature. What is he, a doctor? This is some crazy shit. I like freaky shit, but this is insanity. I keep walking, feeling a slight breeze that ruffles the clear plastic panels hanging from the ceiling. From a distance I see his face. My anger builds with each step, he lifts his eyes. "Who are you?"

I don't say a word, he keeps talking as if I wish to negotiate. "Which whore got out of line? I will take care of it, no problem."

Tilting my head I spot the the ink on his skin and it boils me over.

My veins feel as though they will rip out of my skin as I press the man's neck into the wall, the joints from his neck crack and I can see the edges of the claw tattoo showing from under my hand. "You're not getting out of this." Throwing him back, his body slides to the floor. I stand over him as blood is dripping from his head. "Tell me your plans...did you want her to be your sex slave, till death do you part?"

He looks over, eyeballing a station of what looks like sharp medical instruments. Dashing toward the tray, I push the medical bed before him. I jump up over in his direction.

"You enjoy pain...do you?"

His eyes stare at me as if he's never seen evil up close and personal. My mind flutters back and forth with the images from the video of him attempting to hurt Victoria and the assailant attacking my mother.

I push the bed over, stopping myself from wrapping my hands around his throat. Growling in anger, he steps back as fear floods his eyes and he pleads for me to stop. "I'm sorry for coming after your girl." His hands go up. "I don't even know which one she is."

"That's right, you've had so many."

His courage grows as he lunges after me with his fist, I react quickly, pounding his hand.

He stumbles back two steps. Taking my elbow, I jab in his throat and lock his hand behind his back.

"Pain is what you like. I saw it in your eyes." He is struggling with his feet on the floor. I pull him up, speaking through my clenched teeth.

I twist his fingers and his knees buckle. He yells. "You put your fucking fingers between her legs. She tried to scream and you choked her. You wanted to see the fear in her eyes. What's wrong…is this not fun for you?" He jerks his body free and punches me in the face. That's it, I want him pissed.

He swings back hitting me, my hand grabs his face. "You're not so clever are you?" I drag him by the face, punching his side. I pound his head against the wall. My eyes notice an ax and I go toward it. Grabbing it, I feel the weight from the handle. I can have fun with this.

He is screaming, "No, please don't!" I think he has realized just how sinister I can be. "I won't…please…I'll stop hurting people." Now he is deciding to make a career change? I throw him across the room and he bounces off the floor. I can hear his bones cracking. I stand at a distance, fully extending my arms. Spreading my fingers on the handle, I swing the axe back and then strike the axe, separating his fingers from his hand. Blood spills and his screams of distress echo.

Drew walks in with a gun in hand and shouts. "Rom, stop!" He notices blood across my chest and loses it. His hand pops back the gun. He shoots the man in the shoulder, then a second shot to his leg, the guy falls down.

I yell, "It's not my blood, bruh!" I point in the man's direction. "Look at his head."

Drew's shoulders shrug. "Oh well, I came in here to stop you." I chuckle walking to the face of the man that tortured Tatiana and put his filthy hands on Victoria. Drew's at my side with his gun lowered. The bastard is pleading for us to stop. Without a thought, my hands are at his neck. He falls back and Stanley walks in shouting as if I am his son. Fuck, he found out I came here. Drew drops the gun and a bullet ricochets off the wall. My eyes grow wide seeing Mr. Rodd enter.

"Fuck, you two have killed the man! I had everything I needed to send him to prison." To prison? I thought he was retired. Stanley has fire blazing in his eyes and he snatches the gun from the floor near Drew. Well, at least we saved tax dollars. My eyes lift seeing Uncle Jay at the entrance. Drew and I drop our heads, shit, this is serious if all of them are here. I turn, hearing the man cough and I push forward in attack mode. Mr. Rodd grabs me. Stanley shoots and my chest is convulsing.

"I will only say this once. You two leave!"

Drew's fingers are on my wrist. My chest moves in anger as he tries to distract me. "Come on, Rom."

I turn my head seeing Shaun waiting at the door for us to willingly walk to him. I am perplexed about what is going on. Why would he stop me from killing him? I need answers from my mother. I walk down the hall and through the door. Drew gets in the extended Mercedes and I enter after him. Shutting the car door, Shaun lets down the partition.

"Did you kill him?"

I peek out the window. Why does he care? I muffle through my teeth. "No, Stanley got him."

"I'm taking you to your mother, she needs to speak to you." I shake my head, wondering why I need to speak to my mother now. I have questions but I detest this childish treatment.

"Did you find Victoria?"

He shakes his head and I can hear an incoming call. Elliot has something playing in my ear. I hold my finger to Shaun and the car stops.

"Wait."

It's Victoria, I hear her she's talking to a dispatcher. "Elliot can you locate her?" Drew is looking at me knowing I hear him in my ear.

"You are already where she is, Romel?" I look around across the street as I hear Victoria say she sees police, but they are at a house across the street. I turn noticing a house behind me. I wonder if she's in that house.

"Shaun, I can't leave until I find her."

He puts the car in park. Drew looks at me steady. "I am going with you, Romel."

VICTORIA

The silence stretches on for what feels like an eternity. This drunk culprit has not moved. I feel my fingers around until I touch the cell. I gasp, the phone is still on. My ear makes out breathing. The dispatcher speaks, "Are you still there?"

She didn't leave me. I whisper, "How much longer?" She is trying to gauge me on the phone but I think it might be hopeless all this time, she has not been able to locate me.

"Can you get out of the house?" I shake, wishing she could see me. Lights, I see flashing lights outside. Finally, officers have arrived. She found me! I build the courage to leave, carefully stepping, thankful to my mother for making me learn to pivot my feet with grace. I get to the door, tuning out the wailing from another room. Someone else is in this house. The door is locked.

The phone is at my ear and I hear the lady speaking on the radio. "Are you at the door?" I look but no they are not there.

"Yes." Tears are flooding down my chin and I hear her speaking to the other line.

"She's at the door...she's at the door." She switches in conversation to me. "Is there a window?"

I am looking out, but they are not at the house. I cry for help. "They are at the wrong house." My heart is pounding; this is it, my last words will be spoken to this woman that didn't leave my side. "Please tell them to come back." My breathing becomes erratic. I can hear the guy, I shut my eyes. I know he's behind me, I can hear him breathing. I stay planted by the front door, only wishing I stood invisible.

ROMEL

*W*alking through an old house, my eyes set on the ceiling hanging in different patches with dingy crumbling walls. Ahead of me I see woman with a battered eye holding her hands up to a man coming after her. He slaps her. She is shaking her head. Something about me can't turn away. Part of me can't wait to kick his ass; I step across the room and yank the juvenile from the back of his dark shirt. He falls on his back. Drew is at my side, drawing his weapon I shake my head and he goes to move the female. I shift, looking at the woman, trying to get her to go with Drew. "Run!"

She's in shock and will not move. The piece of shit is backing to the wall, as he turns he reveals the tattoo under his neck. He looks like he is not older than seventeen. He deserves what's coming to him. I grip my fingers around his ankle, growling with fury, yanking him close. My foot sinks in his knee.

He yells in agony, trying to crawl away before I act once more. I lift and slam his boney weightless self ruthlessly to the ground. The lady moves with Drew and I turn away, walking behind her.

A voice captures me and my eyes roam to the top of my head as I realize…the dispatcher is speaking. Elliot has interrupted the call. I can hear a voice shaking saying she's at a door. Regaining my determination and strength, I walk ahead as the night continues to creep upon us. I pace the distance of the hall to the front door where my destiny awaits. Her tone is so pained, I can't say a word as I know now the voice is no longer just in my head, but before me. I reach my hands out toward her as Victoria turns to face me.

I whisper, "Shhh." Her eyes are bright as the stars and she collapses in my arms with relief. I speak in the microphone, "I have her, Shaun."

We stand away from the door and a chaotic rush of police force their way through the door. Our hands are up in the air and behind our heads.

"I was on the phone with the dispatcher," Victoria yells, trying to clarify who we are. One female officer remains next to us as the house floods with the authorities. We do not make any sudden movements until everything is clear.

It feels as if they know who we are as they surround us, pulling us both out of the house. An officer is asking her questions. "Is the assailant still here?"

She nods her head pointing to the back. "Yes…he's sleep."

I speak out, "Another woman is inside." The officer speaks on the radio asking for a paramedic to come inside.

I can hear a police man barking at the assailant. "Show me your hands, right fucking now!" A paramedic is carrying a stretcher inside.

I see Stanley walk up the steps of the porch. Elliot is by his side and Stanley speaks in an apologetic pitch. "I trust you two are well." The female officer nods at Stanley and she puts her hand on Victoria's shoulder.

"You were very brave young lady. Be sure to get yourself

checked, ma'am." She smiles in my direction saluting me. "Mr. Adcock, I suppose." She pats me on my back. "Stay safe." How does she know my name? I shake my head agreeing but perplexed.

"Thank you." We walk further out on the porch giving the police space to work. It looks like the fourth of July out in these streets.

I smirk, eyeballing these two partners in crime; Elliot works with Stanley. I look over his shoulder and spot Mr. Rodd getting in a Mercedes. Shit, they knew all of this. "Thank you Stanley, Elliot, thank you."

I grab Victoria's face holding her close to me. "Vic, you did great. I…" My heart is racing and an unwelcome tug is pulling at my pants leg. I turn and see its Shaun.

"Hey, Romel." Drew is behind him. I can tell he wants to say something but he holds it in for the moment.

Victoria is standing in my arms and the guys tilt their heads. Shaun walks ahead and turns around. "You still have someone waiting on you. Kiss or whatever; let's get out of here." He walks off and Drew is jabbing at Shaun.

Drew shouts out. "Rom, make sure she sees the paramedic before you leave." I tilt my head feeling like I'm on cloud nine, but I'm exhausted as fuck.

Victoria holds me tight. She whispers in my ear, "I see Jasmine over by the yellow tape."

"She will be okay, sweetheart. Let's take care of you."

Victoria looks in my eyes. "Romel…" She is breathing like she did the first time I held her hand. Her voice is soft. "Romel, I see you." I smile knowing she certainly does. I push her hair away from her face.

"On the ugliest days you will remain my beauty always."

She inches up on her tippy toes and I feel her skin rub against my arms. Her fingers grip the back of my head and my lips take her mouth as I see the window into her heart. The passion I have for her overshadows the crowd of police and women being rescued from this monstrous day. Her tongue communicates the desire she has for me. Damn I'm lucky.

"I love you, Vic."

ROMEL

unny how one can think life is going perfect yet it dives straight into a storm. I'm concerned about everything that has occurred and I know from looking at Drew he's on edge. Jasmine stayed at the hospital with Victoria and I get to take a trip to see the one person the family knows will calm me down. The car pulls up to the curb of the back of a club. I see my mother at the entrance. Shaun opens my door and I step out of the vehicle. Drew moves to get out but Shaun stops him from coming.

"He needs to talk to her alone, Drew." His nose flares and he steps back until he sits in the car.

"I will be okay, Drew." He sees my mother and falls back.

Turning my head my mother tilts her chin and I follow her inside. We are walking down a staircase to the basement. Reaching the final step, I stretch my arm to open the door. She goes ahead of me. The room has dim lights and the only person I can see is at the bar.

My mother walks to the bar and orders us a drink. "Two Snakes Bites, straight up."

The man turns as if he is on auto pilot, making our drinks. I position on the bar stool looking at my mother next to me.

"You are so much like Alexander." I wouldn't know, my brother had more time with him than I, but he shares stories with me often as Mr. Rodd.

I frown speaking in a low voice. "Momma, how much of Pops do you think is inside of me?"

The man puts our drinks in front of us. I rub the wooden bar and pick up the glass. "I would say one hundred percent but I know you came from me. A portion of me is still inside of you. Romel, you think like your father when he was your age. I guess that got him into saving people." I sip from my glass, finding it hard to believe. I miss him more and more lately. I set the glass down and I clear my throat to speak.

"I miss him, you know. I think, what do I do without out him?"

My mother's eyes dart in my direction. "You do it every day, Romel...win by living another day."

"I didn't kill the man I wanted to. Stanley—"

She chuckles. "Defeat makes you stronger, mistakes make you wiser. Yet, why do you want to kill someone when you are not a policeman? It's not your job to kill people."

"He hurt Victoria and...his so-called group raped—"

She cuts me off and stands. Her voice is full of authority. "He did not rape me, he tried." I interrupt her as she is speaking.

My voice elevates. "I saw the video."

She grips my throat, and I am confused. I guess it's safe to say my mother taught me to grip people by the throat. "Avenge yourself, Romel, while I offer you the chance." My eyes water and I ache inside.

I shake my head, I put my hands in the air. I offended my mother bringing him up. She takes in a deep breath releasing my neck. I speak in a low pitch, "Fighting for you and Victoria is morally right."

She interrupts. "It can also be a mask, Romel. You accept the responsibilities of your actions. Or does you living justify your acts?" She returns to her seat and picks up her drink. "You are who you are, I love you either way." She sips from her glass. I study her trying to understand.

"Romel, what is your conscious saying? Is your conscious rendering to me?" My head turns away knowing she wants me to tell her the truth. I'm angry and I want revenge.

"I see the hate growing deep inside you." She leans across from me. "The goal in life is for you to know you better than I know you."

I smirk. "How do I compete with that? You are my mother."

"That is one of my roles; face pressed against the wall." She narrows her look. "Fear in my eyes, until my last fighting breath, that will remain one of my roles. You wonder why this happened to me, to Victoria, to Tatiana…"

Wrinkles grow on my forehead. I never mentioned to her anything about what happened to Tatiana. She continues her speech. "Wonder no more who you are and know you better than I know you. Be the master of your conscious." I feel as if I am meeting another side of my mother I have never met before. I know she is a strong woman…her conversation is methodical.

"M'Dear, I saw him attack you, I saw the man attack you."

She has an awkward look piercing in my direction. "And for that you let him rule your conscious. Because you kept how you feel inside you. It made you weak to have him controlling what no other should have control over, Romel." She passes me an envelope.

"What is this?"

"Your father wrote this for you." I'm just now getting it. I hear the door and my head turns. Mr. Rodd is walking in my direction. My mother stands and he speaks to her.

"Mrs. Roselyn Adcock, are you well?" He walks past me and embraces her. She smiles.

"Senior, all is well...I still have a pulse and so does Romel." They have a laugh and I look off. My mother stands behind me and I turn to hug her. "Remember the chance you have, Romel."

A smile grows on my face. "I know the chance you offer me, M'Dear. I didn't mean to speak to you that way."

She steps back and chuckles. "Why speak if you don't mean it?"

"I don't mean to disrespect you." She rubs her hand across my shoulder blades.

"Sometimes disrespect gets you to your true feelings. I am not upset for you feeling, Romel. I just don't want you to think someone raped me. Next time ask me. Have Victoria call me. I know a great counselor." She will not let that one slide I know. My head lowers, and she walks away.

"I love you, handsome."

"I love you too, beautiful." She pushes the door open and Mr. Rodd is staring at the envelope.

"I see you asked your mother about yourself." Looking out the corner of my eyes I ponder his intentions.

"I asked about—"

He cuts me off. "You asked about Xander, I know, I see the package, son."

"How much do you know about my family?"

He clears his throat and the bartender walks in with a glass of wine for him.

"Our family...Your father and I." He twists his fingers as the bartender puts his drink before him. "We were close as you and Drew. Not as stupid."

He reaches for his wine. "Maybe because we didn't hang out at sex clubs." My eyes grow wide and I reposition in the chair. "Perhaps because we didn't spend our money on females. Well our wives, of course." Oh shit, he knows too much.

"Romel, before we move further. I want to know, why you and Drew have two thousand dollars that's to be sent to a female?" He shakes his head. "Don't lie, I'm not interested."

He picks up his glass of wine. Drew looks so much like this man. I gulp at his words. "She needed the money for school."

He tilts his head. "I see...it was a worthy cause."

He leans in closer to me. "I know and will always know more than you, son. This is your senior year. Although you are going on for your Master's at GA Tech, it doesn't mean you fuck up because of a piece of pussy."

I stand, offended by his statement. He hits the table top. "Sit, Romel."

I lower my body. "She's not a piece of pussy, Mr. Rodd."

He sits upright. "I know to you she is not, but as your uncle I want you both to know."

I shake my head understanding he is telling me not to move too fast with her. I switch the conversation. "Did he die?"

"All you need to know is they reinstated the officer."

"Uncle Senior, I thought he was working in Dallas?

"He was until he transferred to Atlanta..." He taps the table. "Enough with the questions. Don't you have a girl to see?"

"Uncle Senior..."

He muffles his baritone voice. "Romel?" He stands on his feet. "Read the letters, Romel. We miss him together, but every day you look in the mirror and you have a gift I can only wish for."

"What's that Uncle Senior?" I am on my feet to his side.

He jabs at my side and chuckles. He speaks in a low pitch with watery eyes. "You get to see him every day. You get to feel his DNA run through your veins daily, Romel. I am thankful for the time I spent with him." He pulls my head to his and points to my chest. "He lives right here, Romel, through your children, your grandchildren, he will continue to live. Your father will forever be a great man, just like you." I embrace him as if my father's spirit has taken over him.

"I will make a promise to you, Romel." I step back as tears release from my eyes. "If we should have to battle another again. We will do it together." I rub my eyes cherishing the moment with my dear Uncle Senior, Mr. Rodd.

THANK YOU

Thank you for reading Last Chance! If you'd like to leave a leave review, you can do so by visiting me me on social media. I'd love you for it!

Breaking Dance

Stalk me anytime!

Come Back for More of Romel and Victoria's story in Your Chance, the continuation of the Chance Series.

Follow J. Bliss on Social Media

FaceBook | Amazon | Goodreads |Website | Blog |Facebook Reader's Group|Instagram|Youtube Channel

ABOUT THE AUTHOR

J. Bliss (1978) was born in Dallas, Texas to NFL star of America's team, Dallas Cowboys and a prestigious English teacher. Her first novella originated from a past radio talk show, based on many callers that called in about having marital problems which mostly stemmed from lack of intimacy. Drawing from her own experiences and struggles, she felt compelled to write Lovers of Convenience.

J Bliss is concluding her Doctorate in English Pedagogy at Murray State University. Her education includes a Master's degree in English at Clayton State University, a Master's degree in Education from Troy University, a Bachelor's degree in Journalism from University of Central Oklahoma, and an Associate's degree in Journalism from Rose State College.

Follow J. Bliss on Social Media
FaceBook | Amazon | Goodreads |Website | Blog |Facebook Reader's Group|Instagram|Youtube Channel

BOOKS BY J. BLISS

Chance Series Titles by J. Bliss

Not By Chance

Taking Chances

Last Chance

No Chance

Additional Titles

Perfect Imperfect Christmas

Perfect Imperfect Christmas II

No, I Do, In My Future

I Do, In My Future

Breaking Dance

Night and Day: Sr. Rodd

Your Chance: Hunted

Legal Chances

Running Back

J Bliss Books Publishing Company

Atlanta, GA USA

www.jblissbooks.com

Cover Design Jamila Harris & Jada D' Lee; Cover Photographer &
Portraits James C. Lewis; Art Direction Jamila Harris

www.ingramcontent.com/pod-product-compliance
Lightning Source LLC
Chambersburg PA
CBHW030917050726
47498CB00003BA/791